PEOPLE
WILL
TALK

Also by Lucianne Goldberg

Madame Cleo's Girls

PEOPLE WILL TALK

LUCIANNE GOLDBERG

POCKET BOOKS

New York   London   Toronto   Sydney   Tokyo   Singapore

This book is a work of fiction. Names, characters, places and
incidents are products of the author's imagination or are used
fictitiously. Any resemblance to actual events or locales or
persons, living or dead, is entirely coincidental.

 POCKET BOOKS, a division of Simon & Schuster Inc.
1230 Avenue of the Americas, New York, NY 10020

Copyright © 1994 by Lucianne Goldberg

Library of Congress Cataloging-in-Publication Data

Goldberg, Lucianne.
    People will talk/Lucianne Goldberg.
        p.   cm.
    ISBN: 0-671-77669-X
    I. Title.
PS3557.03579P46   1994
813'.54—dc20   94-15383
                                                CIP

First Pocket Books hardcover printing December 1994

10 9 8 7 6 5 4 3 2 1

POCKET and colophon are registered trademarks of
Simon & Schuster Inc.

Printed in the U.S.A.

For Dominick Dunne:
National treasure, personal hero, and cherished friend

My heartfelt gratitude to an extraordinary editor, Claire Zion, for her graceful forbearance and absolute professionalism

Prologue

*L*olly Pines was the world's most widely read gossip columnist. Her work appeared six days a week in the tabloid *New York Courier* and reached millions more through syndication throughout the world.

Various commentators, in print and on television, had called her irascible and mean. Others called her unique and showered her with awards. If pressed, even those who lauded Lolly Pines found it hard to say they really liked her. But both groups, detractors and supporters, had this in common: they were afraid of her whims, afraid of her power, and afraid of alienating her and the millions of fans she had acquired.

At sixty, Lolly Pines was the same size she had been at fourteen, barely five feet tall. Like many diminutive women who had fought their way up the career ranks in the fifties and sixties, Lolly guarded her personal and professional life jealously. Being small and dark and possessing a face once described kindly as "distinctive" was a matter of pride to Lolly. She had never cared about being pretty in a conventional way.

Lolly wielded her power not from the downtown offices of the *Courier* but from Penthouse 3 of the Barrington on Central Park West, her rent-controlled fortress.

Everything about the huge old apartment, from its eighteen oversized rooms to its extraordinary disorder, was dear to her. Lolly's parents had left everything behind them when they fled their native Hungary, in 1939, with their eight-year-old daughter. From then on, they refused to part with anything they accumulated in their new life as Americans.

Lolly had continued that practice after her parents' death. As a result, the first two floors of the penthouse were crammed with furniture, photographs, stacks of newspapers and magazines, and boxes containing everything from Lolly's mother's knitting to her father's pipe collection to promotional giveaways that Lolly could not bring herself to throw out.

The third floor was the heart of Lolly's lair. There, three small rooms were filled from floor to ceiling with filing cabinets that contained clips and journals Lolly had kept since the beginning of her career at the now-defunct *Herald Tribune*.

She had converted the largest room at the end of the hall into an office, shortly after her father died. Its glass ceiling rose to a sharp peak to form the roof of the building's northeast tower. It was some nineteenth-century architect's folly, made of four panels of pyramid-shaped glass supported by heavy steel beams. The glass was impossible to clean. Years of bird droppings dappled the outside of the glass panels. Even at night, the light that fell from the sky cast a mottled blue-green glow over the room.

Lolly's desk was pushed against one wall under the eaves. She had not seen its bare wooden surface for years. Clearing it, like organizing her belongings and getting the apartment painted, was among the things she would do—someday.

Someday when the world came to a standstill.

The Friday morning of Labor Day weekend, Lolly had awakened before dawn, as usual. The first thing on her agenda had been to finish her column so that she could break away early for the weekend. At noon sharp, her longtime friend, visiting London columnist Abner Hoon, would arrive to take her to the Hamptons, where the weekend would get off to a glittering start—rain or shine—at a party hosted by investment banker Jourdan Garn and his fashion-designer wife, Tita Mandraki.

By eleven she had finished her work. Sunday's column would be particularly controversial and would make her the center of attention for the final holiday weekend of the summer of 1992.

She reread the pages as they came out of the printer and smiled. Late on Thursday, she had obtained a telephone interview with TV actor Keeko Ram, the star of the top-rated series *Wilshire Boulevard.*

For months the talk of the entertainment industry had been the nasty controversy between the too-pretty twenty-year-old actor, with his double row of black eyelashes and his pale green eyes, and his parents, whom he had accused of squandering the money he had made as a minor. Earlier in the week the dispute had been secretly resolved in an out-of-court settlement. Lolly Pines alone had obtained the whole story. There was enough juicy inside information to fill her entire Sunday column.

The teenybopper icon had never spoken publicly about the matter before he talked to Lolly. To get the story she had had to promise the boy's agent to write the column with a sympathetic spin, telling only his side of the controversy. It was a small price to pay for a bombshell that would vie for the space that Woody and Mia and Murphy Brown were getting in the media.

Other publications would pick up her exclusive, attribute it to her, and once again confirm that, no matter how the world might feel about her personally, when it came to ferreting out information her competition could not get—first and fast—Lolly Pines had no equal.

A great many people who mattered in Lolly's rarefied world were to be guests at the party in the Hamptons that evening.

Lolly was one of the party guests invited to stay on as a houseguest, and with the first Sunday editions of the *Courier* hitting the streets on Saturday night, Lolly, rather than Tita Garn's two-million-dollar decorating job, would emerge as the star of the weekend.

Tita Garn had been somewhat in seclusion after her sensational marriage a few seasons earlier to billionaire Jourdan Garn. The fact that Jourdan had previously been married to Tita's own daughter, Sandrine, was undoubtedly the cause for Tita's low social profile of late.

The phone rang while Lolly was packing. It was her editor, calling to tell her that early that morning Keeko Ram had heaved a girl off the third-floor balcony of the Renaissance Motel in downtown Santa Monica while out of his mind on PCP. The *Courier* had an exclusive on the story, and he planned to page-one it for Sunday. Lolly's puff piece on Keeko would have to be killed, and she had the rest of the day to come up with a new column for the late-afternoon deadline.

Without the scoop, the weekend at the Garns' now looked a lot less interesting. Wearily, Lolly called Abner to cancel their plans. To make matters worse, she had given her assistant the day off.

As she climbed back to her tower office, the headache that had started when her editor called began to pound unbearably. Disregarding the pain, she walked to her desk, flicked on her hard drive, and stared at the screen. When it sprang to life, she closed her eyes against the glare.

She had to be able to look at the screen. Sunglasses, she thought. Perhaps, if she put on a pair of sunglasses, she would be able to type. She remembered that there was a box full of designer samples on the shelf over her desk. She stood up and began to push aside the accumulated debris until she located a red lacquer Ferragamo box under a life-size marzipan bust of Kim Basinger grown dusty and rock-hard since it had arrived to promote the opening of some movie that had closed overnight.

The effort of lifting Kim Basinger's torso high enough to free the box extended Lolly's center of gravity too far for her to regain her balance once she realized she was falling. Panicked, she clutched blindly for the edge of the shelf, pulling on it with her entire weight. The bust began to tip forward. She looked up into Kim's sugary eyes, blank and sightless, falling toward her as the shelf pulled away from the crumbling plaster wall.

1

*A*s Kick Butler jogged around the columns in the Barrington lobby, Mike, the elevator operator, leaned out and grinned.

She whizzed into the elevator, flung herself against the back wall, and took a deep gulp of air.

"Hi, Mike," she said, pushing out her lower lip and blowing out a whoosh of air that lifted her damp red bangs. At twenty-eight, Kick's fresh, freckled face and short red hair kept her looking like a cool breeze even in the dog days of summer.

Mike stood facing the door. "Too hot to be moving that fast, pal," he said.

"What can I say?" she said. "Always on the run. Places to go, people to see. No rest for the assistant to the world's most famous gossip columnist."

"Sure, sure," Mike said dully, and closed the door. "I don't know what she pays you, kid, but I wouldn't trade places with you for a sure thing in the Pick Four lottery."

"Oh, she's not so bad," Kick said with a shrug. It was not a particularly strong defense of her employer. She knew Lolly wasn't a favorite with the building staff. Lolly had always believed that mention in her Christmas column, where she was careful to name all the service staff, was an ample holiday bonus for the little people in her life. Kick didn't think she was paid enough to tell Lolly what the staff really thought of her "gift."

"Here we are," Mike said when they reached the top floor.

"Thanks, Mike," Kick said, stepping out onto the landing and patting her pockets in search of her keys. She pulled the long bootlace she used as a key chain from her back pocket.

She listened to the rattle of the descending elevator as she impatiently unlocked the four Segal locks on Lolly's door. Her door too—when Lolly offered her the job, she had thrown in room and board as an added inducement. Kick had suspected she was being hired as live-in slave, but at the time, she had desperately needed a place to live.

Kick stood for a moment in the long gallery of the penthouse and listened. Sometimes, on a still afternoon, she could hear Lolly all the way up on the third floor shouting into the phone. But the only sound she heard today was the soft tick of the tall case clock on the first-floor landing. Perhaps Lolly had already left for the Hamptons with Abner Hoon. It was around two o'clock now, and Lolly always liked to get places early.

Kick's bedroom was at the head of the stairs on the second floor, her windows overlooking Central Park. At the edge of the right window, she could see the haunch and beak of one of the two stone statues that crouched on the outside ledge. She had named the two ugly things Thelma and Louise. Thelma was the one she could see from her window. During the first few weeks after Kick had moved into the apartment to work as Lolly's assistant-cum-handmaiden, she had come to think of Thelma as a kind of guardian gargoyle watching over her. Late at night, it was to Thelma that she would explain how unhappy she had been before coming to Lolly's. At first it was hard to believe the pain wouldn't last forever.

She knew that if she hadn't been in such a fragile mental state, she never would have agreed to move into the weird old place. Now she was glad she had.

In the year she had worked for Lolly, she felt she had sat at the feet of the master. She had learned not only how people talked but why, and she had learned how a bit of gossip that got into print could have devastating repercussions. At first, she had qualms—reproducing gossip wasn't real work and Kick thought of herself as a trained journalist. But as time passed and she began to realize the effect that Lolly's column had on the world, she began to change her mind, even sharing one of her most prized possessions—something she and Lolly jokingly referred to as Kick's B list.

As a child Kick had started to keep a ledger of sorts. She had traveled widely with her grandmother and over the years had compiled an extensive list of names and phone numbers of hundreds of people she had met in her unconventional early life: doormen at the best hotels, bartenders at trendy clubs, headwaiters at restaurants with three stars or more, celebrity hairdressers, paparazzi, and limo drivers who catered to celebrities not only in New York but, to Lolly's astonishment, in London, Paris, Rome, and jet-set watering holes around the world. These were people who formed the underground army that knew what everyone who was worth writing about was up to. Lolly had built her own list of contacts over the years. It was, of course, too late and never her style to cultivate the "nobodies."

As Lolly had found herself relying more frequently on Kick's list to run down tips and check out stories, she had asked her why she compiled it in the first place. Kick had smiled and shrugged, saying simply that she was a people collector. She saw life as one big connect-the-dots game, and since she believed everyone knew something or someone she might find useful, she thought it might come in handy to remember who people were.

Now Kick pulled a clean white T-shirt from the bottom drawer of her dresser, shrugged it on, and decided to go up to the office to organize her desk. With Lolly gone, she could listen to her favorite rock station as she worked. She began to pick her way up the stairs—space Lolly reserved for the odd and unsolicited objects sent to her by those hoping to be mentioned in her column.

The office phone rang. By the time Kick reached the office door the answering machine had picked up. She could hear celebrity lawyer Irving Fourbraz's gruff voice saying he had a blockbuster story but was leaving his apartment at the Trump Tower immediately and would be out of touch until he reached LA.

Kick stood paralyzed in the doorway, only vaguely aware of the end of Fourbraz's message, blinking her eyes in horror.

Lolly was lying flat on the floor in front of her desk. Cradled against her shoulder was what was left of the marzipan statue of Kim Basinger that had been on the shelf above her computer. The area around Lolly was a mess. It looked as though the shelf had collapsed on her.

Outside of the New York subway system, Kick had never seen a dead person, but somehow she knew in a glance that Lolly would never get up.

She dropped to one knee next to Lolly's body. In the bluish gloom she could see the oozing burgundy gash over her left eye. One of her false eyelashes was coming unstuck.

Kick pressed her lips together so tightly she could feel the edge of each tooth. She reached out and gently pressed the lash back into place. Then she felt Lolly's cheek. It was as cool and rubbery as an inner tube.

Alone in the dim light she could feel her face flush with profound embarrassment. Her relationship with Lolly had been a one of complete professionalism, affable but crisp and unsentimental. To actually touch Lolly's helpless, supine body seemed an act of intimacy of obscene proportions.

She shuddered and stood up, still staring down at the body. Lolly was lying absolutely flat. Her ankle bones touched. The toes of her pumps were neatly aligned, pointing straight up like the dead witch's shoes in *The Wizard of Oz.*

Kick began to shiver. In a half-trance of shock she walked to the rump-sprung couch and picked up the ratty sable coat Lolly used as a throw. Some big cheese at MGM had given it to her years ago, either for putting something in her column or for keeping it out.

The coat had grown stiff and hard and had oxidized to the color of Lucille Ball's hair. One sleeve hung by a few tattered pieces of binding.

Poor dear, Kick thought, lowering herself onto the floor. I have to tidy her up.

She carefully removed what was left of Kim Basinger and set it to one side, then gently covered Lolly with the fur coat, tucking the sleeves under her body.

Lolly, who never left the apartment without getting herself up like Joan Crawford, would have been mortified for anyone to see her in such a state.

Kick had to think. She pushed aside the back issues of *Variety* that had been stacked under the coat and sat down.

It wasn't as if Lolly had any family Kick could call. She did have a lawyer, though. Well, Irving Fourbraz was actually more like a celebrity broker; Kick loathed him. But he handled Lolly's personal legal and tax matters and was mentioned frequently in her column. Surely he would know what to do. Then again, what good was he up in an airplane?

All she wanted was some authority figure between herself and the body on the floor. Someone to take over and assume responsibility for the terrible thing that had happened. Perhaps she should call someone at the paper. She covered her face and leaned forward onto her knees.

"Please, God," she whispered, making the sign of the cross, something she hadn't done since grade school. "I didn't mean it. Truly, in my heart, I was only wondering about her retiring. I never, never, never thought about her dying."

The tiny mean voice that Kick had not listened to since it told her to take the job with Lolly cleared its throat.

The first time she had heard the voice was when it told her to dump a married professor she was having a stand-up affair with (*stand-up* meaning they only did it standing up—in a supply closet in a deserted hallway and once against the fender of his VW bug in a dark stadium parking lot). The voice lived deep inside her mind and never failed to surface in times of crisis. It was the voice that demanded she face down her editor on the Springfield paper and insist that her byline be put on the stories she was writing. The voice warned her to be on guard only minutes before she fell for the man who nearly destroyed her career and crushed her heart, sending her into exile and seclusion.

Now here it was again, responding to her overwhelming feelings of guilt. After a few months of working for Lolly, learning the ropes, she had begun to imagine having a column of her own someday. After all, she was a trained journalist. And more and more of Lolly's columns were based on information garnered through contacts on Kick's B list. Sometimes, late at night, she would speak to Thelma, sitting quietly outside her window, and fantasize about what would happen if Lolly were gone.

"I didn't mean it," she whimpered again. "I never really wanted anything like this to happen."

The tiny mean voice asked, "Are you sure?"

2

Joe Stone, editor-in-chief of the *New York Courier*, sat up on the uncomfortable pullout couch. He looked around for a top sheet to cover his nakedness against the freezing draft from the air conditioner at the foot of the bed. It was about the only thing that worked in the ground-floor apartment Baby Bayer used more as a crash pad than a home.

As he'd expected, there was no top sheet. There seldom was one on Baby's bed.

The naked body lying next to him yanked angrily at the lumpy fiber-filled comforter and moaned.

Joe looked over his shoulder to see if she was really asleep. If he was lucky, he could shower and get dressed before she woke up.

Baby had driven him nuts ever since he had arrived at the paper two years ago. He had still been married to Beth then, but she had been beginning to make it clear that she didn't feel it was worth giving up her job in Washington to follow Joe to New York. Now that his divorce from Beth was final, Baby was still driving him nuts. Baby Bayer drove anyone with even a thimbleful of testosterone in his bloodstream nuts. Guys wanted to either screw her or strangle her. Joe's dilemma was that he usually wanted to do both.

He made it to the bathroom without disturbing her and silently closed the door. The wall phone next to the medicine cabinet silently taunted him. He knew he should call in to double-check on Lolly's column. It hadn't yet arrived when he had left to meet Baby. If there was a problem, he would be pushing things if he waited much longer to deal with it.

Oh, hell, he thought, Sam knew where he was. Good old Sam. The only person in the city room, on the entire paper for that matter, that he trusted enough to tell about his little two-month-old arrangement with Baby. Baby thought that her immediate boss, Petra Weems, the editor of the Grapevine page, suspected, but Baby could never pin it down. Nonetheless, employee dating was a no-no, thanks to a ruling made by the owner and chairman of Courier Publishing, Tanner Dyson.

Joe jumped when the wall phone in the bathroom rang. He managed to grab it in mid-ring and walked to the far corner of the big old bathroom before he mumbled hello.

"Joe? Sam. Sorry to ah . . . disturb you. We got a problem."

"Oh, shit. What's up?"

"Lolly Pines is dead."

Joe sat down on the closed toilet lid. "What?" he said, in shock. "I just spoke to her this morning. She was fine. Jesus, Sam. What the hell happened?"

"She croaked in her apartment. I don't have all the details yet. Her assistant called. We've got a car on its way up there right now."

Joe Stone stood, propping the phone against his shoulder, grateful that there was room enough to pace. "Have you called the old man yet?"

"Not yet. Dyson is out on his ranch. I don't think it's a good idea to bother a vacationing publisher unless someone shoots the President."

14

"Yeah, well, this is close. You better call before he hears it some other way."

"In case I don't catch him, you want to make some kind of a statement for her obit?"

"Try and find Tanner first," Joe said, his mind racing. "What about her column? Don't tell me she didn't get it in."

There was a pause on Sam's end of the line before he answered. "She didn't get it in."

"Damn," Joe said. "She knew I had to have the damn thing by four. Now what am I going to do?"

"You're all heart, Joe," Sam said sarcastically. "The only reason the woman didn't make her deadline is because she died. Cut her some slack."

"Yeah . . . well, Lolly's dead and we're not, Sam," Joe said ominously.

"What's that mean?"

"That means Lolly doesn't have any problems and we do," Joe said wearily. "I suppose we couldn't run the column now even if she had gotten it in."

As Joe reached to hang up the phone, his foot hit a stool next to the tub. Baby's hot rollers crashed to the tile floor.

From the other side of the bathroom door he heard Baby calling in the tiny-baby-girl voice she used when she wanted something. "Joe . . . oh . . . oh. Hurry up, honeeee. I've got to . . ."

Oh, God, don't say it, Joe thought, closing his eyes.

". . . make pee-pee."

"Shit," he hissed. "In a sec, Baby. I just got off the damn phone. Let me finish up in here."

Joe stood over the toilet, urinating as loudly as possible to try to drown out the sound of Baby's voice. It sounded as if her lips were against the crack in the door.

Joe finished and opened the door. "Pipe down, Baby," he said briskly. "I'm coming."

"You could have used the kitchen phone, for Christ's sake," she snarled, pushing by him.

15

Joe padded back to the bed and searched the night table for a cigarette. He found a crumpled pack in a puddle of spilled wine that was soaking Baby's usual mess of nail polish bottles, headphones, *Cosmopolitan* magazines, and a tangle of earrings and bangle bracelets.

He pulled out the last cigarette of the pack he had opened after breakfast. God, he thought as he lit up, a pack, three drinks, and two bottles of wine by the time lunch was over. Insanity.

He glanced at his watch and figured they must have done it three times since they hit the apartment after lunch. At least he got off three times. He never knew with Baby. She came on in public as though she could never get enough. Always coming up with the double entendre, the raised eyebrow, or the lowered lids. No matter what the subject matter, Baby would turn a conversation around to sex.

Whenever she sat down in a restaurant, Baby would lean forward and rest her great breasts on the edge of the table. She was the only woman he had ever known who could unzip a fly with her toes.

For the brief time he had been sleeping with Baby, he'd never known if she truly craved sex or if her little tricks were some kind of nutty controlling device. The fact that she was getting away with something naughty in public seemed to turn her on as much as, if not more than, he did.

At first, she acted as though she had orgasms, squealing and thrashing around, practically bouncing off the wall, but he suspected otherwise. Sure, she liked the foreplay. All the mouth and tongue and finger stuff. He was good at that and really worked very hard to please her. But something told him, some sixth sense, that once he was actually inside her, despite all the moaning and gnashing and tight little legs locking around his shoulders, she never really came. Always, after she was sure he was through, she would hop up and toddle off to the john or the kitchen or worse, without missing a beat, go right back to the story she had been in the middle of telling before they started.

He pushed a thin pillow behind his shoulders and took another deep drag.

His life was out of control. He knew it. His colleagues on the paper knew it. His friends knew it. Even his ex-wife, with whom he had fallen into a sort of armed but amiable truce, knew it.

Beth had come to town recently from Washington, and they had had dinner. She had taken one look at what had once been his guy-next-door face and said, "What the hell have you been doing to yourself?"

How could he tell her? How could he admit that his wan and haggard appearance was caused by the increasing chaos in his life? He longed for the things the world seemed to put such stock in: punctuality, remembering to pick up his socks, honoring his commitments. His life had no order to it. It had excitement, it had tension and erotic interludes, but no poetry of spirit, no sweetness.

Right after the divorce, when he'd been seduced by that sense of chaos, Baby's need to live on the edge had been irresistible. But Baby Bayer wasn't the answer. Hell, she might even be the problem. Certainly things had only gotten worse since he'd given in to her flirting and started sleeping with her.

He rolled over and crushed out his cigarette as he watched Baby swing out of the bathroom, bounce across the carpeting, and disappear into the kitchen.

Her pubic hair covered most of her lower stomach, nearly reaching her navel. It was as dark and wiry as her fluffy hair was lipstick red—although next week it could be platinum blond or coal black. She had a tiny waist that exaggerated her low-slung butt, wide hips, and stumpy, muscular legs. Her upper body was more reasonably proportioned, with small, strong shoulders and high, firm breasts. In profile her face looked like a greeting card drawing of an adorable four-year-old. Full-face scrutiny revealed a pretty face that failed to conceal a deep anger behind the wide-set lavender eyes and at the corners of the cupid's-bow mouth. It might have been a clever brain at war with a baby-girl appearance that drove Baby to try to force people to take her seriously. Few did. The only parts that Joe took notice of were what was between Baby's legs and her ability to cause pain for those who crossed her. He was aware—if not in awe—of both.

Now his personal problems paled in the face of Sam's news about Lolly. He knew Tanner Dyson would be calling around town for him as soon as he heard the news.

It had been Dyson who had given Lolly the huge contract a couple of years ago so she wouldn't defect to another paper, and from that day forward the publisher had never hesitated to use her column for his own purposes, the most egregious of which had been to curry favorable opinion for his beautiful blond second wife, Georgina, formerly of *Fabulous Foods* magazine.

Dyson, for sure, would have the final word on the choice of Lolly's successor, and that, Joe knew the minute he absorbed the news of Lolly's death, was going to be a bitch of a problem.

It wouldn't be just a matter of enticing another big name over to the *Courier*. There was a limited supply. Liz Smith had a fat contract with *New York Newsday*. Billy Norwich was happy at the *New York Post*, and Cindy Adams was already their star. There might be a chance to swipe Richard Johnson from the *Daily News*, but Dyson would have to meet Johnson's price. There were some bright lights around the magazines and weeklies, but they had not yet reached the national recognition Dyson would want. A columnist was only as powerful as his—or her—sources and connections. Dyson would insist on someone who had as many due-bills out as Lolly had died with. The people who fit the profile that he would demand numbered less than a half dozen the world over, and few were likely to sit still for his control-freak meddling.

Dealing with the publisher wouldn't be Joe's only headache. The minute Baby heard the news, she'd be after him to get her a shot at the job. Baby's drive and ambition were as rapacious as her other appetites. Joe shuddered at the thought of all that intensity directed at him.

He heard the sharp *thwap!* of an ice cube tray being smacked against the kitchen sink and Baby's voice calling, "Joe, honeee? I'm fixing you a drink. It's sooo hot."

Joe moaned quietly and held his head. "Thanks, Baby, but I gotta get back into the office."

As he rolled over and sat up he saw her leaning against the side of the kitchen door. She was holding two jelly glasses of dark liquid over ice.

"I thought you took the rest of the day off," she said, advancing toward him.

When she reached the bed, she set the drinks on the floor and knelt between his legs. "That had to be Sam on the phone, right, darling?" She looked up at him. "What did he want?"

"*Umm*," he said, lifting a red curl off her forehead and twirling it among the others. He didn't want to start up again. They had had enough sex for the day. He felt light-headed and anxious about the Lolly situation, and he didn't want to discuss it with Baby.

She lifted her drink, plunged two fingers into her glass, and lifted out an ice cube. Without looking down, she deftly rubbed the ice on each of her nipples, causing them to pucker instantly and stand erect.

"How come he called you here?" she asked.

Joe put his hands on her shoulders and attempted to move her from between his knees. "Oh, nothing. Just some screwup I've got to settle," he said. "Baby, I really do have to get moving."

She put down her drink and, without warning, shoved him backward on the bed and straddled his chest. "What's so important, Joe?" she said softly, rotating her hips. "Nothing could be more important than this."

"Baby, come on, don't," he protested weakly, holding her by the waist to try and keep her from moving. He was beginning to react despite himself. "I can't. I've got to go."

"Why, Joe?" she moaned. "Don't you want some more? *Hmmm?*"

"Sure, Baby, but . . ."

Baby lifted herself, moving slightly back, and forced him to

19

enter her. He tried to move and couldn't. She was squeezing with her knees, holding his torso in a viselike grip.

"What's going on at the office, Joe?" she said, staring down at him, her arms straight, her elbows locked on either side of his head. "I'm not going to let you move until you tell me."

"You gotta let me move, hon," he said with a low chuckle. "I'm going crazy here."

"Tell me what's going on, Joe," she repeated, this time through clenched teeth.

"Okay, okay," he said, breathing heavily.

She loosened her grip slightly, and he was able to thrust higher inside her.

"That was Sam on the phone," he said, between thrusts.

"And?" she asked, with a little shiver.

Oh, what the hell, he thought. She'll find out soon enough anyway. What difference will it make if I tell her now?

"Lolly Pines is dead," he grunted, feeling his climax building.

Baby stopped moving and stared down at him. Her eyes were wild and bright. Her lips parted, and she began to emit a sound like none he had every heard. A low, guttural moan that built as her body began to rotate again, slowly at first and then escalating into such wild gyrations that he wondered if he would be able to stay inside her.

"Say it again," she panted. *"Say it again,* Joe."

"Say what?" he gasped, looking up at her in disbelief.

"About Lolly."

"She's . . . dead," he said, barely able to find the breath to speak as he plunged deeper and deeper.

Baby froze in place, at least outwardly. Inside he could feel the grip of twitching muscles as she threw her head back and screamed in ecstasy. "Oh, God, Joe . . . this is incredible!"

There was no need to hold back. He let himself come. Somewhere in the back of his head he knew what he was feeling inside Baby was something he had never felt with her before.

He had finally given her an orgasm.

3

The police station was only a few blocks away, in the center of Central Park, so it was only minutes after she had called 911 that Kick heard sirens. With the police came the building super, Eddie the doorman, and an Emergency Medical Service crew, and only minutes later a nice man in his fifties from the paper who introduced himself as Sam Nichols. He said he had known Lolly for more than twenty years and would take over the funeral arrangements and make the appropriate calls.

Kick led the way up the two flights of stairs and into the office. Everyone crowded around Lolly's body, speaking in low, authoritative tones. When Kick realized that what looked like a big black rubber sheet was a body bag, she looked away from the medical worker who was unfolding it on the floor. She heard the metallic screech of an industrial zipper. When she turned around, Lolly and the medics were gone from the room. Through the office door Kick caught a glimpse of white-coated arms holding the stretcher bearing Lolly's tiny rubber-wrapped body. They maneuvered her around the newel post at the top of the stairs and disappeared.

Two policemen stayed behind. She knew they were saying something to her about making a report, something about an accidental death, but she couldn't focus on the words. When the policemen left, only Mr. Nichols remained, standing, slope-shouldered, in the middle of the room.

"You gonna be okay, kid?" he asked gently.

Kick looked up at him and nodded. "Thank you, yes."

"Kinda rough, huh?" he said. He was beginning to fidget, as though eager to leave.

Kick drew a deep breath. "I feel a bit unglued. Is there anything I should be doing?"

Nichols looked down at his scuffed shoes. "Officially? No," he said. "I guess the paper's gonna want to put out a big story on her. Maybe you could dig up some background on her. Stuff we wouldn't have on file. She led quite a life."

Kick felt her spirits lift with the idea of something, anything, that might get her mind off feeling so helpless and empty.

"I guess I could look around. I feel kind of creepy going through her things."

"Don't make a bit of difference now," Nichols said.

"Well, okay. If it will help."

Nichols looked at his watch and began to fidget again. "Great. I'll be at the paper. Give me a call if you come up with anything."

Kick thanked Sam Nichols again and walked him down the three flights of stairs.

It wasn't until she had closed the door and turned around that she realized she had no place to be in the big apartment. She didn't want to go to her room. The thought of casually sitting down and watching television seemed almost sacrilegious.

It was nearly six and she was starving. She fixed herself a cup of tea and found half a leftover pizza in the fridge. Then she showered, pulled on her old robe, and climbed back to the tower office. At that time of day, the weird room was at its most eerie.

The sun threw odd shards of light onto the glass ceiling. Through the pigeon droppings, she watched the sky turn indigo as night approached.

She sat down in Lolly's high-backed chair, surprised to see that the computer had been on all along. Strange—it had gone on humming while Lolly's life ebbed away.

Kick sensed that the job Sam Nichols had given her was busywork, a kind way to make her feel useful. But she wanted to really do something. Lolly hadn't been an easy woman to like, but Kick had come to care for her and, more important, respect her. She had taught Kick some important lessons about people and power. Maybe she could write something real for Sam Nichols, use all her skills to bear witness to a remarkable woman's life and at the same time show the *Courier* the stuff Kick was made of. It was time, Kick realized with a growing sense of conviction, to take back her own place in the world. Her wounds seemed healed, and Lolly had taught her a lot about how not to get hurt again. She felt that she was standing on a threshold, poised to step out into her real life. After all she'd been through, she finally felt ready to begin.

Kick Butler's mother, Maureen, died while giving birth to her somewhere over the Atlantic on TransEuropa's Flight 314 from London to New York the day President Kennedy was assassinated. Always fit and slender, Maureen had been one of those women whose pregnancies hardly showed. Even at six months, some friends had sworn she wasn't pregnant at all. At eight months, she had been small enough to evade the airline's regulation against flying the imminently due by claiming she was only seven months along.

She had been determined to make the trip from London, where she was visiting her ailing mother, to New York, because her husband of just eighteen months had been struck by a car crossing 87th Street and lay in intensive care at Mount Sinai Hospital. But labor—or rather, an ominous and violent bleeding

—had commenced halfway across the Atlantic, and by the time the flight landed, it was too late to do anything but try to save the baby. The surgeons managed to do that just hours before Kick's father passed away from his injuries, never having regained consciousness.

Given the sensationally tragic circumstances of her entry into the world, what was always so surprising about Kick Butler was her indomitable good spirits. But then, the tears had all been shed long before she could walk. And the exuberant love of her paternal grandmother, Eleanor, never left Kick much time for self-pity. The implacable lady had gathered up the little bundle of a baby not two days after her parents' deaths, christened her Katherine Maureen, and held her close to her heart for the next two decades. What you've never had, you don't miss, and Kick was happy living with her grandmother in a brownstone apartment in Greenwich Village.

The best part was that TransEuropa had been so mired in bad publicity after the ordeal that the board of directors had tried to bolster the company's image by granting Kick a lifetime free pass for two on the airline. And when TransEuropa merged with Oriental Airways, that little PR gesture became the passport to Kick's truly unusual childhood.

Kick and Eleanor went everywhere. Eleanor had inherited some money and invested it wisely, so they were able to stay at the best hotels the world over. Fearless and friendly, Kick traveled through the world wide-eyed, talking to anyone within earshot and compiling what would become her B list.

In her mind, Kick's future was never in doubt. She wanted to be a journalist. She wrote for her middle-school, high-school, and college newspapers, and after she graduated she went to Columbia's School of Journalism without skipping a beat.

Her grandmother died soon after she graduated, bequeathing to Kick only a little bit of money—most of it had been spent during the traveling years—but leaving her granddaughter a legacy of love that could never be replaced.

* * *

Kick soon discovered how much work could ease her loneliness. By the time she started her first full-time job on a dreary suburban Massachusetts newspaper, she was happy again. At last, she was doing what she'd wanted to do all her life. She was getting paid for her powers of observation and her ability to write about what she saw. Granted, she was observing sewer-committee meetings and school-board hearings, but it was a beginning. She was getting the professional background she needed to return someday to New York and what she considered the journalism big time.

Just after her second Thanksgiving in Massachusetts, a B-list connection got her an interview with Fedalia Null, editor of *Fifteen Minutes* magazine. She spent the weekend before her Monday appointment in the town library reading every copy of *Fifteen Minutes* on file. It was heady stuff. Stylish and quirky, the magazine carried articles by some of the best writers of the eighties. It would be a stretch, but if given the chance she knew she could measure up.

She arrived at the magazine's offices in the Mosby Media Building on East 54th Street in New York City, on a frigid December morning, inwardly reciting her grandmother's perpetual advice like a prayer: "Just be yourself."

The walls of the reception room of the thirtieth-floor executive offices were lined with the framed faces of people who had, according to the Warhol formulation, been famous for fifteen minutes. She was shown into a sweeping office where Fedalia Null was standing behind her wing-shaped desk, wearing a bright pink smock that showed the vague outlines of a full figure and a high collar of pearls the size of Ping-Pong balls. She was pretty, if overly made up, and very, very scary.

"Ms. Butler," Null said, extending her hand. "Come, sit down."

Kick settled into a black bentwood contraption in front of the editor's desk and tugged at her skirt.

"You're a good writer, kid. Good but not slick. We do slick. I give my writers a lot of authority. I like to let them put themselves into a story. I realize this is not quite kosher by old journalistic standards, but it works for us. You ever read *Fifteen Minutes*?"

Kick nodded. "Of course."

"Think you can write slick? Think you can burrow in and figure out who people really are?" Null asked, snapping open a black snakeskin cigarette case. "I smoke," she said. "I don't ask if anyone minds. If anyone jerks me around about it, I tell them they should be kind to a dying woman. Shuts them up."

Kick laughed. She had heard that Fedalia Null was mean. She didn't seem mean at all—just tough. Kick appreciated the difference.

Kick shifted in her chair. "To answer your question," she said, "I think I can write like that. I'd like to try, let me put it that way."

"Do it," the editor said.

"Sorry?" Kick said, blinking.

"I'm not going to hire you," she said. "Putting someone on the payroll here means the goddamn medical plan, withholding, FDIC, all that cradle-to-grave paperwork the fucking government puts us through. You hire somebody, they become your child. If I wanted children, I would have sent for some."

Kick cleared her throat. "Ah, let me understand. You're telling me to 'do it,' but you're not hiring me."

Fedalia Null stood up, walked to the window, and leaned against the sill. "There's a designer up in Harlem," she said, tapping the ash from her cigarette into a pot holding a fake ficus tree. "Someone was telling me about him at dinner last night. He designs funeral fashions. You know, outfits people get buried in. Only he just makes half the outfit. The part that shows. You know, half a suit, half a gown, just the toes of the shoes. That kind of thing.

"I think it would make an interesting feature. You want to give it a shot?"

"Ah . . . yeah, well . . . ah, yeah, sure," Kick said. "I mean, you're serious about this, right?"

"As serious as cancer," Null said, pushing away from the

window and snatching a slip of paper from her desk. "Here's his name and number. I don't give a damn about his hopes and dreams. I want to know the nuts and bolts of such a wacko business. Do it.

"Give me two thousand words. If I like it, I'll buy it and give you another assignment. Three's the charm around here. That's when we make you a contributing editor. Your dreams will be answered. The money is socko. Everything you ever wanted will be yours, and life will be one long dance in the sun."

Kick did the piece. Fedalia liked it. In January, she got two more assignments, one a bizarre gay murder-suicide on Sutton Place and the other a long profile of a twenty-four-year-old woman who had inherited and was operating a fleet of tugboats in New York Harbor.

Kick knew when she handed in the charmed third feature that waiting to hear from Fedalia Null would be excruciating. She had taken a lot of time off to do the magazine interviews. Because she couldn't lie to her boss at the paper, he was aware of what she had been up to. At first he was supportive, but now his own boss was leaning on him, and he had become less amused.

Kick's anxiety about the magazine was compounded by the very real possibility that she could be out of a job altogether and back to square one.

Every day for the first excruciating week, she raced back to her grungy garden apartment in Springfield after work to sit and wait for the phone to ring. She couldn't bear to even put on the television for distraction. When the waiting dragged into the second week with no word from Fedalia, she knew she had to do something to move her life along.

It was time to take one of those risks her grandmother always used to encourage.

The next morning, phone call or not, she would quit her job and go back to New York. Her grandmother's rental in the brownstone in the Village had been lost when she died, but Kick knew she could find an apartment, at least a sublet. She had her small inheritance, not enough to live on, but it would buy meat for any wolf that appeared at her door. What she wanted, more than anything, was to get back to New York to show Fedalia Null that she was making herself available to come on board the magazine. Out of sight was out of mind in the media big-time she so longed to be part of.

By the first Monday in February, Kick was settled in a sublet near Gramercy Park. First thing that morning, she dialed the number for the magazine, identified herself, and was put straight through to the editor's office. She didn't even get a chance to say hello.

"Where the hell are you?" Fedalia demanded.

"Ah . . . I'm here," Kick said, startled. "Here in New York. I quit the paper."

"Hot damn, that's the best news I've had all day. How soon can you get up here? I've got a humdinger for you."

Fedalia's eager reception emboldened Kick to ask, "How was my tugboat piece?"

"Vickie didn't call you?"

"Ah . . . no, not that I know of."

"Damn. I'm sorry, Kick. I guess I forgot to tell her. I've been swamped," Fedalia said apologetically. "I liked it. We're going to use it, probably in the spring. Now, get in here."

Fedalia was on the phone when Kick arrived in the big black office on the thirtieth floor. She waved Kick to sit down, gave the receiver two short pecks with her pursed magenta lips, and hung up. She smiled across at Kick and scraped all ten matching magenta fingernails through her massive hair.

"That was Peter Shea," Fedalia said, referring to the famous journalist. "To be honest with you, I originally asked him to do this interview, but he has a conflict and suggested you. He likes your pieces too."

"Are you sure I can do it?" Kick asked. It seemed to her that something that would have gone to Peter Shea, the magazine's star, might be a bit over her head. Fedalia nodded. "I'm sure. Your work is young and crisp. You have a way of asking about things that older reporters might pull their punches on. I like that. Great answers come from risky questions. And this assignment is definitely risky."

"Okay," Kick said agreeably, although she was wondering what had happened to Fedalia's three's-a-charm rule. Apparently, what she was about to give her was just another freelance assignment. "What is it?"

Fedalia leaned forward on her folded arms. "Lionel Maltby has agreed through his arrogant son-of-bitch agent to sit down for his first print interview."

"Oh, my . . ."

"I can't believe I agreed to all of his agent's bullshit demands. Call me a whore, but every publication in the country wants Maltby, and Irving Fourbraz, agent to the elevated impostors among us, has convinced him he should talk to *Fifteen Minutes*."

Kick was surprised at Fedalia's criticism of Maltby. Nothing she had ever read about the prize-winning author dared call him anything but a genius. "Do you think Lionel Maltby is an impostor?"

"Kinda," Fedalia said, leaning back in her chair. "I don't trust media monsters. He was picked up out of nowhere and given the treatment. I think it damaged something in him. He's never written anything nearly as good as his first book, and yet they keep saying he's brilliant even though his last book was three years late. Personally, I think he got a case of the encore sweats. That's what I want you to find out."

"Interesting," Kick said. "Some people don't even think he exists. When I was in college, my contemporary-lit professor swore Maltby was a pen name for Thomas Pynchon."

"Maltby's real, all right. Alive and well up in Connecticut somewhere with a new book to promote. That's why he's coming out of hiding. Mind you, this is the man who wouldn't even show to pick up his National Book Award."

"For *The Arms of Venus*. I read that. You're right, everything he did after that was kind of blah."

"They were dreck," Fedalia said emphatically. "But because

people were told he was brilliant, they sold like fuzzy dice at Graceland."

Kick remembered Maltby's first book well. She had read *The Arms of Venus* when it was on the best-seller list. She found it bewilderingly obscure and wondered what all the fuss was about. The film rights were sold. A picture was never made, but Maltby's fame was so pervasive Kick once had an argument with a girl who swore she had seen the movie.

Maltby's one and only much-touted television appearance had taken place in prime time, right after *The Arms of Venus* hit the best-seller list. He had been seated on a bulbous sofa with Barbara Walters facing him from another bulbous sofa. After a fawning setup of his singular accomplishment, Walters asked Maltby one of those if-you-were-a-tree, what kind-of-a-tree-would-you-be? questions. Maltby fixed her with a murderous stare, muttered the "C" word loud enough for several million viewers to hear, and walked off the set, not to be heard from again for the next decade except on the pages of his next two books. Through careful handling he remained famous, more for being difficult to reach than for his subsequent literary achievements. Occasionally he would pen angry letters and articles that were published in magazines and newspapers—all from hiding.

"*Whoa,*" Kick said, blowing out her cheeks. "I don't know what to say. Of course. I want to do it. I *can* do it. I guess what I need to know is, do *you* think I can do it?"

Fedalia sighed. "Kick," she said, her tone kinder than Kick was used to. "If you were more experienced, I would take that as a disingenuous remark. To ask it puts the responsibility on me, and I have enough, thank you awfully much. Now, scram. Victoria has a stack of background stuff for you on him at her desk. You can go over it tonight."

"Great," Kick said, gathering her things to leave. "What kind of a piece do you want?"

"I want whatever you find out," Fedalia said, lighting another cigarette and fanning away the smoke. "What I don't want is any of the flyblown lit-crit crap. Anyone who cares about his work knows about it already. What our readers are interested in is where the hell has he been? I want mood, how he lives, what he makes of what his life became. We want to know what he eats, who his friends, lovers, wives are. The invisible hook to the story should be, 'Yo, big boy, what's your *problem*?' You might also ask him why he called Barbara Walters a cunt."

"Okay. Ground rules, please, ma'am."

"Forgive me, Kick, I had to agree to some Mickey Mouse stuff. If any of this bothers you, tell me, and I'll see if I can work something out."

"As long as I don't have to interview him nude with my hair on fire, I'm sure it will be okay."

The deal Fedalia Null had agreed to was a bit unorthodox but nothing Kick couldn't go along with.

A car would pick her up at the main entrance of the the Mosby Building the next day. Kick was to lie down on the backseat and be driven to her first meeting with Lionel Maltby at his country hideaway. Fedalia continued to read from her notes, occasionally glancing up at Kick to emphasize the ridiculous self-importance implicit in such cloak-and-dagger trappings. Maltby had agreed to speak with her for one hour. If things went well, they'd agree to a subsequent few hours. While Fedalia read, Kick wondered if Peter Shea had really refused the interview because Maltby's agent was demanding such foolish guidelines. She quickly dismissed such thoughts as disloyal and gave her full attention to Fedalia.

Fedalia held up one finger. "One more thing," she said. "Maltby has final approval of all quotes."

Kick shrugged. "That's all right with me. I use a tape recorder and I don't misquote."

"Great, then done is done."

"Thank you, Ms. Null. I'm very grateful and excited."

"*Au contraire*, my dear. I thank you," Fedalia said, standing and walking Kick toward the door. "You'll find a large white envelope with the material Vickie's pulled together for you. That's personal."

"Ah . . . am I getting paid for my last piece?"

"That's in the mail," Fedalia said, smiling. "I'm making you a contributing editor. Your contract is in the envelope."

"Truly?" Kick whispered, overcome. "Then you *did* mean it when you said three articles were the charm."

"Well, of course, you goose," Fedalia snapped. "If you'd called me sooner, you'd already be on staff."

Kick hit the big glass doors from the lobby of the Mosby Building with both hands and swept out onto East 54th Street. She made it to the corner of Madison Avenue at a dead run. She felt like Rocky and wished there weren't so many people around so she could have leapt straight up and punched the air. She had never been so happy. Now she understood why composers and artists and people who loved the work they did lived to be so old. If she could just keep writing for *Fifteen Minutes* magazine, she felt she could live forever. Thank you, God, she thought. It can't get any better than this.

At nine sharp the next day, a dark-green Mercedes station wagon eased its way up East 54th Street and pulled to the curb in front of her. A youngish-looking man in jeans and a leather jacket swung out of the driver's seat, looked straight at her, and opened the back door.

Kick waved and scampered across the pavement toward the waiting car.

"Good morning, Miss Butler," the driver said, pleasantly. "I'm Randy, Mr. Fourbraz's driver."

"Hello, Randy," Kick said, sliding into the backseat and grabbing at the hem of her skirt to keep the door from slamming on it. Why was Maltby's agent's driver driving the car? Kick wondered.

She waited nervously for Randy to get behind the wheel before she spoke. "You'll tell me when I'm supposed to lie down back here, okay?"

Randy was trying to nose the big car out into the morning

traffic when Kick spoke. He swiveled his head around and stared for an instant. "How's that?"

She pulled herself forward and leaned on the back of the front seat to explain.

Randy listened patiently until she finished. He had been shaking his head through the whole explanation. "I don't know anything about that, Miss Butler," he said in a bemused voice.

Kick sat back fuming. She couldn't wait to tell Fedalia. The agent must have made all those spy-novel demands just to see how far Fedalia would go to get the interview.

The rest of the trip was spent in silence. They left the interstate and continued for a mile or so on a two-lane road. Without warning, the driver took a hard right and stopped in front of a low wrought-iron gate set in a gray stone wall. He opened his window and spoke into a small metal box on the stone pillar.

"Randy with Miss Butler," he announced.

"Come on down," a disembodied male voice said.

The car wound its way down a very long driveway into a little valley, then reached the crest of a small rise. The bare trees of the dense woods on either side of the road gave way to a shingled house with green shutters looking out over the water of the sound.

Tiny whitecaps in the dark water were being churned up by an offshore wind. Low dark clouds blurred the horizon line and made it impossible to tell where the water ended and the sky began.

To Kick, it looked like a black-and-white movie in which the only spot of color was the red flannel shirt on the man standing in the open door of the house. He was of medium height and wearing brown corduroy trousers and penny loafers.

She was gathering up her coat and the handbag holding her notes, notebook, and tape recorder when the door to her left opened and the man in the red shirt bent down. He was smiling.

"Miss Butler, I presume," he said, pleasantly.

Ummm, Kick thought, nice face, good teeth. This was going to

33

be fun. She liked a face she could flirt with a bit; it made for more interesting quotes.

She pulled herself out of the car and stood up, extending her hand. "Everyone calls me Kick," she said.

His hand felt strong and very warm.

He was a head taller than she. His face was weathered and ruddy. There were tiny wisps of white barely visible at the temples of his brown, collar-length hair.

So this was the great Lionel Maltby, Kick thought, smiling up at him. He was handsome enough to be a cliché. It was a look she didn't quite trust. Men who looked like he did knew its effect and used it. But, hey, she thought, I'm not standing out here in the freezing cold checking out a blind date. Maltby being too good-looking could be worked nicely into her piece.

She was still holding his hand. "Oh, sorry," she said, letting go and looking toward the house.

Maltby turned to the driver, who seemed to be waiting for orders. "You'll be back for Ms. Butler, right, Randy?"

Randy nodded and got back into the car.

So the hour rule was sticking, she thought as she waved good-bye to Randy.

Lionel turned and put his hand lightly on her elbow. "You're just in time, Kick. I need your help."

"Oh?" she said, as they moved across the gravel of the driveway toward the open front door.

"Have you had breakfast yet?"

"Why, yes . . . I have. But I could stand some coffee."

"Great, come with me."

She stood in the small foyer and suppressed a gulp. The big living room was as artfully arranged as a Flemish painting and, despite the grayness of the winter morning, glowed with warmth. The stucco walls were pale yellow, the ceiling beamed in weathered oak. There were wide windows on three sides and a nearly walk-in fireplace on the fourth.

The windows that looked out on the sound were free of

curtains. The floor was covered with a beautifully worn antique Oriental rug. Low, white-cotton-duck-covered sofas faced each other in front of the fireplace. Deep, flowered-chintz-covered chairs were set at angles around the room, each lit with the golden glow of a reading lamp. Tabletops were stacked with current books and magazines. On the floor beside the fireplace sat a large Victorian basket brimming with ripe fruit and nuts.

Maltby took Kick's coat and hung it on a bentwood rack by the door, then gently pressed his palm against the small of her back to guide her toward the kitchen.

The kitchen was enough to make Martha Stewart pitch forward onto her sharpest Cuisinart blade.

The walls were Wedgwood blue, the floor gleaming honey-colored wooden boards. Burnished antique copper cookware and draping plants in blue-and-white wicker baskets hung from the frame of a wide skylight over a double-size butcher-block table in the center of the room. A huge, black Gardiner stove loomed at one end, and navy blue state-of-the-art appliances lined the other walls.

Over the aroma of lemon Pledge and floor wax, Kick could smell something burning.

"Goddamn it," Maltby growled, striding to the huge black stove, where tufts of smoke were seeping from around the door of one of the ovens. He grabbed a mitt and yanked open the door. With a yelp, he pulled out a cookie sheet and flipped it onto the butcher-block table. Four curved, black, rock-hard squares bounced off the tin and onto the floor.

"Waffles," he said, staring at her with innocent eyes. "Formerly waffles, now paving stones."

Kick looked at the black squares and recognized what had once been a frozen product from a box. "You cook a lot?"

Maltby chuckled. "You guessed," he said.

Kick looked around. "This kitchen, it's like a set on a gourmet-cooking show."

"This kitchen came with the house."

"Where are the rest of the waffles?" she asked, looking in the direction of the high freezer. "Let me show you how this is done."

Maltby opened the freezer and handed Kick an open box of waffles. While the door was open, she noticed the freezer was fully stocked with carefully wrapped frozen food, each package marked with the contents and date of purchase.

As the waffles toasted and the coffee filtered, Kick nervously waited for Maltby to finish a call from someone involved with the winter upkeep of a swimming pool located somewhere on the property. Finally, blue speckle-ware plates and mugs were laid out on the table and breakfast was served.

Kick's hour was melting away like the butter on Maltby's waffles. She took one sip of coffee, put down her cup, and asked, "Can we start now?"

Maltby, sitting opposite her at the butcher block took a big gulp of coffee and glanced at his watch. "I'm sorry for the call. No more interruptions. I promise."

Kick took her tape recorder out of her bag and palmed it onto the table next to her mug. Without warning, she clicked her tape on and leaned forward. "Perhaps you could tell me why you called Barbara Walters a cunt."

Maltby had just taken a sip of hot coffee. He slapped his hand across his mouth to keep from spraying the table between them. When he composed himself, he was laughing. "You don't mess around, do you?" he said, reaching for a napkin.

Kick left her face blank and stared directly at him, counting her heartbeats. "I promised I'd conduct this interview by your agent's rules, but he never said I couldn't ask about that incident."

"Rules?" Maltby asked, frowning. His gaze was just as intense as she was making hers. "Who told you I set any rules for this interview?"

"Your agent, through my editor," Kick said, holding her ground.

Maltby threw his head back and laughed. "Oh, those two.

That's a game they play. Ignore them. You can ask me anything your heart desires."

"You're serious," she said tonelessly. "There's no time limit."

"Not at all, Kick," Maltby said, sliding off his stool. "Come on. Let's take our coffee by the fire, and I'll tell you the whole Barbara Walters story and more."

Kick gathered her things, followed him to the living room, and made herself comfortable on one of the facing sofas. As Maltby set a match to an already perfectly laid fire, she glanced out toward the sound.

"Oh, look," she said. "It's beginning to snow."

Great solid white pieces of snow were blowing at a slant against the wide windows. The water of the sound had become strangely black and still.

He looked out the window for an instant, then returned to poking the fire. As the logs caught and flared, Kick was suddenly filled with an odd nostalgia. Only a few times in her life had she been someplace so appealing, so otherworldly that she felt she would never be anywhere as beautiful. Instead of instilling a quiet, happy calmness, those moments filled her with a kind of longing. She had felt that way walking across a London bridge in the fog or standing in front of Notre Dame alone in the moonlight on a summer night. And now, sitting in this beautiful house, seemingly in the middle of nowhere, the water, the fire, the snow, and the tension in the eyes and crooked smile of the engaging man she was alone with filled her with that same feeling, the feeling of wanting something more.

She wanted Lionel Maltby to like her. She wanted him to think she was smart.

This is heavy stuff, the tiny mean voice in the back of her head whispered, interrupting her thoughts. *Be careful, you have a job to do.*

Maltby sat down on the opposite couch. "Before we start, I just want to say what a wonderful surprise you are. I expected a cross between Beatrice Arthur and Golda Meir, and I get a water sprite, a sunflower of a girl who can say 'cunt' without batting an eye."

He hooked his thumbs under his belt and sat back on the couch. *"Ahhh."* he sighed. "I hope it snows forever."

Kick flushed with pleasure. She picked up her tape recorder and played with the volume control.

Easy, girl, she cautioned herself. She hadn't been alone with a grown man with a working brain since Professor Stand-Up, let alone one with crinkles at the corners of his pale blue eyes and sofa-filling shoulders. A famous author had just called her a sprite and a sunflower and told her he was hers for as long as she liked.

She took a long, deep breath, straightened her shoulders, and asked him the cunt question again.

This time he answered it. The Walters interview had come at the end of an extremely trying day in which he had given over a dozen interviews. By the time he sat down face-to-face with Barbara, he was feeling ill used and fed up with the whole process. He had simply lost his temper and said the C-word.

Maltby sat back and began to talk without prodding. And what followed was the smoothest interview Kick had ever done. For every question she asked, she got full-blown, well-shaped answers filled with anecdotes that were both funny and self-effacing. He was open, guileless, and utterly charming, a far different man from what she had expected as she tossed and turned the night before.

Suddenly, just after two o'clock, in the middle of a long story about a trip through Mexico in a lightning-striped school bus during his hippie days, Maltby stopped talking and jumped up from the couch. "Ladies' room is off the foyer," he said, pointing. "Use any towel you find. Stretch your legs a bit. I'll be right back."

Kick was startled by the abrupt change of pace and clicked off her tape.

When she returned from the bathroom, he was not around. She strolled around the room, looking at the books in the bookcases, lifting a magazine or two—he seemed to subscribe to everything. She scanned the room for family pictures, a girlfriend, an ex-wife, little fat kiddies with sand buckets and funny hats. Nothing. There didn't seem to be anything personal or sentimental in the room.

She was standing at the window looking out at what had developed into a real blizzard when she heard him behind her. Maltby was maneuvering a large tray onto the coffee table. There was a bottle of champagne under his arm. The stems of two flutes protruded from both pockets of his pants.

"Got to feed the inner blabbermouth," he said, standing proudly beside his presentation. It consisted of a large bowl of cold fried chicken, napkins, and a small dish of stuffed olives.

"I'm not too good at this. At least I took it out of the bucket."

Kick was touched. It took a very secure man to present a meal out of whatever he could find. Anyway, leftover franchise chicken was one of her favorites.

Kick had finished most of her first glass of champagne before she had worked up the nerve for the next question. "I have to ask you about the women in your life," she said, looking away into the fire that he had freshly stoked.

"*Ah*, the women . . ." he said, smiling wistfully. "Let's have another drink first. Here." He lifted the champagne bottle and waited for her glass. "What time do you have to be back in the city?"

Kick shrugged. "I'm supposed to go to the Philharmonic with a friend," she said halfheartedly. "That's at eight."

"*Ummm*," he said, pouring himself another glass. "Why don't I call Randy and tell him six-thirty? Okay with you?"

"Sure," Kick said, feeling a bit depressed even thinking about when their session would be over. "Fine. Six-thirty would be fine."

The tiny mean voice was back as soon as he left the room to telephone.

It's snowing, it cooed. *It's snowing like mad. Think about it. Cars can't drive in a country blizzard. People get stranded. Happens in Stephen King novels all the time.* The voice turned nastier, taunting her. *Have some more champagne—on the job—while you're working.*

39

Have some more champagne and watch the snow come down blocking the country roads stranding you with this big hot man.

"Shut up," she said aloud, squirming against the cushions.

"Sorry," Maltby said, strolling back into the room.

Kick flushed, thinking he had heard her talking to herself.

He sat down with a big sigh. "It looks like you're stuck with me for a while. Randy says they can't get the plow up his road until this lets up a bit."

"I'd better warn my friend," Kick said. "Can I use your phone?"

While Kick was on the phone, Maltby brushed by her on his way to the refrigerator. He smelled of woodsmoke and lemon aftershave. When she got back to the sofa by the fire, he had opened another bottle of champagne. Her glass was full. He had put an album on the stereo. Chopin filled the room.

They sat silently for several minutes, watching the fire, sipping their champagne, and listening to the music. Kick wished she knew what he was thinking. As for herself, her mind swirled, a combination of champagne, circumstances, and the presence of the most extraordinarily attractive man she had ever met.

As the music paused between movements, Maltby spoke, leaning forward. He leveled his blue eyes at hers and spoke four of the most provocative words in the English language.

"Tell me about yourself," he asked softly.

If she hadn't by then drowned the tiny mean voice with so much champagne, it would have been screaming at her, telling her what she had known since high school. Professional journalists never, never talk about themselves while conducting an interview. A professional journalist must remain neutral, uninvolved.

She couldn't remember exactly when Lionel Maltby slipped across the space between the sofas and sat down next to her. She thought he did it when she got to the part her about her affair with Professor Stand-Up. She knew she was being very witty. Lionel was laughing a lot. They talked for hours.

He touched her only once, a slight pat on the hand. Okay,

twice . . . He casually put his hand on the top part of her knee the time he got up to put another log on the fire. Three times, actually. He did it again when he got up to change the CD to Joachim Rodrigo's *Concerto de Aranjo,* a heartstopping classical Spanish guitar work Kick was familiar with and loved. As the music swelled, she was too dazed to do anything but glance up at him and sigh.

The snow had stopped. The sky over the sound was now clear and pitch-black. Lionel stepped to the window on his way back from changing the music.

"Kick," he said excitedly. "Come here. Look."

She struggled up from the couch, grabbing the arm to steady herself against a swoosh of dizziness that hit her between the eyes. She stumbled against him as she joined him at the window.

Lionel reached out and casually pulled her to his side. "Have you ever seen so many stars?"

Indeed, the sky was punctured with thousands of tiny diamondlike specks of light.

"How do you feel?" he asked, looking down at her.

"A little woozy." She giggled. "God, this is beautiful."

"I want to show you something else," he said, taking her hand. "Come with me."

He walked her through the kitchen and down a long dark hall. At the end of the hall he pushed a heavy door open and flicked on a light. A wide redwood deck dusted with snow stretched several yards along the side of the house facing the water. In the center was a sunken pool of water lit from below. Great plumes of steam rose from the surface of the water into the freezing blackness under the stars.

"I jump in there every night," he said. "It's fabulous. Makes you feel reborn."

"You do?" Kick slurred. "It's freezing."

"Not in the tub," he said, leading her to a wooden cabana arrangement off to one side of the pool. He opened the door and took a long sweatshirt from a hook on the back.

"Here," he said, handing her the shirt. "Put this on. I'll go change. You haven't lived until you've tried this."

He was standing very close. Their chests nearly touched. The vapor from his mouth felt damp and cool on her cheek.

"Are you trying to seduce me in a hot tub, Mr. Maltby?" she asked.

"Don't worry, Kick," he said very seriously. "I certainly wouldn't with a lady who might put it in an article."

He turned and walked further down the deck, disappearing into what must have been another dressing room.

Kick looked at the shirt, then at the hot tub. She had to admit it seemed inviting. Her shoulders ached from sitting all day. At least it would soak out the effects of the champagne.

She stepped inside the wooden cabana and shoved her bag under an old blanket to keep the cold night air from damaging her tape recorder. She pulled off her sweater and bra. What the hell, she thought, pulling the sweatshirt over her head, then pulling off her skirt and panty hose. He was being so sweet and nonthreatening. The least she could do was be a good sport and try something new. Wasn't that what being a journalist was all about? Being curious about life and open to new experiences? She would clear her mind for a bit, then ask him to call Randy. Describing the hot tub would add a nice touch to the story. She would leave out the fact that she got in it herself.

Hugging herself against the blast of cold air that swept up her bare legs and under the loose sweatshirt, she trotted across the deck and eased herself through the cloud of steam and into the luminous, swirling water. She pulled the sweatshirt off over her head, then let herself down onto the redwood bench below the water line and let the water rise up to her neck, thinking that this must be what amniotic fluid feels like to a happy baby.

She closed her eyes and leaned back. Droplets of water bounced against her face and into her hair as she let her limbs relax and bob in the water.

From a distance she could hear Mozart woodwinds coming

closer. She opened her eyes to see Lionel wearing swim trunks. She tried not to notice that he had a terrific body, as she had guessed. He was carrying a portable boom box in one hand and a canvas bag in the other. Kick leaned back and closed her eyes again. "This must be what heaven is like," she said above the low rumble of the gurgling water and the Mozart.

She opened her eyes to see him sitting across from her, handing her another icy glass of champagne.

Kick took a sip and looked up at the cold, velvety sky, so clear that some of the stars seemed to be moving. "We never got to the woman question," she said softly.

Maltby stared up at the stars for a long moment. "There aren't any woman stories to tell, Kick. That is, unless it's just between you and me."

"Between you and me? Well, you know I'm a journalist."

"But your tape recorder's not here?" he said, pretending to peek under the frothy water.

Kick giggled. "No, of course not. Now stop that!" she said, splashing him lightly.

Lionel smiled, then leaned his head back again and gazed at the stars.

He began to speak, softly but firmly, prefacing his words by swearing he never talked about his relationships. He lived them and used them in his work. "But there's something about you, Kick," he said, reaching over and pushing a strand of hair behind her ear. "I don't know . . . I trust you."

There had been two wives. The wife before he got famous, who left him, and the beauty he married after he was famous, who wanted the restaurants and parties but not the loneliness and servitude of being a recluse writer's "life facilitator."

The implication was that the second wife was now out of the picture. Now there was no one. No one to listen, no one to cook and care for him. No one to share in what he was convinced would be his ultimate triumph—the publication of his first really honest work.

Kick listened, luxuriating in the water that was turning every muscle in her body to Play-Doh. She said nothing, merely responding with a nod from time to time.

When the champagne was gone, he stopped talking and sat staring up at the stars for a long time. Finally, he turned to look at her. "You have ice in your hair," he said, reaching across and brushing the frozen specks from the curls around her face. "Let's get out of here before we melt. Wait, I'll get us a couple of robes."

As they walked across the deck toward the house, wrapped in thick terry-cloth robes, he stopped and turned to her. "Do I have to say it?" he asked.

Kick looked up at him. "Say what, Lionel?"

He cupped her face in his hands. "Stay," he said. "Stay here with me. I don't want you to leave."

"Why?" she asked.

He looked out toward the dark water, then dropped his hands. "You know why."

"I want you to tell me," she said, not looking at him.

"I want you."

"I shouldn't," she said, knowing it sounded like yes.

The tiny mean voice said nothing. Smiling is soundless. The tiny mean voice was smiling.

Kick stayed on at the beautiful house in the middle of nowhere for the next three days.

They made love in the big down-filled featherbed upstairs, in a room that looked like one she had once stayed in at a Swiss ski resort. They made love on a fur throw in front of the fire in the golden living room. In a giggling fit in the morning they chased each other around and around the butcher-block table in the kitchen, then made love on it among the English-muffin crumbs and overturned coffee mugs.

Kick thawed out some of the neatly wrapped food in the freezer. She roasted a ham and some chickens for meals taken in front of the fire.

They considered making love on the beach during their walks

along the water's edge, but it was too cold. They settled for starting to make love in the hot tub and finishing on a towel-covered chaise in the cabana.

It seemed they never stopped touching, exploring, melding together.

She would lie awake in the huge, downy bed watching him sleep with one arm over his eyes, trying to figure out what was so different, why what he did to her drove her to near-crazed abandon.

Desperately, she tried to figure out how to make it last. How to keep him in her life indefinitely. She was too in love to play the games she had seen her friends play. To be artful and focused, to scheme a future with him, she would have to have the know-how and a clear head. Anyway, she was too proud to practice the contrived coyness some women used to hold on to someone. Such plotting required a different kind of mind from the one she possessed.

She felt, lying in the great, cloudy haven of his bed, that her very sanity depended on a narrowness of vision. She could concentrate only on what was vital for her to survive the next minute, the next hour, the rest of the day.

As erotic as their days and nights together were, what she was feeling went much farther than sex.

What she was doing, in the deep of the starry nights as she clung to Lionel Maltby's strong, wide chest, was making love with a real man. A man with all the sensitivity, gentleness, and passion she had read about but never expected to experience. It was being held while she had orgasms that lasted so long she thought she was having an out-of-body experience. It was finding one single white rose pinned to her pillow when she awoke in a stream of winter sunlight. It was rolling over to find him standing naked next to the bed with a tray of coffee and orange juice and being carried to the shower where he joined her for more lovemaking.

He found parts of her body she didn't even know she owned

45

and concentrated on them until she begged him to bring her to climax after climax, until she was limp and whimpering, clinging to him and silently praying that time would stop.

Time became her mortal enemy. Time, that element of her life that before could never move fast enough, she now desperately wanted to freeze in place. The passage of time caused the pain she felt waiting for him to get off the phone or finish the paper. The longing she felt, staring down the beach, waiting for him to return from his morning jog, aching for his undivided attention, wanting to melt into his very flesh so they could become one person.

While she waited for him to do hated, ordinary things, she replayed the things he had said, the things that directly related to her, and studied sentences for nuance. Only once had he said something that she could cling to. One morning, when they had held each other in the room upstairs, he had been explaining how the house had been built, a routine and completely mundane subject in which she found poetry. Lazily, he had turned to her and asked, "Could you live in this house?"

She had forced herself to lie absolutely still and wait two, three, four beats before she answered, to cover her shortness of breath. As casually as she could she answered, "Sure," and prayed she had given nothing away.

One afternoon, while Lionel was working at his computer in his study off the living room, she found herself alone in the bedroom holding one of his sweatshirts to her cheek, smelling it, smelling him, and feeling the tears come to her eyes.

Late in the afternoon of the third day her pride surfaced and told her to go before she was asked.

Lionel was sitting at the butcher-block table in the kitchen when she came downstairs. For the first time since putting on his sweatshirt to sink into the hot tub, she was wearing her own clothes. Underneath, her entire body reverberated with the metamorphosis it had sustained, the swift, sometimes violent and overpowering transition from spunky sunflower to full-blown and needful woman.

She knew she would never be the same. She also knew she must keep it light, keep it happy and sweet. Her very heart was in his hands.

He looked up from what he was reading and smiled. "Randy said he'd be here at six," he said.

Kick felt a tiny ping under her left breast. *Randy!* she thought and swallowed hard. *Randy* meant she was leaving. *Randy* meant it was over. She'd had every intention of leaving, but Lionel had made the arrangements, not her. She glanced up at the clock over the stove. Six was only five minutes away.

She pulled herself onto the high stool opposite him. Not trusting herself, she waited for him to speak.

"So," he said, with a teasing glint in his eye. "Think you have enough to start your piece?"

Kick studied her hands. "It's going to be tough to keep it from being some kind of valentine," she said. Her voice caught, and she cleared her throat to cover it up.

He slipped off the stool, walked in back of her, and slipped his arms around her waist.

Please don't, she thought. Please don't come so close. Please don't touch me or I'll spin into a million little pieces. Please, please, please say something about the future. Anything. Don't make me ask. Don't stand so close.

"Kick?"

"*Um-hmmm,*" she hummed, not looking around at him. Outside, she could hear a car's tires on the gravel driveway.

"You'll come back?"

"Why?" she said, immediately wishing she hadn't said it. It sounded too needy.

Lionel, however, took it as the cue she hoped he would.

"Because I want you," he said softly, his lips in her hair.

She sat in the backseat of the green Mercedes in a daze. All the way back to the city she tried to recreate every moment of the

47

past days, only to discover that great joy, like great pain, cannot be recreated or totally remembered. All you can remember is the aura of it.

Could you live in this house? She fixed on the question and repeated it like a mantra. What had he meant? Was it a real question? Was it a foretelling of his own desire?

When she got home, she slipped through the apartment without turning on the lights. All she wanted to do was to get into bed and pretend he was with her.

She dropped her bag on the bedroom floor and pulled out the galleys of his new book. Under it she saw the sweatshirt she had snatched from the chair in the bedroom just before she left. She crawled under the covers wearing nothing but the sweatshirt, remembering his hands on her body. It occurred to her that the tiny mean voice had not said a word since it pointed out that it was snowing three days before.

The next morning she began to write. She typed so fast the machine couldn't absorb the speed and constantly beeped and shut down. After twenty or so pages, the phone rang.

"I'm waiting," Lionel's deep voice announced.

"I just got back!" She laughed, delirious with joy at the sound of his voice.

"Rent a car. I'll pay for it. Bring your stuff and come back. I can't stand it here without you."

That time she stayed with him for ten days. Ten days that replicated the first three.

As desperately as she wanted to be with him, she wanted him to be proud of her. She had to finish the piece. She had to show him how good she was. She couldn't concentrate and returned home to work.

She handed the piece in on a Monday and went to lunch with an old friend, who was in town to shop and see some shows.

With errands to run and chores to accomplish for the rest of that week, she forced herself not to think about why she had not heard from either Fedalia or Lionel.

On Friday she called the magazine to find Fedalia in a meeting.

Against her better judgment she called Lionel, her heart in her mouth when she heard his voice. When she realized the voice was recorded, she quickly hung up.

She spent the weekend trying to read, never straying far from the phone and trying desperately to shake the ominous feeling that something was going on. Something that was out of her control.

On Monday, shortly before noon, her fears were confirmed. She had just set the garbage out when the kitchen phone rang. She picked it up and started to say hello when Fedalia's voice, tight and as unchatty as Kick had ever heard it, said, "Kick, I need to see you right away."

"Hi, Fedalia," Kick said cheerily, pushing the outside door shut. "Is there a problem?" she asked, knowing there was.

"Major."

"My article?" she said flatly, her heart sinking and her forehead beading with perspiration.

"Hop a cab, kiddo," Fedalia commanded. "We need to talk."

Kick's hands were still trembling when she pushed through the heavy glass doors of the Mosby Building. They began to sweat as she followed an oddly silent Vickie down the lacquered hall to Fedalia's office.

Her door was shut as they approached. Vickie opened it and stood to one side. The first thing Kick saw, silhouetted against the big bright window, was a man of medium height with thick long white hair and an ominous, pointy black beard. He was wearing an expensively cut, dark three-piece suit, with glints of gold at the shirt cuffs, and extremely shiny tasseled loafers, so glove-thin she could almost make out the outline of his toes.

Fedalia was standing behind her desk, her face drawn and pale under her vivid makeup.

"Kick," she said, by way of greeting and introduction. "This is Irving Fourbraz. Irving, Kick Butler."

"Miss Butler," the agent said, with what Kick read as sinister formality, bowing his head slightly and not offering his hand.

Kick swallowed hard against her rising panic as she looked from Fedalia to Irving and back to Fedalia.

"Let's all sit down," Fedalia said, gesturing toward the two chairs in front of her desk. Kick and Irving sat down. Fedalia nodded to Victoria, who was standing behind Kick's chair.

"Victoria is going to take notes so that this meeting is on the record," Fedalia said, clearing her throat.

Kick couldn't tell who Fedalia was mad at, her or Irving. Her full lips were very, very thin, and her voice was a register or two lower than usual.

Fedalia sat down and tented her fingers. "Irving has some serious problems with your piece, Kick," Fedalia said briskly.

Irving has problems? Kick thought, fighting the impulse to swivel around and scream at Irving to just butt out. She turned to him and asked, "What's the problem, Mr. Fourbraz?"

Irving crossed his legs, draping a thousand-dollars' worth of suit fabric over a thousand more. "Miss Butler, as you know, we have quote approval. There are quotes attributed to Mr. Maltby in your article that are totally unacceptable."

"You used a tape, Kick? Correct?" Fedalia said, tapping her pen on her desktop.

"Of course," Kick answered evenly. She knew what Irving was up to. She had put things in the story that she hadn't taped. Things Lionel said after their interview was over, so to speak. She pushed the mental picture of the two of them in the hot tub under the stars away from the front of her brain.

There were more things, sweet Jesus, she thought. Things he had told her in bed. She hadn't dreamt there would be a problem. He had been so open and honest with her. Surely, being human, he was painting the picture of himself he was happiest with. In her experience, everyone was a little bit on—on or off the record. No one ever says over a beer or when completely relaxed, "Why don't you write that I'm a shit, that I strangled my firstborn and stole from the Red Cross jar at the office." Everything she had written cast Maltby in a gentle, kind light. There should be no question at all as to her work's validity. It was the things he told her during their private moments that made her story ring true, that made her portrait of him as accurate and telling as it was. Not only had she written the truth, but she had brought her own sense of the man to bear. Wasn't that what Fedalia had bragged about? Giving her writers the freedom to express themselves? But the real question was, What on earth could either Lionel or his agent object to?

Kick turned to Fedalia, who seemed to be waiting for a fuller explanation. "Ms. Null," she said, being deliberately formal, "I swear to you. Every quote, every statement in that piece was spoken by Lionel Maltby."

Kick could see both rows of Fedalia's teeth aligned behind her magenta lips. As she spoke nothing moved. "The tapes, Kick. We'll need to hear the tapes."

Kick looked down at her lap. She couldn't lie. She couldn't tell the truth. "I have tapes," she said feebly.

Irving raised his tanned, perfectly manicured hands in a gesture of supplication. "In that case, ladies," he said elaborately, "I am totally out of line and beg your forgiveness. All we will need is for Miss Butler to provide us with the tapes." He stood up, still smiling, and moved toward Fedalia.

"All *we* need?" Kick asked, her loathing for Irving Fourbraz burning her cheeks. "Are you including Mr. Maltby in this criticism? Did Lionel read my piece and have a problem with it?"

Just saying his name gave her strength. That must have been it—Lionel hadn't read the piece. There was no way he could have seen it and objected. Irving was jerking them all around again. He had a proven track record for that. He was probably bent out of shape because of the things Lionel had said about him, how he hyped his first book when Lionel knew it wasn't all that good, how he manipulated and exploited Lionel from the start. He was covering his own bony ass as far as she was concerned. Well, he wouldn't get away with it. He didn't care about his client. He only cared about his carefully crafted reputation, his fat commission. She put him in perspective by remembering that Lionel would have to earn twenty thousand dollars just for Irving Fourbraz to afford the slick suit he had on. To take the edge off the grim situation, she pictured him as the devil and wondered how his tailor accommodated Irving's forked tail.

"My dear Ms. Butler," he slimed. "Some of the things you claim Mr. Maltby said are very upsetting to him and his family. Even if you do have tapes of some of it, which we doubt, he is insisting that a great deal of what you have written be edited out."

Kick's head jerked up; her eyes locked with his. The word "family" had zinged by her head like a rifle shot. She had to let it go for the time being while she fought for her piece—her life. She looked at Fedalia in disbelief. "You showed Lionel my piece? You never called me . . . you never said . . ." Suddenly she got it. Irving Fourbraz controlled a lot of powerful clients.

"Just a moment, Kick," Fedalia said. She stood and extended her hand to Fourbraz. "If you'll excuse us, Irving, Miss Butler and I need to chat. Thank you for dropping by. I'll call you later. Okay? Vickie, show Mr. Fourbraz out."

Instead of shaking Fedalia's hand, Irving bent down ever so slightly and kissed the air a hair above it. Then he turned and swept out of the office with Vickie trotting behind.

Fedalia sat down and fixed Kick with a devastating you-know-that-I-know-that-you-know-that-I-know stare. She tapped her pen a few more times. Then she sent it sailing wide of Kick's right ear. "You slept with him, didn't you?" she said after the pen came to rest.

"Fedalia . . ." Kick said beseechingly.

"Jesus H. Christ," she shouted. "What turnip truck brought you to town, girl?"

"Come on, Fedalia," she said lamely. "That's not fair."

Fedalia's features moved closer together, and her eyebrows seemed to knit into one straight line. "You bet your ass it's fair," she said evenly.

"But . . ."

"Kick, some of the stuff in your piece is remarkable. It's basically a very telling portrait of what happens to a man who lets other people run his career. But it's also a very telling portrait of what happened between the two of you during that interview. I mean, it's a frigging love letter! And my gut tells me you checked your tape recorder at the door along with your good sense."

"But, Fedalia, I couldn't tape everything," Kick protested, hating that she had to. "He knew he was being interviewed. I mean, once we got to know each other, he relaxed. Things just flowed."

"I'll bet," Fedalia said, not softening her tone. "Pretty tough to operate a tape recorder with both hands on the subject's dong."

Kick was so stunned she just stared at Fedalia.

"Look, Kick, I know what went on up there," Fedalia said a bit more softly. "I also believe he said the things you put in your piece. I know people sleep with people. Secretaries sleep with their bosses, starlets sleep with producers, pool boys sleep with rich men's wives. But did you really have to sleep with Lionel Maltby to get him to say all this stuff? You knew we had an obligation to show Irving the piece. You had to know he wouldn't let the quotes about him pass."

Kick stiffened. "But I thought Lionel would," she said meekly. "Isn't he the court of last resort?"

Fedalia leaned forward and growled, "Get real, Kick. I told you Maltby saw it and he doesn't like it. Doesn't that tell you something?"

Kick fell silent and slumped in her chair. "Fedalia," Kick said, near tears. "I thought something wonderful had happened to us both. It was crazy and beautiful and—"

"And the earth moved," Fedalia said, finishing Kick's sentence. "Spare me the body fluids, Kick. I'd think more of you if you said you slept with him to get a better story. At least that would show an element of risk on your part; wrongheaded but tough-minded. I don't want to hear the L-word. Lionel Maltby is so in love he's talking to a libel lawyer. Irving was up here so he could tell Lionel he had seen you and got the piece killed."

Fedalia's words could not have had a more devastating effect than if each one had been punctuated with a slap.

"All Lionel had to do was tell me the things he didn't want me to put in," Kick said. "Even after he read the piece, he could have called me."

"Kick, if you had been at this a bit longer, you'd know it doesn't work that way. There are rules. When you turned off that tape recorder, nothing that was said counted. In your case, turning it off gave horny old Lionel Maltby a clear shot at you. He sensed you didn't know you were playing in the big leagues. He told you all that delicious stuff to get you in the sack, knowing he could get it killed later."

Kick stood up and walked to the phone next to the sofa. "I'm going to call Lionel and straighten this out right now."

"Save yourself the trouble. He has his machine on. He doesn't want to talk to you."

Kick froze in place in the carpet and turned around. "How do you know that?"

"Because I've spoken to him, at length."

"Lionel talked to you about me? I can't believe he would do that. He even asked me if I would like to live . . ." Kick stopped herself, realizing how foolish she must sound.

"Sit down, Kick," Fedalia said. She sounded war-weary and exhausted. "I want you to promise me something. I'm going to give you some home truth here. When I'm finished, I want you to go downstairs. Take my car. It's waiting in front for me, but I want you to take it. Go home, no place else. Stay off the phone and go to bed. When you come to, you will see what happened for what it is. Promise me?"

Stunned, Kick waited, terrified of what she was about to hear.

"One," Fedalia began, bending back one long index finger with the other, "I've done some phoning around. Lionel Maltby is a womanizer who makes Warren Beatty look like Doogie Howser. He did plan to give my reporter only an hour. He changed his mind when you got out of the car with your great legs and tight little butt.

"Two, Randy could have brought you back at any time. The roads weren't that bad. Maltby told him not to, wink, wink. He also told Randy to check you out. If you were cute enough, you didn't have to put your head down in the car."

Kick pressed one knuckle against the big vein in her temple that had started to throb.

"Kick," Fedalia said softly, "didn't that house tell you something?"

"The house? You were there?" Kick asked. *She was in our house, she seethed.*

"Yesterday, Irving drove me up for a heart to heart."

Kick's humiliation was now complete. The thought of the three of them sitting in the very place she had known such rapture, discussing her like she was some snotty teenager caught shoplifting at the mall, was unbearable.

"Okay. The place is no recluse-writer's retreat. It's a frigging four-color spread in *Architectural Digest.* That's a woman's house, Kick. You think Maltby, who is proud of the fact he can't cook for shit, has a freezer full of time-labeled roasts from Balducci's? You think he has the time to collect jasperware pitchers and stuff them with dried hydrangeas?"

"And how about the makeup? Huh?" Fedalia added.

"What makeup? What are you talking about?"

"Kick, the first thing a good reporter does is open a subject's medicine cabinet."

"But I did. Every morning, to get the toothbrush he gave me."

"Wrong bathroom, sweetheart. If you'd gone into the one across the hall from the bedroom, you'd have picked up and left when he made his first move."

"He said that was the maid's bathroom. I never bothered."

"Well, if you had you would have seen the stuff. Girl stuff, right

55

down to the size seventy-five diaphragm on the upper right-hand shelf behind the Estée Lauder Night Restorative Cream and the Alka-Seltzer. It was still moist. Not warm, mind you, but moist.

"Kick, the man is married. That was his wife's diaphragm. Her name is Basia. She's the art director for an ad agency. The day before you arrived she left on a shoot in Chile."

Kick's face colored with humiliation.

"The problem here, Kick, is that you spent all that time with the man and didn't bother to protect yourself. And I mean emotionally as well as professionally. Instead of snooping, you trusted. Instead of guarding the most precious thing you've got—and I don't mean what's between your legs, I mean your integrity—you let yourself get trapped. You had the power to control the situation, and you gave that power to him."

Kick was desperate not to acknowledge the truth in Fedalia's words. Instead, she lashed out. "So I slept with him," she shouted. "What's that got to do with the fact that what I wrote was good? It was the truth. Lionel Maltby is a brilliant, guarded man. He trusted me to tell the truth about him and I did."

"Listen, Kick, Lionel Maltby isn't brilliant, he's clever. He's a practitioner of what I call the Higher Cute. He smells it when a woman is in awe of him and comes on by being fey and trusting and terribly dear to cover up for his own insecurities. As for being guarded, that's a ploy. He knew if he sounded like he was pouring out his heart, you'd hang on every word. It was an ego trip, he was bored, it was snowing, his wife was out of town. He knew his rat pack of protectors would keep you from using the stuff."

"It sounds to me like you're a part of the rat pack yourself, Fedalia," Kick said, knowing she was treading on dangerous ground.

"Not really. I'm still ready to run an honest piece on Lionel Maltby. But yours isn't it. The pity is that it could have been. Now I don't have a cover story for next month."

"That's it, isn't it?" Kick asked angrily, hoping Fedalia had finished. In another minute she was going to burst into tears. "All you care about is your magazine."

Fedalia stood up. "Well, of course, what did you think? All you should have cared about was doing your piece properly. You've proved you need to do some growing up, Kick, and I don't have the time to raise and train you. Not here."

"So, I'm fired," Kick said flatly.

"Yeah, I guess so. I'm sad about that. Truly."

Kick stared down at the toes of her boots. She felt thick and heavy, as though all the air in her body had been squeezed out and replaced with mud. "I fell in love with him, Fedalia," she said in a small, helpless voice.

"I know you did, Kick," Fedalia said gently. "We all get a blue-ribbon shit in our lives. We're blessed if we learn from the first one. That Maltby can be a real charmer. He sure stuck by you, didn't he?"

Kick winced. "Don't . . ." she said, picking up her purse.

"Sorry. I shouldn't have said that."

Kick turned and slowly headed for the door.

Behind her, Fedalia said, "I'm just as disappointed as you are, Kick. This could have worked."

"Right," Kick said, closing the door behind her.

When she pushed through the lobby doors, she saw Fedalia's big dark blue limousine idling at the curb. She didn't want to get into it. She didn't want any part of anything to do with *Fifteen Minutes* magazine, ever.

She pulled her collar up and began to walk toward Fifth and Central Park. She had to think; she had to sort out what had just happened to her.

By the time she reached the lake at Bethesda Fountain, she had stopped crying. She no longer felt the cold air freezing against her wet cheeks. She was numb.

So that's the way it works, she thought, staring out at the frozen lake, biting her lip to keep to from trembling. That's what having power is all about. You can suck someone innocent into your web, use them, then get your powerful network to get rid of them.

Fedalia wasn't angry because Kick had slept with Lionel. She was angry because she was vulnerable, because she didn't exercise the control Fedalia had given her.

They had surrounded her: Lionel, his absent but very present wife, Irving, Fedalia, even sweet, silent Vickie. They had all conspired while she waited for them to praise her and love her and change her life. They had snuffed her out as though she were a bothersome kitten to be stuffed into a bag and thrown into the lake. Who would know? She was just one more wet cat, drowning.

She turned to go and saw a graffiti-scarred public phone next to a tree a few yards away. She wanted to hear Lionel tell her why he had done it. It didn't matter if he hung up on her. She was too numb to feel any more pain. She had to know.

She fished enough coins out of her bag to buy perhaps a minute of his time and dialed the number of the country house.

Two rings, three—she tried to form some kind of a message for the inevitable answering machine.

"Hello."

It was him. He was answering the phone. "Lionel, it's Kick. I understand you didn't like my piece," she said bravely, shivering in the wind.

"Frankly, I didn't."

"It was the truth."

"There are truths and there are truths," he said, enigmatically.

"I don't think so, Lionel. I just think you have the power to protect what you don't want people to know."

"Well," he said, with a nasty chuckle Kick had not heard in all their time together. "You've learned something, then."

Kick heard some of the coins she had dropped into the phone jangling a refund as she walked away.

She didn't remember walking all the way down to Gramercy Park. She didn't remember getting herself into bed.

She remembered the terribly high fever, then the freezing sweats of the worst case of flu she had ever had in her life.

The doctor told her she had done something to lower her immune system and would need at least a month's rest. Except to get groceries, Kick didn't leave her apartment for six months. Finally, the end of the term of her sublet forced her to make a move. An old friend of her grandmother's put her in touch with Lolly Pines, and Kick took the offer of both job and lodging with a kind of numb relief. She knew she was overqualified for the work, but she wasn't healed yet; she'd have to take it slow. She wasn't going to face the world again until she had the power to protect herself.

Kick stood up and stretched, shaking the cobwebs of memory from her mind. It was all past now. The pain of Lionel's betrayal had subsided to a low ache. Her belief in herself as a writer had returned. More important, her ability to play the game had improved: after all, she'd spent the last year training at the feet of a master.

Now maybe it was pay-back time. Her impulse to send Sam Nichols a real article about Lolly hardened to resolve. Despite their relatively brief acquaintance, she'd gotten to know Lolly better than anyone. And, unlike so many, Kick could say she had honestly liked and admired Lolly. Maybe she could share that sense of Lolly in her piece. Maybe now it was time to step back into the ring, and at the same time do something for the woman who had done so much for her.

4

*B*aby lay very still on her stomach in the middle of the bed, letting the air conditioner blow over her naked body. She was listening for the hall door to slam. As soon as she was sure Joe had gone, she pushed herself up onto her hands and knees and crawled across the mattress toward the phone on the night table.

She had to move fast.

Finding that Joe had smoked all his cigarettes, she located a longish butt, lit it, and punched Georgina's number into the phone. She knew Tanner Dyson's wife was spending the long weekend alone at home.

Georgina had never cared for Tanner's Colorado ranch. It had been his getaway when he was married to his first wife, and Georgina couldn't stand the place. Tanner visited his "spread" and did his macho things with horses, cows, guns. Georgina stayed home and worked on her secret project.

Ever since they married, Tanner had turned the full force of his high energy and controlling tendencies on Georgina, pushing her into society functions and charities she had little interest in other than that her participation pleased the husband that she adored. Lately, Baby didn't know all that much about Georgina's life beyond what she read in the newspaper, but she knew Georgina would do anything Tanner wanted and never let him know she wasn't happy.

The last time they'd talked, about six months ago, Georgina had confided to Baby that she had an idea for combining her journalistic abilities with her knowledge of domestic arts in a project she knew Tanner could never interfere with. Not only was it a field he knew nothing about, she knew he would find it unworthy of his attention and manipulation. She would be able to take full credit when she succeeded.

Georgina had come a long way from her dull background in suburban Columbus. She had the disposition of a saint, the skin of a wellborn English baby, and the coloring of a summer rose. In Baby's view, she was about as interesting as a glass of warm milk, but infinitely more useful.

Baby and Georgina had known each other before Georgina married the distinguished-looking media mogul. Georgina had been a food writer at the paper. Baby's desk was but a partition away from Georgina's. When Baby divined that there was a secret romance going on between the young food writer and the owner of the paper, she made it her business to attach herself to Georgina.

Baby was about to hang up when a breathless Georgina finally answered.

"Hi, sweetie," Baby said in her customary high-pitched greeting voice. Baby seldom identified herself over the phone, assuming, rightly, that anyone who knew her would recognize the voice.

"Baby! How nice to hear from you! It's been an age," Georgina exclaimed.

"Yeah, yeah. It's been way too long," Baby said impatiently. "I just had to call and see if you'd heard the news."

"I don't think so," Georgina said vaguely. "Give me a hint."

"Lolly Pines is dead," Baby said, hoping she had delivered the news with the gravity she intended.

"Oh, that. Yes, isn't it too bad? Tanner's flying back in the Gulfstream. Poor darling, he was so looking forward to the weekend."

God, how like Georgina, Baby thought, dropping the butt of her cigarette into Joe's untouched drink on the floor. You could tell Georgina the world was going to explode on Wednesday and she'd say she'd have to skip it because that was the day Tanner's dark-blue suit had to be picked up at the cleaners.

"Why were you breathing so hard just now?" Baby asked, changing the subject until she could form a new strategy to get Georgina on track.

Georgina giggled. "I was way in the back in the maid's bathroom."

"Why don't you use your own?"

"I'm testing lettuce heads in the tub, and I was right. The iceberg will stay fresh for up to two weeks if you submerge it in water. The Bibb is a bit more fragile. Forget radicchio."

Baby drummed her fingernails impatiently on the back of the phone. Rather than endure a few minutes of household hints, Baby interrupted. Now was the time to strike.

"Georgina," Baby said crisply. "We have to talk."

"Oh, I'm sorry, Baby," Georgina said, sounding slightly hurt. "I do get carried away."

"*Lolly Pines is dead*, Georgina."

"I know, Baby, for pity's sake. But let's face it, she was rather an unpleasant woman. I know she was nice about me and Tanner during the divorce, but that was because she wanted to please him. Frankly, I think they should run Ann Landers in her space and brighten up the paper."

"Georgina," Baby growled. "You don't get it. Baby Bayer is going to be the next Lolly Pines."

"Darling, that's wonderful," Georgina said excitedly. "I'm thrilled. Now, why didn't Tanner tell me that? He must have just forgotten. He was so rushed."

"Well, it's not definite yet," Baby said, rolling over on her stomach and punching the pillow.

"Oh. I thought you meant you had the column already. When will you know for sure?"

"I don't know, but I'd love to strategize with you," Baby said, pulling open the drawer in the night table. She lifted out a bottle of red nail polish, sat up, and began to paint her toenails. "Seeing as Tanner's not home, why don't we meet at the Mayfair for drinks and talk about it?"

"Oh, Baby, I don't know. I'm really out of the scene at the paper. I'm just the owner's wife."

"Just the owner's wife. Right," Baby said sarcastically.

There was a long pause on the line.

"Georgina? Are you still there?" she asked.

"I'm here, darling."

"So? How about the Mayfair? Say, six-thirty?"

"Actually, I'm doing some stain testing. Things are spread out all over the counter in the butler's pantry. I've really got to tidy up before Tanner gets back."

It was Baby's turn for hang time in the airspace between them. She continued to stroke enamel onto her toenails. Finally, she asked, keeping her voice as light as her mounting anxiety permitted, "What time will Tanner be home?"

"Sometime tonight. I don't want him to see all this stuff out when he gets here."

Baby stopped stroking her nails. "I understand," she said, choosing her words carefully. "Maybe we could get together later in the week, then." She paused. "Lunch." Another pause. "We could go to La Caravelle." She let her heart beat for two strokes. "Just like old times."

There. She had said it. She had called in the due bill she had once led Georgina to believe she would never cash.

Knowing she thought better on her feet, Baby swung her legs over the side of the bed. Her heel tapped the bottle of nail polish, sending a long red streak across the crumpled sheet. "Oh, shit," she hissed, yanking at the mess, making matters worse.

"Baby? What's the matter?" Georgina asked.

"Damn," she said, cradling the phone. "I just spilled nail polish all over the goddamned bed."

"Quick, take an old towel and put it under the stain. Then take some remover. Blot. Don't rub," Georgina said.

Baby stood, getting the message loud and clear. Georgina wasn't going to bite.

5

*N*eeva Fourbraz left the auction gallery on Sutton Place South at noon sharp on the Friday before Labor Day. She had waited until the last minute to get something to wear to the Garns' party in the Hamptons that night, and she still hadn't packed for the weekend. Tita Garn's party was *the* place to be that weekend. Everyone was dying to see what she had done with her Hampton house with all of Jourdan's money. Neeva walked briskly up East 57th Street, the hot, humid wind swirling up off the street and sticking her thin linen dress to her stockings.

How she would have loved to go to work bare-legged. She might just as well have gone nude. The other women at the gallery would have fainted at the sight of flesh. As much as she loved the auction business, she could happily have lived without the type of women she had to work with. They took themselves very, very seriously—and their work less so. Their jobs were a chic way to look as if they were working when they really weren't. They all dressed like clones, with their black velvet headbands, serious little suits, and single strands of pearls.

Neeva wished she could dress in a slightly more attention-getting way, particularly since the recent appearance at the gallery of Jeffrey Dunsmore, the one person there who made her laugh. He was the dashing young son of Aubrey Dunsmore, the gallery owner. Jeffrey was such fun and had such a sense of style that she felt a little stodgy around him.

At the corner of First Avenue, she squinted into the crosstown traffic for an empty cab and prayed that Irving wouldn't get tied up at the office. He had promised her he would be back at the apartment, packed and ready to leave for the Hamptons, by no later than two.

She never knew with Irving. There was always something. If she had married an obstetrician or a fireman, her life would have been more predictable. Irving thrived on crisis. By now, she was used to the broken dinner engagements, the canceled vacations, and the nights, sometimes weeks, alone. But if Irving disappointed her this weekend or did anything to louse up going to the Garns' big party, she would never forgive him.

By the time her cab crawled across town in the lunch-hour traffic and deposited her at the West 57th Street entrance of Bergdorf's, she was getting increasingly anxious about the time.

She headed straight for the designer floor. There was no way she could show up at Tita Garn's in anything that was less than fantastic. Halfway down the aisle on the third floor she came face to face with a sight that made her heart sing. There, right in front of her, was a sale rack that had just been wheeled onto the floor. Even more astounding was the first outfit. A beige silk gown designed by Tita Mandraki Garn herself. Neeva's hand shot out, grabbed the tag, and turned it over. The garment was her size and half price. She snatched it from the rack and headed for the dressing room at the end of the aisle.

Inside the cubicle, she whipped off her linen shift, dropped the gown over her head, and smoothed it into place.

It fit perfectly over her slim, fine-boned frame. Neeva had just turned forty, but her small bust was still resisting gravity. She would have killed for longer legs and straight, naturally blond hair. She couldn't do anything about her legs, which she had to admit were shapely if not endless, but sun streaks at the Trump Tower salon made her mouse-brown hair definitely more exciting, emphasizing her wide-set gray eyes. In fact, though her relentless self-criticism kept her from enjoying it, Neeva Fourbraz had a subtle but striking beauty.

She leaned forward and pressed the middle finger of each hand to the top of each cheekbone, then gently pulled upward. It made little difference in the smoothness of her face. There's time, she thought. The plastic surgeon could stay his knife-wielding hand a little longer.

She turned her back to the mirror and looked over her shoulder to check the dress's low-cut back.

"Perfection," she whispered to the empty dressing room. All the dress needed was the freshwater-pearl choker Irving had given her for her birthday and a pair of dressy sandals.

Within minutes she was standing in front of the cashier's desk. Neeva smiled at the salesclerk as she handed over her charge card. The clerk wrapped her dress with great care and left it on the counter while she placed the charge card into a slot in the cash register.

When the machine made an odd beeping sound, the clerk smiled sheepishly and tried again.

"Oh, dear," the clerk said with an embarrassed frown. "This old machine must not be feeling well." She removed the card and reinserted it, only to have the machine reject it again.

Neeva looked up in mild alarm. "What's the problem?" she asked.

The clerk sighed apologetically and held up Neeva's card. "I'm afraid there's a bit of a problem with your card, Mrs. Fourbraz," she said. "Would you mind terribly going up to the eighth floor to see about it? Ask for a Mr. Sasser in Credit."

Neeva was determined to remain cool. She knew it wasn't the clerk's fault. She also knew that there was no point in rushing up to the eighth floor to see Mr. Sasser, whoever he was. She knew what was wrong with her Bergdorf's credit. Irving hadn't paid—again.

"Here," she said. "Use this one." She handed the clerk the gallery Visa. "This card will clear."

If there was one constant in Neeva's life, it was that in times of stress, particularly those having to do with her husband, she could hear her late mother's voice. She had just stepped into the elevator, the dress in a Bergdorf's bag clutched tightly in her fist, when it happened. *"It's that deadbeat you married,"* Rose hissed from that great mah-jongg game in the sky. *"Mr. Zip-What-Is-It is too busy to pay his bills. He has money for a car and driver and his filthy cigars, but he can't pay Bergdorf's."*

When Rose was alive, Neeva would turn to her and say, "Mother, don't start!" Now that she was dead, there was no escape. Rose was like a policeman in her ear, permanently alive in her daughter's subconscious.

When the elevator reached the street floor, Neeva elbowed her way out. Her lips were pressed tightly together, her eyes burning. Trump Tower was just across the street. She would be in her apartment in less than five minutes.

Then she could scream.

As she waited for the light at the busy intersection of 56th and Fifth, she thought how Rose would have loved all the opportunities the last ten years had provided to prove how right she had been about Irv.

When Irving's divorce from his first wife had come through, he and Neeva had slipped off to city hall and got married. If a gossip columnist at the *New York Courier* hadn't printed an item about it, Neeva's mother would have gone to her grave never knowing. At the time, Neeva had no idea how Lolly Pines found out. Now, after years of watching how Irving operated, she knew he had told her.

Rose had been in the Klingenstein Pavilion at Mount Sinai recovering from a heart attack she had suffered in the communal dressing room at Loehmann's Fordham Road store. A nurse had shown her the column. Later that day, when Neeva arrived to feed her mother her evening meal, Rose did not look well.

"Neevila," Rose had moaned from the snarl of tubes that coiled about her ashen face. "Why did you do it?" She pointed to the item in the paper Neeva had hoped she wouldn't see.

"I love him, Ma," was all she could say. "He's a very big man. You'll see."

"Big, schmig," Rose had croaked. "He's a gonif. Anybody who runs off and marries without telling anybody has something to hide."

"No, Ma. That's not why we did it. We were going to tell you as soon as you felt better."

"Dump him," Rose had said. Those were her last words. She died that evening, just in time to miss the next morning's headlines as Irving Fourbraz won an acquittal for Ticky "Boombotz" Shamansky, a former All-Pro wide receiver who had beaten his steroid supplier to death.

The first few years with Irving had been all right. Neeva didn't ask questions. It was not her place. In the last year or so, however, there had been a new tension between them. The Bergdorf's incident was just the latest in a string of unpleasant episodes having to do with money. Just a week before, the treasurer of the co-op board had phoned to say that there had been a "spot of trouble" with Irving's monthly maintenance check. Then there was the nasty bit of business when she had presented her American Express card at lunch with a dealer from the gallery only to learn that it had been canceled. And when she had ordered dinner-party flowers from the Trump Tower florist, she had been told their house account had been closed for lack of payment.

In each instance Neeva disobeyed her mother's internalized demand for decisive action and left terse little notes on the desk in his den, to which he never responded. Irving did not like bad news. Neeva went to great lengths not to be confrontational, but things were getting out of hand. The Bergdorf humiliation was the last straw.

She walked quickly down the block to the residents' entrance of the shimmering Trump Tower, planning the best time to bring up the whole awful subject of money with Irving. Perhaps she should wait until later at the beach house. As she rode up in the elevator, she decided that after a preparty swim and a relaxing drink she would bring it up.

Neeva let herself into her fortieth-floor apartment. She glanced at the mail tray on the faux-tortoiseshell table in the foyer and was surprised not to see the day's mail. Usually the maid brought it up.

Halfway down the long, carpeted hall to the master bedroom suite she understood about the mail. Irving was home and had taken it into his den. He had done what he'd promised and come home early. She pushed open the door to the bedroom. Across the room she could see Irving puttering around in his walk-in closet. She was pleased to see his weekend bag open on his side of the king-size bed.

"I'm home, dear," Neeva called as she walked to her bathroom off the bedroom foyer to quickly rinse the heat of the day from her face and hands.

When she returned to the bedroom a few minutes later, Irving was putting a stack of shorts on the chair beside his dresser.

"For heaven's sake, Irving," she said. "We're only going for three days. You don't need all those shorts."

"Change of plans, babe. Got to go to the coast," Irving said as he patted a pair of monogrammed travel slippers into place in his bag.

Neeva stood in the middle of the Portuguese needlepoint rug with her mouth open, aware that the weekend she had so looked forward to had just imploded.

Irving walked back to his closet and returned with several silk shirts on hangers hooked over one finger.

Speak up! Rose, the marriage cop, shouted in her ear. *You can't let him do this!*

Neeva's instinctive reaction to disappointment was to blame herself. Perhaps she hadn't let him know how much the Garns' party meant to her. She had to say something to let him know how hurt she was. Unable to help herself, she chose the passive-aggressive approach. "I wish I knew what I did to make Bergdorf's mad at me," she said meekly.

Irving said nothing as he folded a long silk dressing gown and smoothed it into his bag.

"Irving," Neeva said, more emphatically, "the clerk asked me to go up to the credit department. Have you paid this month's bill?"

"Call the office on Tuesday," he said without looking up from his packing. "Tell Vivian to send a check."

That did it. "Tell Vivian?" Neeva said, giving up on modulating her voice. "Tell Vivian? I don't want to tell your secretary anything. I want you to take care of our private business. For God's sake, Irving, don't you read the notes I leave for you?"

"I've been busy."

Neeva sat down on her side of the bed. "Irving Fourbraz," she said with a sigh, "the only man alive who can beat Alan Dershowitz to an open mike can't pay his bills on time?"

She knew as the words dropped from her lips that any reference to the way Irving comported himself in public was a surefire fight escalator. Irving's already florid face turned the color of borscht, and the pointy end of his black Vandyke began to tremble as he turned back toward the bathroom. "You realize the only reason I was in Bergdorf's at all was to get something to wear to the Garns' tonight," she said.

"Shit," Irving shouted from the bathroom over the slams and bangs as he assembled his toiletries. He reappeared carrying a large Mark Cross kit and the ludicrous flowered shower cap he wore to keep his shoulder-length silver hair dry so the Trump Tower barber could properly groom it each morning. "This deal on the coast is really hot. I've got to be there."

"What is so goddamn hot that you have to run to LA on a holiday weekend? Don't tell me Spielberg wants to do your life story already."

Irving shot her an angry look. "You've got some mouth on you,

Neeva," he said and turned back to his bag. "It just so happens I'm representing a girl who was brutally attacked by that television brat Keeko Ram. The girl and five witnesses say he did it. If I get out there right away, I can sew this thing right up, so if you want your damn Bergdorf's bill paid, you'll back off."

Irving yanked his valise off the bed and headed for the door. He didn't look back. Neeva waited, listening for the front door of the apartment to slam. When she didn't hear it, she walked to the bedroom door. From there, she could hear Irving on the phone in his study down the hall, and though she couldn't make out the words, the rhythm of his speech sounded as though he was leaving a message on someone's answering machine.

She ducked back from the door and returned to the bed. A moment later, she heard the front door close. With a deep sigh, she reached for the coverlet at the foot of the bed and pulled it over her legs against the chill of the air conditioner. She pulled one of Irving's pillows over to her side and pressed it to her chest.

As she was about to close her eyes, she looked across the room. There on the chair next to Irving's dresser was the stack of shorts he had taken out to pack. He would have to run all over Beverly Hills on a holiday weekend to replace them. There was no way Irving would be able to make a deal without his testicles encased in a cloud of silk. She knew she could phone down to the doorman. Irving was probably still at the building entrance waiting for his car to be brought around. If she called down now, one of the porters would run up and get the shorts.

She lay down and pulled the coverlet up to her shoulders. Then she reached out and turned off the phone. From the aluminum lawn chair in Neeva's mind, Rose smiled.

6

*B*aby Bayer's mouth itched. Each tooth felt as though it were individually wrapped in moss, and there seemed to be some sort of clawed foot grasping the top of her head and pressing its talons into her eyeballs. The only thing she knew for sure was that she wasn't in her own bed. The sheets that seemed to float around her body were linen and so light she barely felt them. The pillows under her head were encased in the same gauzy fabric edged with what felt like inches of heavy Belgian lace. It all smelled faintly of lavender.

Baby was afraid to open her eyes. What if there was someone in the bed with her? What if she didn't know who it was? Her mind whirled with a scene from a movie where the main character wakes up in a blood-soaked bed with a dead body. Imagining the scene, her eyes flew open in terror. Above her hung a transparent tent secured to the ceiling with a white satin ornament. The fabric fell over three sides of the massive bed.

Slowly, she turned her head, sending a cascade of pain down

her forehead. She squeezed her eyes shut, then opened them and looked at the other side of the bed. It was empty.

She tried to sit up and fell back into the pillows.

"Where the fuck am I?" she whispered to the ceiling.

"Oh, shit," she moaned, remembering.

She was somewhere in the vast summer "cottage" that belonged to Tita and Jourdan Garn. The events of the previous evening poured back into her pounding head.

She heard Tita Garn's words again: *"Get this disgusting woman up off the floor and put her to bed."*

With all the strength she could muster, she sat up and pushed aside the gauze mosquito netting. The room she was in was breathtaking. All white, with wide French doors open to a view of the ocean. The balcony that ran the length of the room was ablaze with potted pink and white flowers.

She stood, padded across the white carpeting in her bare feet, and stepped out onto the balcony. She could hear faint laughter and the sound of people talking over the splash of water. She crept to the edge of the balcony and peeked over. Below her were a dozen or so casually dressed people sitting around a shimmering turquoise swimming pool. Everyone had drinks in their hands. White-coated waiters moved back and forth with trays of food on the blue-green lawn between the pool and the ocean.

What time must it be? she wondered, holding her head. The grilled steaks and bowls of salad on the table didn't look like breakfast.

She had to get out of there, but how? The thought of anyone seeing her in a strapless black satin dress and high heels was more than she could bear.

She pulled back from the railing and turned to look for her shoes and bag. Thank heaven she had remembered to put a full complement of makeup in her evening bag before she left the city.

She stepped over the marble saddle of the open door and

jumped back in surprise. A young woman with dark hair and a white nylon uniform and apron was bending over the bed.

"What are you doing?" Baby gasped.

The woman looked up with a start. "Cleaning the room," she said.

Baby found her bag and rummaged around in it for her wallet, silently praying she hadn't been ripped off. The young woman stood in the doorway holding the laundry and waited, her face blank.

Baby walked toward her, extending a five-dollar bill. "Please, could you get me out of here? I don't have a car, and I don't know where the hell the train station is. I have to get back to New York."

The maid made no attempt to take the proffered bill. "Why don't you call a cab?" she said matter-of-factly.

Baby withdrew her hand. "From here?"

"You're not on the moon, miss. Just call information. Tell the cab company you're at Willows, then wait down in front of the house. You go out of town much?"

"How'd you get so smart?" Baby asked sarcastically.

The maid turned and started down the hall. "The University of Michigan," she said over her shoulder, and disappeared into the room next door.

Baby whimpered and sat down on the stripped bed. She shouldn't have alienated the woman. Now she was truly marooned. She stared at the phone and cursed Tita Mandraki Garn for her situation. Boy, she thought, would she do a number on her one of these days. Tita, so fancy with her rich-bitch ways. Didn't she know how everyone talked about her? How she stole her only daughter's boyfriend a few years back. The daughter ended up as some kind of high-class call girl who got lucky and married Jourdan Garn. When her daughter divorced Garn, Tita came along and married him herself. *Sheesh!* It wasn't as if it wasn't in all the papers and magazines. Tita and her man-stealing was one for the books. If Petra let Baby write up the party, she sure as hell would mention all that.

75

Now all she wanted to do was get the hell out of there before she had to face anyone.

Baby had arrived the night before to cover the party with Tony, the *Courier* photographer the city desk had assigned to go with her. He had insisted on smoking a joint outside the gate before they went in and made Baby wait with him against the high granite wall that surrounded the estate.

She felt like an idiot standing there in her little nothing dress and high-heeled sandals while all the limousines and sports cars zoomed up the drive.

"Tony, for Christ's sake, let's go," she grumbled, starting back toward the *Courier* company car Tony had left on the grassy shoulder of the main road. "I wanna do this and get it over with."

"Aw, you just want to be seen," he slurred, pinching off the burning end of the joint and putting it in his shirt pocket. He followed her back to the car.

Joining the line of limousines and sports cars, Tony inched the beat-up company car toward the guards' box at the entrance and pointed to the NYPD press sticker on the driver's side of the windshield. The guard squinted at it, nodded, and waved them on. The line of cars leading to the mansion had slowed to a crawl.

Tony leaned back and rested his wrists on the top of the steering wheel. "Word around the city room is that you're porking Joe Stone," Tony said with a sly grin.

Baby stared at him, her eyes squeezing into tiny slits of hate. "Tony," she said evenly, "you know what you are?"

"Whazzat?" he said, inching the car forward.

"A dick-head greaser."

"I love it when you talk dirty," he said, patting his temples. His hand froze in midair. "Holy shit, look at that!"

Baby turned and looked. Silhouetted against the bright evening sky was the whitest building she had ever seen. The mansion was floodlit from below and seemed to float above the velvet lawn and low shrubs that surrounded it. Wide balconies ran around the second and third stories, making it look more like an ornate riverboat than a house. High flagpoles rose from each corner of the mansard roof, flying gold banners that fluttered in the evening breeze off the ocean. Tall model/actor/waiters in white tuxes and gold bow ties scurried along the edge of the circular drive, relieving guests of their cars and directing drivers where to park their limousines.

Baby slumped down in the seat. "God, this car," she moaned. "Park it, Tony, and we'll walk."

"Like hell I will. I'm as good as any of these poufs. Look at 'em."

"I am looking at them, Tony," Baby said from behind her clenched teeth. "I don't want them looking at me in this rattletrap car. Now, lemme out."

Tony hit the brakes. "So? Go," he said.

Baby got out and then leaned in the window. "I'm going in and mingling. Would you please find me and start shooting anyone you see me talking to? I'll be by the nearest bar."

"Yeah, yeah, yeah," Tony said, motioning her away with both hands.

Baby smoothed her dress, fluffed her hair, and started up the edge of the drive. She couldn't stand working with photographers, particularly Tony. When she had her own column, she wouldn't have to put up with street trash like him.

She joined the crowd milling around the foot of the wide marble steps that led up to a terrace running the width of the house. When she got to the top step, she pushed her breasts up with both hands, repositioned her shoulder bag, and fixed a smile on her face.

Inside the double doors she could see a glistening black marble floor that reflected the lights of more chandeliers than were in Tavern on the Green. Each one was a different color of Venetian glass. The house either had had the most spectacular and authentic renovation known to man or was a case of pure, tacky overreaching. Baby didn't know enough about the subject to pass judgment. She did, however, know what spent money looked like. She knew she was looking at millions.

77

Baby looked to her right and realized her shoulder was brushing against Dan Rather's white sleeve. She turned and tilted her head. "Wow," she said, looking directly at him. "Isn't this fabulous?"

Rather stared straight ahead, his hand on the small of his wife's back.

She could hear music coming from a distance. It got louder as she followed the crowd as it shuffled through the mansion, talking and laughing in that hushed way people have when they are impressed with ostentation but are too cool to show it.

The grand hall let out onto a wide flagstone terrace surrounded by a low wall. Baby scanned the crowd standing in clusters between the terrace and a large white tent. As she snagged a glass of champagne from a passing waiter she heard Lolly Pines's name floating up from a nearby group. She moved closer.

"Was she married?" asked a woman with Nose B on the plastic surgeon's chart.

"Oh, I don't think so," answered Nose A with a honk. "Brandon? Was Lolly Pines ever married?"

A man in a pink Mexican wedding shirt shook his head, "Lord, I don't think so. As far as I know, Lolly Pines was the world's oldest living virgin."

"I heard she was a dyke," said a pair of Porsche sunglasses.

Nose A said, "I know for a fact she got laid once or twice during the Eisenhower administration."

"Who? Lolly?" hooted a magenta mouth. "Are you kidding? Not even then. Lolly Pines's legs had been together longer than the Mills Brothers."

The cluster whooped with derisive laughter, drinks slopping and high heels sinking deeper into the loamy spaces between the flagstones. Obviously the news of Lolly's death had reached outer Long Island. It had probably reached Outer Mongolia for that matter, Baby mused. Too bad. She had hoped to use the news as a conversation starter.

Baby moved on, ears attuned to the cross-talk of a cluster consisting of a Park Avenue lawyer on borrowed time between his indictment and trial; a former call girl turned how-to author; a Wall Street powerhouse who kept an apartment in Baby's building to store his Bob Mackie gowns, lingerie, and blond wigs; and Baby's favorite jet-set couple. He had once had a net worth twice that of Jourdan Garn's and now was secretly broke. They existed on the money his wife made running a clandestine phone-sex operation from the library of their River House duplex.

With the exception of the housebound lawyer, each person in the group assumed his transgressions were secret. They had all been featured at one time or another on the Grapevine page in items not nearly as interesting as those that could have been written.

Baby seldom got to cover big private parties, coveted assignments usually hogged by Petra Weems or one of her sniveling favorites on staff. If the Garns had given their party on any night other than the Friday of a big summer holiday weekend, Petra would be here and not her. Baby intended to make the most of it. She summoned her most radiant smile and elbowed into the group.

"Well, you know why Leona Helmsley is terrified to go to jail, don't you," said the former call girl.

All heads turned.

"They won't let you dye your hair, for one," she said, basking in the momentary spotlight. "Second, her collagen puff is going to drain right out of that upper lip. You have to have it done every six months. And you know they won't let her wear her lashes."

"She won't get her Venus treatments, either," said Mrs. Jet Set.

The women in the crowd shrieked in unison while the men looked from one to the other, bewildered.

When the how-to call girl regained her composure, she said, "Oh, I'll bet there's some big dyke guard that will be happy to do it for her."

"What's a Venus treatment?" the Wall Streeter asked. "I've never heard of that."

Baby moved closer. She had never heard of it either. If this was something new that all the society ladies were into, she wanted to know about it.

"You men aren't supposed to know about it. Absolutely no one will admit they have it done," said Mrs. Jet Set. "Shhhh, girls, don't say another word."

Baby moved in. "Hi," she said brightly. "I'm Baby Bayer from the *Courier*."

The group turned as one, their smiles fading, and stared at her as though she had something hanging out of her nose.

"What's this Venus treatment you're talking about?" As if responding to some dog-whistle signal no one else heard, they turned and moved further down the terrace. Like a group of Russian dancers, only their feet seemed to move.

Miffed but not bowed, Baby turned to see Dave Driks from *Variety* walking by behind her, leering.

"Tough luck, kid. Venus is probably some Hungarian bull-dyke with a diamond-studded dildo. But you wouldn't need a dyke with a dildo, would you, Baby?"

Baby turned her back on him and moved to the edge of the terrace. She grabbed a stuffed date off a tray and looked around for someone who could tell her what a Venus treatment was. She had just brought the date to her lips when a voice behind her spoke too loudly in a exaggerated English accent.

"Isn't it amazing? The more money you have the more privacy you can buy. Then you invite in the masses and let them wander through your house and pull open your drawers. Or pull them down, as the case may be, don't ja know."

Baby turned around and pushed the date into one cheek. Behind her stood a pink-cheeked man in an open white-linen shirt that hung loose to his knees and showed a blotch of matted white chest hair. He had tied a white silk handkerchief around his head to catch his sweat, and he smelled of a warm funkiness underlaid with expensive cologne.

"Hello," Baby said without guile. This man was most assured-ly not her type, but he was someone to talk to.

"Hello, as well," said the Brit, raising his glass in greeting. "I'd shake your hand, but I'm so hot I can't stand the thought of touching human flesh. I don't know how you Yanks put up with this heat. It's positively colonial."

"S'okay," she said, nodding. "I'm Baby Bayer, and no cute remarks."

"I wouldn't think of it," he said. "Abner Hoon here." He inclined his head a bit. The top was bald and bright pink.

"Abner Hoon! The *London Gazette*! I see your column from time to time." Baby said, impressed and relieved to have found a colleague of sorts. "I write for the Grapevine page of the *Courier*."

"The Grapevine page. Are you the one who cribs so many of my items, or is it a joint effort?"

Baby laughed. "We don't steal your stuff nearly as much as Lolly Pines did. Or is it the other way around, Mr. Hoon?"

Hoon held up his hand as though to end the conversation. "Please, my dear. Do not speak of my darling Lolly Pines. I've had far too much champagne to compensate for my loss. She was to have accompanied me tonight, you know. I am stricken with grief."

Baby looked down into her empty glass. "I'm sorry, I didn't realize you were such a close friend," she said sincerely. She wanted Abner Hoon to like her. He was London's premier columnist, a powerful member of the international information loop. Because of the six-hour time difference, an item in a London paper had a longer shelf life and sounded like a breaking story in New York. Petra Weems was a great one for having London items faxed to her for same-day use.

Abner Hoon reached out, placed his hand under Baby's elbow, and gently guided her toward the bar.

"A gin and tonic, my good man, no ice, no lime, no tonic. Might as well, now that I've laid down a champagne base," Hoon said to one of the four bartenders. "And you, Miss Bayer?"

"The same," Baby said with a shrug.

Holding the drinks, Hoon turned back to Baby. "Tell me, how will you write about this party?"

"I won't."

Hoon frowned.

"I just look for items. Dribs and drabs of stuff people say. Who's with whom. Boldface stuff. You know, 'also in attendance was' and then run a long boring list of names. People love that."

"And how many items have we found this evening?" Hoon asked in that peculiar Brit way that might be polite and might be patronizing.

"Just some new beauty treatment that seems to be the rage," Baby said.

"I heard it's some Hungarian woman who uses a dildo on these ladies. She has a private salon somewhere on Fifth," Hoon said.

"Where did you hear that?" Baby asked innocently, trying not to laugh.

Hoon leaned closer. He smelled like a wet dog. "I just ran into Dave Driks from *Variety*. Of course I've known about the woman for some time. Isn't it just delish?"

"*Mmmm*," Baby said, smiling. "Delish."

Hoon suddenly seemed to remember that he was bereaved. "Your publisher, Tanner Dyson, called my car as I was on the way out here. He's organizing a fabulous memorial service for darling Lolly. Isn't that divine?" he said, looking soulful.

"Absolutely divine," Baby agreed, squeezing his hand sympathetically. If Tanner Dyson took the trouble to track Abner Hoon down, either from his ranch or from his Gulfstream en route to New York, Abner Hoon was her new best friend.

"Tell me," she said, "who is going to be at Lolly's service?"

He threw up his hands. "Darling, everyone! You think this party is full of celebrities, wait till you see the undead who crawl out of seclusion for Lolly. The world! The universe!"

"That many," she said flatly. She made her eyes as wide as she could and looked up at him. "Abner?" she said softly. "You know I adored Lolly."

"We all did, darling."

"I wish I could be there."

"Well, of course you'll be there. Why on earth wouldn't you be?"

"Oh, I don't think I'll be invited. I never got around to sitting on Tanner Dyson's face."

Abner recoiled briefly, then chuckled. "It's going to be at the Minskoff Theatre. They'll fill every seat, so come early. You give me your number before you leave, and I'll tell you when and what time."

"You mean it?" Baby squealed.

"Absolutely," he said, extending his arm. "And now, let's think of happier things. Shall we tour the house, see how Tita's been spending Jourdan's money?"

Baby looked over her shoulder, then turned back. "You think we can?"

"Why not?" he whispered. "If anyone stops us, we can say we're looking for the loo."

Baby pressed her lips together and rolled her eyes. If she could see the inside of the spectacular house, she could do a whole thing on it. Maybe even a feature. She loved to get her stuff off the Grapevine page. It rarely happened, because Petra was jealous of her, but if she got a firsthand look at the Garns' renovated mansion, screw Petra, she would go right to Joe with it.

She slipped her hand under Abner's moist arm, and they walked toward the oceanside entrance.

Hoon gazed up at the house as they walked. "I remember this place when Trent Nunnally had it," he said, sounding nostalgic. "The entire first floor was paneled with African mahogany that was shipped panel by panel around Cape Horn. They French-polished it on site. Extraordinary house. I hope they haven't changed too much of it."

The room they stepped into had a double-height ceiling. The walls were covered with mottled, smoked glass shot through with threads of gold. Twin plaster zebras pranced among silk ferns on either side of the mammoth fireplace.

Hoon stood absolutely still as though holding his breath.

"Good Lord," he sighed as he took in the scene. "It looks like Liberace threw up."

Baby's eyes swept the room. "It is horrible, isn't it?" She reached in her bag, pulled out her notepad, and began to scribble.

"Oh, my dear, do write about this. You must. Someone has to chronicle this outrage." Hoon was clearly very upset. More upset than Baby felt was warranted. If Garn's money put green paint over rare old wood, couldn't someone else's money hire a lot of local workmen to restore it? Wasn't that the idea of a trickle-down economy?

"Come," he commanded. "Let us explore what other obscenities these climbers have perpetrated."

As they wandered, Hoon kept up a running monologue of outrage at the insult the Garns had done to the beautiful old house. Baby tuned out. But when she saw Hoon begin to mount the stairs, she pulled up short. "Oh, Abner. I don't think I'm up to it. Let's go get something to eat."

"Come on," he whispered. "There's no way I'm stopping now. Just remember, if we get caught, we're still looking for a loo."

The second-floor hall matched the one on the floor below running the width of the mansion, with bedroom after bedroom opening off of it. Baby and Abner peeked into each, making wisecracks and muffling their laughter as they tiptoed down the hall. At the end was a state-of-the-art spa and a large room that looked to Baby like a Madison Avenue boutique, with low, soft-looking sofas in wheat-colored monk's cloth and racks upon racks of clothes. At first she thought it might have been Tita Mandraki's very big closet, but on closer inspection she noticed that several of the hanging outfits were repeats in different sizes.

She paused as Abner moved ahead to inspect the spa. She could hear the music coming through the windows from the party below. The room and its contents seemed to beckon to her to come closer.

She stepped to the first rack and slowly slid the hangers along the metal piping. Her heart sang. Never had she seen such delicious clothes, such luxurious fabrics and delicate handwork. She pictured herself arriving at Lolly's service in the gold-lamé miniskirt, walking down the aisle of the Minskoff Theatre, all heads turning to stare at her. Or, perhaps, the pale pink chiffon suit, a mass of the smallest hand-tucked pleats imaginable. Each piece felt more buttery and cool in her hand than the last.

She looked down at her tiny handbag, then let her eyes sweep the room. There had to be a way, she thought, her heart beating in her ears. There had to be a way to fold up just one of these incredible outfits. She usually pulled bathing suits she fancied in the store up under the clothes she was wearing. She had never paid for a bathing suit in her life. They were so easy to slip on in a dressing room. Of course, she was limited to those that had no security tag, but for free was more important than color.

She looked down at her cocktail dress. There wasn't enough room to hide a whole dress. She pulled at her skirt. There was enough give in the fabric to pull on the fabulous gold miniskirt and glide away.

As she quickly stepped into the gold skirt, she looked longingly at the jacket and wished she had brought a larger bag. Maybe she would just try it on.

She had one arm in the sleeve of the jacket when she heard a voice from the doorway.

"Is there something I could show you?" There was a sarcastic edge to the words.

Baby turned to see her glamorous hostess silhouetted in the doorway.

That's when she panicked. Her only recourse was to fake a faint.

Right after the thud of hitting the floor, she heard Tita shriek, then footsteps coming up the hall and Abner's voice. What a cool old coot he was. He must have figured out what was going on.

"Oh, my God, oh, my God," Tita had started raving. "Someone help."

Baby stayed right where she was. She even let her mouth hang open just a bit.

"What's the problem?" she heard Abner ask.

"This woman was trying on my things," Tita gasped. "When she saw me, she fainted."

"Oh, dear, dear, dear," Abner dithered. Baby sensed him kneeling beside her right ear. He placed a clammy hand on her forehead and held it there. "Don't you know who this is?" she heard him ask Tita.

"I'm afraid I don't. Does it matter? These rooms up here are private."

Abner removed his hand and stood up. "Then you might provide toilet facilities for your guests," he said grandly. "This lady is from the *Courier*. She is writing a definitive piece for her newspaper on this glorious house."

Baby could hear Tita, who was standing directly over her, sniff. "She certainly has an odd way of getting her story. She was trying on my clothes. I should call Tanner Dyson about this."

"I think what should concern you is this young woman's welfare," Abner snapped. "Now, if you'd be so kind, is there someplace she could pull herself together?"

"There's an empty guest room at the end of the hall, if you must. Just get this disgusting woman off the floor and put her to bed."

Baby thought it was time for her to moan. Maybe Tita would go away if she thought she would have to talk to her. She began to raise her head. Through slitted eyes she saw Tita scurrying down the hall.

Abner leaned very close to Baby's ear and whispered, "Get up, you little twit, and hurry, before someone else comes."

Baby's eyes flew open. "But . . ."

"No buts, little lady. I know what you were up to. If I hadn't pulled your dress over that gold skirt you're trying to pinch, Madame Garn would have as well. Now get up and take it off. We are putting you to bed."

Baby struggled to her feet and pulled off the skirt. She quickly hung it with the jacket and turned to Abner, who was waiting by the door. "Why do I have to go to bed, for Christ's sake? It's over."

"It is not over. If you show up downstairs now, there could be a confrontation. We can't take the chance she didn't believe this little charade. You can't even leave. Only if you stay in bed can I go down and plead illness, and maybe save your job."

Abner led her to the room at the end of the hall and tucked her into bed, clothes and all.

Baby pulled the sheet up to her nose and looked around the room. "I can't stay in here long, Abner. I'll go crazy. Besides, what about my photographer? He'll start looking for me."

"I'll find him and hold him off," Abner said, closing the drapes. "Can you sleep?"

"Christ, no. Not with all that noise right under the window."

Abner reached into the pocket of his slacks and extracted a small silver box. He flipped open the lid and poked around inside for a moment. "Let's see, I've got blues, greens, tricolors, spansules, and all-time bye-byes. I think a blue will do the trick."

Baby sat up, alarmed. "What are you doing? I'm not taking any crazy drugs."

Abner looked up and pursed his lips in impatience. "What do you want to do, love? Lie here and stare at the ceiling or take an hour's nappy-poo until the coast is clear?"

Baby groaned and plopped back onto the pillows. "Oh, all right. But something light. I've got to get up and out of here. One hour, that's it. Then you come and get me, okay?"

"Here," Abner said, handing her a little blue pill. There was a crystal water carafe next to the bed. He poured a glass and handed it to her.

Baby took the blue pill. She put it on her tongue, swallowed, and looked up at her rescuer. "Why are you so good to me, Abner? You don't even know me."

"Oh, yes I do," he said with a half smile. "I'm good to you for the same reason I raise Afghans in the country back home. They are frisky and stupid. Just like you. Qualities I find irresistible."

Baby fell back onto the pillows and closed her eyes. "Thank you," she said. "I think." As little red dots began to dance behind her eyes, it occurred to her that Abner wanted to go downstairs and work the party alone. It was too late.

She passed out.

The short, sharp rap on the door startled Baby. She looked up to see the college-graduate maid standing in the door with fresh linen over her arm. "Are you Baby Bayer?" the maid asked in a bored monotone.

"Ah . . . ah . . . yes," Baby said, taken aback. "Why?"

"They just rang up from the gate. There's a car for you on its way up."

"A car? For me?"

"That's what they said," the maid said.

"How do I get downstairs?"

"Turn right out in the hall, walk to the stairs, go down and out the door."

The maid tossed a folded sheet into the air. It unfurled and floated down onto the bed. "I'd walk straight out if I were you. Don't, like, wander around. They're all talking about you downstairs."

Baby whirled around. "They are? What are they saying?"

The maid smiled. "They're saying Mrs. Garn caught you stealing stuff from her studio down the hall last night."

"That's not true," Baby said hotly. "I'm a reporter. I was here working. I had to look around to write a story about the place. I passed out from the heat and was put to bed with some pill that made me sleep through the night."

"Is that so?"

"Yes, that is so."

"Oh, well," the maid said with a shrug. "Don't let it bother you. You know how people talk."

7

"What is this?" Joe Stone called into the overcooled air of his office. He was standing at his desk in the little glass cubicle just off the *Courier* city room.

He might as well have been shouting into a wind tunnel. There wasn't anyone but his secretary, June, to answer, and she was sitting outside the door with her back to him combing her very high, very big hair in the reflection of her dark computer screen. Joe groaned and slumped in his chair. He had just gotten to the office, but he was already bone tired. The death of Lolly Pines had totally screwed up his long weekend, as it had those of any of the other *Courier* executives who were counting on a few days off.

If Tanner Dyson had to give up his holiday weekend then, by God, so did everyone else.

Now, sitting at his desk, trying to figure out the ten-page fax curled up on his desk and missing its cover sheet, he had no patience for his secretary's little games. She was pissed that she had had to come in on the Sunday before Labor Day, but then again so was he.

He picked up the pages and confronted his secretary's back. "I hate to bother you, June, what with your having a bad hair day and all, but was there a cover sheet with this fax?"

June's comb paused in midair. She turned to squint at the bundle of pages in Joe's hand. "On the floor, probably," she said with a shrug. "It's good, did you read it?"

"Not yet, June," he said in his humor-the-mental-patient voice. "I just got here."

"Yeah. Right."

"Seeing how you've read it, what is it?"

"It's about Lolly Pines. A memoir. By someone who actually liked her," June said. "Sam Nichols dropped it off."

"Impossible," Joe said. "Nobody liked Lolly."

"Whatever."

Joe walked back into his office and scanned the floor for the lost coil that would identify the sender.

The faxes and telegrams concerning Lolly's death had been arriving since early Friday evening. Hundreds of people, no doubt hoping it was true, had wired for absolute confirmation.

Among the papers waiting for Joe had been the memo he dreaded. Tanner Dyson, following some Peter Principle of giving a delicate job to the person least equipped to carry it out without a major diplomatic screw-up, had asked Joe to coordinate the memorial service.

He returned to his desk chair and reached for the cardboard container of light coffee from the Greek coffee shop on First Avenue. It had already started to congeal in the air-conditioned room. As he lifted the cup to his mouth, he saw a piece of fax paper stuck to the bottom.

He peeled it off and read aloud, "To: Sam Nichols. From: K. M. Butler."

Who the hell was K. M. Butler? he thought. Konrad Butler, maybe? Butler was the new ambassador to what used to be the Soviet Union. How did Konrad Butler know Lolly Pines?

He sat back and began to read the rest of the fax. He scanned through it, then put his feet up on the desk and read it again, carefully.

It was good. It was very, very good.

He picked up the cover sheet and stared at it again.

"June!" he bellowed. "Would you mind a lot coming in here?"

His secretary swiveled around in her chair, stood, and slowly, slowly approached the front of Joe's desk.

He pointed to the cover sheet. "Whose fax number is this? I don't know any K. M. Butler."

June squinted at the paper. "*Ummmm*, oh, that's Lolly Pines's fax. That must be from Kick, Lolly's assistant. So that's her last name."

"Where does this Kick person live? I mean, how can I get in touch with her on a Sunday?"

"At Lolly's."

"Lolly's?"

"Yeah, she lives there. I'd love to see that apartment someday. I hear it's the size of Madison Square Garden and full of crap."

"Get me this Kick person on the phone."

"You got it," June said lethargically as she strolled back to her desk.

Sunday morning Kick slept late. It was close to eleven before she struggled down the two flights of stairs to the front door of Lolly's triplex. She half dragged, half lifted the Sunday *Times* from the ratty doormat outside on the landing.

Writing the homage to Lolly—which had taken her all of Friday night and on into a good part of Saturday night as well—had taken a physical and an emotional toll on her. By the time she had faxed it to the newspaper in the wee hours of Sunday morning, she was more exhausted than she could remember having been in years. It wasn't until she had collapsed into bed that she wondered if she had sent the pages to the right number. She didn't have the strength to get up and double-check.

She carried the newspaper into the kitchen and dropped it on the table, then stood listening to the sounds of the empty house. Only then did it hit her that she was indeed alone. Lolly wasn't puttering around with her morning tea. The only sounds were the rattle of the old refrigerator and the ticking of the counter clock.

The silence was broken by the shrilling of the telephone. She was so used to saying "Ms. Pines's office," she almost said it as she picked up the phone. She stopped herself and simply said, "Hello."

"May I speak to Kick Butler?" a man's voice asked.

"This is she."

"Kick, this is Joe Stone down at the *Courier*. I just read the fax you sent us."

Kick sat down in the little chair next to the phone table. "Oh, dear," she said. "I didn't expect to hear from you. I sent that to Sam Nichols."

"Yes, well, he was good enough to pass it along to me."

"That was nice of him," Kick said, feeling a trickle of sweat start down between her shoulders.

"This is an interesting piece of work," Joe Stone said. "I'd like to talk to you about it. Are you free for lunch?"

"Today? It's Sunday."

"Yeah, well," he laughed. "People eat lunch on Sundays, right?"

"When would you like to see me?" she asked, trying to keep the nervousness out of her voice.

"There's a little place called Renaldo's on Seventeenth just off Ninth. Twelve-thirty okay?"

"That's fine, Mr. Stone," she said. "How will I know you?"

"I'll be the one at a table in the back garden with his head turned to the sun," he said. "I was planning to work on my tan this weekend. And you?"

Kick looked down at herself involuntarily. She couldn't remember the last time anyone asked her to describe herself. "Ah . . . tall, short red hair, *umm*, freckles, and no tan."

"Great," Joe Stone said. "See you then."

Kick sat very still. She pictured Stone—heavy, balding, and hungover, with nicotine-stained fingers and a cynical wit. His tie would be pulled down and his collar button missing, a typical tabloid newspaper editor.

Kick raced up the stairs. Once in her room she began to yank open drawers. "Thank heaven," she sighed with relief. There, in the third drawer down, was an unopened package of panty hose.

As she prepared to leave, she went through her usual mental checklist: Answering machines? On. Windows without air conditioners closed in case it rains? Right. Leave note on Lolly's desk lamp to tell her when I'll be . . .

She paused and sat down on the edge of her bed. What was she doing? Lolly was lying on some slab somewhere at Riverside Funeral Home over on Amsterdam, and she was rushing out to a job interview. What would Lolly think?

Well, what *would* she think? Kick closed her eyes and summoned a surprisingly vivid image of Lolly's small, energetic form standing in the doorway, hands on her hips, foot tapping.

What would she say? Kick could almost hear the words echoing in the room.

"Get up and go for it, girl. It's your turn now."

8

*B*aby hated Sundays. Everyone was away. The streets were hot and deserted. She had seen most of the movies around town. Besides, going to a movie alone on a summer Sunday afternoon was beyond depressing.

She was stuck in her messy apartment, lying on her bed in front of the air conditioner, doing her nails.

She had phoned Abner Hoon at the Carlyle twice since she got back from the Hamptons. Both times he was out and she left a message.

Driving back from the Hamptons in the car he'd sent, she had fantasized that he would ask her to lunch on Sunday and she could kill the day solidifying their new friendship. Abner Hoon was as wired as anyone she had known since Georgina Dyson, and she intended to see that she made herself indispensable to him. It was difficult to do, however, if she couldn't even reach him.

She thought about calling Georgina again, giving her one more chance. She was reaching for the phone when she remembered that Tanner would be home by now, for sure. It was next to impossible to have a conversation with Georgina when Tanner was in the apartment.

Though Baby usually saw herself as the victim in any unpleasant situation, in the case of Tanner Dyson's marriage to Georgina, she felt she especially qualified. She was well aware that in marrying the publisher of the *Courier*, Georgina had cut light-years off her social progress in New York. The irony was that, unlike Baby, moving in a powerful circle of important people had never been a goal in life for Georgina.

When the two women had both worked at the paper, as Baby would admit, she had deliberately set about ingratiating herself with Georgina. Still, she had tried to be a good and comforting friend to her, and Baby didn't feel she deserved the way Tanner had used her. It had all happened over two years ago, but the memory still stung.

It was late in the winter of 1990. The paper had been working full-staff around the clock for days with their coverage of the Gulf War. Baby's talents at rooting out tasty gossip items had not been taxed, and for three days in a row the Grapevine-page had been killed and the space turned over to pictures of local-area GIs in desert gear going off to war.

Baby had arrived at work late, as usual, feeling ill used and bored. The only vaguely exciting thing on her dim horizon line had been the arrival of a new editor-in-chief. Advance word had it that he had a great sense of humor, was the fair-haired boy and personal hire of the publisher, and—best of all—his marriage was in trouble.

He was Baby's mischief project for the week.

As soon as she reached the sixth floor, she whipped into the ladies' room to put the final touches on her makeup. She was leaning over the sink working on a second coat of mascara, when she heard muffled sobs coming from the closed stall at the far end of the room.

"Oh, God . . ." the voice from the stall keened.

"Are you okay in there?" Baby called without turning around.

The tormented soul in the booth fell silent.

Baby walked over to the door and pressed her lips to the seam between the door and the wall. "I'm Baby Bayer. Can I get you anything?"

The only response was the loud honking of a nose being blown.

"Are you sick?"

Finally a soft, trembling voice answered. "No, no . . . I'm okay. I'm coming out. Do you have a comb I could borrow?"

"Sure," Baby said brightly, fishing into her bag. She found her comb and frantically began pulling snarled strands of multicolored hair from the teeth. Over her shoulder she saw the stall door open and turned in surprise.

"Georgina?" she asked, not quite believing that the disheveled person with a tissue over her nose was Georgina Holmes from the food page. She had never seen Georgina looking anything but impeccable. Now her eyes were swollen and red, her makeup gone, and her hair, which she usually wore in a sleek French twist, was hanging in limp tendrils around her face. The other noticeably odd thing about her was that she was carrying a copy of the competing morning tabloid. It wasn't like Georgina Holmes to do something so tacky as take the *New York Post* into the john to read.

When Georgina reached to place the newspaper on the edge of the sink, it slipped to the floor and opened to Page Six, the gossip page roughly equivalent to the *Courier*'s Grapevine page.

Baby couldn't help scanning the page. Halfway down was one of those cutesy no-names blind items that Baby hoped to write someday: "What big-time, very-married media mogul is sharing more than crème brûlée with a food editor in his employ?"

So, the rumors were true, Baby thought. The gossip mill had been working overtime for the last few weeks, but no one, not even Baby, who thrived on such tales, could pin it down.

Baby felt a little shiver race down her spine. Her timing could not have been better. Here she was sharing an important moment with someone about to be swept into a highly charged, dramatic situation. Baby would have to move fast to join Georgina in the eye of the storm and make herself indispensable.

Georgina was leaning against the sink, dabbing helplessly at her eyes while fresh tears welled.

"Georgina," Baby said sympathetically. "How can I help?"

"I don't know," Georgina sobbed. "Someone left that on my desk. Oh, God, I can't face going back out there."

Baby looked around the rest room conspiratorially, as though making sure they were not overheard. "Listen," she whispered. "I don't think you *should* go out there feeling this way. We can take the back elevator, grab a cab, and get you home before anyone notices. Where do you live?"

"Seventy-second and Third," Georgina whimpered. "But I can't go home. There are bound to be reporters hanging around my lobby. Tanner's so important. What if someone took my picture? This would be terrible for him."

Baby thought Georgina was being a little paranoid. It was just a blind item, not a front-page story with a shot of Georgina with a big red *A* on her chest. Then again, Georgina's paranoia might work to Baby's advantage. "We'll go to my place. No one will think to look for you there."

And they didn't. Not for nearly a month. In just that brief bathroom encounter, Baby had acquired an instant roommate and a new and exciting life.

As their cab approached Baby's small building in the middle of the block, Baby remembered that, as usual, the bed had been left unmade. Any outfit she had worn that week was in a pile on the broken-down easy chair, and who knew what kind of shape the bathroom was in. The apartment usually looked like a small explosion had taken place, but that day it was particularly bad.

Baby began to apologize as they got out of the cab. "I'm afraid my place is a wreck, Georgina," she said. "I was late this morning and didn't have a chance to pick up."

Georgina was already pushing through the revolving door to the lobby, her scarf pulled far over her forehead Queen-

Elizabeth-tramping-over-the-moors style. "That's okay," she called without looking around, and rushed through the lobby door.

To her credit, Georgina didn't wrinkle her nose or even comment on the state of Baby's one room.

"May I use your bathroom, please?" she asked plaintively. "I'm a mess from all this crying."

Baby rushed into the bathroom and snagged the soiled underwear and towels off the floor.

"Okay, it's all yours," she called, jamming the things into an overflowing hamper behind the door.

She was sorting through the cabinet over the sink, frantically looking for two unchipped tea cups and saucers, when Georgina appeared in the kitchen door. She had washed her face and put on what little makeup she used. Her hair was smooth and back to normal. Baby had never seen her outside the office, and in a different place and light she realized, with a tiny twinge of envy, how flawlessly beautiful Georgina Holmes was. No wonder an older, powerful man like Tanner Dyson had risked his reputation for rectitude and fallen in love with her.

"Baby," Georgina said, "I don't know how to thank you for what you're doing."

Baby turned off the flame under the screeching teakettle. "No problem," she chirped. "I'm sure you'd do the same if it were me." She gave up on cups and saucers and found two mismatched mugs.

"I've made such a terrible mess of things," Georgina sighed as Baby took out two tea bags and plopped them into the mugs.

"Come," Baby said. "Let's sit down. You can tell me what's happened. Then we'll see what can be done about it."

They settled themselves opposite each other in two rickety flea-market bentwood rockers Baby had placed in the bay window, and Georgina began to speak.

Fascinated, Baby listened silently, leaning forward to catch every word. She had always found the details of star-crossed love riveting, yet she was also aware that what she was hearing was the coin of her world, the inside dope on a love affair that seemed on the verge of exploding into a media circus.

Georgina had had no intention of having an affair with the older publisher. She was in awe of him and had been flattered and excited at being singled out to plan and prepare a series of lunches he had scheduled in the executive suite. That had been two months earlier. At first he had been formal and somewhat aloof, treating her as a trusted professional. Not a personal word or a piece of light chitchat had passed between them.

Then one afternoon he had asked her to linger after the chairman of the New York Stock Exchange and two bank presidents had left. He wanted to discuss the next day's luncheon with her for a moment.

She returned to the kitchen to wait for him to call her. She had been slightly unnerved when, rather than summoning her into his office off the dining room, he suddenly appeared in the doorway. Georgina had slipped *La Bohème* into the little tape player she kept in the pantry and was humming as she worked on her menu schedule. She looked up to see him staring into space, a half smile on his face. A lamp in the dining room was backlighting his silver hair, and she noticed that the blue of his shirt was exactly the shade of his eyes.

"Oh, hello, Mr. Dyson," she said, putting down her pen. "You startled me."

"Lovely," he said.

"Sorry?"

"This passage right here," he said, dreamily moving his head from side to side. "It breaks my heart every time I hear it."

It was then that she realized he was responding to the music. "Me, too," she said, listening with him as the aria came to an end.

In the silence between movements he stepped closer. "Are you an opera buff, Miss Holmes?"

"Oh, yes," she said. "My father and I used listen to the Metropolitan on the radio every Saturday afternoon. Those were the happiest hours of my life."

To her utter surprise, he pulled up a high kitchen stool, sat down, and began to ask her what operas were her favorites. He discussed the subject with the intricate knowledge of a person in love with an art form, the way some men talk about fly casting or baseball. He knew far more about everything than she did.

He had been discussing a performance of *Der Rosenkavalier* he had seen in Vienna some years earlier when he suddenly glanced at his watch and stood up.

"Good lord, I've kept Senator Brogan waiting for half an hour," he said.

Georgina had felt bad, as though by listening she had stolen him away from his work.

"I tell you what," Dyson said from the doorway. "If you love *La Bohème*, there's a performance Thursday night. Would you like to go?"

Georgina stared at him, her mind in turmoil. He had asked so casually she wondered if he truly knew what he was suggesting.

He read the confusion on her face and laughed. "Don't worry, Miss Holmes," he said reassuringly. "There would be three of us. My executive assistant, Neal Grant, usually goes with me. You see, Mrs. Dyson is in Paris for the showing. Besides, she loathes opera."

That was how it had begun.

Georgina looked across at Baby, who was hanging on every word. It had started to rain, and the drops made little cracking sounds against the loose glass in Baby's bay window.

"I was so naive," she said. "I found out later that Neal Grant didn't particularly like opera either but went so people would think Neal and I were together."

"So? So? When did it start to get . . . you know, heavy?"

Georgina winced slightly, as though she knew that what Baby was asking was, "When did it get sexual?"

"Come on, Georgina. You wouldn't be in this trouble if the two of you were just opera friends."

Georgina looked down at her tea mug. "Baby, have you ever had an orgasm?"

Baby's mouth dropped open for an instant then quickly shut. "I'm sorry. That's such a dumb question, of course you have."

"I've had 'em on the D train, Georgina," Baby lied, protecting her reputation as a femme fatale. "I can work one up watching a movie all by myself on a Sunday afternoon."

"Well, you're special, I guess. But I'm thirty-one years old and I've never had one before."

"*Sheesh,*" Baby said softly.

"Anyway, after the second night at the opera I finally knew."

"The second night! What happened?"

Georgina leaned forward and whispered, "Baby, we did it in the back of his limousine. We came out of the opera and put Neal in a cab. Tanner's car was waiting with all the others in front of the plaza at Lincoln Center. Tanner had been sitting very close to me throughout the opera. It was like electricity was passing between us. His driver had barely shut the door of the car when we started literally tearing each other's clothes off. I didn't even try to resist. If anything, I was the one who made the first move. I just tore into him. It only took a few minutes. We were thrashing and moaning so violently the driver must have had his own erection. We could have been in a convertible in Times Square for all we cared. He came at the exact instant I did. I thought I would fly into tiny pieces. I've never felt anything like it in my life."

"*Whoa,*" Baby said, deeply impressed. "Our maximum leader? The chairman of the board, our Tanner Dyson, with his tux trousers down around his knees in the backseat? I love it."

Georgina looked stricken and held up her hand. "Baby! Please, you can never, never tell anyone what I just told you. Oh, Lord, I shouldn't have . . ."

"Please, Georgina, please," Baby begged. "You had to tell me. How else am I going to help you?"

"Oh, Baby, you're being so sweet to me," Georgina said.

"All right, so now it's started. You guys are in love? Or did that come later?"

"It's hard to say. All I know is that we couldn't keep our hands off each other. I would go up early to get the luncheons ready, and we would do it in his office. One awful time I was completely naked bending forward over his desk, he was way up inside of me, and his secretary knocked on the door."

Baby's mouth dropped again. "Tanner Dyson does it doggy style?"

"Baby," Georgina said, lowering her eyes as the color rose in her pale cheeks.

"Well," Baby said with a frown. "You're the one telling the story. It's just that I'm seeing Tanner through totally different eyes. He sounds fantastic!"

Georgina bit her lip. "Not only that," she said softly. "He makes me come with his tongue. He kind of flicks it, you know. He keeps doing it until I scream, then he, you know."

"Screws you, right? *Arghhhh!* I love it," Baby hooted. "No wonder you're in this fix."

"I shouldn't have told you. It's just that it makes me crazy thinking about it. We want each other all the time. We've even left Neal sitting at a restaurant table and walked out before our order came just so we could do it."

"Where do you go? You can't go to his place."

"That's the awful part. He offered to rent me a suite at the Carlyle, but I said no. We do it in the car. Mostly we do it in the office. He won't come to my place because he's afraid the doorman will recognize him. You know some of those doormen make calls to the gossip columnists."

"Really?" Baby said, her eyes hooded.

And so the great escapade began, with Baby as Georgina's protector and the lovers' go-between. Tanner and Georgina now used Baby as a beard and her apartment as their hideout. Tanner had the place professionally cleaned, got a full-time maid to pick up after Baby, and offered all kinds of time-fillers to Baby herself, embarrassed that he had to ask an underling to leave her own place in order for him to be with his beloved. There were orchestra theater seats, the use of his limousine; Neal Grant, who wasn't half-bad-looking but a little uptight for her taste, took her to "21" and Mortimer's, to—God help her—a basketball game, on buggy rides in Central Park, and to the ballet. Rumors started at the office that Baby was having a thing with the chairman's assistant, and she was teased for sucking up to management. Little did they know.

Then Georgina missed her period. She was terrified. When the doctor told her she had an ectopic pregnancy and advised surgery, Georgina panicked.

She called Tanner, crying, from the nurses' station outside the doctor's office.

What Georgina didn't know was that she and Mrs. Tanner Dyson had more than Tanner in common. They shared a gynecologist as well. Minutes after Georgina left, another call was made from the nurses' station.

Baby stood by her friend throughout the divorce ordeal. They lunched together often: the maître 'd and waiters at La Caravelle protected the two women from intrusion until the whole exciting and dreadful mess was over.

On a moonlit summer evening when the gods sent an onshore breeze that blew the aroma of the Hudson River to the Jersey shore, Baby stood beside Neal Grant on the fantail of Tanner Dyson's yacht and listened to a Manhattan Superior Court judge marry Georgina Holmes and Tanner Dyson.

Baby got very drunk on very good champagne, outjumped a deck steward to reach Georgina's tossed bouquet, and was about to put the moves on Neal Grant in the lounge when Tanner loomed in the passageway. He asked Grant to excuse himself and walked toward Baby on the couch.

"I have a little something for you, Baby," he said, reaching into the pocket of his white linen suit.

Baby's eyes widened. Such a lovely phrase coming from a wealthy man, she thought, smiling up at him.

Tanner handed her a robin's-egg-blue box tied with a white satin ribbon. "Just to say thank you for everything," he said tightly.

Baby slowly opened the box, savoring the moment. Inside was a spray of diamonds, a crescent-shaped pin the size of her thumb.

She gasped. "Oh, Tanner, how beautiful," she breathed. "This wasn't necessary."

"I think it was," he said, reaching into his jacket pocket. "I also have a piece of paper I'd like you to sign."

Baby frowned and reached for the folded paper. There were two pieces, one a photocopy of the other.

"Me? Sign something? I don't get it."

"Read it," he said.

Baby looked down at the page and felt the buzz the champagne had provided burning away as she read.

I, Minerva Teresa Bayer, known professionally as Baby Bayer, swear and attest that I will not speak, write, or otherwise broadcast my knowledge of any relationship between Mrs. Georgina Holmes Dyson and her husband, Tanner Woodruff Dyson, prior to their marriage, now or at any time throughout my lifetime.

I have received as compensation for this irrevocable undertaking a piece of jewelry valued at thirty thousand dollars. Should I break this agreement in any way, I will forfeit that amount plus one hundred percent damages to Tanner Dyson's attorney of record at the time of the infraction.

Baby looked up at Tanner through narrowed eyes. "What the fuck is this, Tanner?" she growled.

"You just read it. It is what it is."

"Its a piece of moose shit, that's what it is."

"Baby, you've had too much to drink," Tanner said, backing away as she stood up.

"Right, and you should thank your lucky stars I have or you could kiss your heartbeat good-bye," she shouted.

"Calm down, Baby. This is just a formality. A man in my position can't tolerate someone out there who might someday talk about details best left private. Life is short. You could go to work for a rival newspaper someday and be asked to do a profile on me. I have to be protected."

"Why, you two-faced bastard," she snapped. "I've a good mind to go up on deck and show this to Georgina."

"Baby," Tanner said, as calm as she was furious. "I don't think Georgina needs to know about this. Surely you don't think she'd take your side over mine. Not after what we've been through to be together."

"I still won't sign," she snarled.

"You can sell that jewelry tomorrow. The only reason I bothered was because Georgina wanted you to have a nice gift. Thirty thousand would make a down payment on a proper apartment, my dear."

"Oh, something wrong with my apartment, is there? It was good enough for you to fuck in."

Dyson made a face.

"I won't sign this."

Tanner began to pace. Baby pulled herself onto a barstool and poured a shot of hundred-year-old brandy into a dirty glass someone had left on the bar.

Tanner cleared his throat. "Baby, sign that piece of paper and when Lolly Pines leaves—and I have reason to believe this may happen—her column is yours."

Baby took a throat-searing swallow of brandy and coughed hard enough to bring tears to her eyes. "Lolly's going to leave?" she said, choking.

"I have reason to believe the *Daily News* may make her an offer. I don't want that known, however."

"I'll sign."

Lolly never left the *Courier*. Now, two years later and Lolly good and dead, Baby was tired of waiting. She closed the nail polish bottle and held her fingers up in front of the air conditioner. She wanted that column so badly she could taste it. And she'd do anything to get it. It was time to make her move.

Sitting alone in her messy apartment, Baby remembered the few notes she had made at the Garns' party. Maybe it made sense to go into the office when no one was around and write it up.

When she arrived in the newsroom an hour later, she was relieved to see that there was no one around the Grapevine space. She could hear the phone on Petra's desk ringing in her office. Without a second thought she marched in and picked it up.

"Grapevine," she said in a bored tone.

"Oh, hello. This is Irving Fourbraz in Los Angeles. To whom am I speaking?"

Baby's body stiffened with excitement as she congratulated herself for being once again in the right place at the right time. "Why, hellloooo, Mr. Fourbraz," she cooed. "You don't know me. I'm Baby Bayer. I saw you on *Larry King* just last week, and I couldn't help wondering if you are that handsome in person." Fourbraz had been on TV to talk about that dreadful Keeko Ram.

There was a moment's pause. When Irving replied his voice sounded deeper than before. "What did you say your name was?"

"Baby Bayer, sort of like Kitty Cat or Pussy Willow," she said with a little giggle. "Now, what can I do for *you*, Mr. Fourbraz?"

9

*I*rving Fourbraz hung up the phone next to the bed in his suite at the Beverly Hills Hotel wondering what a Baby Bayer looked like. She had sounded young. She was probably one of those anorexic brats who fiddle around a newspaper office until they find some Wall Street yuppie to marry them. How ironic it was that he should learn about Lolly Pines's death from someone like that. No wonder he hadn't been able to reach her.

Losing Lolly was a blow. He felt a twinge of guilt that she had been dead an entire day before he heard about it. But, hey, he thought. He had had something to celebrate. He'd gotten Dave Kasko at the *World* to agree to advance seventy-five grand for the Lopez girl's story. The beauty part was that he wouldn't have to pay anything out to the girl for a while. She wasn't going anywhere.

Anyway, his little party sure had been worth it. Not an hour earlier he had closed the door of the suite and shaken his head in amazement. Phew, he thought, Madame Dee-Dee had pulled out all the stops when she sent that one around.

Her name was Monica. She had cost him a yard and a half, but when he thought about it, fifteen hundred bucks wasn't a bundle for nearly eight hours of the greatest tail he'd had in years. And a looker too, like Ursula Andress's baby sister.

Sheesh, who the hell but him remembered Ursula Andress?

He had to stop even mental references to anything that happened before, oh, maybe, Iran-Contra, before the Gulf War. Nothing mattered that happened before yesterday, actually. The world belonged to those in love with the new.

Fifty-nine. Scary. Only a hairpiece away from sixty.

What if he had a heart attack with one of these hookers? What if the LAPD or the NYPD or the Miami or Atlantic City police found him, like John Garfield, with his silk shorts on backward because some broad panicked getting his body dressed?

Poor Neeva, people would say. Poor Neeva, married to a schmuck like Irving Fourbraz who can't keep his heart beating long enough to get his pants on right. And as for his son Jason, the publishing genius, he hadn't spoken to him since the divorce, and he doubted if the kid would give a shit.

He couldn't think about that now. He wasn't dead. He was hungry and he had a deal to lay off. He needed Lolly Pines to help him make it work. His luck, she died. Go figure.

Maybe that Baby Bear, Bayer, however she spelled it, would prove useful. The Grapevine wasn't as powerful as Lolly's column, but it was something.

He wondered if he should have made the dinner date with her for tomorrow night. He hoped to hell she was a looker. He would wait until after they had drinks at the St. Regis before he actually booked a table for dinner. Irving Fourbraz did not dine among his peers with dogs.

10

*G*eorgina heard the oven timer go off and licked the deviled egg off her fingers. There was one more sheet of potato puffs to bake.

She slid the cookie sheet out of the top oven, placed it on the big butcher-block center island, and slipped the rest of the hors d'oeuvres into place.

She had baked and sliced a Virginia ham earlier. Eight dozen tiny beaten biscuits were ready, as was the crabmeat starter and the *filet en croûte* and the rice pilaf.

She was determined to have everything done and put away in the walk-in freezer before Tanner got home from the office. He would not be pleased if she wasn't able to give him her full attention.

He had had a trying enough weekend. He loved the ranch so. To have to leave for any reason was upsetting enough, but to come back because of the death of a colleague made it even more unpleasant.

Georgina had never known Lolly personally, even though they

both worked for the *Courier* at the same time. Lolly never came into the office, and in any case Georgina would have been beneath Lolly's notice. Until she married Tanner.

Looking back, it seemed as though everything and everyone who mattered to her in life had faded into the background the day Tanner walked into the little executive kitchen and asked her if she liked opera.

From that day forward, she had one focus: making Tanner happy. If the wonderful life that had just happened to her had a dark cloud at all, it was that deep in her heart, Georgina felt she was an impostor.

Tanner thought she was beautiful. Tanner had not known, nor would he ever know, what she was like when she first came to New York.

The Georgina Holmes that Tanner had never known was not statuesque. She could not have been correctly called full-figured or even heavy. That Georgina had been enormous. That Georgina had been fat.

At sixteen she wore a size 2X, which meant she had passed the whale's position on the food chain; passed size 16, where salesladies, when they saw you, looked as though they had swallowed a flying insect; passed the sizes that sent you in your stained raincoat to places with demeaning names to squeeze into the sad conspiracy of sizes that started at 1x. Georgina learned early that a 1x woman is just as capable of preening and prancing in the company of 4xs as a size 4 is on the runway of a suburban fashion show.

In high school and college her mother blamed Georgina's size on hormones and glands. Later, when she began a career in food design, she had a professional excuse. How could someone cook all day without tasting and testing?

Georgina had never had a real boyfriend. There was Rupert in high school, who was relatively the size of her leg. He liked to touch her breasts and giggle. Then there was Karl at college, who followed her around until driven away by the taunts of other students calling him a "chubby chaser." But until Tanner Dyson swept her into his arms in the back of his limousine and pulled her dress up, she had never felt the passion of a man, let alone been entered.

In 1980 she was living at home in a Columbus suburb and commuting to her job as a food designer's assistant at a Columbus advertising agency. Because she had no social life, she had time for a second job writing a chatty household hint and recipe column for the food workers' trade union house organ. Through that connection she was offered, sight unseen, a job in New York arranging photo layouts for *Fabulous Foods* magazine.

The job called for more trickery than truth. It meant painting an anemic-looking roast turkey with crankcase oil to give it a golden glow. It meant spraying mounds of fruit with baby oil so they wouldn't discolor under the lights and touching up green spots on bananas with a magic marker. It also meant handling food all day. By the time she had been in New York for six weeks, she had oozed her way up to a 4x.

Then she met Bobby Max.

Bobby Max Kilgore was so flamboyantly gay he practically floated. In Bobby Max's words, he wasn't just out of the closet, he was over the top. In the late seventies and early eighties gay men in New York had seized the right to be and do whatever they fancied. Their new, glittering, and often bizarre bars and clubs provided a gigantic stage upon which every fantasy could be played out. The music, the drugs, the nearly circular promiscuity gave those in the life every reason to believe that it was one endless, seamless, hilarious, and hallucinogenic party that would never end.

Bobby Max Kilgore lived across the hall in Georgina's East Side apartment building. Several days after Georgina moved in, her copies of *The New York Times* began to disappear from her doorstep. She would hear the delivery man plop it on the floor out in the hall. When she went to retrieve it, it was gone. An hour later, when she was on her way out the door to work, the *Times* would have reappeared. When she picked it up, it was mysteriously warm to the touch, as though it had been sitting on a radiator.

The situation remained a mystery until, one Sunday morning, there was a brown scorch mark on the front of the classified section.

More amused than angry, Georgina took the paper and, in her caftan, padded across the four feet of carpeting between their doors.

It took several minutes for the door to open on the chain. A bloodshot eyeball peeked out at her.

"*Ummmm?*" an androgynous voice inquired through the slit in the door.

"Hi, I'm Georgina Holmes. I live in Four-A. Are you, by any chance, ironing my *New York Times* every morning?"

The door opened a bit wider, and she could see it was a young man in his twenties. He had a brush cut and an almost pretty face. "Why not, darling," he said, lowering his voice. "The royal footmen do it for the queen when hers gets wrinkly."

"Well, it's really not something I require," she said lightly.

"You're not angry with me, are you?" he asked, sounding hurt.

"No. I just find it odd. I'd rather you didn't. If you want to read the paper, I could leave it for you on my way home."

"I live in the moment, darling. I can't wait a whole day."

"I'm sorry," Georgina said.

He opened the door wider. He was wearing a black satin shirt, open to the waist, and black cotton jeans. "Please come in?" he asked plaintively. "I've just made fresh coffee, and I have some divine jelly doughnuts. I get them on my way home from dancing. The bakery opens at seven, so they're fresh, fresh, fresh."

Georgina paused. She hadn't had a conversation with another human outside her office since she'd moved to the city, and the lure of a fresh jelly doughnut was irresistible. "Okay," she said hesitantly. "But just for a few minutes."

"You can't have to go to work. It's Sunday. Unless maybe you're a priest. You aren't, are you?"

Georgina laughed. "No, I'm a food designer."

"*Ooooo*," he said, clapping his hands. "You make things out of food? If I scramble up a whole bunch of eggs could you make me the gazebo at Kensington Palace?"

Georgina stepped into the apartment. "Sure," she said, taking him seriously. "If I mixed them with enough paraffin."

The apartment was a mirror image of hers except for what looked like light-years of painstaking work. The walls had been stippled pale orange, and the window treatments must have taken hundreds of yards of the most beautiful floral-patterned chintz. The furniture was an eclectic mixture that seemed to have been rescued, mended, and refinished. The effect was cozy and overwhelmingly pretty.

Bobby Max told her over coffee and truly delicious doughnuts that he was a window designer at Bloomingdale's. He hadn't paid for anything in the apartment except the television and stereo. The rest had been either street finds or glommed from leftovers at work.

They spent most of the afternoon talking and laughing, discovering how much they had in common. They were both from small towns. Bobby Max was from a one-chair-barber-shop town in the Texas panhandle, where he was "completely misunderstood." They both had an interest in things artistic, only Bobby Max's sensibilities were far more daring and advanced. She left, late that afternoon, feeling as though she had found a soul mate. For the first time in her adult life she had spent several hours with another human being who didn't seem to notice that she was fat.

Over a period of weeks Bobby Max included her in the life that swirled in and out of his apartment, introducing her to his friends, asking her over for impromptu dinners. He helped her hang her new curtains and put down a rug.

Then, late one Saturday afternoon, he asked her if she wanted to go dancing that night.

She tried not to show her surprise. He could have asked her to go hot-air ballooning and not have shocked her more.

"I don't dance," she blurted out from her favorite spot in the corner of his couch. There, she could pull one of his big satin pillows over her midsection.

Bobby Max stopped puttering in the kitchen long enough to stick his head out the door and frown at her. "Everybody dances," he said flatly. "Paraplegics dance, babies dance. All you have to do is do it."

"You don't understand," Georgina said softly. "I've never danced in my life. No one ever asked me to."

"Darling," he sang. "When you dance with us, you don't have *a* partner. You have three *hundred* partners, a thousand partners. You'll see."

"Bobby," she said forlornly. "I have nothing to dance in."

"Yes you do," he called. "Put on something shiny, and I'll knock on your door at midnight sharp."

"Midnight! I'm in bed before that," she protested.

"Not tonight. Actually, even midnight's a bit too early."

"I don't have anything shiny."

"Do too," he shouted over the crunch of an ice tray being loosened.

"What?" she said, challenging him. All she wore were flowered polyester 4x dresses with floppy bows at the neck and big loose jackets.

"Your black and silver thingy."

Georgina thought for a moment. Black and silver thingy? "Oh, Bobby," she sighed. "That's a caftan. That's just for sitting around the house. Half the time I sleep in that rag. I can't go out in that."

Bobby walked into the living room and put a tall glass of iced tea on the coffee table in front of her. "Of course you can. Go get it. I'll show you."

Reluctantly, Georgina walked across the hall and retrieved the lifeless garment on the bathroom hook. The caftan was made out of several yards of black rayon shot with silver Lurex. There was nothing distinctive at all about it except the shine of the fabric and the multitude of figure flaws that it covered.

When she returned a few minutes later, Bobby Max had laid out a tray of cosmetics on the dining room table. Next to it was a rainbow of scarfs, feather boas, long beads, and tassels.

He pulled out a dining-room chair and held it for her. "Sit," he commanded. "We are about to create Lady Lilith, Queen of the Night."

Georgina sat down without protest and watched as Bobby Max plunged his hands into her thick mouse-brown hair. "First, we're going to color-rinse this. Then we're going to bring it up, up, up. Then, I think, bangs."

"Wait, wait, wait," she protested. "I've never done anything to my hair, ever."

"I can see that, darling."

It took three hours to create the new Georgina. When the transformation was complete, she took one look in Bobby Max's mirrored closet door and burst into tears.

Bobby stood in back of her and said nothing. It was as though he knew instinctively that her tears were not from disappointment or shock. They were tears of joy.

Whatever he had done, from the dark-gold shine of her hair to the dramatic makeup that showed her eyes and the planes of her face, it was more than magic. The stranger staring out at her was nearly beautiful.

Bobby Max waited until she got control of herself.

"Wait," he said. "Put this on."

He handed her the lifeless caftan and, once she'd put it on, reached for a long silver lamé scarf. He looped it around her neck, tied it into a huge bow over one shoulder, and carefully fluffed it. "There," he said grandly. "A Celebutante is born."

Georgina went dancing.

She traveled in a group of six, with Bobby Max as Master of the Revels. The night began at the Ice Palace on West 57th Street, where the thumping vibrations of the music could be felt out on the sidewalk.

Georgina had never seen anything like it. Inside the cavernous room, a mass of beautiful men danced in the near darkness as a single entity. Around the edges of the vast dance floor, low couches held a jumble of arms and legs, torsos and heads. When she realized what the bodies were up to, she averted her eyes.

Then Bobby Max grabbed her and, pumping his shoulders and hips to the beat, swung her into the mass of bodies. She stood for a moment, bewildered, and then, involuntarily, began to move in sync with him. She felt the blood rush to her cheeks and threw back her head. Over the music she screamed, "I'm dancing! Everybody, I'm dancing! In my nightgown!"

Georgina was at last free.

She began to feel as though she had been invited to join a secret society. She had known gay men before. She had worked with many of them in the design business. She had noticed them in groups, standing by themselves laughing and talking. They seemed very exotic to her. Now she was with them, if not of them, as she was treated far more specially than they treated each other. She was treated like a star.

She would rush home from her job, where she was fat, shy Georgina who didn't get the punch lines to jokes, who blushed at anything slightly off-color, and put on her other self. Then, made up and swathed in one of her growing wardrobe of glittering caftans, she would join her adoring courtiers for the party that paused but never ended.

Georgina's caftans began to get looser. Her daytime skirts with the big cabbage roses and little blue bonnets began to droop at the waistband. She began to have to loop the closing over itself and pin it to keep them up.

Her cheekbones began to show and her breasts, once simply an indistinguishable part of her protruding stomach, became clearly defined.

On the job she had no appetite for polishing off the leftover cream puffs from a shoot. Where once she would have eaten an entire display of potatoes lyonnaise for lunch and taken home a doggy bag of creamed chicken, she now picked at a container of yogurt and washed it down with Perrier.

In her night world, there was about as much interest in food as there would have been in proper child-rearing techniques—except for the handful of M&M's or popcorn to assuage the "munchies" from the pot.

Food was replaced by feedback from the boys, who would shriek with glee as her new body began to reveal itself under the pounds and pounds of fat.

One morning she woke up and discovered she had something she never knew was there. Hipbones! She had a waist! She had hips! She had a body!

Over the next few years, members of Bobby Max's little band began to drop away. Tanta Boufanta moved to Florida to open a salon at the Fountainebleu, then someone heard he got sick. Big Sam moved in with a male model who died mysteriously. Someone killed himself; someone else got a job in California and never called or wrote. One by one the clubs closed.

By the mid-eighties the only club worth going to was the enormous Saint, where women were not permitted. Bobby Max tried to no avail to get the people who operated it as a "private club" to make an exception for Georgina.

By the late eighties, when Georgina was offered the job on the *Courier,* the dancing had pretty much stopped. There was the Pavilion at Fire Island Pines in the summer, of course, but the whole atmosphere was different. Something awful was happening and the party was over.

The day Georgina got the job on the paper, she rushed home to tell Bobby Max, who by that time was working for a fabric house in midtown.

It was a blistering hot day in June that would not be cooled by the onset of evening. When Bobby Max opened the apartment door, a blast of hot air greeted her.

"Good Lord, Bobby," she had said, putting her bag down on the chair beside the door. "Turn on the air conditioner. You'll smother."

"I'm comfortable," he said, taking the bottle of wine and baguette she had brought for their usual dinner.

When he took the wine, their hands brushed. His was clammy

to the touch. She looked at him. There were beads of sweat on his forehead and upper lip.

"How can you be comfortable, sweetie? You're sweating."

"It's okay," he said.

"It's not okay," she protested. "And what are you doing in a long-sleeved shirt?"

Bobby Max slowly walked to the sofa and sat down. He stared into space for a long moment, then looked up at Georgina. There were dark circles under his eyes.

"You look stunning, darling," he said. "Peach is your color. That suit is you, you, you."

Georgina glanced down at her suit. She had splurged on an Adolfo knock-off for her interview.

"Thanks, dear," Georgina said. "Apparently it worked."

Bobby's face lit up. "You got it!" he said, breaking into a big grin. "I'm thrilled! Doesn't that mean I get the *Courier* for free?"

Dear Bobby Max, she thought, always looking for his sliver of someone else's silver lining. Ordinarily, when she had some triumph in her life, large or small, he was far more effusive. Presented with the momentous news of a new job and twice the money, he would normally have leapt to his feet and swung her around the room singing "We're in the Money" or some other appropriate show tune.

That day Bobby Max sat on the couch and tried to sound happy for her.

"Honey, what's the matter?" she said, sitting down next to him.

Bobby Max hugged himself. He didn't look at her. "Nothing, really. I think I caught a chill. That idiot Resnick had me in the warehouse until nearly midnight last night filling the order for the redo at the Helmsley Hotel."

"Bobby . . ." Georgina said. "Midnight used to be when the parties started."

They sat in silence for a while, staring sightlessly at Peter Jennings with the sound off.

Bobby Max's current lover left for San Francisco the day Georgina took him to the doctor.

She spent all of her free time the following year taking care of Bobby Max. There were weeks in the hospital on the AIDS ward, where at Christmas everyone got a free bottle of Elizabeth Taylor's perfume and the halls reeked. There were as many weeks at his apartment, which, while Bobby's case was high drama, was so jammed with stuffed toys, gag gifts, dying flowers, deflating balloons, videos, books, and magazines that Georgina finally scooped it all up and pitched it out. Bobby Max didn't seem to notice. He was getting worse.

During the last weeks, when changing the diapers and cleaning up the food he couldn't keep down got to be too big a job, she hired a day nurse and phoned Big Sam. Big Sam moved in to stay at Bobby's and help out at night.

It was Big Sam who called the paper one evening when Georgina had to work late on a special section on Easter ham.

Bobby had his eyes open when she got to his apartment. He was now in a hospital bed, and Big Sam had cranked it up so he could see the TV. Georgina pulled a straight-backed chair up to the side of the bed and took Bobby's hand. They laughed together when Delta Burke said, "I know about old people, I've dated 'em."

The laughing was too much for Bobby, and he started to cough violently. Big Sam walked over and turned off the TV. When the coughing subsided, Bobby lay back exhausted.

"What can I get you?" Georgina asked. "A little juice? I put some fresh cranberry in the fridge this morning."

Bobby lifted one finger on the hand she was holding and moved it as though beckoning her to come closer. Georgina leaned toward his feverish face. "What, love?" she asked softly.

"You know the crewelwork on the chairs in the Helmsley lobby?" he whispered.

She didn't, but she nodded her head "yes."

"It's fake," he said, and closed his eyes.

After Bobby Max died, the black hole in Georgina's heart formed a scab that was protective enough for her to feel numb. She needed the numbness. In the following year she would go to funerals for Big Sam and Willy Wonka. Tanta Boufanta didn't have a funeral. He was cremated in Miami.

By the time she was asked to plan the executive luncheons for Tanner Dyson, everyone was gone.

Georgina dimly noticed the egg timer going off. Now she smelled the results of her inattention. There was smoke seeping from around the door of the upper oven. She jumped to her feet and yanked open the door just in time to save the potato puffs.

The potato puffs were overkill, really. The AIDS patients to whom her butler, Grover, delivered the food she cooked each week had little appetite.

As she absently scrubbed at the cookie sheet, she thought about Baby's phone call on Friday. She'd always known Baby was ambitious, but was surprised—and a little disappointed— that she would try to get Georgina to use her influence with Tanner. She and Baby were hardly close anymore. Besides, Tanner seemed to freeze up whenever Baby was mentioned.

Georgina never really understood why. She knew Tanner was a very private man. She understood that he was jealous of friendships she made that did not include him, and she could put up with that, even though at times she was terribly lonely for someone she could be herself with and not just Tanner's wife.

Being Tanner's wife was wonderful. As wonderful as being Lilith had been. But look what had happened to Lilith's world. It disappeared into anguish and death. How could she know a similar fate didn't wait for her life as Mrs. Tanner Dyson? Then what would she do? Who would she be?

She thought about the lettuce heads soaking in Selma's back bathroom and the other little testing projects hidden away around the apartment. Was producing a book on such unimportant subjects as getting chewing gum out of a bath mat going to be enough protection against what awaited a woman who marries a man twice her age? Georgina knew she would never want for material things or financial security. None of that had mattered to her anyway. What she wanted was to feel, permanently and with no sense of masquerade, the way she had felt the night Bobby Max pulled her out onto the dance floor in her grungy housecoat. The way she felt when, in front of a totally accepting world, she had lifted her arms, thrown back her head, and let the sense of being herself set her free.

11

*K*ick was only going downtown and yet it felt as if she were crossing into the Twilight Zone. Her luncheon date with Joe Stone was strictly business. The best thing that could happen at lunch would be a job offer, or even just a one-shot assignment. The worst thing was already happening. In a few short minutes, she would be face to face with a man.

As the rattletrap taxi jounced down Ninth Avenue it seemed to be aiming at and hitting every open pothole and discarded pop bottle in its empty Sunday path.

Kick bounced around on the backseat, making a mental list of other men she had been face to face with in her year of hiding in Lolly's tower. She counted seven.

There were the two Chinese delivery boys, one from the Hunan on Columbus, the other from Yu So Fat's Take Out Kitchen on Amsterdam. There was Leroy from Winged Foot Messenger Service, who was permitted to pick up at the penthouse door. Then there were the two doormen, the super, and

Mike, the elevator man. Oh, and a repairman from Manhattan Cable.

She had conversed in person with eight men in one solid year.

Wow. Eight humans with penises, presumably, and deep voices asking her, "Which toilet is stuck?" and "Could you sign here, please, miss?" wasn't exactly a social life. How the hell was she going hold up her end of lunch with a male human who lived his life on the cutting edge of what was happening in the world?

Small talk. That's what was needed. Light, amusing, not-too-inane small talk that would show Joe Stone that she was not only educated and sharp but happening, with it, in touch with the nineties.

What had happened to her? She had never been afraid to meet strangers. In all her travels, at school, on the paper, she had always found strangers the most entertaining people in the world.

But Joe Stone was a man. That was the problem. A man who had the power to change her life if he liked her. She had never worried about people liking her. They usually did. Just because the last man in her life had betrayed her didn't mean they were all out to do her harm.

As the taxi approached the corner of Ninth Avenue and West 17th Street, Kick leaned forward.

"Here! Right here!" she shouted to the driver over the sounds of the radio and the chassis shaking itself apart.

Driving around the block just to be able to get out in front of the restaurant would cost at least a dollar more. Whatever she was getting herself into by meeting Joe Stone for lunch, a continuing income was certainly not guaranteed. Every penny she had in the bank was going to count, especially since she'd have to start looking for an apartment. Legally, the co-op board would have to give her a month or so grace period, but the wrecking crews were sure to be lining up.

Plunging from the sunlight of the street into the darkness of the restaurant's front room blinded her for several seconds. When her eyes grew accustomed to the cool gloom, she could make out a long bar to her left, checkered-cloth-covered empty tables, and a bright rectangle of light at the end of the room that apparently led out to the garden where Joe Stone said he would be working on his tan.

A heavyset man was leaning against the back of the bar, arms folded, watching a soccer game on a big TV mounted overhead.

As Kick moved further into the room, the bartender dropped his arms and walked toward her. "Miss Butler?" he asked.

Kick blinked, thinking, Thank God. He's not coming. I can turn around and go home. I don't have to do this to myself. I can teach at some East Side prep school and maybe someday marry the gym teacher.

She nodded and smiled. "Yes, I'm Miss Butler."

"Joe's out in the garden."

Oh, well, Kick thought. I didn't want to marry a gym teacher anyway.

Kick headed toward the back door. Her feet felt as though she were dragging lead weights. I'm fine, she thought. My face is fine, my mind is fine, I'm in all-right shape.

Just as she took the small step out into the shaded garden, she looked down and wished she had bigger breasts. Somehow, a more pronounced chest would have given her the extra confidence she needed. Men looked at breasts first. No matter how enlightened they pretended to be, no matter how hard they tried to look you in the eye, the minute you looked away, their eyes moved down to your chest. That was one of life's grim givens. It was only women who had big boobs who said they didn't matter.

Kick was relieved to find the garden was almost as cool and airy as the front room had been. Leafy branches of giant plane trees crossed overhead, dappling the tablecloths and flagstone flooring. Seated at a table in the center of the garden was a man in his early forties with dark-brown hair and a good jaw. His head was back and his eyes were closed.

As Kick approached his table, she noticed, with sneaky pleasure, that the closed eyes were open just a sliver. He was watching her from under his lashes. She had reached the edge of the table before he raised his head with a startled gesture that was only slightly affected.

"Hello there," he said.

He stood, pushing back his metal chair with a cringe-producing scrape along the stone floor.

"Joe Stone," he said extending one hand and holding his napkin against his crotch with the other.

He was wearing a navy-blue polo shirt tucked neatly into a pair of chinos. He wasn't at all the rumpled, sweaty creature she had imagined he would be. He had bright, straight teeth, important eyebrows, and a face that could only be described as nice.

"Kick Butler," Kick replied tentatively, hoping her handshake was firmer than her response. As she smiled directly into his eyes, she felt her body tense.

"Is this all right out here?" he asked, gesturing toward the chair next to his. "We could go inside."

"Oh, no," Kick said, a bit too enthusiastically. "This is lovely. It's like one of New York's hidden places. I probably walked down this block a hundred times when I was a kid and never knew it was here."

"Ah." He grinned. "A fellow New Yorker. We are a rare breed. I grew up in Riverdale."

Kick laughed as she sat down. "For a kid who grew up in the Village, Riverdale was the Great North Woods."

Joe chuckled, then looked over her shoulder. "Ah, my man Gino to the rescue."

Kick turned as the bartender reached in front of her with a wide-stemmed glass heaped with clouds of what looked like shaved ice. He placed a second glass in front of Stone and removed one with its contents reduced to water.

"You want the fettuccine for you and the lady, Joe?" Gino asked, standing back a bit.

Joe smiled at Kick and winked. "I'll make it. You got bacon, Gino?" Joe said, a grin playing at the corners of his mouth.

"No, you won't," Gino grumped. "The last time we let you in the kitchen, you set fire to the overhead rack. Relax, I'll make you the pasta."

Kick watched Gino as he shambled back into the restaurant, feeling as though she were watching a lifeboat sailing away and leaving her stranded. She turned back to Joe, her mind searching frantically for something to say. "I get the feeling you come here a lot," she ventured.

"Only because I hate to eat out," Joe said with a slow grin. Kick noticed with gratitude that his gaze had not yet wandered to her chest. "I live on the next block."

"It's a great neighborhood," Kick said, trying again. Mentioning the neighborhood provided an opening for him to say something about his living circumstances. He didn't.

"So, Kick Butler. What was a nice girl like you doing working for a dragon lady like Lolly Pines?" he asked, sitting back and stabbing at his ice cloud with the stubby plastic straw.

"I was very fond of Lolly Pines," she said carefully. "She is . . . was . . . an extraordinary woman."

"Who never made life easy for her assistants."

"That was not my experience," Kick said, listening to herself. She sounded arch and argumentative. She tried again. "Working for Lolly was the most fun I've ever had on a job. I used to look down my nose at gossip until I discovered that practically everything one reads or hears is gossip, including the front page of *The New York Times*."

Stone held up his palms in a truce sign. "Sorry. I shouldn't presume. I guess I have an old-school disdain for gossip columnists."

"I learned a lot from Lolly. Someday, I'd like to be the newswoman she was." Kick knew she'd better say that with a smile and leave it alone. The last thing she wanted was for him to see her as needy.

Stone leaned back and tucked the corner of his napkin over his belt buckle. "You been in this business long, Kick?" he asked, with only the tiniest edge of superiority in his voice.

"Columbia J school, two years local reporting in the boonies, six months off to think great thoughts, and just about a year with Lolly."

"That's long enough for you to stop being humble. That piece you sent me was damn good writing."

Kick's leaping heart caught in her throat, and at the same moment Gino arrived carrying two heaping plates of pasta in each hand, and a basket of bread on the turn of his elbow.

"We would have waited for two trips, Gino," Stone said.

"Yeah, well, Uruguay is about to score, for Christ's sake," Gino grumbled as he maneuvered everything onto the table and then left.

"Why don't we drink to Lolly?" Kick suggested.

"Of course," Stone said.

Their eyes caught as they touched glasses. There was something behind his eyes, as though he wanted to ask her something more personal. She knew she should do the girl-thing and ask him about his work, his life, his goddamn hopes and dreams for the future—none of which she cared about just now. Joe Stone had only one thing she cared about, the power to put her back to work writing. She didn't want to tell him anything personal. As personal as she wanted to get would be to look him right in the eye and tell him she was out of a job and nearly homeless.

She took a sip of her frozen drink and put down her glass. "So, here I am, out of a job and nearly homeless."

"Come and work for me," he said without a moment's hesitation.

"For you?" she asked, stunned.

He had said "come." "Come" had traveling connotations. It sounded like earrings and suits with big shoulders. It sounded like those pumps they say feel like sneakers but don't because sneakers don't have heels and pointy toes and kill your calves.

Joe laughed and shook his head. "Somehow I don't hear a careerist's ring of joy and exultation."

"Sorry," she said with a wan smile. "I'm surprised enough to give you an honest reaction. I don't mean to sound unenthusiastic. What I guess I need to know is are you talking about an office job or something else?"

"Something else," he said.

"Something else? You mean something else having to do with writing?"

"A feature," he said. "On Lolly Pines."

"A feature on Lolly! Now that's something I'd love to do. But why me?"

"Why not you? That short article you did on her was terrific. You're up there in her place with access to her files. Who better? Our fearless leader, Tanner Dyson, wants a big Sunday magazine piece on her. It would probably be syndicated, so your byline would appear in many other papers. I'll pay you decently. Then, if you do a good job, there'll be other assignments. You game?"

"Absolutely. Game and delighted," she said, grinning.

"It won't be easy. She's been profiled in everything from *Mirabella* to *The Wall Street Journal*. I'd like something different. Something we don't know about her. Do you know if she kept any journals or diaries that you could get your hands on?"

Kick thought for a moment. "Well, her apartment is crammed with stuff. I don't think she ever threw anything out. I could look. When do you need it?" she asked.

"As soon as you can do it."

"I'll do my best," Kick said, meaning it. She was so relieved she could hardly eat. It wasn't a solid job offer, but her career-camel's nose was certainly inside the tent. "I'll start going through her things this afternoon."

As they began to eat in earnest, Joe Stone spoke without looking up. "Tell me about the six months you took off to think great thoughts."

Kick was glad she had just put a forkful of pasta in her mouth. It gave her time to let the question sink in. The last thing she wanted to do was talk about that time. The good food, the sunshine, the pleasant surroundings didn't alter the fact that one of her worst fears was being realized, the job seeker's nightmare —the résumé gap.

She couldn't lie about it, and yet if she told the truth, she would be speaking of a completely inappropriate, not to mention painfully personal, experience that had nothing to do with whether or not she could write a profile on Lolly Pines.

She chewed longer than she had to and finally had to answer. "I got involved in a bad personal relationship. It threw me for a while, but I'm fine now."

"A man?" he asked, shifting his pasta to one cheek.

"*Ummm*," Kick said.

"Lionel Maltby."

Kick dropped her fork but quickly retrieved it. "How do you know about Lionel Maltby?"

"Oh, people talk."

"But I'm not worth gossiping about," she said, trying to keep her voice even and low. She felt a moist haze forming on her upper lip and dabbed at her mouth with her napkin.

"People who get involved with famous people are always worth gossiping about," he said. "But, to be fair, Fiddle Null is an old pal of mine."

"Remind me to put Fedalia on my permanent hit list," Kick said with a dull feeling of betrayal. Being talked about was a new experience, and she didn't like it.

"Lionel Maltby is a rat," he said, tearing off a hunk of bread. "But I guess you know that."

"I didn't at first. I learned the hard way."

"There's no easy way. That's what I learned the hard way."

Kick was so grateful for the chance to redirect the conversation, she spoke too loudly. "You did? Tell me about it."

Joe Stone shrugged. "Not a big deal unless it's happening to you. I married a woman who was interesting and difficult. Then she just got difficult. Especially about her career versus mine. I'm divorced now. I can understand why it took you so long to get over your trouble with Maltby. It's too bad it had to affect your work."

"It sure did that," Kick said, wishing desperately that a jet would crash into the restaurant and they could drop the subject and busy themselves with helping the dead and injured.

"Thank God, I had the *Courier*," he said, pursuing it. "It's so hectic there I didn't have time to think about it until I got home at night. Scotch helped."

Kick saw her opening and seized it. Now was the time to tell him how much she liked the paper. It worked. He seemed almost grateful to hear someone say they liked the tabloid and launched into a fascinating examination of the media in general.

Kick, who had been absorbed for so long with Lolly's need to know whether Warren Beatty would marry, if Leona Helmsley would ever go to jail, and determining the details of Ivana Trump's divorce, found herself listening intently.

From time to time he would ask her something, and she would answer with quick, nearly flip answers, hoping to deflect him from returning to any discussion of Maltby. Whatever she said, he seemed to find it amusing. He would laugh heartily and mercifully go back to more journalism war stories. He had had a colorful life: the last dying days in Saigon as a kid with a *Rolling Stone* assignment, a stint in Beirut, and a few ducked bullets in Panama before being hired as editor of the *Courier*.

By the time Gino took their coffee order, Kick felt relaxed enough to ask about Lolly's replacement.

"What's going to happen to Lolly's column?"

Joe Stone moaned and ran his hand over his face. "And here I was having fun," he said.

"Sorry."

"That's okay. It's just that I know I'm going to be pecked to death by ducks. Too many people want the job. Too many unqualified people. And I don't think the paper wants to spend what it would take to bring over a name."

Joe glanced over her shoulder and signaled for the check. Kick looked around to see Gino, who had been standing in the doorway, disappear inside.

When she turned back, Joe was leaning forward on his folded arms. "This is the best lunch I've ever had," he said, grinning.

"Ever? In your whole life?" Kick asked, laughing a little.

Joe frowned and thought for a moment. "There was a time I was covering a NATO conference in Paris. I had lunch in a little Rive Gauche café overlooking the Seine . . ." he began, then shook his head. "Nope, no competition. I was alone."

She knew he was kidding. It felt nice. "I think my best lunch was in an old wine bar in Fleet Street my first Christmas in college. A friend's father who worked for the London *Times* took me there. It was raining and cold, and the place was full of reporters who decided they'd rather drink and tell stories than go back to work."

"El Vino's."

"Right! Do you know it?"

"Of course. I logged a lot of hours at El Vino's. I can't say I remember the food."

"It wasn't about food, really. It was the sense of community. I don't have a real family. It was just me and my grandmother. That afternoon at El Vino was the first time I was with people whose profession made them family. It changed my life."

Joe slipped his credit card on the check Gino handed him and passed the bill back. "You know now, of course, that you based your decision on a bunch of drunks who would rather lie than work?"

"Sure, but I've never regretted it."

"You really love this racket, don't you?" Joe said, pushing his chair back.

"Yup."

"Well, let me see what I can do about that."

As they walked across the uneven flagstones of the empty garden, Kick felt his hand resting gently on the small of her back. She hoped he couldn't feel her trembling.

131

12

Joe hadn't planned to walk back to the office after his lunch with Kick, but by the time he reached Eighth Avenue he knew a hot, sticky cab ride would ruin the way he was feeling. It took him a block or two to identify what was going on inside his head. Gradually, he realized that for the last two hours he had liked himself. He had enjoyed being himself.

He tried to remember what he had expected Kick to look or be like. When he had called her for lunch, none of that was particularly important. He knew she had to be on the ball to work for Lolly. That was enough. What he really wanted was to get the feature on Lolly assigned to the right person.

The last thing he expected was the freckle-faced gulp of fresh air that breezed into Gino's backyard. Not only was she disarmingly bright, but she was one of the rarest of female creatures in the New York nineties: a woman who listened.

Compared to his angst-filled couplings with Baby, a plate of pasta and a summer's chat with Kick Butler nourished his soul like a Brandenburg Concerto.

Walking next to her as they left the restaurant after lunch, he had placed his hand against the small of her back. He had felt the cool, firm flesh under her summer dress, and perhaps he had imagined it, but he swore when he touched her she was trembling.

It hardly seemed possible that there was a female left in New York who could tremble at the touch of a man's hand.

He had to do something about Baby. It would not be pretty or easy. As long as Lolly's job was up for grabs, she would hang on like a ferret.

Lost in thought, he looked up to see a couple headed toward him. They were dressed in basic Sunday-in-New-York shorts and T-shirts. The man was pushing a baby in a stroller, an older child rode his shoulders, water gun at the ready. The woman had her arm looped through his.

As they passed, he was overcome with nostalgia, a longing so profound he felt dizzy and stepped closer to the building he was passing to get into the shade.

The feeling lingered as he regained his stride. How odd, he thought. He was not a particularly sentimental man. He had married Beth because it seemed like the thing to do. Most of his peers had simply moved in together. But at the time, having the courage to make a legal commitment to someone else had a certain style, a classiness that had made him feel good. Although he would never have admitted it at the time, he found the promise of emotional permanence enormously appealing; he found he didn't even mind the possibility of children. As it turned out, the marriage had provided neither. Not until this moment had he realized that he was still looking.

Maybe the chaos of his life was just a reflection of how much he hated being single. He wanted a relationship that didn't require a fighter's stance, dukes up, bile rising. Somewhere between *Casablanca* and *Fatal Attraction*, being heterosexual had become an ordeal.

It would be too easy if Kick Butler turned out to be the answer

133

to his need for life's sweetness, but at least knowing she existed gave him hope.

Whatever he had with Baby, it wasn't sweet.

After his afternoon with Kick, he knew what he had to do. He had to take control and get his life back. The only question was, how?

Joe waved to the lobby security guard as he turned into the entrance to the *Courier* building and stepped into an empty elevator.

As he turned the corner into the corridor that led to his office, Joe was annoyed to see Baby coming toward him, her ankles crossing each other in the mincing camel walk she affected when she wanted attention paid to her figure. She was clutching a computer printout against her ample chest.

Christ, he thought, she's lying in wait for me.

"What are you doing here?" he asked gruffly as he picked up his pace to imply that he had pressing business to get to.

"Same-ee-same to yoo-hoo-hoo," Baby trilled, letting her eyes drift slowly down his body.

Joe swung a right into his office. He knew, without looking around, that Baby was only a few feet behind him.

He quickly stepped behind his desk and sat down, hoping the barrier would encourage her to keep her hands to herself.

"What's up?" Joe asked, stacking papers to appear rushed.

"Goodness, it's chilly in here," Baby said coyly, as she eased one hip over the corner of his desk. "As a matter of fact, Baby's been chilly all weekend. Somebody hasn't called Baby to warm her up."

Joe glanced up at her and wondered how he could ever have thought Baby's pout was cute. "Somebody has been preoccupied. In case you forgot, this paper has lost its star columnist."

Baby edged her hip further onto the desk and crossed her legs. She was still clutching the printout against her cleavage. "I don't see why that should take your time," she pouted.

"It does when the publisher drags you into the office to help plan a memorial service," Joe said flatly.

"Is that why you had lunch with Lolly's secretary today?"

"She isn't . . . wasn't Pines's secretary. She's a reporter."

"My, my, aren't we on the defensive."

"How do you know who I had lunch with?"

"You just told me," Baby said smugly.

"Baby," he warned, glowering at her.

"Okay. When I got to the office, June told me you went to Renaldo's. So I called Gino and he told me the woman you were with was named Butler. So then I called Sam and . . ."

"Okay, okay, okay. Jesus, Baby, you don't quit, do you?"

"What's the secretary want to do? Take over her boss's column? What have we got here, Eve Harrington from hell?"

"Baby, what do you want?" Joe asked, exasperated.

"You know, Joe," Baby said, looking up at the ceiling, "I'm just as sorry as all get-out that Lolly died. Shit happens. But there is another gossip writer on this newspaper."

Joe rolled his chair back so he couldn't see all the way up Baby's micromini. "You have something there you want to show me, Baby?"

She lowered her head and closed her eyes as she spoke. "Just a little item for tomorrow's Grapevine I just happened to pick up." She smoothed the paper out on the desk in front of Joe. "Right there, at the top."

Joe read aloud the item she was pointing to with a bright orange nail. "Celebrity lawyer Irving Fourbraz said today that he plans to file a twenty-million-dollar lawsuit for assault against TV throbber Keeko Ram . . ." Joe stopped reading and handed the copy back to Baby.

"What?" Baby whined.

"No good."

"I got that item from Irving himself," Baby said proudly.

"Baby," Joe said in a world-weary voice. "The only remarkable thing about this item is that Fourbraz is now feeding you stuff instead of Lolly. We can't say he *plans* to file. Anybody can call in and say they are *going* to do something. We only print it when they do it. You know that, Baby. Now, what are you *really* telling me?"

Joe had known Irving for years and couldn't stand him. With Irving, every move was a flex—the darting eyes, the tie strokes, the occasional hitch of the Gucci belt. Worse, Irving Fourbraz was a shyster.

"Well," Baby huffed, tossing her head. "I think it's quite a coup to have Irving Fourbraz giving me stuff. I'm sorry you're not impressed. I'll tell him so tomorrow. I'm having drinks with him at the St. Regis and probably dinner."

Joe began to shuffle papers again. "Well, that's great, kiddo. You might also tell him I still remember a book deal he fucked up for a friend of mine. Just mention Eddie Soames. He'll get the picture."

"Is he married?" Baby asked, running the tip of her tongue over her front teeth.

"He was when he died. He killed himself when he couldn't return a hundred-thousand-dollar advance. They took his house. No thanks to Irving K. Fourbraz."

"No," Baby squealed angrily. "I meant Irving. Is Irving married?"

"Oh, Jesus, Baby," Joe moaned. "I don't know. What's the problem? You don't have drinks with married men?"

"Of course I do. I just like to know when I make a new friend if he's married or not."

"Get up, Baby," Joe said, tugging at a stack of papers under her butt. "You're sitting on something I'm working on."

Baby slipped off the desk and leaned over his shoulder. "*Oooo,* the invitation list for Lolly's service," she said excitedly. "My God, look who's going to be there! We can go together, right?"

"No," Joe said without looking at her. He could smell her perfume, though, and it was disturbing.

"No!" Baby shrieked. "What do you mean 'no'? You have to go with me."

"Get real, Baby. The entire staff will be there. I can't walk in with you, and you know it."

136

"But it's business. No one will think anything of it if I'm with you, Joe. Come on," she pleaded, stroking his shirt sleeve. "Please."

"Irving Fourbraz is invited. Why don't you get him to take you? This thing isn't until the end of the week. You'll have plenty of time to give him some head by then."

Baby yanked her hand away and turned on her heel. "You are a real shit, Joe Stone," she snapped. "Probably the biggest shit I have ever known."

"I doubt that, Baby," he muttered, pretending to read.

"I'll get you for this," Baby said, heading for the hall.

"I'm sure you will," Joe replied.

He watched her through the glass partition as she stormed down the corridor, flipping her fuzzy, currently red hair.

Joe put down his papers, turned, and looked out the window. Through the space between two warehouses across the street he could see one of the Circle Line boats slowly making its way up river, its decks packed with holiday tourists.

Baby was right. He was a shit. That was why Beth hadn't followed him to New York, or even tried to work out a compromise. She was tired of living with a self-centered, career-driven, thoughtless, uncaring shit.

He shouldn't have spoken to Baby the way he did. She was pushy and a flake, but she didn't deserve such treatment. Maybe she would team up with Irving Fourbraz and leave him alone. Wouldn't those two be a combo? he thought, smiling to himself. A veritable media Bonnie and Clyde.

13

*N*early a thousand people attended the memorial service at the Minskoff Theatre on Times Square the Thursday morning after Labor Day.

The service was scheduled for noon. Georgina had just gotten out of the limousine in front of the theater with Tanner and two of the *Courier's* executives when she spotted Baby in the middle of the crowd moving into the lobby.

As Baby turned to speak to someone, Georgina saw that she had done something bizarre to her face. Her eyes were beaded and giraffed with fake eyelashes that gave her a look of fixed surprise. She was wearing a saffron-colored straw Abe Lincoln hat and a mini-tent-dress made of yards of orange and yellow chiffon that swirled around her tiny figure.

Upon entering the over-air-conditioned lobby, Georgina noticed that the television film crews and still photographers were showing a proper funereal restraint in spite of the celebrity crowd. Several camera crews actually stepped aside to let the mourners pass.

Tanner said a few words into a bouquet of extended micro-phones, then held up his hand and moved on. He showed Georgina to her seat and excused himself to go backstage to organize the others who would be sitting on the stage for the service. As Georgina arranged herself and glanced around, she could see Baby's hat sticking up above the other heads a few rows in front of her. It bobbed up and down as Baby talked first to the man on her right, then to someone in the row in front of her.

After a brief musical presentation by the Tewesbury Consort, a string quartet Tanner particularly liked, he rose to speak quite movingly about Lolly's long career. Georgina continued to glance around as he spoke. It was a fitting tribute to Lolly that all her favorite bold-facers had shown up for her last event.

Tanner finished his speech by reading telegrams from celebri-ties, then began to introduce someone as Lolly's oldest, closest friend. Abner Hoon got up from his seat on stage.

Hoon was resplendent in a silver cravat and wore an incongru-ously large calla lily lashed to his lapel. He spoke of his early friendship with Lolly with what seemed like real affection. As Abner returned to his seat, Georgina glanced down at the printed program in her lap. Walter Cronkite was scheduled to speak next. He was seated on the stage right next to Tanner. Georgina gave Tanner a little wave when she caught his eye and smiled when Walter mistakenly waved back.

Just as Tanner was about to get up to introduce Walter Cronkite, Georgina saw Baby's vivid hat rising. At first she thought Baby had picked an extremely awkward time to run to the ladies' room, but when she realized Baby was headed down the aisle toward the steps to the stage, she gasped and looked at her program again. Baby's name was nowhere to be found.

Nonetheless, Baby mounted the steps to the stage and walked across to the lectern, her bright orange spike heels flashing between the vases and pots of flowers in back of the footlights.

Tanner, seated at the far end of the row, started to rise from his spindly little chair. Georgina could see how angry he was, but he glanced around the room, then slowly sat again. Clearly he had decided he would only make matters worse by trying to stop Baby from doing whatever she was up to.

Fortunately, someone had provided a small lift behind the lectern to accommodate Abner, or Baby would have looked like Queen Elizabeth's talking hat.

Baby unfolded a sheet of paper, cleared her throat, adjusted the microphone, and waited until the murmur in the huge auditorium had subsided.

When all was quiet, Baby began to speak in a low, soft voice. After a few lines, Georgina realized she was reciting the lyrics to "Wind Beneath My Wings," which she had transposed to the past tense, complete with hand gestures.

"I never told you, you *were* my hero . . ." she intoned. "My dearest Lolly, you were the wind beneath my wings."

Georgina felt a kind of cosmic squirm lurch up her spine, over her shoulders, and down both thighs. She couldn't remember the last time she had felt so uncomfortable. There was something so ick-making about spoken, transposed lyrics. What could Baby possibly be trying to accomplish? Here it was high noon at a memorial service in front of everyone who had ever been profiled in *Vanity Fair* and *Fortune* magazine—not to mention Baby's employers—and Baby was crashing the ceremony with a performance that was nearly ravishing in its vulgarity. Georgina felt as if she was watching the arc of Baby's career heading straight for a brick wall.

Finally, Georgina's psychological root canal was over. Baby stopped speaking. With a bizarre flourish, the Tewesbury Consort beneath the stage struck up "Wind Beneath My Wings." Georgina concluded that Baby had provided them with the sheet music ahead of time.

To Georgina's utter amazement, Baby strode off the stage to the surge of music and deafening applause.

All heads turned as Baby and her hat moved up the aisle and she took her seat. Georgina craned her neck and for the first time saw that Baby was seated with that dreadful Irving Fourbraz. When Irving leaned close to Baby's ear and said something,

Georgina was sure that not only had they come together but that Irving must have put her up to the extraordinary act she had just witnessed.

The service continued for another forty-five minutes without further incident. Georgina was so eager for it to be over, so she could find out what really happened, that the rest of the speakers' words didn't register.

When the service finally drew to a close, Tanner thanked everyone for coming, and the theater began to empty.

Tanner's limousine was waiting directly in front of the canopy. Out on the sidewalk, Georgina waited for Tanner to join her, speaking briefly to people from the paper who came up to greet her. She was standing with Tom and Meredith Brokaw when she spotted Tanner. His index finger was to his lips as he approached the car.

He leaned over and whispered, "We're giving the Brokaws a lift. Don't say anything about Baby."

It wasn't until later, after the reception, that Georgina experienced the last of the surprises Baby had wrought on that extraordinary day. Tanner, who had not spoken Baby's name since their wedding day, casually pronounced her performance "rather touching."

14

Nearly two weeks had passed since Lolly's memorial service, and the *Courier* had still not replaced her. Running in the space that had been hers for years was a ragtag column pulled together from wire copy and less-than-exciting items picked up as the paper's reporters moved around the city.

Georgina knew Tanner was concerned about Lolly's replacement, but since her death he had been wrestling with complicated labor problems at the paper, and Georgina had barely seen him. He left early in the morning and arrived home very late at night.

Last night she had waited up for him and made him promise he would come home for dinner the following evening. She wanted to spend some time with him. She had a special reason.

Alone in her big designer kitchen, she hummed happily as she prepared Tanner's favorite meal.

She had just finished breading the veal croquettes, shaping them to look like pork chops. Recently, she had taken to including a tiny witticism or two in each meal she prepared for

Tanner. She loved their evenings at home as much as she dreaded the charity balls and the four-star-restaurant meals and the dinner parties in the enormous apartments up and down Park and Fifth avenues that belonged to the people in Tanner's life.

She always tried to make each meal a bit special: heart-shaped meat loaf, Jell-O molds topped with smile faces—a lemon wedge for the mouth, orange-slice eyes, and a strawberry nose. She made meals that would have been not only hooted out of the test kitchen at *Fabulous Foods* but sneered at by the people with whom she now socialized. Georgina was one of the youngest wives in the group of couples they saw most frequently. She didn't think of any of them as friends—not in the old-fashioned sense of friendship. They were business and civic leaders, people from banking and the media, whose lives crisscrossed with Tanner's. Most of the couples had grown children.

The other wives thought it was sweet that Georgina cooked for her husband and, Georgina thought, were a bit patronizing about asking her for recipes for their cooks.

Tanner, trying to take some of the sting out of the occasional remarks, made a big deal of her skills, telling people she had been one of the country's foremost food designers before they married and reminding them that she had been in full charge of the *Courier*'s executive dining room, where she pleased heads of state with finicky appetites.

Georgina noticed the little smiles and nodded heads with the sinking feeling that no one thought that whipping up a nice hot meal made her an interesting person.

The croquettes began to snap in the frying pan, a sign that they needed turning. Georgina slipped off the stool beside the butcher-block island and looked for the spatula to flip them. They were brown-gold and crispy, just the way Tanner liked them.

She checked the oven window. She had only to make the cheese sauce for the cauliflower casserole and brown some onions and mushrooms for the croquettes. Later, she would whisk the pecans into the boiled sugar for the caramel sauce to top the banana dessert.

Georgina smiled, thinking how the meal she had prepared would shock a strict nutritionist. It was not only monochromatic but loaded with fat, calories, and cholesterol. She didn't care. Tonight was special, and Tanner's mood was key to the success of her plan. Tonight she was going to tell him about her secret project.

Georgina had sent the manuscript for her household-hint and cookbook to the only person in publishing she knew. Rona Friedman had been a copy editor at *Fabulous Foods* when Georgina worked there; she'd left to become an editor at Winslow House. Georgina knew that manuscripts submitted without an agent were often returned from publishers unread. Still, she hoped to hear from Rona any day now.

She wasn't completely sure how Tanner would take the news. Apart from her cooking for the AIDS reach-out project—which she instinctively kept private from Tanner—this would be the first truly meaningful thing she had done that he had no part in. All of her other work, the ball committees, decorating, planning parties, while carried out by Georgina on a day-to-day basis, had been instigated and approved by Tanner.

Publishing a book was different. It was something permanent, something real in which the attention would be focused on her. She desperately wanted Tanner not only to approve but to be enthusiastic. For everything to work she had to approach him with great delicacy.

She remembered the advice she used to give interns who worked in the test kitchen at *Fabulous Foods:* "A perfect meal comes from starting early and keeping the flame low." She would take her own advice—bring up the subject early at dinner and keep things calm and pleasant until the idea sank in.

She had just enough time to bathe, change into something Tanner would find fetching, and watch a few minutes of the news so she could discuss what was happening in the outside world at dinner.

Twenty minutes later, she had just finished applying her eye makeup when she saw Tanner standing behind her in the mirror.

She smiled at him and lifted her cheek, laughing softly as he nuzzled her face and neck.

"I don't know which smells better, dinner or you," he said.

Georgina closed her eyes and took a deep breath, relieved that he seemed to be in a cheerful mood. There was always the chance that something—at the paper, with the unions, with the lawyers, with the competition, anything—could have happened during the day that would have sent him home in a sullen frame of mind.

"How was your day, darling?" she asked as usual.

Tanner removed his suit jacket and slipped it onto the mahogany valet for Grover to brush and steam. "It looks like Cindy Adams has turned down our offer to take over Lolly's column. She won't leave the *Post*. Our search committee is back to square one."

Georgina turned on the dressing stool. She wanted to ask if he had considered Baby. Seeing his pleasant expression as he unbuttoned his pale blue shirt, she decided the subject was too risky at the moment and left it alone.

Tanner stepped into his dressing room to toss his shirt into the hamper. When he returned to the bedroom, he was wearing a monogrammed terry-cloth robe, a signal that he was going to the lap pool in his gym off the terrace. "And what did you get up to today, sweetheart?" he asked.

"Some fun things," she said enigmatically. "You go have your swim. I'll tell you all about it at dinner."

Later, seated at either end of the long dining room table, they snapped their napkins loose simultaneously.

Grover leaned forward, poured Tanner's wine, and waited for him to taste it. After Tanner nodded his approval of the selection, the butler stepped to the sideboard and lifted the silver tray of Tanner's favorite veal dish. Selma stood behind him waiting to serve the other dishes.

"Another extraordinary meal, my darling," Tanner said, spooning hot cheese sauce onto his cauliflower. "There isn't a restaurant in town that can compete."

"Thank you, dear." Georgina smiled across the glowing expanse of mahogany. She wished he would start a conversation so she could listen for openings to casually bring up the book. It wouldn't do to just jump in with such news.

She watched him contentedly cutting his food, raising it to his mouth, and chewing, until she could stand it no more.

"I was thinking about an old friend today," she said lightly, knowing that would get his attention. 'Old friend' might as well have been a code phrase between them. It meant someone she had known B.T.—before Tanner—to him, that dark, mysterious forest in which she had dwelt before he met her.

Tanner put down his fork and tilted his head ever so slightly. "Oh?" he said, raising his silver eyebrows a millimeter. "Who would that be?"

"Rona Friedman. We worked together at *Fabulous Foods.* She was a copy editor. She could think up more names for meat loaf than you could imagine."

Tanner was sensitive to any mention of not only former friends but also anyone not in their immediate circle who might attempt to use her. He lowered his eyebrows. "Is your friend Rhoda still with the magazine?" he asked without inflection.

"Rona," Georgina corrected pleasantly. She took a sip of her wine.

"Sorry, *Rona.*"

"No, she's an editor at Winslow House Publishing."

"Ah," Tanner said, brightening. "Rob Roy Kadanoff, a six-handicap golfer. I played with him at Burning Tree not too long ago."

"Who is Rob Roy Kadanoff?" Georgina asked, confused.

"The chairman of Winslow. Grand fellow. I like him very much."

Georgina sighed inwardly. "That's nice, dear," she said, managing a smile. She should have known. If possible, Tanner always made a personal connection with any topic. It could be an annoying habit. In this case, it might work in her favor.

"Anyway," she said, returning to her conversational plan of attack. "I'm waiting to hear from her about a book project."

Except for the twitch of a tiny vein at the corner of Tanner's left eye, his expression remained the same.

"Book project?" he said dully.

"Yes," Georgina said quietly. "I sent her my manuscript."

A matching vein on the right side of Tanner's head began to twitch. "Excuse me?" he said. His eyebrows dropped a notch. "You sent her what manuscript?"

Good Lord, Georgina thought. Why would he think a publishing house would contact her out of the blue?

"Oh, dear, I'm sorry, Tanner. I seem to have gone about this from the middle rather than the beginning. I've been working on a . . . oh . . ."—she opened her palm and waggled her hand back and forth—". . . a sort of a combination cookbook and household-hint collection. You know, like a survival manual for people who work full time and still want to run a nice . . ." Her voice trailed off as her attention became riveted on Tanner's reaction.

It took a moment for her to realize that Tanner was on the verge of laughter. He had picked up his napkin and was holding it over his chin and mouth to hide his struggle to hear her out. Reflexively, she started to laugh herself. But it was an imitation of a laugh. Inside she was furious. How dare he laugh at something so important to her?

"Tanner?" she finally said, helpless to go on.

Tanner gave in and threw his head back, dropped his napkin, and howled. When he brought himself under control, he apologized, shaking his head again.

"I really don't see what's so terribly funny," she said, giving up any effort to hide her annoyance.

"Oh, Georgie, I'm such an old poop," he said, wiping his eyes. "You know what I thought when you said . . . well, when you . . ." He burst out laughing again.

Finally, he got himself together enough to explain. "You know

147

what I thought? I thought your friend had come after you for a tell-all. You know, *How I Married a Millionaire*. That kind of garbage."

"Tanner," Georgina said sharply. "How could you dream I would do something like that?"

"Darling, forgive me. I wallow in such sensationalism all day I have been corrupted. I'm truly sorry. Now, tell me all about this book you've written, you sly one. When did you find the time?"

The fun of it was all gone. Georgina pushed a floret around her plate without looking up. "I have time," she said quietly. "I'm sorry it isn't something more dramatic, but that is my field."

Tanner nodded to Grover, who was hovering with a bread basket. He selected a piece before he spoke. "That explains the bathtub full of lettuce."

Georgina pressed her lips together. "Oh, dear, you saw that? I deliberately put them in the back bath so you wouldn't be bothered."

"Oh, I wasn't bothered. I just happened to take some shoes back for Grover to clean, and there they were. I couldn't imagine. I meant to ask what they were there for."

Georgina smiled. If Tanner would rather discuss lettuce heads in the servants' bath than the fact that she had written and was planning to publish a book, she should be grateful. At least he wasn't angry, and that had been all she was concerned about.

"Well, I don't know if you can ever use this bit of intelligence, but lettuce keeps in submerged water for up to two weeks."

"Is that the sort of thing you have in the book?"

"Along with a lot of other new stuff. Things that aren't in the current books."

Tanner put down his fork and reached for his wineglass. "What kind of money is your friend talking about?"

"Tanner, the book hasn't even been accepted yet."

"You realize, of course, you should have had your agent send it out. You shouldn't speak to this Rona person directly."

"Tanner, darling, I don't have an agent," she said in the same tone she would have said she didn't have a sky-diving instructor. Having an agent seemed so cold-blooded. Rona was a friend. It had never occurred to her to submit the manuscript through an agent. How could she sic a pit-bull agent on an old friend?

"Well, if you want to pursue this project, darling, I'll give Irving Fourbraz a call this evening."

"Irving Fourbraz," she gasped. If he had dropped a dead animal onto the table, she would have been less alarmed. A moment ago Tanner was accusing Rona of being an opportunist. He didn't know that during the terrible days before Tanner's divorce, Irving Fourbraz had had the nerve to track her down and ask if she wanted to sell her story. "Darling! I hardly think advice on how to keep one's hollandaise from separating is Irving's cup of tea. I just saw him on some panel discussing the girl that TV star nearly killed. She's going to write some kind of a book about all the famous people she's had sex with. The raciest thing in my book is how to whiten graying lingerie."

Tanner drank off the last of his wine. "Georgie, dear, if you're serious about the publishing business, you not only must have representation, but you should take advantage of our contacts," he said patiently. "Now, after dinner I'll give Irving a call. He can get in touch with Bob Kadanoff in the morning."

Georgina studied the back of Grover's snowy cuff as he removed her plate. She wished she hadn't gone to the trouble of making dessert. What she wanted to do was leave the table and not talk about the book anymore. She knew she was slumping, something Tanner hated at the table. She couldn't help it. What had she started here? Within minutes her little project had become the undertaking of a high-powered lawyer/agent and the chairman of a multimillion-dollar publishing concern. Her little time filler was being sucked into the old-boy network like Kitty Litter up a Dustbuster.

Mercifully, as soon as Grover took Tanner's plate, Selma pushed through the swinging kitchen door with the dessert tray.

Tanner's eyes widened at the sight of the bananas Foster.

He took a serving, making the expected comments about how many laps he would have to do in the morning.

"Darling," Georgina said, bracing herself to start the discussion up again. She had to get the book thing settled or she would have a sleepless night. "Don't you think Irving Fourbraz is a bit high-powered for a project like this?"

Tanner's fork paused in midair. "Irving knows how to make authors into celebrities."

"Sweetheart, I don't want to be a celebrity. I'd just like to get my little book published. If people like it, I could do another one. I don't have to be turned into a Julia Child. I don't need to be made into something I'm not, like Irving was doing with that poor girl on television."

She could see Tanner's eyes glazing over. He wasn't thinking about what she wanted. He was thinking about a new project. Something else he could control. She would try another tack.

"Don't you think you should save your contacts with agents and publishers for when you write your memoirs?"

Tanner perked up. "They'll still be around if I ever do that. At the moment, I do think you need protection, my sweet."

"From what? Someone's going to sue me because my marble-swirl cake has uneven nut distribution?"

Tanner didn't laugh. He glanced up at Grover, who immediately stepped forward and eased Tanner's chair back so he could stand. "Let me call Irving and at least get things started," he said, tossing his napkin onto the table.

"But . . ." Georgina started to protest, then thought better of it. She accepted another half a cup of coffee and told Selma she could clear the table. She wanted to sit quietly for a moment.

This wasn't the first time Tanner had taken over something she could have handled herself. In the past his interference had always been on a small scale. When she told him she needed some new clothes, he called the president of Saks and had a personal shopper bring things to the apartment. When she wore open pumps to the Heart Ball and smashed her big toe in the revolving door at the Pierre, he called the head of orthopedic surgery at Mount Sinai and had a foot specialist come to the hotel to look at it.

Georgina finished her coffee and pushed back her chair. She couldn't stop Tanner. His feelings would be so hurt.

15

*K*ick hadn't spoken to another human in so long she'd begun to wonder if she was real. Lolly had been dead for nearly three weeks; her memorial service, nearly two weeks ago, was already history. And Kick really hadn't spoken to anyone since her lunch with Joe Stone. She rubbed her aching neck and leaned her head back against Lolly's desk chair.

She had been at the word processor at the top of the penthouse since dawn that morning, pounding out the feature Joe had asked for. On the desk and the floor around her stood yellowing stacks of files so filled with dust the air in the room seemed to sparkle when light hit it.

She sat very still, listening to the distant sounds of the city. The old penthouse never seemed to be completely silent. There was always a vague hum of traffic on Central Park West far below and trucks honking or grinding gears on the side streets. It was amazing how sound could carry twenty stories into the sky even in the dead of night.

There were also times, now that she was alone in the apartment, that she swore she heard sounds inside coming from the floors below. It was probably her imagination. Did furniture sigh? Was it possible that the possessions in the more than a dozen closets mumbled to each other when they thought no one was around?

"Arghhhhhh!" she screamed, reaching both her arms high above her head and stretching. "I'm losing it," she said aloud. "This place is driving me batty. Maybe I should rent a room to finish this piece."

It was being surrounded by Lolly's *things* that was depressing her the most. In all the reading she had done about Lolly's life in the last couple of weeks, nothing explained why she had so relentlessly collected stuff. It wasn't as though there were anyone else who could ever use it once she was gone. Then it dawned on her. Lolly had never thought she was going anywhere.

But who was going to sort out the mess?

Maybe she should try to reach that sleazebag Irving Fourbraz again. In the past two weeks—she'd been trying to reach him since the day after Labor Day—he hadn't responded to any of her messages. Lolly must have left some kind of instructions, even if she did think she was immortal. As her lawyer, Irving would have seen to that.

During her first days with Lolly, it had taken only a couple of calls from Irving's office for Kick to realize that he had no idea who she was or that they had ever met. At first it had angered her. Now she was grateful. There was no way she could have spoken to him if he had remembered he had once gotten her fired.

Kick looked at her watch and sighed. Too late; it was after business hours. She'd been so caught up in her work, she'd never noticed the passage of time. It was definitely time for a break. She decided to go get the mail, then see what was languishing in the refrigerator.

Kick made her way down the stairs, rolling her shoulders to release some of the tension. Computers were hell on the neck. She was starting to open the locks when she noticed that someone—Mike, probably—had brought the mail up for her and shoved it under the door. That was nice of him; he knew that Kick had been holed up here working.

Kick shuffled through the pile: bills, bills, bills. What was she supposed to do with them? Damn that Irving Fourbraz. At the bottom of the stack was an envelope from his office. Oops, sorry, Irving, Kick mentally apologized. She opened it eagerly, scanned the contents, and slid to the floor, her back against the wall.

She shook her head, stunned. Buried in all the legalese, two points stood out. The good news was the rent on the apartment was paid up through the end of the year—a little arrangement Lolly had with the management. Jeez, only $800 a month. No wonder the co-op board had hated her.

The bad news was Lolly had left every blessed thing in the apartment, and the responsibility for getting rid of it, to one Katherine Maureen Butler.

Kick's first reaction was one of great sadness. Lolly really had been alone in the world if the only heir she could think of was someone she'd known for only a year, and an employee to boot. Her fame and power had isolated her even more than Kick had realized.

Then doubts began to creep in. Was this Lolly's final manipulation, pressing Kick into servitude from beyond the grave? "No," Kick moaned. "Please, Lolly, thanks, but no thanks." How was she going to sift through three lifetimes of accumulated junk? This was too much. Just getting rid of the piles of newspapers and magazines in the gallery where she was sitting would be an enormous task.

Kick stood up and looked around, taking stock. She wandered into the living room, noting the threadbare brocade upholstery on the couches. The doors of the huge mahogany armoire gaped open; they couldn't be closed against the objects stuffed on its shelves. The portrait of Lolly over the fireplace badly needed cleaning. The tables squeezed in between the upholstered pieces were covered with *things:* souvenirs, plaques, boxes containing God knew what.

The dining room was, if anything, worse. The walls there were lined with boxes. A breakfront wall held unopened bottles of spirits—ghosts of Christmases past—along with carefully washed plastic food containers, bits of string, and bulging shopping bags from stores that had gone out of business before Kick was born.

Kick was too dispirited to explore the wing that contained Lolly's father's library and the maids' rooms. She felt overwhelmed—how could she cope with all this? Maybe it was a mistake, maybe she hadn't understood Irving's letter. To hell with business hours, going through channels. This was an emergency.

Kick made her way upstairs to the office, the letter clutched in her hand. She located Fourbraz's home number in the Rolodex and dialed. The phone rang three, four, five times. She was about to hang up when a woman answered.

"Hello, is Mr. Fourbraz in?"

"No," the woman said curtly.

"Well . . . ah, it's really important that I reach him. My name is Kick Butler. I'm . . . I was Lolly Pines's assistant, and I just got a very upsetting letter from Mr. Fourbraz."

"Why am I not surprised."

"Sorry?" Kick said, baffled at the woman's sour tone.

"Irving's hobby is to upset people," the woman said, sighing. "I'm sorry, I shouldn't have said that. I'm Neeva Fourbraz. You've caught me in a rather bad mood."

"I'm sorry too," Kick said. "But, well . . . you know who Lolly Pines was, right?"

"Of course."

"It's just that your husband's written me saying Lolly has willed me all her earthly belongings, and I'm, well, freaking out."

"No, kidding. That whole triplex?" Irving's wife said, showing a flicker of interest for the first time. "From what Irving's told me about that place, you're going to need a strong back and a shovel."

"How about a forklift?"

"I'd offer to take a message for Irving, but I don't know when it would ever get delivered."

Kick sat back and held her head, cradling the phone on one shoulder. "Oh, Lord, what am I going to do?"

"You could put it all up for auction," Neeva suggested. "I know something about how to go about that if you'd be interested."

That figures, Kick thought. What a pair those two are. Irv jiggers things so people inherit crap they can't handle, and his wife "conveniently" knows how to take it off their hands. "I'll keep that in mind, thank you, Mrs. Fourbraz," she said, feeling drained. "If you wouldn't mind just leaving some kind of note that I'm trying to reach your husband, I'd be most grateful."

"I'll try."

After she hung up, Kick walked to the dusty little bar Lolly kept behind the office door and poured a very dark scotch into a clean coffee mug. She took a big slug, then carried the mug down the hallway toward the stairs.

When she got to the second floor, she paused and took another slug. The full impact of what she had to deal with finally hit.

Now that she was focusing on the meaning of Lolly's bequest, she had little doubt that she was the owner of some very valuable things. Besides the furnishings, there was some jewelry, mostly big costume stuff from the forties. Lolly's old designer clothes alone would have been enough to make Diana Vreeland weep. But surely the cost of disposing of all the junk would eat up whatever profits there were.

As she continued down the stairs, Kick resolved to call Neeva Fourbraz the next morning and dump the whole mess in her lap.

16

*T*wo hours later, Baby Bayer's knees were locked firmly behind Irving's head in the middle of the king-size, fur-covered bed in Ian McCaulley's pied-à-terre in the Beekman Tower. The London-based actor used the place only a couple of times a year. On the other hand, his agent and attorney, Irving, used it regularly.

Irving was about to do something that, Baby had told him, and he believed her, drove her crazy. He pushed himself halfway off the bed and withdrew himself so that just the tip of his penis touched her. He paused until she begged him to come back, then slammed inside her until she screamed and shuddered in rapture.

Irving had begun mentioning his erection halfway through dinner with Baby at Le Cirque. When the check came, he had to ask Sirio to bring him his raincoat from the checkroom before he could safely leave the table. The restaurateur, ever cool in emergencies, had given no indication whatsoever that Irving had not arrived with a raincoat in the eighty-degree heat, nor that Irving had no such garment on the premises.

A raincoat subsequently arrived at the tableside over the arm of a blank-faced waiter. Irving quickly snatched it onto his bulging lap.

He kept his head down as they left the crowded restaurant, ignoring several tentative waves from other tables as he passed.

The raincoat remained protectively over his arm in the cab, through the lobby of the Beekman Tower, and in the elevator up to his absent client's apartment.

When they were safely inside, Irving dropped the raincoat on the settee in the foyer, unzipped his fly, and revealed himself in all his tumescent splendor to Baby. Baby, as was her usual custom, squealed with delight and pulled him into the bedroom. Within seconds, they were both nude and locked in passionate coitus on the wolf-snout fur on Ian McCaulley's king-size bed.

He had never known anyone or anything like Baby Bayer. From the moment they laid eyes on each other, the sexual electricity had begun to flow. They had seen each other every day since their first date at the St. Regis. Irving couldn't remember what he had expected the girl who answered the phone at the *Courier* to be like; all he'd cared about was planting an item about his representation of the Lopez girl. Baby Bear could have looked like Margaret Mead for all he cared. He sure as hell didn't expect the hot little number who arrived at his table at the St. Regis. Baby, it turned out, possessed what, for Irving, was an irresistible combination in a woman—boobs, snappy looks, and a ratlike cunning.

In the days that followed he became totally distracted by her. Meetings were shifted, appointments canceled or postponed. Calls went unreturned as pink message slips littered his desk, to Vivian's utter frustration. He and Neeva had virtually stopped speaking. He knew she was pissed about bills piling up and his never being home, but she knew he was a workaholic when she married him. She knew he had to spend a lot of time entertaining clients, attention always had to be paid—so suddenly, what was new?

To get a weekend with Baby, he told Vivian and Neeva he was running back to the coast to work on the Lopez deal. Instead, he cabbed to Ian's with flowers and champagne and found Baby waiting in the lobby.

Baby was a fireball, a tightly clenched fist of wild sexuality and drive. In all his years of practicing sex as a hobby, he had always involved himself with women who, ultimately, wanted something from him—his power, his influence, whatever. Baby seemed to want only two things: his body and his mind.

He had never felt better than he had during the heady two weeks since they met. Whenever he was with her, he felt as though a spotlight was trained on them. People stared at them in the street. Heads turned in restaurants. Cab drivers gave him winks and grins when he paid the fare.

He loved it. He loved Sirio's raised eyebrow when he arrived at Le Cirque three days in a row with Baby on his arm. To him, the men in the room were staring at him with envy, dirty movies running in their minds.

Baby didn't look like the women who pushed lettuce leaves around their plates in posh restaurants. They wore ice-cream-colored little suits and had pipe-cleaner legs. Baby looked as though she ate three meals a day and dressed to show it off, twisting her tight little ass an extra spin as she walked, bouncing along in the highest heels he had seen outside of a strip show.

He found making an entrance with her as intoxicating as any business triumph he had ever experienced. By her mere presence Baby had figuratively given him the biggest dick in town.

Irving, a man not given to introspection, found himself forced to analyze her effect on him. The conclusion he reached was that, aside from the way she looked and acted, what excited him the most was the way he excited her.

She hung on his every word, laughed at his jokes so genuinely that he began asking everyone he came in contact with if they had any new ones. When she wasn't laughing at his wit, she was asking him about his work, telling him how clever he was, offering support, and agreeing that anyone who crossed him was a "shit," a "bastard," or a "dumb fuck."

Best of all, Baby couldn't keep her hands off him. He had never experienced such a crosscurrent of lust and protectiveness. He wanted to do something for her, but she never asked.

The wolf fur was beginning to chafe the skin of his knees and elbows. If they hadn't been in such a red-hot frenzy when they got to Ian's apartment, he would have thought to pull the damn thing off the bed.

He pulled out of her again and waited, smiling down at her as she loosened one arm and groped between his legs.

"*Oooo*, honey, don't take it away," she whimpered. "Gimme that big thing." She thrust her pelvis forward and threw her head back against the headboard as if in pain.

Irving had seen his share of triple-X films. Nothing Baby said in bed was anything he hadn't heard before from blue-veined, pimply-backed porn queens in badly lit videos. He had heard the same sexy phrases from thousand-dollar-a-night call girls and casual pickups in hotel bars. But never had he heard them as he lay atop a creamy-skinned Barbie doll looking up with huge blue eyes, her perfectly shaped peach-colored mouth whispering as it was now, "Please, honey, please. Put that big hot cock back in me. I want to feel it all the way up to my throat."

He wouldn't deprive her any longer. He shoved himself home, moving in perfect rhythm with her body as she moaned, "Fuck me, lover, harder, harder," over and over again.

Baby always screamed when he gave her an orgasm. Her whole body would go stiff for a few moments, as though she was in the front car of a roller coaster. She would scream a long, throaty sound, break into a deep shudder, and then fall limp under him, covered with his sweat.

He rolled off her, soaking wet and as hard as he was when he started.

"What's the matter, honey?" Baby asked from his armpit as she ran her hand down his damp stomach, grasping his erection. "You didn't come!"

"I didn't want to," he said, panting for air. He didn't want to tell her he couldn't. He was in good shape for pushing sixty. He jogged, worked out at the health club on the top floor of the Friars Club, and swam vigorously, when he could, in his Hampton's pool, but nothing could keep the plumbing from slowing down. It was enough to hear her scream and feel her shudder beneath him. He would finish up later. He knew she would see to that. Baby gave the best head he'd ever had.

Baby pushed herself up on one elbow, resting her chin on his chest. "Why doesn't Mr. Happy want to come?" she asked in a little girl voice. "I like it when Mr. Happy comes. It feels sooo good."

Baby had started calling his penis Mr. Happy and holding conversations with it in baby talk since the first night after "21." No one had ever actually chatted with his penis, and Baby's adoration of it almost made him jealous.

Irving ran his fingers through the blond ringlets falling onto her forehead. He raised his head and kissed her gently on the mouth, "Later, doll baby. Gotta take a little rest here."

He glanced down at his watch as his hand rested on her shoulder. He had been out of touch for more than six hours. His service would be loaded with calls by now. Ever since Baby's item on him and the Lopez girl had alerted the talk shows that there was fresh meat available, the pace of his life had escalated to a frenzy. The past week had been a blur of sorting through offers for movie-of-the-week deals, and from drooling tabloids, talk-show invitations, and requests for exclusive magazine profiles. Thanks to a cooperative and easily "tipped" doctor on the case, he had been able to keep the girl in the hospital until he had the whole media package arranged. The story in the *World* would only whet the appetite. There were overseas sales to be arranged, *Paris–Match*, the Brits, and with a name like Lopez, every Spanish-speaking country in the world. Not to mention every country where Keeko Ram's series was in syndication. The kid was a demigod in Italy. There was no telling what they would pay.

Producers for Donahue, Sally Jessy, and Oprah had offered to set up their cameras at the foot of her goddamn bed, but he knew such an appearance would do nothing but take the edge off her story. He could wait. Leaving her at City of Angels was as safe as if she were in jail. He could control the timing and content of her interview with the *World* and save the really juicy stuff to sell off in one huge deal.

He looked down at Baby, feeling the even rhythm of her breathing against his chest, and wondered how many "Babys" he had left in his life. Maybe she was the last.

Suddenly he was overcome with a sense of panic. He tried to imagine life without her in it. His life had never been dull. He had seen to that. For years he had lived on the edge, piling deal upon deal, scheme upon scheme. By twisting, turning, leaping out of the way of fate like a broken-field runner, he had usually come out on top.

His marriage to Suzanne had dissolved mainly because she wanted her own mental space to write. He had gotten her work ghostwriting for some of his celebrity clients and, in one case, for a one-book novelist who had blocked when the book became a huge success. But Suzanne wanted her own slice of fame, and their life together became a battleground. Suzanne resented him, his kid wouldn't speak to him, and they both wanted out. By then, he already had a compliant, never-complaining Neeva waiting in the wings, and it was easy to move on.

He thought of Neeva and supposed he had made her happy.

If she knew about his extracurricular activities, she pretended not to. There was no way any woman could understand a man's need for what ballplayers called their "strange": the random sexual opportunities available to any powerful man who wanted them.

There had always been available women. The girl in the next seat on the red-eye; the cute waitress with the cuter butt; and, when the need was too immediate to sustain the small talk and the candlelit dinners it took to score some casual strange, there were always the pros.

Each girl was different, sometimes startlingly so, but the cooing creature snuggled in his arms at that moment was unique. He felt he had stumbled upon a unicorn in the concrete forest. Keeping her in his life was more important to him than any scam or deal he had ever perpetrated. He had to have her . . . but how? She didn't want his money. She was too independent to let him keep her, even if he had the money, too smart to continue to put up with stolen romps in borrowed hay, and if he wanted her so badly, the jungle had to be full of younger, bigger dicks who wanted her too.

He looked down at his eighteen-karat Rolex again. It was getting late. He would have to slip into the apartment as it was. The last thing he wanted to do was wake Neeva and have to start inventing his evening.

Reluctantly, he pulled his left arm out from under Baby's shoulders and swung his feet over the side of the bed. He was about to stand up when he felt a hand slipping around his hip and cradling his balls.

"Don't," Baby whispered. "Don't get up. I want to kiss Mr. Happy. He hasn't come yet."

Irving put his hand over hers and smiled at her over his shoulder. "Next time, dollface. I gotta go. I gotta call my service."

Baby made a face and looked up at him imploringly. "It makes me so sad when you have to go," she said, softly.

"Me too."

"I know you have to. You sure you don't want give it one more try?" she asked, releasing his testicles and rolling over on her back.

He turned around and brushed her cheek with his lips. "It's okay. I had a wonderful time. Just a little too much to drink. Come on, sugar tits. We gotta get dressed. I'll take you home."

"When will I see you?" Baby asked, her eyes pleading.

"Tomorrow. We'll have lunch or dinner, whatever you like."

"Can't," Baby pouted.

"Can't what?" Irving asked with alarm.

"Can't tomorrow. I gotta work."

"Shit," he hissed.

Baby pulled the second pillow under her head and sat up, watching Irving's eyes slide down to her breasts. "I just hate it there. I could be doing so much more than talking to press agents for Chinese restaurants and following up on crap Petra Weems doesn't want to do," she said, staring off into space.

"Like what, honey?" Irving asked, leaning forward and taking her right breast into his mouth.

Baby released a long, shuddering sigh. She wanted her announcement to Irv that she was after Lolly's column to be carefully timed. Up until now she had never quite trusted him, but she had had enough love affairs to know when the relationship had crossed the line and a man was hopelessly hooked. If she was ever going to get Lolly's column, she would need Irv. It was worth the risk to tell him now. She reached over and traced the large veins on the back of his hand with one fingernail. "I could be doing Lolly's column. I'd be damn good at it," she said softly.

Irving kept circling her nipple with his tongue. Of course, he thought as he licked away, how perfect. When Lolly was alive, she was a nightmare. She lived by a quid pro quo that kept him jumping. Not only had he handled her legal matters for nothing, but she always demanded a tip or item in kind whenever she put his name in the column. It wouldn't be like that with Baby. He didn't even want to question whether she was qualified or not. What did he know? Suddenly, his ability to make Baby happy had taken on a whole new dimension.

"So ask," Irving said, between tongue flicks.

Baby turned her head to one side. "I can't. Tanner Dyson hates me."

Irving's head jerked up almost involuntarily. "Tanner Dyson hates you? What'd you ever do to him? Guy's nuts. Why would he hate my Babykins? Nobody hates my Babykins and lives." He was teasing, but apparently, from Baby's hardened expression, she was dead serious.

He clasped her chin and pulled her face around so that he

could look at her eyes. They were filled with tears. "Oh, sugar, don't do that. I'm sorry. What happened with you and Dyson? Jesus, I know the man. Have for years. What happened? He try to screw you or something?"

Baby looked away. "Promise you won't tell?"

"Cut my heart out."

"He married the best friend I had in the world."

"The second wife? She's a looker."

Baby rolled over on her stomach really getting into the story. "Well, she wasn't always. She used to be fat, I mean, really gross. I didn't know her then, but she showed me pictures. After she got skinny, she hooked Tanner. I protected her when the press was hounding her before his divorce."

"Yeah, I remember that. The tabloids had a field day with that one. I called her once to see if she wanted me to help her sell her story. She acted like I was looking to sell her left tit. She wouldn't remember."

"So anyway, I guess old Tanner thought I was some kind of a threat because I was so close to Georgina . . . He didn't want me around after they got married. Some kind of sick jealousy. Frankly, I think he was afraid I knew too much."

Irving reached over and tickled her stomach. "God, I wish I'd known you then. We'd have taken this town by storm by now."

Baby pulled away from him and stood up. She padded naked across the rug to the dresser where she had left her handbag. She carried the bag back to bed and sat down opposite Irving, her legs spread, permitting him a view that nearly made him swoon.

"I got this out yesterday," she said, handing him a legal-size white envelope. "I want you to have a look at it and tell me if it's legal."

Irving sat up and took the envelope. Fascinated, he pulled out a document written on heavy bond. Halfway through it he turned to Baby. "What the fuck is this?"

"Keep going."

He finished reading and shook his head. "Jesus H. Christ, Baby. I suppose he kept a copy of this piece of shit."

Baby shrugged. "Of course, Tanner does everything by the book. He's the most tight-assed man alive. He was so wild about Georgina, so controlling. I think half of making me sign this was just showing off, letting me know that now that he'd married my friend, he was the boss. Also you gotta remember, the two of them had been shredded in the press. His ex-wife was telling the world what a rat he was. Georgina's parents were hounded by photographers. They even followed her mother to a supermarket. Georgina hadn't lived with her parents for years. I think Tanner was a little nuts by the time they actually got married."

"A lot nuts, if you ask me," Irving said, shaking his head. He'd seen a lot of crazy legal stunts in his time, but this one took the cake. How a man in Tanner Dyson's position could expect a young female employee to sign a statement that she would never speak or write about his personal life and expect to collect damages if she did was loony.

Irving flicked the page with a snap of his thumb and middle finger. "You know, don't you . . . Minerva," he said, pulling away from the little slap she aimed at his shoulder, "I could sell your story about Tanner's romance for ten times what this piece of crap stipulates even if it was legal."

"Sure, that would get me Lolly's column real fast," she sneered. "That's what he promised if I kept my mouth shut."

"So? How come I don't see your pretty face on the top of page ten each morning?"

"Because he was bullshitting me, that's why."

"The bastard," Irving mumbled, squeezing her hand.

"What do you want to know about this, hon?" Irving asked, replacing the page and handing the envelope to Baby.

"Is it legal?"

"Come on, sugar, give me a break."

"I'm serious."

"First place, it's a piece of crap. Un-fucking-enforceable. Worthless. The thing itself makes a great story. The guy must have been crazy to even think he could get away with it."

"I figured," Baby said, with a cute little shake of her head.

"That's just what I wanted to hear." She dropped the envelope into her bag and snapped it shut.

Irving looked at Baby with a mock scowl. "Baaabbeee, you are up to something," he singsonged. "What are you planning to do with that letter? You've had it for years."

Baby lifted her chin and looked down her cheekbones at him. "Tanner made me some promises when I signed that. But Lolly's been dead for over two weeks. I heard he made an offer to Cindy Adams, so there's no way he could deny he was lying. The bastard is going to make good or else."

To his astonishment, Irving was beginning to get another erection. Nothing excited him more than intrigue and evening a score. This was a situation he was born for.

"Look," he said, rolling over on his back, "even Mr. Happy is paying attention."

Baby laughed and swung back off the bed. "As soon as the timing is right, I'm going to have a little talk with Mr. Tanner Dyson."

Irving didn't know shit from shinola about the inner workings of a newspaper and less about what it took to be a syndicated gossip columnist. However, he knew fat opportunity when he saw it.

"You'd be great at that job, Baby," he said. "Christ, you're smart, you got balls, you'd be able to promote the column on talk shows . . ." His voice trailed off. Nothing in their brief relationship could possibly have led Irving to know whether or not Baby could write, but he had seen how she handled herself when she spoke at Lolly's memorial, and he knew from showbiz. The girl was a natural. The people in the Minskoff that day were eating her up.

"And here I thought I was going to put in a word for you with Dyson," he called to Baby as she stood at the bathroom sink running a wet face towel over her naked body. "Damn! You got that guy in the bag, sugar."

Baby tossed the towel into the tub and reached for one of Ian McCaulley's toothbrushes. "If I don't get that column, I'm going to need an agent to get me top dollar for my story," she said, speaking around a ball of foam as she scrubbed her teeth. "You know anybody?"

By the time they reached the street in front of the Beekman Tower, he was already working on a plan for Baby's future as a star.

17

Once she was inside her apartment, Baby saw the light on her answering machine blinking. The display said she had one message. She would check it later. It was probably the office jerking her schedule around again. All she wanted at the moment was to get into the shower—fast.

She stripped off her clothes, leaving them in a heap on the floor, and stepped under the pulsating water.

She wished Irving Fourbraz didn't sweat so much. It drove her nuts. Fucking him was like flying and swimming at the same time. He also had hair on his back, something Joe Stone didn't have. Joe Stone could also come without her having to give head. She supposed Irv was just too old, but he tried. Oh, how he tried!

She also wished they didn't have to do all their screwing at the tricked-up pad at the Beekman. But Irving said her place, smack in the middle of midtown, was too dangerous. Anybody could see him coming or going. Like the doorman and elevator operator didn't notice at the Beekman? The way she figured it, Irving had taken one look at her housekeeping and decided he liked the

Beekman place better. After all, the man did live at Trump Tower with a wife and a full-time maid. Orange rinds under the bed and underwear in the fridge probably turned him off.

Even so, the actor's place wasn't paradise. It was choked with heavy furniture. Huge pillows covered with cut-up Oriental carpets were strewn all over the place. Everything was so massive, so macho-baroque in scale, the guy just had to be a queen. Irving, however, thought the apartment was hot stuff and raved about the actor's taste. All she knew was that the place gave her the creeps and that there were exactly one hundred and twenty gold-cord rosettes holding yards of puckered tapestry that was tented across the bedroom ceiling. She had counted them in time to Irving's thrustings.

She had known five minutes after she met him face-to-face what Irving would be like in bed. She had been there before. The Irvings of the world were men who thought with their dicks, who liked women to talk baby-talk to them, to give them names like Snookie or Snake or Tiger or Big Boy. Irving's prick's name was Mr. Happy. It wasn't much bigger than his thumb, and the last two times she had been with him he went soft after the second time they did it. She ignored it so he would and went right on telling him what a great big fella Mr. Happy was.

She couldn't imagine women naming their vaginas. But, to be fair, she supposed if she had something hanging from her body that jerked her all over town, she'd want to be on a first-name basis with it too.

There were other things she knew about the Irvings of this world. They wanted you to talk dirty. That's why she started counting the gold rosettes in the ceiling. She was trying to think up ten other ways to say, "Fuck me."

She liked the fact that Irving was recognized by famous people. She liked that he was a celebrity himself. She even found his knowledge of the law and how to get around it sexy. But she doubted that she could fall in love with him, mostly because he had been so easy to run to ground. There was no real challenge in the Irvings of the world. But, boy, could they be useful.

Baby had learned early how to get ahead. While her competition in school or on the job were working their buns off, getting extra credits, working overtime, and sucking up to whoever it was that controlled their lives, Baby knew to target the guy in charge who thought with his dick.

That's what she thought she was doing when she zeroed in on Joe Stone. It was a big miscalculation. She should have known he was thinking that way only because he was freshly divorced. He was feeling failed and vulnerable, and sex was the only thing that made him feel better. Now that he had made it clear that he wasn't going to help her get Lolly's job, she found him a lot less interesting. The final straw was when he didn't even want to be seen with her at Lolly's service. She hadn't spoken to him since.

She lifted her hair to let the hot water pound against her neck and shoulders, rubbed raw from the English actor's stiff tapestry pillows, and thought about Irving's table at Le Cirque.

She had eaten at the restaurant a couple of times before, with unimportant PR people at tables so close to the kitchen she could have fixed her own meal without leaving her seat. When she arrived with Irving, the headwaiter did everything but get down and dust his shoes. Before she knew it, they were being seated at the first table just inside the entrance. Anyone who came in had to notice them. A lot of people stopped and spoke to Irv. Everyone who did had a recognizable face. The same thing had been true at "21", but the people there weren't nearly as familiar to her. Except, of course, the mayor. He had stopped beside their table and talked for nearly five minutes, keeping his entourage cooling their heels by the door. Irv introduced her to everyone. "This is Miss Bayer," he would say. "She writes for the *Courier*."

When Irving told the mayor that, the mayor asked her to have her assistant call Gracie Mansion and put her name on the list for his monthly press lunch. "Sure," she had whispered to Irv as soon as the mayor and his entourage left. "My assistant! I'm lucky they don't make me bring my own toilet paper to work."

Irving wasn't uninteresting to be with. At least she didn't have to come up with sparkling conversation. All she had to do was

171

ask him about himself, then put her mind on cruise control—just as she did with her body later.

She would mentally glide along, laughing at his jokes—most of which she had heard in high school or college, when they weren't funny either. While the left side of her brain was in neutral, the right was working on how she was going to play the next hand with the powerful Mr. Irving Fourbraz—Mr. Fixit.

She squeezed a bottle of bath gel and let the contents trickle between her breasts and down her stomach as she considered the most interesting aspect of listening to Irv.

Each self-serving story he told involved a celebrity and was peppered with tidbits of information that would have taken her weeks of digging to turn up.

A lot of the people he talked about were his clients! She wondered how some of these poor schmucks who were cheating on their taxes and wives and robbing other people blind would feel if they knew their lawyer was filling her ear. Yikes, how she could use those stories someday. Her mind swirled with the thought. No wonder Irv and Lolly Pines were so tight. The man was a gold mine.

From time to time during their meals, Baby would excuse herself, run into a booth in the ladies' room, sit down on the can, and make notes. Pretty soon she was going to have to start carrying one of those tiny little tape recorders in her bag.

Petra Weems, the bitch, would kill to know some of the information Baby was picking up. She couldn't wait to casually mention a few things and watch Petra's face drop.

She was standing at the sink, deafened by the roar of the hair dryer, when she thought she heard the phone. She switched off the dryer in time to hear the machine pick up.

"It's me, sugar tits," Irving's voice breathed onto the tape. "I just got home. I'm sitting here thinking about you and Mr. Happy is hard as a rock."

Twenty minutes earlier, the elevator man at the Trump Tower had been sitting outside the bank of elevators in the residents' lobby, with his feet resting on a tall marble ashtray, when Irving arrived. The man snapped to his feet and made a half turn into the paneled car.

"Good evening, Mr. Fourbraz," he said in his most formal voice.

"How 'ya doin', Matthew?" Irving asked as he stepped into the elevator, not really interested in the answer. He had just checked his watch. It was well after two. Neeva would be asleep for sure.

He opened the door to the apartment as soundlessly as possible and tiptoed down the carpeted hall toward his den. At the end of the hall he could see their bedroom door was slightly ajar. The room was dark.

He made a quick turn into his den and checked the answering machine. There were calls. He listened again for any possible sound from the bedroom. The only sound was the ticking of the antique clock on his desk and the hum of the air conditioner. He quietly closed the den door and sat down in the leather wing chair beside the answering machine.

There were two calls from Vivian frantically asking where he was, the second saying the *World* had called wanting to know when Maria Lopez would be strong enough to see their West Coast stringer for the interview. There was a call from Keeko Ram's lawyer in LA, a shriek of fury he would handle tomorrow.

The last call, to his surprise, was from Tanner Dyson. He rewound the tape and listened to it again, not quite believing his luck. Irving loved it when good things happened of their own accord and not because he had manipulated them in any way.

"Good evening, Irving," Tanner's disembodied voice rose from the tape a second time. "Tanner Dyson here. My apologies for calling you at home, but I have a matter of some urgency. I'd like you to represent my wife on a little publishing matter. Would you ring me at my office tomorrow?"

Irving sat for a long moment, smiling into the darkness, remembering a spot on Baby's upper thigh that was particularly ticklish. He was picturing her lush underbrush when he realized he was getting an erection. He knew it was late, but he couldn't resist. He had to talk to her.

He listened again for any sounds coming from the bedroom, then snatched up the phone.

He let it ring four times. The machine picked up. He knew she would answer if she knew it was him. He cupped his hand over the receiver and said, "It's me, sugar tits . . ."

18

*N*eeva had turned off her light early that evening. Usually she read until Irving got home, but considering the current coolness between them, she wanted to be fast asleep when he arrived.

She and Irving had been staying out of each other's way ever since the weekend of the Garn party. The few times their paths had crossed they had maintained a polite but distant reserve.

Still, little humiliations had begun to pile up. More department stores were calling. The Trump Tower garage called about the June, July, *and* August parking fees. It was very upsetting. Irving had to have money. His practice seemed to be booming, if one could judge by the papers and television. He had been in the *Courier* again just recently. It was an item that had to do with the seamy TV-star case he had been working on.

The latest embarrassment had come earlier in the week. Hildy Bornstein, her friend from nineteenth-century European paintings, told her Irv had been at Le Cirque with some blond two days in a row. Hildy's husband had been just a few tables away both times and said that Irving was being very cozy with her.

In better times, Neeva would have asked her friend what her husband meant by "cozy." Now she didn't want to ask. She was too afraid of what the answer might be.

Neeva had been raised to be afraid.

Her therapist once had her make a list of the things she was afraid of. The list went on for several pages. At the top she wrote the biggies. Most of all, she was afraid that people wouldn't like her; that she had said or done something wrong; that she wasn't good enough.

When she was little, she was afraid that the Russians were coming; that there would be snakes in the toilet when she lifted the lid. On her list, she had included being fat, the wind, and Republicans. She was terrified that her parents would divorce and she would be sent to a Christian orphanage. There would be a plaster dead man bleeding from a cross over her pillow, and the main course each night would be a bowl of mayonnaise.

When she got into Hunter College as a fine arts major, she was afraid of everything from failing a course to getting a menstrual stain on the back of her dress. In graduate school, she was afraid she wouldn't be able to write a dissertation; when she finished it, she was sure she'd be accused of plagiarism and sent to prison.

Painstakingly, the therapist made her understand that up until then, her life had been a struggle to control what was happening to her. In the beginning, she was too small and lacked the vocabulary to speak up for herself. By the time she was grown enough and could speak up, she had had a spokesperson for so long she was still helpless.

That insight made her come to terms with her relationship with her mother. That was fine. Then she had to deal with why she replaced her mother with a husband who did the same thing.

The therapist helped her figure out that fear of being afraid was what had made her choose Irving. He was a surrogate Rose: sure of himself, fearless, and strong. David Niven he wasn't, but he seemed so in control of his life that Neeva felt sure he could take charge of hers. What she had done was perpetuate the circumstances that made her afraid. Small wonder her doctor changed her Valiums from yellow to blue shortly after she returned from her honeymoon.

"You should talk to someone, Neeva. Something isn't kosher with him."

Rose's nasal voice twanging in her ear was the last thing she wanted to hear. She should have known Rose would be on the job; she always was when Neeva lay awake worrying.

In Neeva's mind's eye she saw Rose seated at a bridge table with Eleanor Roosevelt, Golda Meir, and Mrs. Gerwitz, the butcher's wife from Jerome Avenue. Mrs. Gerwitz was dripping with jewelry purchased with the money Mr. Gerwitz had stolen from Rose over a lifetime of overpricing brisket and baby lamb chops.

My daughter thinks a two-days-in-a-row blond for lunch isn't trouble? Rose was speaking to Eleanor Roosevelt, who knew a thing or two about other women. *My son-in-law can't see a client in his office? He has to take her to the Jackie Kennedy restaurant? He can't come home for dinner like a human being? The man with thirteen telephones and one in his pocket can't call up?*

"Mother, don't," Neeva breathed into the dark. She turned over restlessly. She knew Rose was right. Rose was always right. But what could she do? Confronting Irving was as hard as confronting her mother.

Neeva knew she would have no freedom until she did something about Irving. But what? How could she leave him? Her job at the gallery didn't pay enough to live on. Assuming she even kept the job—business had been going badly. For months the supposedly recession-proof auction businesses all over town were feeling the economic crunch. Dunsmore and Street had been luckier than most, but by early fall it, too, was in trouble.

Dunsmore and Street dealt in upmarket household effects: minor estate jewelry, items of good value but not extraordinary pieces; decorative art; bric-a-brac; and old silver. People who liked to dabble in antiques and objets d'art and smaller dealers were D&S's mainstay customers, but now even they were not showing up for the midweek auctions.

Neeva just knew if a layoff was coming, she would be one of the first to go.

Just the thought of waking up each morning with no place to go and nothing to do was terrifying. She was afraid of losing not only what little sense of independence she had but also the work she truly loved. To her, the auction business was a constant treasure hunt. She never knew when a battered cardboard box would contain something rare and valuable or the bidding on a mediocre painting would suddenly skyrocket out of sight when two dealers went at each other. There was a history to everything that came into the gallery that she found fascinating. Objects one thought rich and powerful people would never part with cropped up all the time. It was fascinating, stimulating work, and she didn't ever want to leave it. Now she was afraid she would have no choice.

There were two things she knew for certain as she tossed and turned alone in the king-size bed in the Trump Tower: she wanted to stay in the only work that made her happy and she had to make more money.

She began formulating the defense she would offer her boss Aubrey Dunsmore on that terrible day he would call her in to tell her she was being let go. She would remind him of her one great coup. She had correctly identified a Rafael Senet Perez that had been in a crate of dusty early nineteenth-century paintings. The Perez had gone for several thousand dollars above the Dunsmore and Street price. Still, Aubrey couldn't keep a person on hoping for a repeat of such a fluke. As Irving liked to say, "You're only as good as your last act." Her last act had been too long ago.

There was the hope of getting the Lolly Pines estate. Surely, Aubrey would keep her on if she brought in that business. But that would only perpetuate the status quo. She had to make *more* money, not the same amount. Her thoughts were going in circles. If she couldn't think her way out of this mess, maybe she deserved to stay in this loveless half life with Irving.

She thought she heard his key in the lock.

She rolled over, shut her eyes, and listened. It took exactly eleven seconds for Irv to walk from the front door to the bedroom unless he stopped in the powder room off the foyer. When he did that, she could see the light filtering down the hall. She opened her eyes and checked. Utter darkness. She waited for several minutes. Irving was probably checking his answering machine.

In the darkness, something caught her eye. One of the tiny red lights on the night-table phone lit up, covering her pillow with an eerie blush.

It wasn't like Irving to call someone back at this hour. Maybe something was wrong. Cautiously, she reached out and picked up the receiver and listened to Irving's first sentence. And a few more phrases.

She hung up. She couldn't hold the phone any longer. Her hand was shaking too much.

This wasn't a loveless half life. This was a living death.

19

*S*cattered, and often hidden, throughout the publishing world are women who are the backbone of the industry, a silent army of educated, docile worker bees who do the real work.

They do not dine at the Four Seasons or get their pictures in *People* magazine or profiled in *Vanity Fair*. They are not invited along on private jet rides to the south of France when famous authors throw ego parties. They never sun themselves on decks in Big Sur or play tennis on the velvety courts publishing money builds in the back of best-selling authors' mansions.

They stay in their windowless offices and make some kind of sense out of reams of word-processed drivel.

At night they struggle aboard homebound subway trains with heavy shopping bags filled with manuscripts to be read and evaluated, and on weekends they watch the favorite TV shows they'd taped to watch later, when they've finished the eye-glazing work that the editor who bought the work has foisted off on them.

They are sometimes invited to the glittering parties that launch the book that they made readable. They then spend a week's salary on an outfit that doesn't look that much different from what they wear to work.

At these parties they get to watch the editor who acquired the work get his or her picture taken with the author. The one who really did the work is rarely introduced to anyone at these parties, most certainly not the author, for no one wants it known who actually deserves the credit.

Knowing their place, the good gray wrens stand at the back of the room drinking warm white wine from plastic glasses and talking to the author's agent's secretary, who doesn't get any credit either.

Rona Friedman had been a wren at Winslow House for five years. She had been working as an assistant editor for a food magazine when she took what all her colleagues told her would be the dream job at Winslow House.

The job turned out to be all right except for the Kafkaesque aura cast by her immediate boss, the editor-in-chief.

Paper-thin, perpetually indignant, Pearl Grubman was a woman with the people skills of a maximum-security-prison guard. She was careful to hire women who were too decent, too respectful of the word business, to risk her contempt and their jobs by talking back. Pearl tormented them for their letting her torment them. As hard as Rona tried to keep her head down, stay out of the line of the woman's fire, and quietly do her job, Pearl found a way, at least once a week, to reduce her to a tongue-tied child with irrational criticism, snide personal remarks, and dismissive responses to any idea Rona proposed.

It did little to comfort Rona that all the women huddled along her hall at Winslow House were equally abused.

Each morning Rona arrived at her cubicle, lifted the manuscript she had put aside at the close of business the day before, and reluctantly began to edit as she waited for her mail.

Jason Fourbraz, the cute Juilliard kid from the mail room, was the one truly bright spot in Rona's day. Jason's mother, Suzanne Deavers, was a mid-list romance novelist who had ended a tumultuous marriage to Jason's father, celebrity agent/lawyer Irving Fourbraz, when Jason was just a kid. Jason spiced his morning mail deliveries with office gossip and tales from his other life as a pianist with a Village jazz band.

Rona looked forward to his visits as much as she dreaded the arrival of the manila envelopes he dropped on her desk. The envelopes invariably were addressed to her from the listings available in publishing directories in every public library. They were random submissions of work that bordered on the illiterate. She would ignore them until the end of the day, when she would reluctantly open and read them, then type a kind rejection note, and send them back to their hapless authors.

That was why, when Jason swung his lanky form through her door, she didn't even glance at the thick envelope he had under his arm.

"Help me, Rona, help, help me, Rona," he sang in a sexy half-whisper as he bopped toward her desk. He pulled the envelope free and held it with both hands, swinging it in time to his singing. He lifted the package head high and, swooping it from side to side like a landing spacecraft, dropped it on her desk with a thud that made her jump.

"'Morning, Jason. I think the name in that lyric is *Rhonda*," Rona said, eliminating a dangling participle with a brisk pen stroke. Pearl had given her a manuscript to edit on trekking in Nepal. The work was this month's pet. Pearl had been to Nepal with her husband the previous summer. Last month's pet project had been on shingles. Pearl suffered from bouts of the irritating disease. Rona had edited a book on garden soaker systems when Pearl had a planted terrace. Rona had also edited several books on multiple births—Pearl had twins—as well as the joys of bottle feeding, the physiology of twins, and sibling bonding.

Jason leaned over her desk trying to read what she was working on. "Uh-oh," he said. "Looks like Madame Pearl stuck you with another one. Is that Nepal?"

"*Ummm*," Rona said, still not looking up.

"That thing's a dog. It won't sell a hundred copies. She tried to stick Kathy Strickland with that one last week."

"Then how come I got it?" Rona asked, turning a page.

"'Cause Kathy's been here long enough to know to call in sick."

Rona tossed down her pen and leaned back in her chair. "Why didn't I think of that?" she asked wearily.

Jason propped one hip on the side of her desk. "Because you, my sheltered one, have not yet learned how to outwit Pearl the Squirrel. You could have gotten sick too."

"Sure, and gotten fired for it."

"So?" Jason asked, poking around in the tin of hard candies Rona kept on the corner of her desk. He selected a lime sour ball and popped it into his cheek. "You'd be free. You could get a good haircut and go to med school."

Rona snatched the candy tin out of Jason's hands as he reached for another. "Jason, the things you call her are going to get back to her one of these days. She will skin you alive."

Jason lifted his chin and gazed down at her. "Men born with phenomenal talent and possessed of a detached and sovereign aura are not skinned alive by dried-up editors with Chia Pet hairdos. Besides, my father would rotate her tires."

"I thought you didn't speak to your father," Rona said suspiciously.

"I don't. My mother does," he said, cracking the candy between his back molars. "Whenever he gets behind in the alimony payments, they have lunch and he tells her how terrific he is to distract her."

Jason craned his neck across the desk looking for the candy tin Rona had hidden. "You got any wintergreen? I love wintergreen."

"What's today's pile of junk?" she asked, dumping the rest of the hard candy into her top drawer and reaching for the envelope. "Maybe I finally get to buy something. I've done nothing but Pearl's castoffs for months."

Jason hooked one hip over the corner of her desk, sat down, and tapped the envelope. "Take a look at the return address on this one," he said with a sly grin. "This just might give the old star fucker her first orgasm since she and Charlie Manson got it on."

Rona made a face. "What are you talking about, Jason?" She lifted the package and squinted at the name in the upper left corner. "Oh, my God! Georgie," she squealed, grabbing the package.

"Well, excuuuuse me. *Georgie*, yet. That's one the tabloids forgot."

"Georgina Holmes. I used to work with her. She's an old friend. I can't imagine what's in here."

"Well, open it, Chickie Bean, and find out."

"I will," Rona said enthusiastically, without moving.

"When?"

"When I'm ready, Ja-SON," she snarled behind clenched teeth.

"But I want to see," he said in a mock whine.

"Beat it, Jason."

"You don't suppose it's an exposé, do you?" he said wide-eyed. " 'How I fucked Tanner Dyson and found a zillion bucks.' Listen, Rona, if she's not represented, just let me know and I'll speak to dear old Dad. There might be a nice little kickback in it, if you get my drift."

"Yeah. *Right*," Rona said. "Go."

Jason loped toward the door. He turned and opened his arms wide. "One day I shall own this establishment. Then I shall free you from your bonds of servitude and shower you with bubble gum and peanut sprinkles."

"Beat it, Jason, you're weird," Rona said, repressing a giggle.

Rona waited, listening to Jason singing a not-half-bad version of Aretha's *Respect* over the rumble of his mail cart as he moved down the ninth-floor hall to pester other editors. He was annoying at times but awfully cute.

As soon as he was out of earshot, she tore open the envelope and pulled out the neatly printed pages. At first glance it looked like a finished work.

She turned the stack of pages over and read the cover page. *"Handy Hints for the Harried Housewife,"* she read with a sinking heart. Oh, no, she sighed silently.

20

Jeffrey Dunsmore dressed the way rich people dress when they don't want people who might hit them over the head to know they are rich.

He wore vegetable-dyed T-shirts under neutral suits with immaculate white running shoes. That was during the day, when he hung around his father's East Side gallery.

What New York's muggers didn't seem to know was that the T-shirts were hand-finished silk and one hundred dollars a pop and his suits—never the same one twice in a given work week—were made by his personal tailor in Milan.

Restaurant captains and downtown-club door gorillas knew his clothes were expensive. Models and heiresses knew it too.

Neeva knew what he wore at night only from the pictures in the glossy magazines. His club uniform seemed to be a tux—with a black silk T-shirt.

As Neeva hung up the phone in her cubicle at the back of the gallery, she could see Jeffrey standing near the front door in an intense conversation with one of the dealers who came to every auction.

She felt terrible. She had lain awake the night before after hearing those vulgar, humiliating words—*"It's me, sugar tits . . . Mr. Happy's hard as a rock"*—until Irving was asleep. Then she got out of bed and curled up on the living room sofa, huddled under her mink coat, with the storage tag still dangling from the sleeve. She had felt utterly alone. Even Rose seemed to have given up on her. The sleepless night on the living room couch had left her head throbbing, and when she moved it too quickly, the big muscle in the back of her neck seized into a spasm.

Staring absentmindedly at Jeffrey, she sat thinking about the call she had just taken. Lolly Pines's assistant wanted her to handle the sale of the stuff in the incredible penthouse on Central Park West.

If Neeva hadn't been in such a state, she would have been thrilled. She knew the answer to all her problems might be at hand, but she was so exhausted she couldn't seem to focus on it. Instead she studied the effect of the overhead lights playing on Jeffrey's blue-black hair. Every now and then, when he raised his hand to pass it through his hair, a heavy gold ring on his right little finger caught in the light.

Jeffrey had spent several years bumming around Europe "studying art history"—his father had said with a sly wink—after he graduated from Brown. For the last couple of years he had been coming in to buy special pieces from dealers for his own collection.

Neeva didn't feel exactly maternal toward Jeffrey; he was only six or seven years younger than she was. She felt more like a big sister who flirts innocently with an adorable little brother.

"Jeff?" she called when she heard him saying good-bye to the man he had been talking to.

Jeff turned and headed toward her with a long, easy stride, his hands deep in the pockets of his full-cut trousers.

He entered the room and swooped into the chair facing her desk.

187

"Neeva, my weakness," he said with a broad grin. "Good morning. How's my favorite girl?"

Neeva knew she was, technically speaking, an attractive woman, but somehow she never felt as pretty as she did when Jeffrey flirted with her. Still, she said with a sigh, "It's not a good morning, Jeffrey. Not good at all."

"Who's making my Neeva unhappy? Tell me and I'll take care of it."

Neeva sighed and leaned back in her desk chair. "Jeffrey . . . you know everything. I mean you move around in some very fancy circles."

"Who says?"

"*Women's Wear Daily*, Richard Johnson, Liz Smith."

"Oh, them," he said. "They say that. My press agent says that. They just repeat it."

"Jeffrey Dunsmore, you don't need a press agent," Neeva said with a wry smile. "I've seen photographers leap out of nowhere to get your picture."

"Only when they can't find JFK, Jr.," he said, teasing. "Now, what were you going to ask me?"

"It's kind of personal."

"Oh, yum. What?"

"Do all men . . ."

"Yes, yes," he said eagerly, leaning forward.

"Do all men cheat?"

Jeffrey pressed an open palm to his chest. "You're in the auction business and you ask such a question?"

"I don't mean that. What I mean is do all men . . . screw around?"

"You're talking married men, right?"

"Well, married . . . committed . . . involved with one woman."

"*Hmmm*," he said, sitting back. "That's a goody."

"I know you're single, but you must know a ga-zillion people. Would you say that married men, in general, are unfaithful to their wives?"

188

Jeffrey put his fingertips together and pretended to be deep in thought.

"I would have to say, in general, by and large, under some circumstances, without any real scientific basis for my opinion . . . I don't know."

"Jeffrey, I'm going to smack you. You do too know. You just won't say because men stick together."

"What's the matter, sweet thing, Irving working too late these days?"

Neeva fought it for a heartbeat and then gave in and burst into tears.

Jeffrey leaned forward and grabbed both of her hands. "Ah, honey, don't. I'm sorry. I was just teasing," he said, stroking the back of one of her arms. "Geez, it looks like I hit a nerve."

Neeva reached for a tissue and pressed it against her eyes, then her nose.

"S'okay," she said. "I just had a bad night."

"I'll say," Jeffrey said sympathetically. "What can I do? Anything. I know, I'll get a bottle of champagne. We'll hire a hansom cab and ride around the park until lunch. Then I'll take you to Mortimer's for lunch."

"Jeffrey, hush and listen to me for a minute. I need some business advice. You're the only one I can talk to."

"Good. I think I'm better at business advice. My personal advice makes women cry," he said with a big grin.

She had never noticed how perfectly even and white his teeth were. Clearly the product of dentistry as expensive as the private schools and summer camps he had attended.

Neeva straightened her shoulders and lifted her chin. "I got a call this morning about a lot on the West Side. It's a penthouse, three floors."

"A penthouse? You mean the Lolly Pines estate?"

"You know about it?"

"Everybody in the business knows about it. We've all been drooling waiting to hear who owns the stuff. I hear the old trout didn't have any heirs."

"She does now. I just talked to her."

Jeffrey's handsome face brightened. "The stuff is clear?"

"Apparently so. Lolly Pines left everything in the place to her assistant, a woman named Kick Butler. I just spoke to her. She wants me to set up a sale as soon as possible."

"Hot damn!" Jeffrey whooped, smacking his hands together. "Does Dad know about this?"

"Not yet. I wanted to get some advice first."

"Hey, didn't I read that your husband represented Lolly Pines? No wonder she called you. You're on the ball, my friend."

Neeva stiffened and lowered her eyes. "Irving won't be involved in this at all, Jeffrey."

"Even better," he said with a smile.

"Jeffrey, do you have any idea who your father is going to be letting go? What I mean is, am I on the list?"

"Gee, I don't know, Neeva. I know there's going to be quite a bloodletting when it comes. Why? Do you think you might be laid off?"

"It's possible. Whatever happens, I've got to make more money than I make here."

"I see. And . . . ?"

"Jeff, you've handled some auctions on your own. If I wanted to do it too, what kind of money would I have to have up front?"

Jeff's eyes widened. "Well, that all depends."

"It's important. I don't have much, just a little trust from my mother. I'm also concerned about how your dad would feel about it. Those are my two major problems."

"I can't imagine Dad would mind. He's crazy about you. He'd much rather see you launch your own business than have to lay you or someone else off."

Neeva's mood lightened. She was glad she'd taken Jeffrey into her confidence. "Okay, let's assume I have Aubrey's blessing. I'd hate to lose his friendship by setting myself up as competition. What immediate costs are we talking about?"

Jeffrey reached for a spiral notepad on her desk and uncapped a heavy gold pen. He began to jot down items on the pad. "Let's see. You'll need to advertise. I can get you a good deal on a printer. If this woman wants to do this in a hurry, there won't be enough time for a really classy catalog, but that's okay. The Pines name will make up for that. You'll need a publicist; use mine," he said, looking up with a wicked grin. "Then, you need a secretary to handle the calls. You can have my friend Sal do the appraising. He owes me. You'll need an auctioneer and temporary staff for the exhibition and actual sale. Then there's trucks, moving men, renting storage and sale space . . . *hmmm.* It won't be cheap, my sweet. Figure . . . *um* . . . fifty thousand to do it right. Of course, you could see a nice profit when it's over, providing the stuff isn't total garbage."

"Fifty thousand!" Neeva pinched the bridge of her nose between a thumb and forefinger. "You're depressing me, Jeff. What was I thinking of? I have barely half of that."

Jeffrey studied the list for a long moment, then capped his pen and grinned. "I know where you could get the other half. Take in a partner."

"Oh, Jeffrey," Neeva said, her momentary enthusiasm draining away. "I don't know anyone who's nutty enough to invest in this."

"Yes, you do."

To Neeva's utter surprise, Jeffrey slid down onto the floor of her office and knelt in front of her. He clasped both of her hands and looked up at her imploringly.

"Beautiful, smart, lovely lady. May I be your partner?" he said grandly.

Neeva began to laugh. "Jeffrey, get up," she whispered urgently, glancing toward the door.

"Let me be your garbageman. Take my money and my mind. I will only waste it on wine and limousines."

"For pity's sake, Jeffrey!"

Jeffrey pulled his long frame up from the floor. He was still holding on to her hands. "I'm dead serious, Neeva. I'm bored out of my skull. Besides, I'm sentimental about Lolly Pines. The first time my name was in the paper was in her column. She had me at a party I didn't go to with a woman I didn't even know. I knew I had arrived. Come on, girl. Let me in on this."

Neeva gently removed her hands and looked up at him. Just the expression on his face was enough to convince her he wasn't kidding around. "What would your dad say?"

"My dad would shriek with joy that his playboy son had finally decided to do some heavy lifting. Come on, let's go ask him right now. Then we'll go have lunch to celebrate. This afternoon you'll take me up there, and we'll have a look. Whatever there is, we'll get our money back and have some fun."

Fun, Neeva thought. She couldn't remember doing anything fun for so long that, at the moment, it sounded like a life-sustaining goal.

Mortimer's was, as usual, packed. Neeva was relieved that she had chosen a bright red suit that morning. As she and Jeffrey waited at the front door for Glenn Birnbaum, the owner of the "in" little bistro on Lexington Avenue, to seat them, she could feel the staring eyes all around her. Mortimer's was the place where gossip started in Manhattan's smart set, and she could just picture cartoon balloons over people's heads asking what Mrs. Irving Fourbraz was doing on Jeffrey Dunsmore's arm. She recognized a few familiar faces who would know that Irving Fourbraz's wife was out to lunch with a handsome young man, but it wasn't enough to make the columns. Not unless she and Jeffrey did something outrageous, and that wasn't going to happen. This was business. Albeit glorious, new, exciting business that was still their secret.

It took them several minutes to reach their table. Jeffrey seemed to know, and have to speak to, half the people in the room.

Jeffrey had just ordered a bottle of champagne when he looked toward the door, ducked his head, and lowered his voice.

"Here comes a woman I know from the *Courier*. Don't turn around. She's headed this way. I'm going to get us some publicity if that's okay with you . . . partner."

Neeva smiled, grateful for Jeffrey's youthful, take-charge attitude toward the venture that she still didn't quite believe was happening.

"This is crazy, Jeffrey," she whispered. "What do we call ourselves?"

"*Hmmm,* I really shouldn't use *Dunsmore,* my dad might feel that was pushy."

"And I sure don't want to use Fourbraz," Neeva responded with a grimace. From the look on Jeffrey's face she could tell his journalist friend was getting closer. "Quick, Jeffrey, what champagne did you order?"

"Why . . . ah . . . ah . . . Moet et Chandon. Why?"

"Chandon Gallery," Neeva blurted out.

Jeffrey snapped his fingers. "Perfection. Chandon Galleries, make it plural. Think big."

Neeva was still laughing when Jeffrey stood and spoke to someone over her shoulder.

"Hi, sweetheart," he said exuberantly. "Come meet my partner."

Neeva turned to see a snub-nosed blond smiling down at her.

"Neeva, this is Baby Bayer from the Grapevine page of the *Courier,*" Jeffrey said, then turned to the blond. "Baby, this is my partner in Chandon Galleries, Neeva Fourbraz."

"Fourbraz," the blond said flatly as her smile snapped shut. "That's a most unusual name. Are you related to Irving Fourbraz?"

"Yes," Neeva said pleasantly, her hand suspended in midair. "Irving is my husband."

"How do you do," the blond said. She ignored Neeva's hand until she sheepishly withdrew it but continued to stare at Neeva's face as though checking for sloppy makeup.

"Why, Jeffrey," the blond bubbled, regaining her composure. "You have your own gallery? When did this happen?"

Jeffrey shot a glance at Neeva. "Recently, Baby, very recently. Our upcoming auction might interest you. We'll be handling the Lolly Pines estate."

Baby Bayer gasped. "I'd like to talk to you about that, Jeffrey. May I call you this afternoon?"

"Sure, you have my number. But Neeva here is the senior partner. Why don't you call her?"

"I'll call you later, Jeffrey," she said pointedly, giving him a fast air kiss and moving toward her table without even a glance at Neeva.

"Sweet," Neeva said in a dull voice, watching the woman distribute more air kisses to some man sitting against the exposed brick wall that ran along the side of the restaurant.

"Not," Jeffrey said, looking up as the waiter served the champagne. "But useful."

Neeva picked up her glass and held it toward him. "My toast first," she said.

"Okay." He grinned, lifting his own glass in response.

"To Neeva and Jeffrey's excellent new adventure . . ."

". . . and to Chandon Galleries . . . wherever they are."

They touched glasses and drank.

True to form, Neeva realized that she was afraid—this time afraid to be so incredibly happy.

21

*R*ona had gotten stuck on the Number 6 train and was ten minutes late for work. By the time she reached her office, Jason was standing in front of the door leaning on his mail cart.

As she stepped past him into her office he whispered, "Where have you been? It's shit city, babe. The Vile One is loose."

Rona looked up at him. "Is she looking for me?" she whispered back. "I mean me, specifically."

"Is Benihana her plastic surgeon?"

Rona felt her lips set in a thin, grim line. "Jason, don't fuck around. Did she actually walk down here or did she send Sheila? There's a big difference."

Jason raised his chin and gazed the length of the long corridor. "I saw the face of the Moondog myself."

"Oh, God," Rona moaned. "How long ago?"

Jason turned back to his cart. "At nine sharp."

"What did she want?"

"I'm supposed to know? She doesn't speak to peasants. But I

195

saw her come in here. When she came out, I heard her tell Kathy she wanted to see you in her office at ten."

"How long was she in here?"

"Only a couple of seconds."

"Ten? Oh, Christ." Rona sighed. "Did she ask nicely or did she snarl like she usually does?"

"She was so sweet I just now snapped out of my diabetic coma. Miss Perfect Executive. Where was that glass ceiling when we needed it?"

"You know how she got the job, Jason. Everybody knows," Rona said, tossing her raincoat onto the hook of a wooden tree behind the door.

"Tell me she didn't use sex. The mental picture is too revolting so soon after breakfast."

Rona walked to her desk and sat down. "Lionel Maltby," she said flatly.

"Figures," he said casually. "My father represents Lionel Maltby." He lifted Rona's snow-globe paperweight. He shook it, making it snow on the penguin trapped inside, and put it down. "The old fraud."

Rona looked up and gasped. "Jason, that's blasphemy around Winslow House. Do you know how much prestige we get from being his publisher? Pearl takes credit just because she bought his first novel."

"Did she buy his second?" Jason asked, cocking his head to one side.

"Of course."

"Then that makes her as big a fraud as he is, because he didn't write it."

Rona frowned up at him. "Jason, there's a lot of bullshit shoveled in this business. You don't have to believe all of it. There is no way a best-selling author like Lionel Maltby, with a wall full of awards, doesn't write his own novels."

Jason stood up and jammed his hands into the pockets of his twill slacks. "Wrong."

"Oh, Jason, how can you say that?"

"Because my mother wrote it. She got a flat fee. It paid for two years of boarding school, my braces, and new joysticks for my busted Atari."

Rona felt her chin drop. She stared at Jason for a long moment. There wasn't a doubt in her mind that he was telling the truth. "Oh, my God," she whispered. "Your mother. Doesn't she write bodice rippers for Haden Books? Suzanne Deavers, right?"

"Right. Remember *Kiss Me Until Dawn?*"

"Of course," Rona said, impressed. *Kiss Me Until Dawn* was one of the first really hot historicals of the early seventies. "How did your mother get together with Maltby?"

Jason lowered his dark brows at Rona and scowled. "Guess."

"Daddy dearest. Damn," she breathed. "There's no way Pearl didn't know about this, right?"

"No way, pussycat."

"And you've known this since you were a little kid. How could you not talk about it? It must have been rough."

"Surely you jest," Jason said grandly. "I've told anyone who will listen. But talking about something that's true and wrong only works when it cuts across the power structure. You think the guys I hung with were impressed? You think my girlfriends rail against the injustice of it all? Forget it. This is talk I save for when it will do my mom some good and put my phony old man in his place. I don't know how the opportunity will present itself or when, but I got time."

"Oh, God! Time. What time is it?" Rona said, panicking.

Jason checked his wrist. "Five to ten. You want an escort? I'll go with you. I don't want to miss this."

"Give me a minute," Rona said. She wanted to check her desk for clues to the possible reprimand that awaited her down the hall. She scanned the room pretending she had Pearl's eyes. What would displease her? Rona had no personal photos stuck to anything; she was careful about that. She had no hot plate, no cup warmer, no open containers of food remnants, all Pearl no-nos.

Other editors had been reprimanded, but never by Pearl

directly. She delegated housekeeping reprimands. If she found obscene sayings or cartoons pinned to bulletin boards or the sides of their computers. If windows were left open. If desks were not cleared upon leaving. Some rules changed weekly. Last week she wanted any houseplants that were not completely healthy removed. Rona took her African violet home. It was lush and wonderful, but it might turn on her overnight and throw a brown leaf.

Rona checked behind the door, where she usually kept her bike, allowed only because Pearl rode one to work. It was free of forbidden packages, rain boots, mufflers, or dress pumps for when she wore her Reeboks.

Her desk passed an equally careful inspection.

Rona sat down with a sigh. What the hell does she want? She pushed herself back up out of the chair, knowing the only way she would find out was to get down the hall to Pearl's corner office and get it over with. She found herself almost curious and oddly calm. Whatever it was, and it couldn't be anything good, she was prepared to defend herself—for once.

Some years earlier, after a savage divorce, Pearl Grubman had spent a great deal of her settlement money on plastic work— Winslow House's medical plan didn't cover cosmetic surgery. She had her face and eyes lifted and every tooth in her mouth capped. The face work gave her a skeletal look and the caps were so even and large the dentist apparently had decided against making them really white.

The combination of tight skin and gray teeth drained her face of any character it might have had. But it was Pearl's eyes one had to watch. They were framed by long brown bangs that tapered down her high-boned cheeks and looked like nothing so much as the eyes one sees through the slit of an assassin's hood.

Apparently breastless, she was given to wearing turtleneck sweaters with high, exaggerated tube collars that made her head appear to swivel like an owl's.

Pearl's door was open as Rona approached, having waved Jason off. Rona rapped on the side of the door with one knuckle.

"You wanted to see me?" she asked brightly.

Pearl was sitting at her desk, her back to the door. At the sound of Rona's voice she spun around in her chair. She swiveled her head without moving her shoulders and shouted, "Rona!"

Rona jumped, then started to giggle. It was more a nervous tic than laughter. "Hi, hi," she said, wiggling her fingers in a useless little wave.

"Sweetie! Come in," Pearl said, still shouting. "Love the outfit. Very Ralph Lauren. It's you."

Rona glanced down for an instant to remind herself what the hell she had put on that morning and saw a Gap denim miniskirt, a tattersall shirt she lifted from her little brother years ago, and a tapestry vest she found at a Village street fair.

"Sit," Pearl commanded.

Rona sat, thinking *good doggy*.

Rona looked around Pearl's office, known around the company as the Winter Palace. Set in a corner of the building, it had windows on two sides, shimmering silver vertical blinds, and a mahogany wet bar in the bookshelves that ran the length of one wall. Pearl had brought in a wicker love seat and chairs covered with a tight little pattern of wildflowers, none of which went with the industrial-gray carpeting and silver blinds.

Pearl stood. "Love your hair. Tell me how you've been?"

Pearl's tone was very just-us-girls, a tone Rona hadn't heard since the Christmas party the first year Rona came to Winslow House. Having thrown back too many rum and cokes, Pearl had put her arm around Rona's shoulder and asked her all kinds of questions, proving she had read Rona's résumé carefully. She told her how impressed she was with her and how she was going to be the star editor with a big, big future at Winslow House. The next morning Pearl had passed her in the hall without a word.

"I've been great, Pearl. Just . . . ah . . . great." She pawed around in the spongy tundra of her small-talk reserve. All she could dredge up was, "How 'bout those Mets?" and "Gettin' any lately?" Men were lucky, their small talk was so much more accessible.

She decided to wait Pearl out. She glanced over Pearl's shoulder to where a vertical line of photographs was hung between the windows. The largest photo, framed in black lacquer with a gold mat, was, of course, of Lionel Maltby. He was sitting on a craggy outcropping, his thick hair blowing across his craggy face, wearing a craggy plaid wool shirt.

There was Pearl with British columnist Abner Hoon on a banquette at the Russian Tea Room, where they celebrated the publication of his collection of articles on the royals; Pearl with Dr. Sonia Wiener, who wrote *Change Positions, Change Your Life.* Pearl's all-time best-selling sex-book acquisition. Rona remembered having edited it over one Christmas break with an impacted wisdom tooth. Below Dr. Wiener was Pearl with Southern humorist Randy Bagley, whose last book was called *Different Is Nice But It Sure Ain't Pretty.* Rona had given up her share in a house in Provincetown to edit that one last summer. The book had been dedicated to "My muse, Pearl Grubman, who cast herself before my swine."

Rona tented her fingers and broadened her smile. "So?" she said, trying to sound cheerfully expectant.

"Rona," Pearl said, having modulated her voice to a lilt. Now she sounded like the Church Lady. "I understand you are a good friend of Georgina Dyson."

Damn, Rona thought, the only one who knew that was Jason, and he wouldn't have told Pearl if she had put hot paper clips under his eyelids. Somebody was meddling, and she had a creepy feeling she'd better be careful about her answers.

"Well, ah . . . we worked together at *Fabulous Foods,*" Rona offered cautiously. "I'd say we were more office pals than close friends. She was a very talented food designer."

A tiny muscle at the side of Pearl's nose, one of the few the plastic surgeon left usable, twitched. *"Fabulous Foods?* The magazine? You worked there?" Pearl, the résumé reader, asked.

"Right."

"*Ummm,*" Pearl said, dropping her eyes in apparent disappointment. "That was before she married Tanner Dyson."

"Long before."

"So you must have gone to the wedding?" she asked, her expression brightening with anticipation.

"Oh, no. As I say, we were office friends. We sort of lost touch after I left to come here. Not long after that, she left to go to work for the *Courier*. That's how she met Tanner Dyson."

"Then you never met him?" Pearl asked, her face closing again.

"Actually, I did."

Pearl's taut face switched back to hopeful.

"I was standing in front of Bloomingdale's one night when a big limo pulled up Third Avenue and Georgina called out the window. They drove me home. He's very good-looking and quite nice."

"They . . . drove . . . you . . . home," Pearl said slowly. "Ah-huh, I see."

"I guess you're asking because Georgina just sent me a manuscript," Rona said, knowing that was as close as she dared get to challenging Pearl to tell her how she knew about the manuscript in the first place.

"Right," Pearl's face resumed its mask, her thin lips closing over her long gray teeth. Pearl's sense of entitlement was so total Rona knew she could ignore the implied question. "I noticed it's not in the log. We rather like to have submissions put in the log."

Pearl's eyes burned into Rona's collarbone. Pearl had a hard time looking directly at anyone, preferring the middle distance of the body—collarbone, belt buckle, and in some cases, crotch.

"Sorry. I was going to do that today."

"*Ummm.* And have you read it?"

"Oh, yes," Rona said. Thank God.

"And . . . ?"

Rona pinched the bridge of her nose against an oncoming killer headache. "Pretty ordinary stuff. We kind of covered the same territory with Nancy Gillian's *Happy Homes.* Then of course there's *The Whole Dirt Catalogue.*"

"*The Whole Dirt Catalogue* is not a Winslow House book," Pearl said in an instructing-the-retarded tone.

"That's my point. I don't think we can compete."

Pearl leaned back and lifted a pink phone slip from the pile on her desk. "Do you know what this is?"

"Sorry, Pearl, I just got here."

"Of course," she said with a sour smile. "This is my second call from Rob Roy Kadanoff since nine o'clock. That's the time we start here, by the way."

Never complain, never explain. Rona reminded herself glumly. Pity old R. R. Kadanoff doesn't have to take the subway. "I take it Mr. Kadanoff is a friend of Tanner Dyson."

Pearl extended her ribbed cashmere neck to its fullest. For the first time the assassin's eyes in the E.T.-like head bored into Rona's face. "Buy Georgina's book, Rona," she hissed. "Offer fifty to start."

Rona stood and smoothed the sides of her skirt. "Fifty," she said evenly.

"Go up in twenty-five-thousand increments. If he gets you over one hundred, call me in."

"One . . . hundred . . . thousand dollars?" Rona said, trying not to choke, reminding herself that this was Pearl the paper-clip queen, who had her secretary slip them off of submissions before mailing them back. Pearl, who would question dessert on an expense-account lunch. Pearl, who spent Winslow House money as though it were blood dripping slowly from her own slashed wrists.

"That's right," Pearl said. "Let him keep foreign rights if he pushes."

"Excuse me, Pearl. I missed something. Who is this 'he' I'm throwing money at?"

"Here," Pearl said, extending her arm. Between two scarlet nails dangled a scrap of paper. "This is Irving Fourbraz's phone number. He's representing her. You do know who Irving Fourbraz is?"

"Yes, Pearl. I have a TV," Rona said patiently, and took the slip of paper. "I'll call him right away."

She walked down the hall holding the paper with two fingers, much as Pearl had.

Pearl.

Hate is exciting, she thought. There is a heat in it that is oddly warming.

22

*A*bner Hoon's instrument of pleasure was the telephone, and his drug of choice was dish.

There was a phone in his little Triumph, a phone in his ever-present briefcase, and phones in every room of his shabbily genteel apartment just off Sloane Square. In the last few years he had started to carry a Wizard, a palm-size computer into which he was able to program the thousands of phone numbers he needed to exist.

For thirty years he had carefully built, layer upon layer, his global network of contacts, much as Lolly Pines had done. And barely a day had passed in all those years that he hadn't devoted at least a half-hour's phone conversation to her. For someone as involved with the workings of the world as Abner, a half-hour was an extraordinary amount of time.

It was not until his first morning back in his flat in London that he truly felt the impact of Lolly's death. He found himself reaching for his bedside phone. He got as far as punching in the

U.S.A. code before he realized what he was doing. Slowly, he put down the phone. His life had irrevocably changed.

The following day he arranged his phone schedule minus the Lolly half-hour. At first he felt a twinge of grief whenever he turned to the page in the *Courier* where Lolly's column used to run, but by the third week with no Lolly, he began to wonder, idly, when they were going to find a replacement for her. Life, after all, went on.

On Monday morning Abner arrived in the seedy city room of the *London Gazette*, the last tabloid left on Fleet Street, at precisely eight o'clock, as was his habit. He could have done his work anywhere, but he much preferred the theater of the city room, where he could be seen and heard plying the gossipist's trade.

He had just started reading a fax copy of Liz Smith's column in *Newsday*—sent to him each morning by the *Gazette*'s New York bureau—when his phone console buzzed.

"Hoon here," he said in the especially flutey voice he saved for phone greetings.

"Mr. Hoon?" It was the city-room phone receptionist. "Kensington Palace on line two."

Abner snapped to attention and stood up. He always stood at his desk when Princess Margaret called, not only out of old Tory respect but also to let his colleagues know he was speaking to a royal.

When he heard Her Royal Highness's voice, a protracted pronunciation of his name that sounded like "Aaaaahb-nuh," he cradled the phone on his shoulder and slipped into his suit jacket.

"Good morning, ma'am," he said, loudly enough for those sitting around him to hear. "Thank you, ma'am. A most eventful trip . . . Yes, yes, awful shock."

He paused and listened to the princess tell a long-winded anecdote about the time she had been at a table at Aly Khan's villa in Sardinia with Lolly Pines. He wasn't listening carefully. He was searching his mind for something riveting to pass along to the princess. He knew she only phoned him for gossip she wasn't likely to read in his column. Gratuitous gossip was Abner's coin, and he spent it freely.

The princess signaled the approaching end to her story when she began to laugh and snort simultaneously.

"Oh, my, your Highness, that is pure Lolly. What a marvelous story, but of course, I shan't breathe a word," he said with a nasal guffaw.

"Oh, the Garn party . . . Yes, yes, of course. The whole purpose of my trip, ma'am."

Good Lord, he thought. What could he tell her about the dreadful Garn party except that it was drippingly hot?

Suddenly he remembered something he could pass along from the soiree. It would have to be embroidered a bit, but, as with all his tattle, the truthful essence would remain intact.

"Well, ma'am," he said, lowering his voice to a near whisper. "Everyone . . . all the ladies in New York are having this new treatment done. It's really too risqué for the phone . . . *ummm* . . . *ummmm.*"

He looked around to see who was listening. All heads turned back to their work as he cupped his hand over the phone. "Well, Your Highness. It has to do with this ersatz Hungarian countess named . . . ah . . . named . . ."

He thought quickly for a Hungarian-sounding name. "Yanna, yes, Yanna. She is all the rage. What she does is called the Venus treatment. It has to do with . . . shall we say, a very special kind of hair styling. How should I put this? Ah, below the waist."

He listened to her delighted response. "Yes, yes . . ." he said enthusiastically. "Oh, my, yes . . . very expensive."

He knew he had the princess's rapt attention. Now his imagination moved into high gear. "Rather like topiary for the nether regions; zebra stripes, flora, hearts, all sort of inventive designs." He paused for an instant wondering if he should push further. "And . . . I'm told—even coats of arms."

He listened while the princess hinted around about Madame Yanna's availability. Would she travel? How could she be discreetly contacted?

"Yeeessss, well, I suppose I could. It would take some phoning about. A crown? I don't see why not, Your Highness. It seems to me it would work. Yes . . . yes . . . well, let me see what I can find out. Will I be seeing you at Lady Duncan-Knolls' on Thursday? Marvelous, marvelous. Ta for now, thanks awfully for ringing."

Abner hung up without bothering to suppress a wheezing chuckle. If he were a betting man, he would have laid odds on the story reaching his ear from another venue before the sun set. He could only speculate as to what services his invented Madame Yanna would be providing by nightfall. God help him if the princess really wanted . . . No, he told himself, returning his attention to the fax machine that was still humming away, impossible. Not the princess.

He glanced down to see the *New York Courier*'s Grapevine page in the earlier edition of the paper inching across his desk. When the fax cutter thumped across the finished page, he picked it up.

A little black book found in the Santa Monica motel where Keeko Ram's party got out of hand earlier this month may be introduced into evidence at the upcoming inquest. Seems that Maria-Louisa Lopez is an "actress" who up until her unfortunate and speedy exit over the balcony railing of the Santa Monica motel worked for an international escort service to the jet set under the name of Monica Champagne. It seems Ms. Champagne had more celebrity friends than just baby-faced TV throbber Keeko Ram. Sources say some of the names will not only have official Washington shook up but will give Queen Elizabeth a bad case of the tiara trembles. Miss Lopez-Champagne is in the hospital in Los Angeles and not expected to be well enough to appear in court this week to press charges. Her attorney, celebrity lawyer Irving Fourbraz, will do it for her. Stay tuned.

When he started to read the item, Abner recognized it as the tired old Little Black Book Story. Whenever a call girl made the headlines, the follow-up story invariably involved a little black book. Never, to his knowledge, were the contents of little black books ever published, but it did serve to keep the story alive when there was no news to report. However, when the words "Queen Elizabeth" jumped off the page, he knew he couldn't ignore the implications. What if there was a book? What if there were names that would interest the *Gazette* readers as much as, if not more than, the Americans?

He glanced up at the wall clock and cursed. It would still be the middle of the night in New York. But it was worth the risk of being rude.

He consulted his Wizard and tapped Baby's home number into the console.

He listened to the click, click, clicking of the fiber-optic cables deep under the Atlantic, then slammed down the phone.

"Busy," he muttered in disgust. How could anybody in their right mind be on the phone at three o'clock in the morning?

It would take him another five minutes to get the overseas operator to force through the line with an emergency call.

Baby rolled over on her stomach, put the phone receiver on the pillow for a moment, and leaned over the side of the pullout couch to retrieve what was left of an anchovy pizza on the floor. From the receiver she could hear Irving moaning. He was jerking off from his library phone and was just about finished.

She took a big bite, shifted it to her right cheek, and panted, "Do it for me, sugar, I love it when you come." She shifted the hunk of pizza back and began to chew slowly, periodically making low groaning noises.

"I'm gonna come, doll," Irving said. At least that's what she thought he said, he was panting and thrashing about so hard. She could hear the leather chair he always sat in squeaking away.

Baby tore off a piece of crust, popped it in her mouth, and chewed. "Shoot it, sugar bunny. Shoot it all over me." She listened to more panting and squeaking, suppressing a yawn. She was exhausted. It was after three.

There was a snapping on the line. Baby thought Irving was doing something weird with the receiver and rolled over with a groan of boredom.

"Ms. Bayer. This is the London operator. We have an emergency call for you from a Mr. Abner Hoon."

Baby sat bolt upright, her foot narrowly missing the edge of the pizza box. "What the fuck?"

"Baaaabbbeeee!" Irving shrieked. "Honey cunt! I'm coming."

"Irving," Baby shouted. "Irving, I gotta get off."

"I know, sugar tits, use your hand, a candle, anything."

"Irving, I mean I gotta get off the phone. Didn't you hear that? It's an emergency call coming through."

"Ms. Bayer? Will you take the call?"

"Oh, shit," Baby hissed. "Irving, people can hear you. Operator? Is Mr. Hoon on the line?"

"Hoon here," a flutey voice said over another moan from Irving. "Is that you, Baby? What's going on?"

Baby started to hoot with laughter. "Irving," she said between yelps. "Hang up, for Christ's sake."

"Yeah, yeah," Irving slurred. "Okay, dollface. Love you."

Baby didn't even respond to Irving. She was too excited that Abner Hoon was calling her. She heard him click off the line and bounced to the edge of the bed.

"Abner? I'm here," she called. "How *are* you?"

"Simply super, my dear. What was all that racket on the line?"

"Oh, ah . . . nothing. Just saying good night to a friend."

"He sounded as though he was in some distress."

"No problem, Abner," Baby said. "Gosh, it's great to hear from you. What's up?"

"I just read today's Grapevine. The item about the Keeko Ram girl," Abner said lightly.

"You saw it? How? It's in tomorrow's paper."

"It's in your early edition, darling. I have it faxed to me before nine our time," he said, sounding a bit smug.

Baby flopped back onto the bed. "Of course," she said, "Silly me."

"Listen, Baby . . . about that item. Can I assume it's yours?"

The excitement of having Abner call was instantly replaced with the cold sweat of getting caught. Irving had fed her that item. They both knew there was nothing to it, but there hadn't been anything about the girl in the papers for days. He thought maybe a foreign angle would respark some interest. That's why she put in that crap about the queen.

"Baby? Are you still there?"

"Oh, yes, Abner, ah . . . the cat . . . ah . . . was trapped in the bathroom," Baby said lamely.

"About the item," Abner persisted. "What is that reference to the queen all about? We'd be interested."

"What makes you think I wrote that, Abner?" Baby cooed.

"Now, Baby, I know you and Irving are an item. I've refrained from putting something about it in my column. I wouldn't want anyone to question your . . . professional ethics."

Baby wanted to change the subject.

"Maybe she's one of the girls who Concorde over and do the Prince of Wales," Baby said.

"The Prince of Wales?" Abner scoffed in a highly offended tone. "I'd have to seriously doubt that."

"Benny Hill then?" Baby was having fun. What harm would it do? Let Abner get sucked into the game along with everyone else.

"Baby, you're not being coy with me by any chance, are you?"

"Me? Coy? Why Abner, how could you think that?"

"Then you can assure me that she had something to do with—let's call them clients—here? I mean important people. Names."

"Oh, absolutely. No doubt about it," she lied, rolling her eyes at Abner's gullibility.

"Baby?"

Oh, goody, she thought. He was beginning to whine. She loved it when important people whined at her. "What, Abner?"

"If you get anything along those lines, would you ring me immediately? My office, my home, the car, on my cellular phone . . . anywhere, anytime. I'll fax you the numbers."

"Sure, Abner," she lied.

"Now, I have a goody for you. I found out what the Venus treatment is."

"*Oooooh*, do you know?"

"*Ummmm*."

"Tell."

"Are you sure you don't have something for me on the girl?"

Baby thought for a moment. She knew she'd better give him something. Getting on Abner's network was important. But she dared not give him something that wouldn't check out. It was one thing to hint and tease, quite another to deliberately stick someone like Abner Hoon with a bad item.

"Well, I can tell you this, but you have to cover me."

"I always cover a source, my dear."

"Irving has signed on with one of the weekly tabloids for the Lopez girl's exclusive story."

"Which one?"

"Tell me about Venus."

"In a minute," Abner said with increasing agitation. "Was it the *World*?"

"*Ummmm*, could be."

"How much did they pay?"

"Big bucks. He did the deal right from the hospital. She was lying there at City of Angels trussed up like a Christmas goose. Irving marched right in and made the deal. Irving owns every word she speaks in perpetuity."

"City of Angels?" Abner asked blithely. "That's in Los Angeles?"

Baby was getting annoyed with his questions. It was late, she was tired, and she didn't like the way he said "Los Angle-ease," either. "Yes, Abner. Now, what's a Venus treatment?"

"Well," he said, exhaling elaborately. "How can I put this delicately? It has to do with . . ."

Baby settled back into the pillows. Another few minutes on the phone wasn't going to kill her.

* * *

Baby was late for her Wednesday lunch date with Irving at Café des Artistes. Sitting in the back of a cab she had urged to speed uptown, she practiced the dialogue she'd planned to have with Irving ever since she had run into Jeffrey Dunsmore at Mortimer's the week before.

Once she and Irving were seated facing each other on a red velvet banquette opposite the bar, she waited until they were almost finished with their first drink. She was about to launch into what was bugging her when Irving's phone buzzed in his briefcase under the table.

Baby repaired her lipstick while Irving took the call. She was getting used to his constant accessibility and had learned to tune his conversations out. Unless he screamed. When he screamed, as he was doing now, he got her attention.

"What do you mean they kidnapped her!"

The tissue Baby was blotting her mouth with hung from her wet lips as her hand froze in midair. Every head within earshot turned in fascination.

Oops, Baby thought. Abner Hoon. City of Angels.

Oh, well. Irving should know better than to trust someone like her with classified information.

"Don't lie to me. You're a bigger whore than your daughter. How much did those Brit bastards pay?" It was Maria Lopez's mother, and what Baby was witnessing was Irving's deal for the girl's story blowing up in his face. Apparently, Maria Lopez had made her own deal with the *London Gazette*, and her mother was now trying to make Irving believe that she had been kidnapped from the hospital.

Baby hadn't known Irving long enough to know if he could be any madder than he was at that moment, but from the color of his face and his bulging eyes, she doubted it. He slammed the phone on the table so hard she expected it to smash into little pieces.

"Irv, sweetie, take it easy," Baby whispered urgently.

"Take it easy? Take it easy!" he blurted. "Those guys at the *World* are going to have my testicles flying from their car antennas. How could that broad do this to me?"

"How much did they pay you?"

"Fifty," Irving groaned, and reached for his drink. "Okay, seventy-five. I had expenses."

"I assume they'll want the whole seventy-five back when the *Gazette* runs the story."

"Shit!" Irving hit the tabletop hard enough to make their glasses jump. "Two-faced bitch! Tries to tell me the girl was kidnapped. She got tired of waiting for the money and signed another deal. Just because she hasn't been paid, she thinks she doesn't have to honor our agreement."

"Irv," Baby said quietly. "You spent her money, didn't you?"

"Details," he grunted. "Whose side are you on?" Irving ran his hand across his receding hairline. "Christ, this screws up everything."

"So, just pay the *World* back," Baby said lightly.

From the look in Irving's eyes at her lighthearted suggestion, there was no doubt as to the root of his excessive anger. He took another long pull on his scotch and soda. "I need cash," he muttered, looking around the room as though he might spot someone to put the touch on. "Where the fuck am I going to get cash?"

"That's a lot of cash, honey."

He leaned against his velvet seat back. His face was now drained of color under his perpetual sunlamp tan. "Shit," he said. It was more a sigh than an expletive.

"Irving," Baby said, leaning toward him and speaking through clenched teeth. "Why don't you just write a check?"

Irving hooked his thumbs under his belt and bit his lower lip. "What am I going to cover it with, babe?" he snapped. "Like you said, I spent it. That money is gone. Kaput. I had expenses. I need cash, folding money, long green, and I've got to get it to Dave Kasko before the shit hits the fan."

Baby didn't like the sound of this one bit. "I could go give this Kasko guy a blow job."

Irving didn't seem to notice her sarcastic tone. "You're good, honey, but not seventy-five grand good."

Baby remained silent.

"Let me think for a minute, babe. There's gotta be a way," he said, raising his hand to signal the waiter. "You want another?"

Baby nodded, then leaned closer. Now was the time. "Listen, Irv. What about your wife?"

Irving stared back at her. He had never even mentioned his wife to Baby. She was not something they discussed.

"What about my wife?" he said.

Baby was relieved at least that he hadn't tried to deny he had one. That would have been truly dumb, but even smart men got dumb on that subject.

"She's got to have money," Baby said, determined to force him to discuss the subject.

"Neeva? Money? Ha." He snorted. "She's part of the reason I'm so tapped out."

Baby stared down into her fresh drink for a few minutes, intently stirring it with the little plastic stick tourists thought was a straw. Irving was lying through his caps, and she didn't like it.

"Baby?" Irving said softly, brushing the back of her hand until she looked up. "How do you know about my wife?"

"I met her a few days ago," Baby said, looking somewhere over his shoulder. She wished she could work up a tear or two, but her ducts weren't cooperating.

Irving lowered his drink without taking a sip. "You met her? You met Neeva? Where the hell did you meet Neeva?"

"At Mortimer's," Baby said, finally looking at him.

"Oh, yeah."

"She was having lunch with her partner."

"Her partner? Neeva has a partner?"

Baby was amazed he could keep a straight face. "In her new auction business. Wait, I have my notes."

Baby pawed around in her purse and plucked out a little red leather book. She flipped it open and read. "The Chandon Galleries, Irving." She was so furious he was lying to her, she all but shouted his name.

"What are you so pissed about? What did I do?"

"They're going to auction Lolly Pines's estate."

"News to me."

"Bull-boring-shit, Irving Fourbraz. You were Lolly's lawyer. Now your wife is gonna make even more money for the two of you auctioning her things. You sit here poor-mouthing, telling me your wife spends you dry, while all the time she's a big-deal gallery owner. Now you're pretending it's all news to you. Where am I in this picture, huh? Huh?"

"Baby . . ." Irving said helplessly, his face flushed, this time with embarrassment at the scene she was making.

"You know I deserve Lolly's job. Are you trying to get it for me? No. But you don't hesitate to throw wifey a piece of the Lolly action. Thanks for nothing, Irving. Thanks for fucking nothing."

"Calm down, Baby. I thought we were working out my problem here. How come you started up with all this stuff?"

"You don't know what a problem is, Irving. You're lying to me about your wife and how much money you have. I was all set to be sympathetic until you goddamn lied to me. You just want me to listen to your fantasy problems while you do nothing to help me with mine."

There was no way she was going to admit she had been planning to pounce on him before she even arrived. The fact that he was in trouble and vulnerable—if he really was—was just plain good luck. Her anger at him was further fueled by having witnessed him blowing a lucrative deal. Seeing the man in her life outfoxed by some hooker was not pretty. Slick, clever Irving didn't look so clever anymore.

"Irving, you don't want to help me. You just wanted a hot fuck. Well, you can just go fuck your fancy-ass wife and leave me alone."

Finally, the tears came. Baby made no attempt to staunch the flow. She wanted everyone who was staring to see them.

"Baby, Baby," Irving protested, trying to push her back down into her seat. "Calm down. You don't understand. My wife has nothing to do with us."

Her free hand swept across the table, collecting her scarf,

notebook, and purse as she wrenched her shoulder out of his grasp.

"Yeah, yeah, yeah," she snarled. "The check is in the mail. This won't hurt a bit and I'll only put it in an inch. Tell me another one—asshole."

Furious, she slammed out of the bar, through the main dining room, and headed for the door, interested eyes following her all the way.

It wasn't until she had crossed Broadway that she realized she had scooped up Irving's portable phone in her sweep of the table. She dropped it into her purse and stepped off the curb to hail a cab.

She was tired of waiting around for Irving to use his influence to get her Lolly's job. This always happened when she counted on a man. She hadn't met one yet who didn't, in the end, let her down. She sat on Joe Stone's face for months and look what it got her. Now she'd wasted her time with Irving. He wasn't going to do a damn thing for her.

She spotted a cab moving through the light at the corner. She waited until she could see the driver's face, then placed two fingers to her lips. She liked to watch their expressions when they heard the piercing whistle she had perfected. This time, the driver responded by slicing across two lanes to get to her.

Once inside the cab she pulled out Irving's phone and placed a call to London.

23

Wednesday afternoon, Neeva let herself out of Lolly's penthouse, tired but pleased with the day's work. It was truly amazing to her that anyone could have accumulated so much stuff in one lifetime, but to her and Jeffrey's delight, there *was* gold buried under the rubble. As she hailed a cab cruising down Central Park West, she thought about how much her life had changed in only a week.

The afternoon of their celebratory lunch at Mortimer's she had called Kick and taken Jeffrey over for their first look at Penthouse 3. Kick had greeted them as if they were paramedics, throwing her arms around Neeva momentarily and pumping Jeffrey's hand several seconds too long. Neeva had explained the standard arrangements—ten percent on big-ticket items, twenty percent on things valued at less than $2,000—to Kick on the phone earlier, so she suggested they get right to it.

On the guided tour Kick graciously provided, Jeffrey remained utterly silent. At first Neeva thought he was simply being professional, not wanting to remark on the value of anything he

217

saw. After Kick walked them back to the foyer and let them out, thanking them profusely for rescuing her, Neeva realized that Jeffrey wasn't so much professional as he was stunned.

He waited until Kick had locked the door behind them before he leaned toward Neeva.

"Do you believe this?" he breathed. "I've done a lot of these graveyard runs with my dad, but I don't think I've ever seen anything like this."

Neeva tried to suppress a giggle. "It is remarkable, isn't it? Kick tried to warn me, but I had no idea."

"This is critical mass, Neeva. Didn't the old nut ever throw anything out?"

"I don't think so. It's a good thing she died when she did. Another year and this place would have caved through the floor."

Neeva and Jeff returned to Neeva's office to work out the details of how they were going to deal with a project neither one of them had realized would be so complicated. It was close to midnight that night before Jeffrey had completed the workup of their immediate expenses and gave Neeva the bad news.

Their start-up expenses had to cover renting warehouse space, hiring a moving van, a Dumpster permit and equipment for trash, daily cash payments to workers and the appraiser, and another pair of hands to catalog each item.

Jeffrey's enthusiasm never flagged. It was Neeva, of course, who got scared. It took Jeffrey another hour that night to calm her down, to reassure her that there were far more valuable items in the penthouse than either of them could have imagined. The fact that it had belonged to Lolly Pines made even the weird old junk a potential gold mine. They were on their way to a smashingly successful sale.

Neeva insisted on putting up her trust fund first. They needed twenty-five thousand immediately, all the money Neeva had in the world. The next morning she went to Chase Manhattan Bank, cashed in her mother's trust, and put it into a new account. The bank promised to messenger checks marked "Chandon Galleries" to her as soon as possible.

Neeva and Jeffrey had started work immediately that day, sorting and flagging trash versus sale items for the movers. It had been fun working together. Neeva smiled, thinking of Jeffrey's energy and enthusiasm. He was really something special.

She was still smiling when she pushed through the revolving doors of Trump Tower. There was a bulky manila envelope from Chase Manhattan waiting for her at the concierge's desk. Her new checks! The concierge also handed her a message from the appraiser saying that the tall case clock on the penthouse landing was eighteenth-century Chippendale, rare and valuable enough by itself, to bring them a profit.

Neeva closed her eyes for a moment, feeling a bit dizzy with the news. Her luck was holding. She had been on her own for only a few days, and already she and Jeffrey knew that under the mountains of rubbish there were indeed treasures, important pieces that would guarantee an attention-getting auction, big prices, and a delicious profit after all the bills were paid.

The clock could be added to the other items that would be featured in the display ads she planned to run, along with the two grime-encrusted Federal Pembroke tables she had uncovered under a pile of old clothes in a back hall and two early nineteenth-century Paris porcelain urns that Lolly had kept pencils in.

Exhausted but exhilarated, Neeva looked at the envelope in her hand. The checks were the first tangible evidence that she was truly in business for herself. The dream that had started in her frightened mind as a seemingly half-baked bid for emotional and financial freedom was starting to come true. Just as the elevator door opened, she turned to see the concierge rushing across the lobby toward her.

"I'm sorry, Mrs. Fourbraz, I forgot to give you a message. Mr. Fourbraz was in earlier. He said to tell you he'll be out this evening."

Neeva's happy delirium faded. She nodded grimly. "Thank you, Manuel."

She stepped into the elevator with a nod to the operator.

Why did Irving bother? He was out every night but still kept up the pretense of leaving her a message. She wished he wouldn't. It only reminded her of the ongoing tension between them. Her work in the penthouse had permitted her to maintain a state of denial about what or who was keeping Irving occupied and out night after night.

The part of her brain that knew Irving was having an affair had gone numb. As long as he wasn't rubbing her nose in it, she could bear it. The only thing she wished he would do was pay some bills. The envelopes in the lobby mailbox contained more and more charge-account bills from angry stores. The envelopes had ominously changed color in the past month. Most were now a bright and angry yellow.

Neeva had no intention of paying any of them. She had stopped charging anything. Unpaid bills had always bothered her, but knowing she hadn't charged anything at least left her guilt free. She was now living in a different world. It was her world, and messages from Irving about his whereabouts weren't any part of it.

She let herself into the apartment and tossed her keys on the silver dish on the foyer table. Hugging the envelope containing her new checks to her chest, she kicked off her shoes and padded into the bedroom. She sat on the bed just holding the envelope, savoring the anticipation.

Finally, she started to open it. As soon as she did, she realized there was something wrong. The envelope looked as if it had been opened, then clumsily resealed. Tendrils of fear licked at Neeva's heart. She found herself moving at a run to Irving's wood-paneled den. It smelled, as always, of lemon furniture polish and cigar smoke. Neeva walked to Irving's untidy desk, telling herself there was absolutely nothing to worry about.

In the middle of a pile of papers was . . . one of her new checkbooks. A slip of paper lay next to it. It was a deposit slip from her new account. She turned it over. On the back, someone had written "Neeva M. Fourbraz" several times. It looked almost exactly like her signature. She picked up the checkbook and flipped through it. She immediately saw that the first check was gone.

Trying to remain calm, Neeva picked up the phone and called the Chase information number listed in her checkbook. It didn't take long to discover that her worst fears were true. The check was cashed. She dropped the phone back into its cradle.

Irving. The bastard had forged a check and cleaned out her account. And the half-hearted way he had tried to cover his tracks was insulting in its clumsiness.

She didn't care if Irving had taken the money for a quadruple bypass. If he told her the son he never talked about or spoke to needed a liver transplant or if Mafia hit men were waiting in the lobby to remove his legs, nothing justified what he had done. Nothing.

The only times Neeva had ever been in a bar by herself were when she arrived early to meet Irving. Then she would smile sweetly at whoever was on the door, tell them she was expecting her husband, take a discreet table against the wall, and order Perrier until Irving showed up.

She never thought of the bar in the Oak Room at the Plaza as a bar. It was too elegant, with its high ceiling, burnished wood paneling, and high windows facing Central Park. The Oak Room clientele was usually better-dressed, better-looking than the patrons of most other meeting places around midtown. The management was careful about suspiciously dressed and madeup women and kept a watchful eye on behavior that wasn't absolutely correct. A woman her age, dressed as she was, in a proper little gray silk suit, could easily be a guest in the hotel and wouldn't have any problems having a quiet drink alone at the end of the day.

The captain just inside the Oak Room entrance bowed slightly from the waist and smiled as she stepped through the door. There were a few couples scattered at tables around the elegant room. There were more people at the bar, some men standing behind several women on stools.

"I'm alone," Neeva told the captain. She held her chin up and her shoulders back for a look of confidence she didn't feel.

The captain held his smile. "For dinner?" he asked, gesturing vaguely in the direction of the dining room to his right with a large menu.

"Just drinks, please."

"Would you prefer a table or the bar?"

"A table, please."

"Right this way, ma'am."

As the captain headed toward the corner near the window, Neeva changed her mind. The laughter and chatter coming from the people at the bar made it seem less conspicuous than sitting alone at a table.

"I think the bar," she said to the captain's dark shoulders.

Instantly, he turned around and held out his arm. "My pleasure," he said. "Right this way." He led her to a stool at the far end next to the mirrored wall. "Will this be all right? We're pretty full this time of night."

Neeva smiled and slipped onto the stool. "This is fine, thank you. I have a nice view from here."

"You'll let me know if you'd like to stay for dinner," he said pleasantly, and backed away.

Neeva didn't know what to order. She usually only had wine with dinner. Everyone around her seemed to be drinking some sort of hard drink. She was studying the others' drinks when the bartender slid an inverted glass triangle on a high stem filled with clear liquid in front of the man to her right. A lemon peel bobbed on the surface. The glass was slightly frosted and glistened in the half-light of the dark room.

The bartender turned to Neeva and smiled. "What can I get you, miss?"

Neeva smiled nervously and looked at the drink he had just served. "Is that a martini?" she asked.

"That's right. Gin, straight up, with a twist. Is that what you'd like?"

She couldn't remember ever having had a martini. She had

heard endless jokes about how lethal they were. People didn't drink or talk about them much anymore, but a martini always sounded so sophisticated, somehow reckless, and she supposed they were dangerous if one drank a lot of them. But what could one drink do to her now except blunt her simmering rage at Irving?

She crossed her legs, steadying herself by holding on to the thick leather rim of the bar. "Yes, I'll have a martini."

She slowly sipped the icy gin, listening to two men down the bar discuss a show they had seen. As she sipped her drink, letting its numbing effect warm her body, the two men became more interesting. Their suits were too pale for New York, and when the one with the dark blond hair went to the men's room, she noticed his tan shoes. His trousers were an inch too short, and she could see he was wearing ankle-length socks. After he returned, Neeva continued to listen to their conversation. They were engineers in town for a meeting at the Marriott. They were from Illinois and played golf a lot. The taller one with dark, receding hair had been in the Marines, and they both had played football in college.

By the time she finished the first drink, the blond one was deep into a story about a painting he had seen in a window on Second Avenue. The man in the shop had quoted him a dreadfully high price, telling him it was an original nineteenth-century oil.

Neeva stared at the bottom of her glass, poking the lemon twist around with one finger. She felt wonderful, calm and yet slightly excited at the same time. Now she knew why people talked about martinis. Why hadn't she discovered them before? Then again, if she had, she would have been a drunk by now. They were magic. Early starts in life, she thought, feeling philosophical. Early starts for everyone, then when someone got to be her age, they'd know how the world worked and not get surprised by the bad things. If she had shot Irving the day she married him, she would be out of jail by now.

She started to giggle at her own joke. Feeling foolish, she quickly put her hand to her mouth. As she checked along the bar to see if anyone had noticed, she caught the blond man staring at her and quickly looked down at the fresh drink the bartender was sliding under her chin.

The pounding in her right temple had stopped. The hard, aching muscle across her shoulders had turned to pliable mush, and her mind felt wonderfully floaty and calm. A second one could only prolong the feeling.

"How was that?" the bartender asked with a friendly grin.

"Great," Neeva said, beaming, "but I didn't order this one."

The bartender banked his head in the direction of the two engineers. "The gentlemen down the bar sent this over."

Puzzled as to just what her response should be, she looked over at the two men. They were smiling at her with fresh drinks held aloft.

Neeva smiled back and nodded. She pulled the drink toward her, spilling a bit on her hand, and lifted her glass in the air as they had. She curled her lip over the edge, feeling the hot-cold liquid sliding down her throat and wondering if she was supposed to talk to the men or just say thank you.

The couple who had been sitting between her and the men paid their check and slipped away. The two men went back to talking about the painting. She heard her own voice as though someone else was speaking. "I wouldn't buy that painting if I were you."

Both men turned.

"I know that shop."

The blond man blinked. "You're kidding. At Second and Fifty-third?"

"Um-hmm," she said, putting down her glass. "That's the one. They do all those paintings in the back. It's practically a factory. Were you interested in the snow-capped mountain scene or the desert flowers with the red sky?"

The two men looked at each other in appreciative surprise. The blond one took a step closer. In the light from the back of the bar his suit looked almost pink and had a little textured weave to it. "Actually, the one I priced was a forest with a stream in it."

"With a tiny deer at the edge of the stream?" she asked.

"I think it was a bear," he said with a sheepish expression. "The guy said it was done in Europe and was one of a kind."

"Ah, yes, the bear. They only put one bear painting in the window at a time. Trust me, if you wanted to do your house in wall-to-wall bear paintings, they could help you do it. Same painting over and over again all the way down your living-room wall. I pass that shop every morning. Lots of bear paintings. There are a lot of tourists in town. I guess they sold all the deer."

Both men laughed simultaneously. Their laughter had a very similar effect to the way the second drink was making her feel. It was exciting to have two strangers think she was amusing.

When they stopped laughing, the shorter, blond one kept smiling at her. "Are you waiting for someone or would you like to join us?"

"Please," the other one said, pulling the empty stool between them away from the bar. "I'd love to know how you know so much about fake art."

Neeva hesitated for a moment, taking a sip of her drink as a stall. They were both so friendly and unthreatening. If they really wanted to know about art, they had picked a subject she certainly was comfortable with.

"Sure," she said. "Why not?"

As she slipped off her stool, the bartender lifted her drink and followed her down the bar.

"I'm Ned," the blond one said, offering his hand as she moved around to join them.

"And I'm Tom," said the other.

"My name is Neeva," she said, shaking both their hands. "Thank you again for the drink."

"Do you live here, Neeva?" Tom asked as he helped her onto the stool. "I'll bet you do. You look like a real sophisticated New York lady to me. Doesn't she, Ned?"

"Bring the lady another," Ned said forcefully to the bartender.

Later, Neeva would remember the meal. They ate in the big

dining room next to the Oak Bar, where Ned had made reservations earlier. She ordered a salad but didn't eat much of it. The men both had big brown-black steaks, bloody at the center. They had taken their drinks with them to the table. By the time they sat down Neeva felt rather than tasted her fourth drink. It felt sharp and wet.

Tom had been in charge of the ordering. It was difficult for him to make himself understood because Neeva and Ned were laughing and being silly.

Neeva was aware that he was telling ancient, unfunny jokes that all seemed to start with "So, this guy walks into a bar," or "So, this sailor brings home this parrot." She had heard them all before. Still, under the circumstances they all sounded hilarious and fresh. She couldn't stop laughing.

Some red wine came during dinner and then some champagne. It seemed as though someone from another table had sent it over, but she couldn't be sure until a couple stopped to speak to them. Ned grabbed the man's wrist and wouldn't let go until he told everyone a joke about a gorilla with diarrhea.

Neeva was pushing at a wine stain on her skirt and thought she heard the other couple mention a club somewhere. There was too much loud talking and shoulder punching going on to hear over the ringing in her ears.

She didn't remember the check coming, but it must have, because suddenly they were standing out in front of the Plaza, laughing at something Ned had said, as a cab pulled up.

Neeva sat wedged in the backseat between the two men, who were teasing the driver about his name. Her eyes had stopped focusing some time ago, and she couldn't make out his face card.

She looked out the front window of the cab as it whizzed by the Trump Tower at the corner of Fifth and 56th, so close she could almost touch it. It was all gold and shimmering in the night.

"I live there," she giggled, falling against Tom's shoulder as she tried to point at the building. He slipped his arm around her shoulders.

"Didn't I tell you, Ned? This is a very sophisticated New York lady."

The cab headed at a very high speed down a deserted Fifth Avenue.

She remembered a wide man with a thick neck standing under a canopy in a dark part of town. He waited while Ned came up with a fistful of cash before he let down a velvet robe in front of a door.

She remembered dancing fast to loud rock music somewhere where it was dark. Ned kept shouting, "Do the Monkey," over the music. "Do the Mashed Potato." "Do the Funky Chicken."

Neeva kept on dancing, thinking she was in a time warp.

She remembered sitting at a crowded table, practically on top of Ned. He was kissing her neck and his hands under the table were moving up and down her inner thigh.

He had just plunged his tongue down her throat when she felt a hand on her shoulder and heard someone say, "Neeva? Is that you, Neeva?"

She put both hands on Ned's chest, pushed him away, and looked around. Jeffrey was standing over her, frowning.

She couldn't remember if she introduced him. Probably not; she didn't know anyone's last name.

Later, the only thing she could remember saying to him was that she was celebrating "because Irving stole all my money. Chandon Galleries is out of business, Jeffrey. Isn't that a hoot?"

She couldn't remember what he said. The next thing she knew he was gone, and she was kissing Ned again.

Later, in an elevator that smelled of stale perfume and cleaning fluid, she remembered she had seen Jeffrey. It seemed like a dream, so she pushed it out of her head and let the sound of "Moon River" flowing from little speakers in either corner of the elevator car wash over her.

When the door opened she looked down a long corridor with dull, greasy-looking carpeting. "Is this the Plaza?" she slurred.

"No, baby." Ned laughed, holding tightly to her elbow. "We just drink at the Plaza. This is home sweet home."

She remembered more drinks in thick short glasses with no ice in a room where the television set was chained to a metal loop in the wall.

Then she was lying down naked and wasn't sure how her clothes had come off. She felt Ned's hands on her breasts and stomach and then between her legs. She knew it was Ned because his breath smelled the same as it had when they were kissing.

Somehow his mouth was between her legs and he was talking. He was telling her things. Talking to her about her. How she looked and smelled and how smart and funny she was. He was talking to her about how she didn't have to worry, he'd take care of everything. He took her hand and made her help roll the condom on. As she clung to his back it didn't feel a bit like Irving's back. It was cool and broad and hairless.

She must have slept for a while. She remembered hearing voices from the adjacent room, and laughter. She felt Ned's hand against her thigh and rolled over. Instantly he was on top of her again, entering her. She ran her hands down his back.

It wasn't the same back. It was thinner, less fleshy. Where Ned's knees had been well below her own, the knees on top of her now were even with hers. The feet rubbing against her feet had socks on, and the latex-covered penis pushing inside her was wider and shorter.

She drifted off. It wasn't sleep. It was some kind of floating, high above the city. She remembered it being very airy and quiet in a sky filled with stars. There was a metal chain in her hands, trailing behind her, and when Irving floated by in a pair of salmon-colored pants and white patent-leather loafers, she looped the chain around his neck and strangled him.

When she woke up safe in her own bed the next morning, she couldn't remember exactly how she'd gotten there.

24

*L*ate in the afternoon of the day of her fateful lunch with Irving, Baby finished her kidnap story in a white-hot fury. She had considered writing the truth—that sneaky Abner Hoon had bought the girl, not stolen her—but a kidnapping was much more dramatic. She snatched it out of her printer and swung down the aisle to Petra's glassed-in office.

She breezed in and dropped the pages onto the desk.

"Maybe you want to run this by Joe," Baby said with a sly smile. "He might want to give it a tad more space. Say, page one."

Petra looked up at her with the blank expression she used to mask her true feelings about Baby. She dropped her hooded eyes to the page and read the item. When she finished, she held up one finger. "Wait," she said without comment on what she had just read.

Petra reached for her phone and hit three buttons.

"Joe. Petra. Listen to this," she barked, then rapid-fired Baby's "kidnapping" item into the phone. She listened for a moment then hung up.

"Joe said it was great, right?" Baby asked.

"Joe said it's great if it checks out. This is the first time I've heard about this. How do you know this woman was kidnapped?"

"Trust me, she was."

"A person is considered kidnapped if they are forcibly taken from point A to point B. That means against their will."

"I know what kidnapped means," Baby said, squeezing her eyes into little slits. Sometimes she enjoyed lying to Petra just for the sake of it.

"You mean two men hired by a London tabloid walked into a big public hospital and walked out with a woman who is involved in a major Hollywood scandal, and you are the only one who knows it? Somehow I think there's something missing from this story. Maybe like verification. *Hmmm?*"

"My sources are absolutely airtight," Baby continued defensively.

"Your sources?"

"Yes, people very, very close to the case."

"Would you like to share their names with your editor?" Petra asked in the you-will-eat-your-peas voice she used to make Baby feel three years old.

"No, I would not," Baby answered in the same tone.

"Did you call the *London Gazette* to verify this?"

"Absolutely," Baby shot back. "They have her, as they told me, in a very safe place."

"Well, you better have their names on my desk in the next ten minutes, or we won't be running this."

"I want to see Joe," Baby said, furious.

"So, go see Joe," Petra said, opening her hands palm up, in a gesture that told Baby Petra would just as soon give the problem to someone else altogether.

Baby snatched the printout off Petra's desk and stormed out of the office.

"Cunt, cunt, cunt," Baby hummed under her breath as she hurried up the aisle toward Joe's office. "Cow, cow, cow. Big, sweaty cow."

As she swung into Joe's office, he looked up from whatever he was reading. "You and Petra fighting again?"

"Joe," Baby whined. "She wants my sources, and I promised."

"I'm assuming your biggest source is your new squeeze Irving Fourbraz."

Baby looked down at her shoes. "You know about me and Irving," she said sheepishly.

Joe leaned back in his chair and smiled. "Get real, kid. Twenty-one, Le Cirque. You are your own best item." He raised his hand in the air as though delineating a headline. " 'What girl reporter has been playing suck face on the best banquettes in town with one of Gotham's most powerful married mega-agents?' Underline the *married*."

"Can it, Joe. He's a terrific source."

"He probably tells you a lot more stuff over at Ian McCaulley's pad at the Beekman Tower."

Baby's jaw fell. "How do you know about the Beekman Tower?"

"My dentist has an office in the building. If I hadn't had to have a root canal last week, I wouldn't know."

Baby sighed and sat down. "May I sit down?"

"You're down."

"So, are you going to use it? I think it's hot."

"Irving won't. It makes him look like a fool."

Baby shrugged. "I don't care."

"You check it out with the *Gazette*?"

"Yup."

"Who, Abner Hoon?"

"Correctomundo."

"That figures. I heard about the two of you at the Garns' party."

"Oh," she said, looking away and clearing her throat. "So? My story. It's too good for the shitty Grapevine page. It really is."

"That's why I'm going to move it up. We've got a front-page problem. No one got shot today. It'll look good there. Go punch it up a bit. Recap the Keeko Ram stuff. Call the girl's family for some quotes. Do a little rundown on how the Brits do this kind of stuff and why. You know what to do. I'll get photo on this right away."

Baby lurched up out of her chair with a shriek and started to throw herself across Joe's desk.

Joe stood up and backed toward the window. "One step closer and I'll have security throw a bucket of cold water on you."

Baby righted herself and smoothed her dress. "Thanks, Joe," she said softly, meaning it.

Joe smiled. "You're welcome, Baby. It's a good story. I don't care what you had to do to get it. You're a pro."

Baby turned to go, feeling her cheeks flush.

"Oh, and, Baby?"

"Yeah," she said, turning, thinking for an instant he was going to change his mind.

"I'm sorry I was such a shit about taking you to Lolly's service. I had a lot on my mind that day."

Baby grinned. "How did you like my little speech?"

Joe paused for an instant. "It was okay, Baby," he said slowly. "But it probably would have sounded better in the original pig Latin."

25

*K*ick awoke early Thursday morning with a vague feeling of anxiety about the day ahead. Her article for Joe was finished, but now she had to address herself to a chore Neeva had insisted only Kick could accomplish—the morbid task of cleaning out the personal things in Lolly's bedroom. That was the one room the workmen had refused to touch as they bumped and banged around on the floor below while she struggled to complete the piece, barricaded in the tower office. From time to time Neeva would slip notes under the door to keep from bothering her. Most of the notes were questions about what she wanted to do with the things the men didn't want to throw out without asking.

Kick fixed herself a cup of coffee and went to Lolly's bedroom to begin. At least the job would distract her till she heard from Joe.

She sat at the huge old dressing table in Lolly's bedroom and pulled open the middle drawer. She exhaled with fatigue when she saw the contents. The other drawers were no less depressing. There were boxes of old Cover Girl loose powder, dried up Dark

Lady mascara wands by the dozens, hairpins, dead lipstick tubes with once red, now black, stubs inside. Everything stuck to everything else, covered with some milky residue now hardened and slick, all dusted with pale pink powder. She scraped everything into the industrial-size garbage bag Neeva had given her and wiped her hands on the legs of her filthy jeans.

At first she tried to save anything that might be of some use. There were packets of unworn stockings; boxes and boxes of unopened packages of false eyelashes, corn plasters, and fake fingernails; and bottles of nail polish and perfume. There was also an odd little statue on top of the dresser; Kick found it when she removed the costume beads Lolly had draped over it, concealing the figure entirely. The sheer amount of stuff was making her sick to her stomach. Her lungs filled with the stale smell of Lolly's signature perfume, a cloying oriental scent she had had made up especially for her at Elizabeth Arden. It smelled all right on her living body. It was as though when she died it all went bad.

When Kick had been working on the article, she smelled the same scent on all the documents, diaries, scrapbooks, and old photos she had to paw through on the third floor trying to sort out the chronology of Lolly's career. Lolly had known and kept notes on everyone who had mattered for the past thirty years. There were wonderful pictures, and though mostly torn and yellowed, they showed Lolly as she once had been.

There was Lolly, one platform shoe locked around an unsuspecting Sheila Graham's ankle, as the two rivals pushed toward a mopheaded Paul McCartney; Lolly, notepad in hand, seated next to Marlon Brando. Lolly with Norman Mailer, Richard Burton, Truman Capote, Leonard Bernstein, Brigitte Bardot, and every president since Eisenhower. Lolly on a deck chair between the Duke and Duchess of Windsor. Lolly with Irving Fourbraz and JFK's girlfriend Judy Exner.

Kick had woven it all into a seamless tale, being very careful to keep her personal relationship to Lolly out of the story. When she had finished, she printed it out and reread it. She liked it. It was one of the best things she had ever written. She lovingly stacked up the pages, slipped them into the cleanest envelope she could find in the clutter, and called the messenger service.

That had been more then twenty-four hours ago. If Joe wanted it to make the Sunday paper, he would have to let her know before the end of the day.

She stepped over a plastic garbage bag full of shoes to send to Goodwill and walked to the window to check Thelma. Kick pushed open the window, leaned out, and patted Thelma's pitted haunch. She would miss her concrete friend.

She suddenly shivered against a gust of cool air. To her surprise the morning breeze held a hint of fall.

She loved fall. That was the real start of a new year. New clothes, new pencils and books, new classes of new kids. It was fall when she first saw Paris. It was nearly fall when she stepped out of her apartment for the first time after six months of pain and took a cab up to the weird old penthouse on Central Park to begin to forget once and for all about Lionel Maltby.

The muffled ringing of the phone on the top floor sent her spinning out of the bedroom, cursing the fact that the office telephone had no extensions. It had to be Joe.

She charged into the office, zigzagging around the boxes, and lunged across the desk, frantic to get the phone before she had to talk over the answering machine message.

"Sorry, Kick," were Joe's first words.

Kick sat down, her mind going blank with fear. "You're sorry," she said dully.

"I really liked the piece. I really did," he said.

"Oooookay," she drawled, desperate to hang on to whatever cool she had left. Joe was killing her story. It wasn't the first time an editor had killed something of hers. It had happened from time to time at the paper. It had happened big time at *Fifteen Minutes* magazine. It wasn't fair to blame Joe, who had no way of knowing he was tearing up her ticket to the real world.

235

She listened in stunned silence as he told her again that the piece was terrific, that she was a "hell of a writer," and that it really wasn't his decision not to run it.

"You're going to tell me who killed it, right?"

"This is awkward."

Kick said nothing.

"Kick? You still there?" he asked.

"By a thread." She sighed.

"If it had been anyone else fooling around with the magazine, I could have stopped it."

"What are you saying, Joe?"

"The publisher has hijacked the space," Joe admitted sullenly.

"Tanner Dyson? I thought he was the one who wanted my piece in the first place."

"He did. Now he's decided he wants to run a big feature on his wife."

"That's cute," she said sarcastically.

"Beyond cute. It's total chutzpah, for my money."

"What did she do, run up chintz curtains for his yacht all by her wittle self?" Kick asked bitterly.

"Now, now," Joe said.

"I'm sorry, Joe. I'm just disappointed . . . and exhausted for that matter. There's no way you could hold on to it and run it in another issue?"

"*Ummm*, not really. The Journalists Society is planning a testimonial next month. We might just run a collection of what people have to say and call it a day on Lolly. Life goes on, Kick. What can I tell you?"

Kick sighed deeply. She didn't want to argue with Joe. He was just doing his job. "I'm curious, Joe. What did the beautiful and talented second Mrs. Dyson do to rate a layout in the magazine?"

"She used to be a food designer for *Fabulous Foods* magazine. Dyson has a tie-in with one of our supermarket advertisers. You know: Mrs. Tanner in a ball gown steaming clams at her Norwegian ceramic stove. Mrs. Tanner in a hacking jacket serving tea on the terrace."

"I knew I should have learned to cook," Kick said, grateful that she wasn't having this conversation face to face. Her lower lip quivered.

"Not to put too fine a point on it, kid, I don't think cooking was what did it. You remember all the stuff in the papers about Georgina Dyson a couple of years back? They made her out to be a femme fatale. She's not really. She's very sweet."

"Why do I have the feeling sweetness had nothing to do with it either?" Kick said dejectedly.

"Listen," Joe said, brightening. "I feel bad about this. Let me cheer you up, at least. How about dinner?"

Kick's eyes swept over the chaos around her. "I'd like that. This place is turning my brain to Silly Putty."

"Call you at six, then," he said, sounding more upbeat than before. "And don't take this too hard, Kick. You might be able to sell the piece to a magazine down the line."

"Sure, Joe, sure," she said wearily. "Later."

Jealousy wasn't an emotion Kick had had to deal with much in her life. She had never lost a boyfriend to another woman or a job to someone brighter, better, nicer. Unlike so many people she had known, and with the sole exception of her brief relationship with Lionel, she never felt herself tricked or oppressed or given the short end of the stick. But something had happened. Had she lost her touch? Did she ever have a touch to begin with? Was it too far-fetched to think people were taking her name literally? Perhaps when the world heard the name "Kick," they got a subliminal message to aim one at her head.

When the phone rang again, she could just barely bring herself to answer it. The day had only just begun. Maybe worse was to come.

"Kick, it's Neeva." There was something funny about Neeva's voice. It kind of wobbled.

"Hi, Neeva. You coming over?"

"I don't think so," Neeva said softly.

Something was wrong. Kick glanced at her watch. It was a little after nine. "Is everything okay?"

"No. I have a terrible hangover."

"You, Neeva? You don't strike me as much of a drinker."

"I'm not. It's just that . . ." Her voice broke, and she couldn't finish whatever she was trying to say.

Now Kick felt truly concerned. Even though she was married to the schmuck of the century, Neeva seemed like a nice lady to her, and Kick hated to hear her cry.

"Neeva, tell me," Kick pleaded.

There was a long silence. Kick could hear the muffled sound of Neeva blowing her nose. "I'm not going to be able to go on with the auction," she finally said.

"What? Why not?"

"Well, something terrible has happened."

"Neeva," Kick gasped. "What?"

"My husband forged one of my new checks. I'm wiped out. I can't even pay the bills I've already run up."

"My God! Irving? Oh, Neeva, I can't believe this."

Kick was stunned. She'd never liked Irving, and she knew that professionally he could be a real sleaze, but to steal money from his wife!

"I don't know what to do. The truckers have to be paid tomorrow. I postdated a check to the appraiser. I know this isn't your problem, Kick, but I think I'm losing my mind."

"Neeva, stop crying and tell me, where is Irving?" she asked, refraining from adding, "the bastard."

"I don't know. He didn't come home at all last night. He must be in some terrible trouble to do this but my whole world is falling apart."

"Does Jeffrey know?"

"Oh, God, Jeffrey. Maybe he knows. I ran into him last night. I think I said something to him. I can't remember. I'm too mortified to call him now," she said between sobs. "He had such faith in me. He thought I was a grown-up, and I've let him down. I've let his father down. He was so proud of Jeffrey, of us."

Kick spoke very slowly, making sure Neeva would understand. "Neeva, are you dressed?"

"I've got sweats on. Why?"

"That's fine. Walk out of your apartment, hail a cab, and get over here. Now. This minute. I don't know how right now, but we're going to fix this thing. Then we're going to fix Irving."

26

Georgina's antidote for depression had always been food. In the past she had eaten it. Now she just cooked . . . and cooked and cooked. It was only ten-thirty, on Thursday morning, and already six sheets of Toll-House cookies had steadied her hands when they began to tremble. A Swiss mocha Bundt cake stood cooling on the butcher-block table, the product of another nerve-calming hour before dawn. When the clock moved passed nine o'clock and she knew Rona Friedman would be in her office, the preparation of a salmon mousse and a crock of liver pâté kept her from reaching for the phone.

When everything was finished, she carried the food to the Sub-Zero freezer in the pantry only to discover there was no more room. She stood staring at the results of the cooking marathon that had started the morning after Tanner had insisted he involve Irving Fourbraz in the sale of her manuscript. Thank God she had her AIDS-project deliveries to make use of the madness of it all.

She sat down at the butcher-block island in the kitchen and

began the daily wrestling match with herself called "Don't Call Rona." It was a losing battle, she decided. It was better to know something, than bear the unknown.

What if Irving had somehow screwed up the deal? Since the evening she had mentioned the book to Tanner, there had been dead silence except for Tanner's call from the office the next day telling her not to "worry your pretty head." Irving was going to take over and get a very nice deal for her.

As each day passed with no call from Rona saying she had even received her manuscript, she became more anxious. What if Rona had gotten a call from Irving, been deeply offended, and dumped the whole thing in the trash. She remembered hearing editors complain about writers' agents, when she was at the magazine, and their annoyance at their interference and demands. Maybe that's what had happened at Winslow House. What if it had been lost in the mail or misdelivered. What if? What if? She couldn't stand it any longer.

She took a very deep breath and reached for the phone.

"Ms. Rona Friedman, please," she said to the female voice that answered on the first ring.

"This is Rona."

"Rona . . . it's Georgina. Georgina Holmes," she amended, hoping to invoke the old days.

"Georgie! Wow! Hey this is great. How are you? Gee, I'm so glad you called. I got your manuscript. I was going to call you. I really was but . . . it's just that . . . well, I was just waiting to . . ." Rona's voice trailed off into what seemed like an embarrassed dead end.

"I should have called you before I sent it."

"No . . . no, hey listen, no problem."

"Yes, well, I was just wondering if you'd had a chance to look at it."

"Yeah, sure, I looked at it. I mean I read it. The whole thing. I'm delighted you thought of me."

This was like pulling teeth, Georgina thought. Why was Rona being so vague? She was speaking as though the line were tapped. "So? What did you think?" Georgina finally asked, hating that she actually had to ask.

"Look, Georgie," Rona said in a half-whisper. "I really shouldn't even being discussing this with you. I mean with Irving Fourbraz involved, it's all out of my hands."

Georgina's heart sank. "Oh, dear." She sighed. "That wasn't my idea, Rona. My husband is a friend of both Irving and your chairman. I could ask Irving to just step aside if it's awkward for you."

"*Krikees*, Georgie, don't do that," Rona said in mock terror. "You've made me the office genius. My boss didn't know I was alive until she found out you sent your book to me. Besides, the bidding is up over a hundred grand as we speak. I just assumed someone would have called you by now. You mean to tell me no one has?"

How could all this be going on without her knowing about it? "Who would have called?" Georgina said, in stunned disbelief.

"Well, Irving for one. He's your agent."

"But who is he talking to if not you?"

"Oh, I'm just a little fish around here, Georgie. I just open the mail and read my eyeballs out. I started the bidding, but with a big deal like this, he's speaking directly to the chairman."

Georgina was mortified. "Rona, I'm so sorry. You're not mad at me are you?"

"Don't be silly, Georgina. Of course not. Everything's fine."

"No, it's not," Georgina heard herself shouting. In the distance she could hear the doorbell, then Selma speaking to someone. She glanced up to see the maid standing in the door. "Rona, when this is all settled, I'd love for you to come for lunch. Promise?"

"Sure, Georgie, I'd like that. It's been a long time."

Georgina set the phone down, feeling dreadful, and looked up at her housekeeper. "Yes, Selma," she said, with a sigh.

"Some people are here from the paper, Mrs. Dyson," Selma said. "A reporter and some photographers. They want to know where to put their things."

Georgina blinked in confusion. "What people? What things? I'm not expecting anyone."

Selma looked over her shoulder. "Well, there's a lot of camera equipment, screens, umbrellas, all kinds of stuff."

Georgina pushed up out of the wing chair behind Tanner's desk and strode angrily into the hallway. Through the archway at the end of the hall she could see there were three men in blue jeans, draped with camera gear, standing in the middle of the pale Aubusson rug. A woman clutching a tape recorder was staring out a window onto the terrace.

"Selma, I don't know who these people are," Georgina said with mounting alarm. "Why did you let them in?"

Selma looked distraught. "They said Mr. Dyson sent them to do a magazine shoot."

Furious, Georgina told Selma to offer them some iced tea and tell everyone to wait. She closed the library door and rushed to the phone. Once she reached Tanner's secretary, the woman said she would have to page him. He was somewhere in the *Courier* building, but no one seemed to know where.

When he finally came on the phone, he seemed rushed and annoyed.

"Tanner, dear," Georgina said, trying hard to be calm. "There are some people from the *Courier* here, photographers and a reporter. They said you sent them. What is going on?"

"Darling, I've been so rushed. I forgot to tell Nadine to call you. I thought a nice story on you in the Sunday magazine would help with negotiations on the book. Irving tells me they're well into six figures."

"You suddenly have all that space in next Sunday's magazine?" she asked skeptically.

"Oh, we moved some pieces around," he said blithely. "I just thought it was an opportunity we shouldn't pass up."

"I see."

"They'll want to get pictures of you in the kitchen, darling," he said. "I hope you have something on hand that will make a nice picture."

243

Numb with shock, she felt as though she had been hijacked by forces beyond her control. First Rona, now this. It was more than she could bear.

"Yes," she replied, sounding like a robot. "I have something that would make a nice picture. I have a lot of things that would make a nice picture. I have a salmon mousse. I have dozens of cookies. I have a Swiss mocha cake and a whole crock of goose pâté. Will that do, Tanner?"

"Wonderful, darling. I must run. I'll call you later to see how it all went."

Georgina sat still, holding the dead phone in her hand. Why hadn't she said something? Why hadn't she protested? She wasn't ready to have her picture taken for anything. Her hair was a mess. She hadn't sent Grover out yet, so there were no fresh flowers in the house.

She knew Tanner was trying to help, using his influence and power again, unselfishly trying to get her career going. Why couldn't she say something? Why couldn't she just have told him not to spring something like this on her?

In her heart, she knew why. She couldn't because she was a formerly fat girl with few friends and a dim future. She couldn't because, in her heart, she also knew she didn't deserve to be Mrs. Tanner Dyson. It was something that just happened, and she should be grateful.

Out in the living room she could hear the people from the *Courier* asking Grover about electrical outlets and whether there was enough current out on the terrace for the lights.

She looked around the kitchen. Selma and Grover had swiftly tidied up the last of the cooking pots and pans. The place, as always, was immaculate. It was as if nothing had gone on in the room since she started cooking at dawn. The life around her was picture perfect again. Later, Grover would load up the station wagon with all the food she had cooked and whisk it away to the warehouse kitchen for the AIDS patients.

She checked her hair and makeup in the black glass door of the upper oven. It was time to go have her picture taken. Time to do what Tanner wanted her to do. Time to do something that would make him happy. Tomorrow she would cook and freeze a whole turkey. No, a whole Thanksgiving dinner. It would keep in the freezer for two months. Then she would make some pies; pecan, pumpkin, cherry, blueberry. She was thinking about the pies as she walked into the living room, smiling broadly at the strangers waiting for her.

27

*B*aby sat in the back of a cab heading downtown and reread her piece to make sure the desk hadn't changed the way she'd written it. Joe had splashed it all over the front page of Thursday's paper. Somewhere photo had gotten a hold of a bosomy picture of "Monica Champagne." Probably from her Los Angeles escort service. Joe knew cleavage on the front page would sell a lot more papers than pictures of Florida real estate scattered by Hurricane Andrew.

Anchored at either end of a red streamer at the bottom of the page were two small pictures, one of Abner Hoon, the other of Irving wearing a tux. The copy between the pictures read: "Super Agent Irving Fourbraz represents kidnap victim." Under Abner's picture the caption read: "London gossip columnist involved. See Page 4."

Baby quickly turned to page four and snapped the paper open on her lap.

The LA woman who alleges TV idol Keeko Ram attempted to murder her when he pushed her off a motel balcony last month has been spirited from City of Angeles Hospital in a daring twist that threatens a transatlantic legal battle for the rights to her story.

Baby skipped down the page to see if the legal department had left in the important part—the revenge part—as far as she was concerned.

To her disappointment, it had been moved to the jump page. She found it in the continuation back by the television listings.

In a statement issued by his office yesterday, New York celebrity lawyer and media deal maker, Irving Fourbraz, claimed the London tabloid *Gazette* kidnapped the woman after learning that an address book turned over to the LAPD contained some of the most glittering names in British society. According to a source close to the negotiations for Ms. Champagne's story . . .

That would be me, Baby thought, with a smug smile; it was fun to be her own source.

. . . attorney Fourbraz had already sold exclusive rights to Ms. Champagne's life story to an American supermarket tabloid shortly after she was injured. A spokesman for the *World* said that they did not know Ms. Champagne's whereabouts and that they were attempting to reach Mr. Fourbraz to confirm their exclusive right to her story.

London Gazette gossip columnist Abner Hoon is believed to have been involved in the alleged abduction. Hoon told the *Courier* yesterday afternoon, "I am completely unaware of any 'kidnapping.' I have never heard of Ms. Champagne and I am only vaguely familiar with the name Keeko Ram."

When told that Keeko Ram's syndicated television series

had been appearing on British television for two seasons, he replied that he "never watched television."

Mr. Fourbraz could not be reached for comment. His office said he was out of town and issued his statement for him.

Baby closed the paper and sighed deeply. She couldn't wait to fax the story to Abner. Let him twist in the wind when he read her completely fabricated quote. There wasn't a damn thing he could do about it.

She whipped the paper open again. "Damn," she whispered. They had dropped a line she had hoped to sneak by the copy desk. Right after Abner's ridiculous denial that he watched TV, Baby had written: "Mr. Hoon was recently in New York to undergo what society insiders say is the hottest weapon in the beauty wars known as the Venus Treatment."

When she wrote it, she had a pretty good idea that the line wouldn't make it through, but it was worth a try. Oh, well, she thought, she'd find some other way to let Hoon know she'd had his number all along about the damn Venus stuff. It wouldn't hurt to let him, as well as Irving, know how she felt about being lied to. She didn't need Abner on her side, not with a page-one story and the inside information to keep it going for a while.

She settled back for the rest of the ride, glancing out the window every time the cab slowed down, to see Monica Champagne's breasts leaping upward from every corner vending box and newsstand.

Wherever Irving was, he was having a cow. The story would make him look like an idiot to his other clients. Already the guys at the *World* had to be having kittens. Wait till they found out he'd spent the advance without giving a cent to his client.

Monica's breasts were on every desk and stacked in the corridors as Baby moved toward her cubicle. A few heads rose as she passed and called out.

"Way to go, Baby!"

"Great story, kid."

It was mostly the men who spoke to her, the ones who

ordinarily stared at her butt or breasts when she passed their desks. A lot of staffers didn't look up at all.

Screw 'em, she thought, letting her heels hit the tile floor a little harder. Fuck 'em all. She'd show them. She knew she would never win any popularity contests around the city room. She didn't give a damn. They would change their minds soon enough. As that great philosopher Elizabeth Taylor said, "There's no deodorant like success."

There was a coiled fax standing on end in the middle of her desk. She unfurled it and saw it was a handwritten note from Abner: *"Saw your story. Terribly awkward for me, Baby. Phone as soon as possible. Affectionately, A Perturbed Abner."*

"Hard cheese, old sock," she muttered under her breath as she crushed the fax and sent it sailing toward a wastebasket on the other side of the aisle. It narrowly missed Petra's shoulder as she moved rapidly toward Baby's desk.

"Tanner Dyson called to congratulate you on your story," she said flatly.

"Tanner Dyson called who?"

"Me. I thought you'd like to know."

"What, does he think I'm deaf? He can't call to congratulate *me?*"

"I'm still your boss, Bayer."

"I'd like to speak to him myself," Baby said. She had been thinking the whole time she put together the Lopez story that it was time to strike. If she was ever going to get Lolly's job, she knew she should push for it while she was hot.

Petra pointed to the phone on Baby's desk. "You know the extension. Call him up yourself," she said, making it sound like a dare.

"I want to see him personally," Baby said with a pout.

Petra shrugged. "I can't stop you," she said, turning back toward her office.

"Wait. I want you to call him and make an appointment."

Petra turned back to face Baby with a look of utter disgust. "You . . . have . . . got to be kidding." Baby leaned across her desk and squeezed her eyes at Petra. "If you don't, I'll tell the next person I see in the ladies' room that I saw you shoplifting in Saks."

"You'll what? What are you talking about?"

"You know," Baby said coyly.

"Bayer, I think you've lost what you laughably call your mind. I haven't been in Saks for five years." Petra was in an absolute rage.

"Who's going to believe that once the rumor gets started, *hummm?* You know how that works, don't you Petra? Just the way the rumor you started about me and Joe Stone worked. It just flies around the building." Baby lifted her hand and swooped it out into space like a gliding bird.

"That wasn't a rumor, and you know it," Petra shouted.

"Suit yourself," Baby said brightly. "Now, if you'll excuse me, I have to go to the ladies' room."

"All right, all right, all right. I'll call Dyson. But I swear to you, Bayer. You'll pay for this."

"Thank you, sweetie," Baby trilled, fluffing her hair. "Ask him to make it as soon as he can, would you? I expect the talk shows to be calling. After all, I'm now the Monica Champagne expert."

After Petra stormed back to her office, Baby announced to anyone within earshot that she was taking no calls.

She cleared her desk of back paperwork and made enough phone calls to meet her daily allotment of items for the next day's page. By noon, Petra sent word, rather than tell her in person, that the publisher would see Baby in his office at ten sharp the next morning.

Elated, Baby decided she had worked enough for one day and sailed out of the office. She needed time. Time to get her roots and nails done and to buy a new outfit. Time to make several copies of a certain "un-fucking-enforceable" piece of paper she wanted to have with her when she met with Tanner tomorrow morning—just in case their meeting didn't go her way.

28

*I*rving opened his eyes and quickly closed them against twin stabs of pain in his temples. The bedroom ceiling in his apartment was smooth, a pale mushroom color. The ceiling he had just seen had ornately carved plaster rosebuds and leaves swagged with plaster vines and ribbons. A huge crystal chandelier hung from the center of the alien room.

His tongue explored something painful under an upper-molar-bearing bridge. His mouth tasted as if he had been chewing cigars. Behind that flavor was the sour tang of consumed scotch.

He kept his eyes closed and moved his hands up his clothed body. He was beginning to remember. He was on the couch of the Ed Sullivan room of the Friars Club on East 55th Street.

Christ, he thought, who's seen me in here? He painfully lifted his head to see if the door was closed. Members could do a lot of boorish things in the club, but spending the night in one of the public rooms wasn't done. He must have been plastered. He couldn't even remember how he had gotten there.

Every muscle in his body protested as he tried to sit up. He looked down at the carpeting, instinctively trying to find his shoes in the dim light that filtered through the heavy curtains.

Sluggishly, he moved his mind backward, trying to piece together the past angst-filled twenty-four hours.

He remembered Wednesday's lunch at des Artistes with Baby; the phone call from the duplicitous Maria's mother. He remembered Baby flouncing out in a high snit just as the waiter put their lunch order on the table. What had she been so pissed about? Something to do with Neeva. "Shit. Neeva," he moaned, and dropped his head into his hands. He had been so crazed, and it had seemed so simple.

All summer Vivian had been warning him that he was headed for financial meltdown, and he had ignored her. There was always another deal or a way to rob Peter to pay Paul. Gradually, however, he'd begun to see that Vivian was right.

Their house in the Hamptons was a money pit. His other real-estate holdings around town weren't worth half what he had paid for them. The Trump apartment was way too expensive to carry. It had seemed a piece of cake in the mid-eighties when he bought it, but ten grand a month wasn't as easy to come by now. The car and driver, the restaurant and club bills, the MGM Grand at the whiff of a deal. It all added up.

What he had in the market had slowly turned to crap. He wasn't doing nearly enough legal work and was spending too much time spinning his various deals or commenting on media scandals on television talk shows. He didn't even want to think about his problems with the IRS.

It was desperation that had driven him to set up the Maria Lopez deal. It had cost too much in both time and money. It was pushing his luck to do it in the first place.

His affair with Baby had clogged his wheels. Until she came along, he could juggle a dozen deals at once, chase ambulances going in seven different directions. The most reckless thing he had done, by far, was talk to Baby so much. If he had just stayed with the interchangeable bimbos who had serviced him for years, he would be fine. Getting tangled up with someone who traded in talk was a fatal mistake. Now, pissed at him and thinking only of her overweening ambitions, she was like a loaded gun aimed directly at his balls.

After she had stormed out of the restaurant, he had returned to the office to start phoning around to find money to cover the botched deal with the *World*. He had to get it before they discovered Maria was gone.

It was humiliating to get into such a state over a relatively paltry sum. A few grand never meant anything. Usually he would dip into his office slush fund, but that was long gone. There was money in the pipeline—royalties, fees owed. He might have a few days before the knuckle draggers at the *World* found out what was going on, but it wasn't worth the risk. They knew too much about the way he worked. He had to raise seventy-five grand immediately, and a tabloid wouldn't take plastic.

By two he saw that his attempts were futile. Exhausted and at his wit's end, he went back to the apartment to take a nap and get a second wind. As he passed through the lobby, the concierge handed him the mail. There was the usual stack of bills, some catalogs, and a bulky manila bank envelope addressed to Neeva. Curious, he lifted the flap and looked in.

It had been so easy.

He hadn't even bothered to question why the hell Neeva had twenty-five grand in a new account. Seeing it made his head spin. Twenty-five grand wasn't enough to pay off Kasko, but it sure as hell would give him the biggest *cojones* in the Friars' card room. He made it to the bank just as the doors were closing.

The money! His open palms flew to his chest, then frantically down his body and into his pants pockets. His jacket? Where was his jacket? He located it on the arm of the sofa and plunged his hands into every pocket. He found his wallet. There were two tens in it. His cigar case was empty. The American Express receipt for the uneaten goddamn des Artistes lunch was still there.

What the fuck had happened to the money? He couldn't have

253

lost it all. How could he? He was up ten grand at one point. Then fifty. He moaned and rolled over on his side and went back to trying to piece together how it had happened.

The game he had cobbled together didn't get under way until nearly eleven o'clock.

By midnight, driven by scotch and desperation, he was going strong. Danny Mann, a press agent, had folded. Maxy Bakus was borrowing heavily from Irving's cigar case. By one he had half a dozen high stacks of black chips lined up in front of him. Straight flush, four of a kind, full house—he was on a roll. Then, nothing. By two A.M. he was tapped out. The two tens in his wallet were the last of Neeva's mystery money, and he was still in the toilet. Eventually he would have to face Neeva, but that was the least of his worries.

He didn't want to think about how he got to the Ed Sullivan room or worse, who carried him there.

He glanced at his watch more for the date than the time. Damn. In his frantic marathon of phoning around town for help yesterday afternoon, he had made a lunch date with Tanner Dyson, hoping that somehow, with Tanner's powerful contacts, most particularly his long friendship with Lord Mosby, the owner of the *London Gazette*, he could extricate the Lopez girl from the Brits. Then Tanner could buy her story himself.

In any case, once she was back in the States, he could remind her that they were too truly partners in sin for her to turn her back on him. He had the goods on her, and he could let her know that while the truth might damage him, it would utterly destroy her. After all, who had more credibility? If she wanted to see a dime—whether it be from the *World* or the *Courier*—she'd better be prepared to give him his share of it. And that would be more than enough to pay back the *World* and make the kind of profit he'd originally planned on.

All Irving had to say to get Tanner to see him was that he wanted to go over publishing plans for Georgina's book and Dyson cheerfully agreed to the lunch at noon at the Friars.

He painfully pushed himself up off the low couch. He had to get himself cleaned up. There was just time enough to get up to the health club on the top floor, take some steam, and get a shave. Hopefully, there would be a porter around who could press the sleep wrinkles out of his suit and run down to Paul Stuart's for a clean shirt.

He managed to get up to the health club, undress, and plunge into the steam room without running into another member.

He sat down on a damp stone bench, his head wrapped in a towel, wishing he had made his appointment with Dyson in a quieter place. The Friars Club dining room could take on the atmosphere of a fraternity smoker at noontime. Any conversation was in danger of being either interrupted by some back-slapping bore or monopolized by any number of gasbags. In an atmosphere of wall-to-wall egos, the delicacy of his mission could be seriously compromised.

By quarter to twelve, freshly shaved, clean, and pressed, Irving made his way down to the dining room feeling almost human. What he needed was a Bloody Mary to get rid of the buzz in his head.

There were only two other people in the dark-paneled dining room when he entered. He strolled to the bar where Murphy, the day bartender, was bent over the sink washing out beer mugs.

"Top of the mornin' to 'ya, Murphy," Irving said in a forced Irish brogue.

"And the balance of the day to yourself, Mr. Fourbraz," Murphy said, putting down a mug and wiping his hands on the bar towel looped over his belt.

"Lemme have a Bloody, would you, Murph?" Irving asked, doing his best to sound chipper. His eye fell on an open box of Las Palmas beside the cash register. "And let me have a couple of cigars, Murph. Put 'em on the tab."

Murphy nodded, handed him two five-dollar cigars, and moved down the bar to mix his drink. "Saw your picture in the paper this morning," Murphy said nonchalantly.

Irving had just unwrapped and lifted a cigar to his lips. His hand froze in midair. "My picture? Where? What paper?"

"I think it was the *Post*. No, wait a minute, the *Courier*. You mean you didn't see it? Oh, well, I guess you get your picture in a lot," Murphy said with a shrug as he poured a long stream of tomato juice into a tall glass.

The *Courier*, Irving thought with rising panic. That had to be something Baby did. The bitch! What is she trying to do, kill me? It took most of Irving's self-control to sound calm. "That's interesting, Murphy. What was it about?"

" 'Bout that girl the TV kid almost killed. Something about her being kidnapped by some English paper."

Irving sat, speechless. She did it, he thought. She goddamn did it. Probably called it into the paper on his own damn phone.

Irving couldn't think straight. He could feel his heart hammering under his brand-new Paul Stuart shirt.

He had to call Vivian. She could read the story to him. Then again, maybe there was a copy around the club. Reflexively, he patted his jacket pocket for his phone and cursed Baby again for taking it.

"Hold my drink," Irving said to Murphy, who had just dropped a long stalk of celery into Irving's Bloody Mary.

He had started down the curved staircase to ask the first-floor receptionist to find him the paper when he saw Tanner Dyson at the foot of the stairs.

He stopped dead in his tracks. Tanner was smiling up at him, assuming Irving was coming to greet him. There was no escape.

Tanner's hair was the color of aluminum, WASP aluminum that looked nearly iridescent next to his sunlamp tan. As Tanner made his way up the stairs, several men heading up to the dining room greeted him with great ceremony. The Friars Club was a bit rough and tumble for the likes of Tanner Dyson, and no doubt the others were surprised and flattered to see the media mogul in their presence.

As Tanner shook hands and spoke briefly to the other men on

the stairs, Irving studied his clothes with mild envy. It helped that Tanner kept himself in excellent shape and his weight down about ten pounds more than necessary. His ramrod posture and reed slimness made the European cut of his custom suit fit to perfection.

Irving waited at the head of the stairs, wishing to God he knew what was in the paper.

Dyson finally broke away from the others with a politician's handshake, one hand shaking, the other cupping an elbow, and hurried up the stairs.

"Hello, Irving," he said, as they shook hands at the top of the stairs.

"Tanner," Irving said brightly.

"I hope I haven't kept you waiting. I know you're a busy man."

Irving sighed with relief. Tanner had given him his out.

"Luckily, I just had a court case postponed. I've been locked up with Judge Markus all morning."

"Oh, if I'd known I'd have brought you a copy of today's paper," Tanner said as they moved toward the entrance of the dining room.

"I certainly heard about it. You can fill me in. What are you drinking, my friend?" Irving asked, cheerfully clasping Tanner's left shoulder pad as they approached the bar.

"Perrier with lime, thanks," Tanner said.

The two men settled themselves at a corner table as a waiter followed with their drinks.

"So," Tanner said, carefully crossing his legs, as though mindful of the knifelike crease of his trousers. Tanner gave Irving the gist of Baby's story, implying that they had splashed it on page one more for the girl's picture than the story itself.

"Well, no harm done," Irving said blithely, trying to give the impression that his involvement was just par for the course in the fast track.

"It looks like the Brits pulled a fast one," Tanner said, taking a sip of his Perrier. "I'm glad it won't complicate things for you,

Irving. Actually, it's fortunate we had this lunch date today. Now I can get the *real* story."

Irving studied Tanner's face. There was just a hint of a leer in his request.

He had to punch up the girl's story. If he could get Tanner intrigued with her background, maybe that was the way to go. Better to rope him in than to put himself in the degrading position of having to ask a favor of a more powerful man. Maybe there was enough of a newsman in Dyson to maneuver him into the picture as a competitor to the Brits. It was worth a try.

Baby had told him enough about Tanner's early relationship with the tit-heavy lemon soufflé he dumped his first wife for to know that Tanner was not only unsophisticated in the ways of women but a downright sucker for sex. Inside information was a powerful tool.

Irving removed the celery stalk from his Bloody Mary and set it aside. He had to strike now, or he would lose his shot.

"What you said about the Lopez girl is on target. You don't know the half of it," he said, wiggling his eyebrows.

"Oh?" Tanner said, his face brightening in lascivious delight. "How well *do* you know your client, Irving?"

Irving leaned forward and lowered his voice to a bedroom whisper. "Intimately," he said. He sat back and took a long sip of his drink and waited for the dirty movie in Tanner's brain to roll. "But first I want to talk about Georgina's book. I have some terrific ideas. I want to talk to Bob Kadanoff about a series of books. I think we can really build her into a big personality. She's got a lot of style. Your idea of a Sunday piece on her was brilliant. That ought to give Winslow House just the push we need. Monday, I'll set up a meeting . . ."

"Sounds great, Irving," Tanner said briskly. "I trust you implicitly. I think Georgina would be thrilled. Lord knows she's got enough ideas for a series of books. You go ahead. Do what you have to do."

Tanner's tone was too hurried, his attitude too pliant. He was walking right into Irving's trap.

"Now," Tanner said, leaning forward slightly. "Tell me more about this Lopez girl. Did you actually . . . you know."

Bang! Irving's trap slammed shut.

When Irving got to the bit of fiction about how he himself had given Lopez her "stage" name after watching her masturbate with a champagne bottle, Tanner switched from Perrier to scotch on the rocks.

When he began to list the names of people the girl supposedly told him she had had sex with, Tanner waved away the waiter bearing luncheon menus for the second time.

It was public knowledge that Tanner's media empire had been threatened with a hostile takeover during the eighties. The man involved, a sanctimonious Bible-quoting prig named Arnold Elihu, had eleven children that he trotted out for the media at the drop of a Minicam. This was right about the time of Tanner's messy divorce, and Elihu made a great deal of Tanner Dyson's character during the eight months that he made Tanner's life a living hell. Tanner ultimately kept his companies, but his hatred of Elihu remained white-hot.

Perceiving that Tanner's purient interest was a bottomless pit, Irving launched into a long story, making it up as he went along. He billed it as something Maria Lopez had told him about a three-way S-M party with a prominent New York businessman. Suddenly, Irving interrupted himself and slapped his forehead for effect. "Jesus," he gasped. "It just occurred to me. You gotta know this guy."

Tanner looked across the table bug-eyed. "I do?"

"Yeah, yeah, yeah," Irving said, ostensibly searching for the name. "He wanted the girls to tie him up with their panty hose. Damn . . ." He snapped his fingers. "Short guy, bald, bought out Penn Media a year ago. You were involved with him on some deal a couple of years back? I forget exactly when . . ." Irving let his voice trail off as though still searching for the name.

Tanner was looking around the room to see if he could be overheard. "Good Lord, Irving. You don't mean Arnold Elihu?"

"That's the guy! Elihu," Irving said, snapping his fingers once again. "So, anyway. The girls agree to tie him up. Then, he offers them another grand if they'll flick his nipples with a cigarette lighter."

Irving's mind was running at double the speed of his mouth. He frantically tried to remember if Tanner had any children, particularly daughters, by his first marriage. It was worth a shot to make Maria's friend in the scene fourteen years old.

He glanced across the table at Tanner's rapt expression and decided not to chance it. One thing Irving always prided himself on was knowing enough to quit while he was ahead.

Irving waved for the waiter, confident his mission had been accomplished.

They both read the menu for a moment, then Tanner cleared his throat.

"Look, Irv," he said, with a studied, casual air. "What do you think it would take to get the girl away from the Brits?"

"You mean kind of a rekidnapping?"

"Actually, what I was thinking was that I could assign someone to track her down. If the girl wants money, that's not a problem. The Elihu involvement puts a much bigger spin on this story. Don't you think?"

Irving paused for a moment as though considering the idea. Actually, he was going weak with relief. The plan was working. "Well, yeah . . . but, boy, this is a rough one. We'd have to move fast. I dunno. I don't think it could be done."

"What about going to the Brits directly, buying her back? Billy Mosby is a good friend of mine. He may be the queen's third cousin, but he likes a buck as well as the next man."

"Nah, that could backfire. They would know we were on to something. They'd keep her for sure, then."

Tanner asked the hovering waiter for a chef's salad and iced tea. Irving quickly ordered the same, wishing they didn't have to eat at all. His whole plan was going swimmingly.

There was a moment of silence while they waited for the waiter to move on.

Tanner leaned forward. "I've got it," he said calmly. "I know exactly what we can do. It's tricky, but I think it will work. I have a meeting tomorrow morning with a young reporter that one of my editors suggested. Petra Weems says she's difficult but fearless. She may just be the one to solve our problem here. Let me try my idea out on her first, then we'll talk."

Irving was sorry the subject of Maria Lopez was closed. He rather enjoyed turning Dyson on. Now they would have to go back to nano-talk about the lemon soufflé's goddamn book.

29

*K*ick opened the door to find a much calmer Neeva than the one she had spoken to an hour before.

As she stepped through the door, Neeva handed Kick a grease-splotched paper bag from the French bakery on Columbus. *"Pain au chocolat* to feed our souls," she said with a wan smile.

Kick opened the bag and closed her eyes in rapture when she smelled the fresh chocolate-stuffed croissants. "Oh, God, how did you know?" she breathed. "I love these things. There's nothing to eat here but two cans of SpaghettiOs. I'm starving."

"I didn't know how you liked your coffee," Neeva said, reaching into her tote bag and pulling out a jar of instant. She'd spent enough time in the apartment going through Lolly's things to know how poorly stocked the kitchen was. "I've got Sweet'n Low and some half-and-half too."

"Come on," Kick said, gesturing toward the stairs. "Let's go up to the tower and pig out."

The two women settled into the office. Kick sat at the desk, while Neeva sat on the old couch, balancing a mug of instant coffee made from water Kick had heated on the hot plate that shared the closet with the Xerox copier.

"So," Kick said, carefully placing a pastry on a piece of bond on the desk. "You seem a little less frantic now. Anything new?"

"I screwed up my courage and called Jeff," Neeva said with a deep sigh of relief. "He says not to worry. He'll pay the immediate bills."

"Sweet guy," Kick said, chewing slowly.

"The sweetest."

"So, you're back in business."

"I guess, only twenty-five thousand dollars in the hole."

"We'll make that back, won't we?"

"I guess so," Neeva said tentatively. She took a sip of her coffee and thought for a moment. When she looked up at Kick, her eyes were pleading. "Kick, I don't know what I'm going to do about Irving."

"What do you want to do?"

"I want to leave him," Neeva said.

"That sounds doable."

"Have you ever been married, Kick?"

"Nope. Crazy in love but never married."

"Why not?"

Kick shrugged. "I dunno. I guess I've spent my twenties figuring out who I am. Sounds selfish, doesn't it?"

"No, it sounds smart. I never had that. I was raised to define myself through a man. My mother drummed that into me. I went through college and graduate school waiting, like Sleeping Beauty, for the right man. Even my job, which I love, was partly a way to meet men. Then I met Irving. He was so strong, so smart. I felt, no matter what, he would take care of me. I was absolutely nuts about him. But there was one small problem."

"Oh?" Kick asked.

"He was already married."

"Ooops," Kick said, wanting to add, *of course.* "Any kids?"

"One, a son. Jason. A very bright, very sweet boy who must be twenty-one, twenty-two, now."

"You're not sure how old he is?"

Neeva looked down at her coffee cup. "No. His mother did her best to turn him against Irving. At first I thought it was cruel of her. Now I think I understand better. Anyway, Irving barely sees him."

"So, clearly, Irving got a divorce."

"Right, but you don't know what I had to do to make that happen," Neeva said with a sigh. "I completely turned myself wrong side out. Irving's wife was a writer. She had a career. Irving didn't like that. She was demanding. Irving didn't like that, either. She didn't believe Irving walked on water. Irving really didn't like that."

"But you were different," Kick said.

"That's the story. It wasn't hard for me to turn myself into the placid, obedient, adoring little girl. That's how I was raised. I made the half life we had together so pleasant, so hassle-free that I eventually won. If you can call having Irving marry me winning."

"What's changed?" Kick asked, feeling a private kind of relief that she wasn't the only one who had been tricked into betraying herself for love.

"It's been gradual, really," Neeva said, glancing in the pastry bag, then shaking her head and twisting the top closed against temptation. "I began to see that Irving was all flash. His stealing the money my mother left me was the final straw."

"It was also grand larceny," Kick said, outraged. "I think you should call the cops."

Kick could see Neeva's eyes filling.

"Neeva?" Kick said softly. "I know we don't know each other that well, but if there's something you want to get off your chest, I'm here for you."

Neeva looked back at Kick and bit her lip. "Irving is having an affair," she blurted out.

Since Kick had already identified Irving as a member of the Lionel Maltby school of intersexual relations, she wasn't surprised. But she was furious for her friend. "Oh, Neeva. How can you stand all this at once?"

Neeva shrugged. "Not well. Last night, after I found the money gone, it was all too much. I went out and treated myself the same way Irving treats me."

"Huh?"

"Like garbage," Neeva said quietly. She lifted the bakery bag and held it toward Kick. "You want this last one?"

Kick shook her head. "What happened last night?"

"It's pretty gruesome. You sure you want to know?"

"Of course. But I have to warn you. I'm a writer. My memory is a registered weapon."

"Fine. Just change the names to protect the guilty."

"Go on."

Neeva pulled the last pastry from the bag with two fingers, studied it for a moment, and took a big bite. She chewed and swallowed before she spoke.

"I went to the Oak Room, got blitzed on martinis, and picked up two conventioneers."

"Neeva. You?"

"Wait, it gets worse. We went to some disco in hell. I went back to their hotel and screwed both of them. At least they practice safe sex in the Midwest."

"That's a relief," Kick said.

"One of the guys left his socks on," Neeva said, giggling, as she dusted the crumbs off her hands.

Kick couldn't help it. She pitched forward onto the desk and roared. "That's like a porno movie," she said when she sat up and wiped her eyes. "When did they bring in the Doberman pinscher?"

"I shudder when I think of it. Plus having run into Jeffrey at that disco. I was so mortified it took all the strength I had to call him this morning. He was sweet. He really was. He didn't even bring it up."

"Oh, you poor dear. You must feel rotten," Kick said. "I hope to God you didn't tell them who you were."

"No, but they know I live in Trump Tower. I volunteered that bit of snobbery when we drove by the building."

Kick extended one finger to pick up the stray crumbs on the piece of paper on the desk. "Maybe they thought you were Ivana. I can't wait until that rumor hits the columns."

"Kick, do you think I need to see a shrink or something? I mean, wasn't that a sick thing to do?"

Kick made a face, then shook her head. "It's understandable. People do goofy things when they're hurt. If I were you, I'd pretend it never happened."

Neeva put her coffee cup down on the side table and curled up on the couch. "Well, I've made up my mind. I'm not going to put up with this life anymore," she said, with quiet determination. "When Jeff told me he would bail me out on the bills, I took it as a sign. I have to bail myself out of this marriage. This project and Jeff's encouragement have made me like myself for the first time. I want to feel like that all the time."

"What are you going to do? Where will you go?"

"I don't know. I can't stay in that apartment any longer. He can move his current bimbo in, for all I care."

"Neeva, you can stay here. I've been sleeping in the office to stay out of the way while you and your people work, but you can sleep in Lolly's room if you don't mind the chaos."

"Oh, Kick, that's so nice of you. Let me think about it, okay?"

"About the bimbo, do you know who it is?"

"No," Neeva said, with a sigh. "But somehow I don't think she's the first for Irving. Now that I look back, I think he's been screwing around for as long as we've been married."

Kick walked her coffee mug to the little sink behind the door.

"I'm having dinner with the editor of the *Courier* tonight," she said, as she rinsed out her cup. "He knows everything that goes on around town. Someone has to have seen Irving with this woman. I'll check it out."

"Oh, Kick, would you?" Neeva said eagerly.

"No problem."

"Is this a big date tonight?"

"*Umm,* kind of," Kick answered with a sly grin.

Neeva stood and shook the crumbs from her sweats. "One has to look smashing, right?"

"Yeah, smashing," Kick said, frowning. "I have a choice between a black dress one size too small and a black dress one size too big. I don't dare buy anything new right now."

"Come on," Neeva said, picking up her tote bag.

"Where are we going?"

"I'm taking you to Saks. My treat."

"Neeva, you can't do that," Kick protested.

"I'm doing it. Don't argue."

"I'll pay you back."

"That won't be necessary. It's Irving's card. It's the last one I have that's paid up. We might as well take advantage of it."

Neeva and Kick capped an afternoon of carefree shopping with tea at the Mayfair and giddy plans for Neeva's new life. By the time they parted, Neeva had agreed to accept Kick's invitation to stay at the penthouse until she could make other arrangements. She would go pack a few things and come over later.

It was late afternoon when Neeva helped Kick into a cab with all her shopping bags. Kick gave her a spare set of keys and promised to be quiet if she got in late. Just as the cab started to pull out into traffic, Neeva ran into the street and leaned in the back window. She kissed Kick on the cheek. "Thank you for being a friend, Kick."

"You're welcome," Kick said. "It isn't difficult."

"This whole Irving business is very painful to me. Once I get over the pain, I guess it's all economics."

Kick thought for a moment, then nodded. "I think that was the original last line of *Gone With the Wind*," she said with mock seriousness.

Neeva giggled. "Kick, you're a nut."

"A nut who's on your side," Kick said, rolling up the window. Just before it reached the top she pushed her lips out the last two inches and called, "I love my new dress!"

30

*T*he phone in the penthouse foyer was ringing as Kick unlocked the door.

Joe wanted to know if she would have dinner at his apartment. She eagerly agreed. Nothing told one more about a man than a look at how he lived.

She dressed in the wonderful outfit Neeva had given her, a black knit sheath with matching jacket by Nicole Miller. It was the most expensive outfit she had ever owned. She had protested letting Neeva buy it, until she tried it on. For the first time, she understood why someone would spend eight hundred dollars for something to wear. It had melted over her body like warm fog. Neeva had gasped as Kick turned slowly around in the three-way mirror. Under the sleek fabric was a figure Kick had forgotten she had.

She quickly showered and put on the outfit again. If possible, it felt even more luscious than it had in the store. She would never have bought anything like it by herself. If, indeed, she had helped

Neeva get through a trying day, Neeva had done a lot for her morale, as well.

As she was leaving the Barrington, it began to rain. Ordinarily, she would have trundled down into the subway for the run downtown. The subway in this dress was unthinkable. Maybe getting back into the real world was all a trap. You spend a lot of money to look good, more money to protect it, then you have to have it cleaned. What the hell, she thought, and hailed a cab.

Joe's building was one of New York's nondescript, mud-colored apartment houses with a fire escape climbing the facade. It was sandwiched between a drug-rehab clinic and an auto-body shop only a block from Renaldo's, where they had met.

When she stepped from the elevator on the top floor, Joe was standing in his doorway wearing a knee-length canvas apron that read *"I Got My Job Through the New York Courier."*

"Whoa," he breathed, moving his eyes down her body. "Look at you. I'm speechless."

Kick smiled and looked down at herself. "Neat, huh?"

"Ahhhh, there are about nine other words I'd choose. Neat isn't among them." He pulled off an oven mitt and took her hand. "Come on in. It will take me a moment to get my eyes back into their sockets."

Kick stepped into his foyer while he closed the door. "What's that wonderful smell?" she asked.

"I've got garlic bread in the oven."

"He cooks," she said gleefully. Kick walked toward the living room. "Now that's the perfect smell for a rainy night."

"Give me your coat."

"I'll do it. You go tend to your bread."

"Thanks. I better," he said, turning back to the kitchen. "There's a coatrack on the back of the bathroom door. Help yourself to wine. I'll be right out."

Kick moved into the room. It was just what she expected. Books were everywhere. A table in the corner held a Mac and a printer. There was a battered but comfortable-looking couch in front of a working fireplace and unmatched club chairs on either side.

She helped herself to the open bottle of wine in a bucket on the coffee table. She glanced at the small fire in the fireplace as she carried her glass to a pair of sliding doors that looked out onto a dark, wet rooftop.

She took one sip and felt her throat close. The tightness in her chest began to radiate to her shoulders and neck. Her hand on the stem of the wineglass began to tremble noticeably. She quickly put the glass down on the edge of a bookshelf and hugged herself to steady her hands.

What the hell is happening to me? she thought as her breath came in short gasps.

She listened for a moment and knew. It was the music. The volume was turned so low she hadn't noticed it at first. It was also the books, the fire, a man cooking, lousy weather.

God help me, she thought, pressing her forehead against the cool glass of the sliding door. I'm having a déjà vu attack. My first night back in the world as a human and I've come full circle.

"How're ya' doing?" Joe called out.

"F—f—fine," she croaked. "Just fine. Take your time."

"I hope you like meat loaf and mashed potatoes?"

"My favorite," she called back, praying she sounded normal. She walked toward the kitchen and peered around the corner. Joe was looking into the open oven.

"Okay if I use your bathroom?"

"Sure," he said, looking up with a grin. "I . . ."

Kick didn't hear the rest of his sentence. She bolted for the john, locked it, and leaned against the door, sweat beading her forehead. She walked over and sat down on the closed toilet, feeling as though she was going to faint.

She had to get it together. This was crazy. Was she going to flip out every time she saw an open fire? Were men in kitchens a phobia she was going to have to live with?

"Stop it," she told herself, hammering her fists on her thighs.

271

"This isn't Lionel. This is nice. This is good. Joe is a friend. This is not going to hurt."

The tiny mean voice she hadn't heard since the day she found Lolly dead on the floor cackled from some deep crevice in her brain. *That's what you thought about Lionel.*

She sat very straight and took little panting breaths, thinking of it as a sort of Lamaze for giving birth to her grown-up self.

"Madame, dinner is served," she heard Joe call in a stagey English accent outside the bathroom door.

She cleared her throat. "Be right there."

She stood in front of the mirror over the sink and pinched her cheeks to relieve the green pallor. She wished she had thought to bring her bag in with her. Her hair could use a fluff and she needed some lip gloss. She moved closer to the mirror and looked into her own eyes. "Calm down, Katherine Maureen. Calm the hell down. This is a nice thing. Enjoy."

Joe was standing proudly by the food-laden card table when she returned to the living room. "I hope you don't mind if we eat sooner than later," he said, holding the back of her chair. "I find if I sit around swilling cocktails, somehow dinner never gets served."

"Not at all, I'm starved," Kick said surveying the table. "Joe, this is spectacular. How come you know how to do all this?"

Joe retrieved her glass from the bookshelf, poured more wine, then held her chair. "Simple survival," he said, taking his seat. "I spent a lot of time eating cold pizza by the kitchen sink. But I've recently decided I deserve a more civilized lifestyle, even if I have to provide it myself. This menu, in fact, is the first I've mastered."

"How long were you married?" Kick asked, both out of curiosity and because she remembered enough about men in social situations to know that if she got them talking about themselves, she didn't have to do anything but listen.

During dinner, Joe did indeed do most of the talking, responding in full to her somewhat personal questions. At one point she apologized for sounding like a reporter conducting an interview, but she could tell he was flattered by her interest.

When they finished, Joe popped up to clear the table.

"You relax," he said, reaching for two brandy snifters on a bookshelf next to the table. "There's brandy. If you'll pour, I'll bring coffee."

Kick was feeling immeasurably better. She poured two brandies and settled back into the soft, worn corduroy pillows of Joe's couch. The music had changed to soft rock only slightly louder than the wind outside. The cat, who Joe said was named Geraldo, had appeared from some secret cat place during dinner and had since apparently decided Kick was okay. He leapt into her lap and went to sleep. She rested her brandy snifter on his plush back and stared into the fire.

Joe reappeared with a tray of two mugs and a Chemex pot of coffee and placed it on the coffee table. "How many people do you know who still own a Chemex?" he asked, pouring them both a cup.

"Two." Kick laughed. "We found seven coffee pots in Lolly's pantry. One was a Chemex."

"Collector's item," he said, taking a seat in one of the club chairs by the fire.

Kick liked that. If he had sat down beside her on the couch, she would have been uncomfortable. It would have been too predictable a move.

"That was absolutely delicious, Joe," she said, meaning it. "It was so nice of you to go to the trouble."

"I like comfort food," he said, grinning. "Sort of an antidote to the days I spend awash in violence and sex."

"I'm embarrassed to admit, I didn't get to see the *Courier* today."

He turned and poked the fire. "Too bad. We had two fellows you must know on our front page."

"No kidding. What was on the front page?"

"Well, the biggest thing was Monica Champagne's chest. Our readership demands that. But at the bottom of the page we had Irving Fourbraz and Abner Hoon."

Kick eased Geraldo off her lap and leaned forward. "Monica Champagne?"

"The Lopez girl in the Keeko Ram case. Her working name is Monica Champagne."

"So, go on. I know Irving Fourbraz represents her, but what does Hoon have to do with it?"

"His paper kidnapped the girl. Hoon's supposed to have been involved with setting it up."

"What?" she asked, completely surprised. "Can that be done?"

"I don't think it was a kidnapping at all. I think the girl cut a better deal with the Brits. Left Fourbraz out in the cold. But he'll recover. He's a pro at the game. Anytime a good-looking woman figures in some scandal, we can count on Irving turning up as both her agent and lawyer."

Kick held her palm over her glass as Joe lifted the brandy bottle again. "Does Irving fool around?" Kick asked, trying to sound disinterested. "I mean, you don't suppose he's having an affair with this Monica, do you?"

"I don't think so. I doubt he could handle two at the same time."

"What does that mean?"

"His current squeeze works for me."

Whoops, Kick thought. Maybe she'd better drop the subject for the moment. She didn't want to sound too eager. "So, how is Irving taking all this? He must be furious."

"No doubt. He's probably trying to get on the Concorde with a loaded gun. I heard he sold the exclusive rights for the story to the *World* for six figures. Now the Brits are tormenting him, saying they plan to do a book."

"A book?" Kick asked in disgust. "How could someone do a whole book on a call girl who gets lucky with a big TV star—if you can call being thrown off a motel balcony lucky."

"The word around is that she's got a bigger story to tell. Seems she was a jet-set hooker with a lot of clients in London. That's why the Brits were interested."

"I take it your information comes from the reporter who did the story."

"Right," Joe said. "Baby Bayer. You probably saw her do her number at Lolly's memorial service."

"Oh, yes. The one who recited 'Feelings.'"

"'Wind Beneath My Wings,'" Joe corrected.

"Why, Joe, what a sweet thing to say," she said, then waited for his reaction.

He reached out and cuffed her knee playfully, refusing to give her the benefit of a laugh.

"What an odd woman," she said. "Is she a good reporter?"

Joe turned and looked at the fire. "Yeah, she's good. She gets the story. I can't say that she's a great writer. Now, you, my friend, are a great writer."

Kick grimaced. "Sore subject."

"I'm really sorry about that piece, Kick. You know it had nothing to do with the way you handled it. It was all office politics. But I have an idea."

"Uh-oh," Kick said apprehensively. Now that her Lolly piece was dead, she just wanted the subject to go away.

"Seriously. I'd like to pass it along to a friend of mine."

"Who?"

"Fiddle Null."

Kick cringed. "Geez, Joe, you're handy with the salt for old wounds."

He held up his hand. "Hear me out, Kick. It's a shame to waste your piece. Why don't you let me send it over to her? If she doesn't like it, nothing's lost. Fiddle's a terrific editor; I think she'll agree it's a good piece."

"I don't know, Joe. I don't think I'm one of Fedalia Null's favorite writers. I mean, she did can me."

"From what she tells me, she was pressured into it by Irving. Fiddle runs one hell of a magazine, but she has one fatal flaw. She has a tendency to cater to powerful people. She needed Irving's clients more than she needed another writer. It's a jungle out here, Kick."

Kick stared into the fire. "Out here . . ." she repeated wistfully. "I guess I'm out here again. I'm just beginning to realize what a sheltered life I've been living up in Lolly's ivory tower."

"Welcome back," Joe said softly, reaching over and lightly touching her arm. "Don't be frightened. You have a friend."

Kick pulled her eyes away from the flames and looked at him. The sweetness she saw in his expression caused a lump to form in her throat. "Thank you, Joe," she said looking away. "That means a great deal to me. More than you know."

Joe reached across the coffee table and picked up Kick's coffee cup. "Here, let me get you some hot."

Kick sat watching the fire, thinking about Joe's offer. Maybe she should let him do it. The worst that could happen would be that Fedalia would remember her without fondness, stuff it right back in the envelope, and tell Joe not to bother her with amateurs. Still, she wanted to think about it.

Joe returned from the kitchen with a fresh cup of coffee.

Kick leaned forward and took a sip. "You make good coffee, Joe Stone," she said smiling up at him. "And superior meat loaf and, as Ross Perot would say, world-class mashed potatoes."

"More brandy?" he asked, reaching for the bottle.

"Uh-uh," Kick said, swallowing. "I've got to go, really."

"I wish you'd stay a while," Joe said, his eyes moving down her dress again.

"I saw that look," Kick teased.

"That obvious, huh?"

"Yeah . . . but nice. Not grounds for a harassment charge. Nice."

"You know I want you to stay. We could play Monopoly. We could get out my collection of baseball cards. Or we could go to bed and make passionate love."

"Nah, that's okay," Kick said, laughing. She pushed herself up out of the low couch and sidestepped the coffee table. "I never play Monopoly on a full stomach."

"I could wait four or five hours," Joe said meekly.

Kick smiled at him over her shoulder as she walked to the

bathroom to get her coat. "Anyway, Geraldo looks like a watcher. If there's anything I can't stand, it's being watched."

Kick returned from the bathroom to find Joe shrugging into a suede jacket.

"You're cold?" Kick said.

"I will be if I go outside without a coat. I'm finding you a cab."

"You really don't have to, Joe. I'll hail one right downstairs."

"The street is a seething mass of our more aggressive brethren hungry for fresh female flesh and wallets," Joe said as they stepped out into the hall. He pulled the door shut and double-locked it.

When they reached the street, the rain had stopped. There were no cabs on Joe's street, so they picked their way between the puddles and walked to the corner of Eighth Avenue.

"So who's Irving Fourbraz having an affair with? I love celebrity dish."

"Just between us?"

"Of course," Kick said lightly.

"My reporter, Henrietta Hat."

Kick, who was walking a few steps ahead, stopped and turned. "Baby Bayer? That's interesting. Is that how she got all those items on Maria Lopez?"

"Probably," Joe said under his breath.

Kick sensed that he didn't really want to discuss it further. That was fine. She didn't need the details. She had the information Neeva needed, and that was enough.

"I'm not crazy about Irving Fourbraz, but he has my sympathy," Joe said.

"Why do you say that?"

Joe stopped walking and turned to face Kick. He put both hands on her shoulders. "Look, Kick, I plan to see more of you, if you're willing."

"I'm willing," Kick said, nodding enthusiastically.

"I just want you to hear this from me. You know how people talk. It will only be a matter of time before you find out that Baby and I had a . . . thing . . . once."

"A thing," Kick said without inflection. "You mean an affair."

"That doesn't quite describe a relationship that was something between a drinking contest and a fistfight. Whatever it was, it's over. Thank God."

Kick laughed, giving Joe high marks for at least telling her. He was right. She would have heard about it. "Thank you for telling me, Joe," she said as they resumed walking. "Now I'll tell you something."

"Okay," he said.

"Between us?"

"Right."

"Irving's wife is a friend of mine. She's going to leave him and stay with me for a while, until she gets settled somewhere."

"Yikes," Joe said, grimacing. "Did I just get myself in trouble?"

"No, but I am going to tell her about Baby. I'm sorry. I guess I tricked you into telling me."

"That's okay," Joe said, cheerfully. "But, as they said in *Tea and Sympathy*, when you speak of me . . . be kind."

"I'm not going to speak of you at all," Kick said, squeezing his arm. "I never reveal a source."

Suddenly, Joe's arm shot into the air, and a cab screeched out of nowhere and pulled to the curb. As Kick turned to say good night, he put his arm lightly around her waist. "I won't kiss you good night until you promise you'll think seriously about letting me submit your piece to Fiddle Null."

"I don't like the deal," she said, looking up at him. The yellow light from the streetlamp showed the tiny creases at the corners of his eyes, which made him look as if he were smiling even when he wasn't. "How's this sound? If you kiss me good night, I'll promise to think about it."

Joe leaned forward and slowly pressed his lips to hers. His mouth was slightly open, not enough to be terribly sexy but enough to make something flutter in her chest. Then he stepped back.

"Are you thinking?"

"I'm thinking about thinking," she said.

"How about thinking about my time?" the driver snarled. "My meter's running, ya know."

They both laughed as Kick slid into the backseat.

"I'll call you," Joe said through the window.

"Soon."

"How about an hour?"

"It only takes me twenty minutes to get uptown," she yelled as the cab started to roll.

31

*B*aby chose black spandex. The top pushed her breasts up without showing too much cleavage. The bottom hugged her hips, thighs, and rear as snugly as a girdle and called attention to her muscular legs. If she was going to show Tanner Dyson she meant business about getting Lolly's column, she was going to involve his eyes and his gonads first. If he balked, she had a copy of the wedding-day agreement in her purse, right next to Irving's phone. As a final touch, she fastened the diamond pin Tanner had tried to buy her off with between her breasts.

She gave her hair one last poke with a rattail comb and smiled. Irving, the bastard, wherever he was, would be crippled without his precious telephone. She hoped he was suffering. More than anything, she wished she had been with him when he saw her Monica Champagne story.

"Mess with me, will you," she said to her reflection in the bathroom mirror, still seething over the lies she believed he had told her about his wife and their money. She hated it when people thought she was dumb. That's what lying to someone did—told them you thought they were dumb. The worst was to have someone you were fucking lie to you. Exchanging body fluids with someone should mean you have a pact, an unspoken agreement not to lie to the other person.

Of course, *she* lied to guys, but that was different. A girl had to protect herself.

She flicked on her answering machine, double-locked the front door, and strode through the lobby with the firm determination that when she returned that evening, she would have what she felt was rightfully hers—Lolly Pines's column—or else.

The rain that had been soaking the city on and off since the night before had finally stopped. Baby was relieved not to have to cover the effect of the black spandex with a raincoat. She wanted a little street feedback before her meeting.

She got it as she waited for a downtown cab at the corner of Second Avenue.

"Hey, doll, wanna do the wild thing?" yelled the driver of a beat-up blue van gunning his engine as he moved through the intersection.

"In your dreams," Baby yelled, flipping him the finger, and yanked open the door of a yellow cab that screeched to a halt in front of her.

She knew that all the secretaries at the desks that lined the dark wood corridor of the executive floor were staring at her as she stepped off the elevator. She gave a little extra swing to her hips as she moved, head up, toward the big double doors to Tanner's office.

Baby blinked against the light of the large window at the end of the vast room. In the distance, the shimmer of the East River nearly blinded her.

Tanner's tall, thin body was framed against the window. His silver hair created a translucent glow around his head. Did he work standing up? Baby wondered. Had he stood when he heard the secretary buzzing? The effect was a clever one, calculated to give the feeling that he eagerly anticipated her visit, while implying that he had a limited amount of time.

"Good morning, Baby," she heard him say. She couldn't see his face at all. He must have practiced this, she thought. It was all very Darth Vader and utterly disconcerting. If anyone had an ounce of fear or apprehension about meeting him, they would be too paralyzed to sit down.

"Good morning, Tanner," she said, moving slowly in a very straight line toward him. She was annoyed that the lighting prevented her from seeing if his eyes moved down her body. She knew he was besotted with Georgina, but she'd never met a man who didn't at least look.

"Please," he said, gesturing to one of the two austere Harvard chairs in front of his desk.

They both sat down. Baby languidly crossed her legs. There, that was better, she thought. Now she could see him. He was, as always, beautifully dressed. He wasn't wearing a jacket, no doubt trying to look like the rough, tough journalists on the floors below but ruining the effect with a tiny TD monogrammed a third of the way down his chest and large gold knots at his French cuffs. The pale lavender of his shirt was echoed in the alternate stripe of a lavender-and-gray silk tie. He had the same sunlamp tan he had when she first met him during the hectic Georgina days and didn't look a day older. Georgina was probably responsible for that. She probably gave Tanner sponge baths with camphorated oil to keep the basal cells in his skin from erupting in response to all that fake sun.

"This is most serendipitous," Tanner said, folding his arms on the glossy top of his big desk.

What the fuck does he mean by that? Baby wondered. She didn't trust him as far as she could heave his mahogany desk. "How is that, Tanner?" she asked in her best Marilyn Monroe voice.

"If we hadn't already made this appointment, I would have sent for you myself."

"Oh," she said, thinking: You bastard. I know this game. It's the old dangle and disarm gambit. She had used it herself many times when she knew someone was displeased with her. She would head them off with a promise of goodies to come. In her case, it always involved the promise of some sort of sex treat. In this case, she was sure Tanner would play to her ambition.

"First, let me congratulate you on the excellent work on the Monica Champagne story," he said pleasantly. "Circulation tells me that edition did bigger newsstand sales than the *Post's* Marla Maples 'Best Sex I Ever Had' story. Shows you the power of a good scandal, doesn't it?"

"Or of a couple of extremely large breasts," Baby said with a sultry smile.

"Perhaps," Tanner said, clearing his throat. "Now, I know this is your meeting, but there is something I'd like to discuss with you first, if that's all right with you."

Baby thought for a moment. "Okay," she said slowly.

"You seem to have a lock on this Maria Lopez story. It's my feeling that we should stay on it. What I'd be interested in most particularly is who her big-name clients have been."

"I don't see how it can be done, Tanner. Not without her. That's the reason the Brits took her in the first place. They want her English clients."

Even though Tanner's icy eyes began to warm, she didn't trust him. "Baby," he said, leaning forward. "There's no one on staff here who could pull this off except you."

What the hell is he up to? Baby thought. He pretends I don't exist for years and suddenly I'm hot stuff? "Pull what off, Tanner?"

"I want you to find Maria Lopez. Offer her however much money she wants and get her story."

Baby leveled her eyes at him and said nothing.

"I'd like you to leave for London immediately. Wherever the girl is, Abner Hoon has to know."

"Don't tell me you're planning to offer Hoon money," Baby said sharply. "I don't know how he feels about this Lopez story, but he'd never risk losing his column. The *Gazette* would can him for sure."

"I'm not suggesting that, Baby," Tanner said in a somewhat

patronizing tone. "How you get the information out of Abner Hoon is part of the assignment. It's my understanding that the two of you are friends. I heard you were very cozy at the Garns' party over Labor Day weekend."

Baby rolled her eyes. "Nobody, *nobody* in this town keeps their trap shut, do they?"

"I'm sure the two of you made an attractive couple," Tanner said, leaning back and grinning annoyingly.

"We weren't a couple," Baby said angrily. "And if you have some idea in your head that I can seduce Abner Hoon to find the Lopez girl, you are barking up the wrong sexual proclivity."

Tanner leaned forward and lowered his silver eyebrows. "Baby, you'll be staying at Claridge's. All expenses will be taken care of. Can you be on the next Concorde flight to London?"

It was too tempting. All of this would somehow get back to Irving. It would drive him nuts if she was responsible for yanking his client out from under the noses of the people who'd stolen her from him. Joe Stone was bound to hear about it. So would Petra, the bitch. She didn't know how she would manipulate Abner, but she had a few hours to think about it.

"No problem," she said, recrossing her legs and slightly arching her back. She brushed an imaginary speck from her spandex top to check her cleavage. "I'll need something to wear."

Tanner smiled weakly and shook his head. "All right, Baby," he said with a sigh. "I'll take care of that personally. This was my idea. You do understand that this entire arrangement is confidential? It's between you and me."

Baby raised her chin and lowered her eyes. "No one else knows about this?"

"No one."

Baby didn't believe him. She leaned forward and skewered him with what she felt was her killer look. "Did Irving Fourbraz think this one up? As you know from my story, he's in deep doo-doo financially over this. Did he ask you to try and get her away from the Brits?"

"Do you know Irving Fourbraz?" he asked calmly.

"Not personally," she said, matching his tone.

"Then let me assure you, Irving would never ask such a favor. He has no idea I am speaking to you. Neither does anyone else. I can't afford leaks. If either of us tells anyone about this, we'll lose it. You know how people talk."

"Tell me about it," Baby said sarcastically.

"Do we have a deal?"

"Maybe. There's one more thing. Suppose I find her and she tells me everything. What's in it for me?"

Tanner stood, indicating that their time was up. "If you do this for me, Baby, you'll have Lolly Pines's column as soon as you get back."

Baby sat speechless for a moment to make sure she heard him right. "You mean that?" she asked.

"I meant it when I told you on my wedding day. I still mean it," he said, moving around the end of his desk.

"But why have you waited . . . I mean . . . she's been dead for almost a month. You could have told me before this."

"Perhaps. But I'm telling you now. After all, that's what you came up here to ask, right?"

"Yeah . . . yes, but . . ."

Tanner had moved so close to her she could smell his cologne. There was barely enough room between them for him to bend his arm and offer his hand. His fly was even with her face. "Do we have a deal?"

Baby stood up and tried to smooth her skirt without bumping into him. It was an awkward move, again calculated to keep her off guard.

"Okay," she said tentatively, shaking his hand. "Yeah, we have a deal. Who do I see about tickets and stuff?"

"My secretary has everything you'll need. Stop by her desk on the way out. She can answer any questions. She knows where you're going but not why. Don't fill her in."

Baby nodded. Her head was spinning. It seemed as though she should be asking for more information, but she couldn't think of what to ask.

She walked slightly behind Tanner as he moved toward the door and opened it. She was halfway out when it dawned on her that she had no more of a guarantee of Lolly's column now than she had at Tanner's wedding.

"Hey," she said, whirling around. "How do I know you'll actually give me the column?"

Tanner smiled. It was a slow, slightly twisted motion around the mouth. His eyes looked positively arctic.

"Why don't you just hang on to that document you have in your bag? I can't imagine you didn't bring it with you."

Baby's jaw dropped. Reflexively, her hand went to her shoulder bag, pressing it to her hip.

"I thought so," he said, dropping his smile.

"But how did you know I'd bring it?" she asked, completely befuddled.

"You're a very smart young woman. One of the most ambitious I've known in my long career. Every time I've heard your name, I've thought about that document. I'm a little surprised it took you so long to challenge me with it."

Baby couldn't pinpoint what she was feeling. It was familiar, and yet she hadn't felt this way for a very long time.

"Good luck, Baby. Please be in touch as soon as you arrive. I want to follow your every move."

With that, Tanner gently closed the door in her face.

It wasn't until she heard the solid clunk of the brass catch on the door that she identified what she was feeling.

It was profound embarrassment. She had come to see Tanner to trick him into giving her what she wanted. Instead he had gotten her to do precisely what he wanted her to do. She had agreed to a damn near impossible assignment and still had only his promise that she would get Lolly's column.

Until now, she believed she had never met anyone who was a better manipulator than she was. She had met the master.

32

*K*ick awoke to green-blue morning light streaming through the glass ceiling of the tower room. It was bright enough to tell her that the rain clouds of the night before had cleared away. Her back felt as though she had been mugged; maybe sleeping up here in the relative peace and quiet wasn't such a good idea. But there was something about this room that made her feel good. It felt like it belonged to her.

When she sat up and leaned back, something hard and unyielding poked her. She got up to investigate and found, attached to the wall behind the couch, a rusty contraption that looked like a ship's wheel. It seemed to be held in place by thick wires that ran up the wall and disappeared into the trim that surrounded the ceiling. Evidently, the thing had been covered by the back of the couch for years.

Lolly had once said that her father raised orchids in this room years ago. Kick supposed the thing had something to do with raising and lowering racks of flowers. She shrugged, then folded up the bed, shoving the couch over so she wouldn't lean back on the contraption again.

Too lazy to go downstairs to the kitchen, she heated some water on the hot plate and spooned out some of the coffee crystals Neeva had brought over. She wondered if Neeva was awake. When she'd gotten home last night from her dinner with Joe, the door to Lolly's bedroom had been closed. Kick assumed Neeva'd been exhausted from moving her things out of the Trump Tower apartment and had gone to bed early.

Kick finished her coffee and pulled on her robe. It was after nine, and she and Neeva needed to make plans for the day.

On the second-floor landing, Kick tapped lightly on Lolly's bedroom door. When she got no answer, she knocked more loudly and then slowly pushed the door open. Lolly's big bed hadn't been slept in. There were no suitcases, nothing on the dresser, no signs at all that Neeva had indeed gone home and packed her bags after leaving Kick in the cab. Had she changed her mind about moving in for a while? Just then, the office phone rang. That would be Neeva, calling to explain. Kick ran up the stairs.

"Hi, Neeva. What's going on?"

A cool, official-sounding voice replied, "Is this Ms. Kick Butler?"

"I'm sorry, I thought this was a friend of mine. This is Kick Butler. How can I help you?"

"This is Nurse Driggs at New York Hospital. A Mrs. Neeva Fourbraz was admitted last night. She asked me to notify you."

"Oh, my God. What happened? Is Neeva all right?"

"Well, apart from the fact that her husband tried to kill her, she's fine."

Kick slammed down the phone. Within seconds she had found her Reeboks and pulled on a sweat suit that was tossed over the back of a chair. She grabbed her bag and raced down the stairs.

A bored receptionist in the main lobby of New York Hospital looked up from her copy of *People* magazine. Through hooded eyes she told Kick which wing and room Mrs. Fourbraz was in.

"Is there a problem getting in to see her?" Kick asked hurriedly.

"Not unless you got a problem," the woman said, dropping her eyes back to her magazine.

Kick studied the woman for a moment. "I don't have a problem."

"You do if you're not family."

"I'm her sister," Kick shot back.

"Then you don't have a problem."

"Thanks for all your help," Kick muttered, racing for the elevator.

Kick wandered the halls of the third floor unchallenged for a good five minutes before she located Neeva's room. She tapped on the half-open door with one knuckle. She thought she heard something and nudged the door.

"Neeva," she called in a loud whisper.

There was a rustling from the bed near the window.

"Who is it?"

"It's me, Kick."

The body in the bed rolled over, sending a cascade of pages of *The New York Times* skittering to the floor. "Kick, they said they would call you, but one never knows," Neeva said, pulling at the pillows in order to sit up. "I'm so glad you're here. Want some coffee?"

"Neeva," Kick said sharply, noting Neeva's neatly arranged hair and fluffed nightgown. She looked a long way from being an attempted murder victim. "What the hell is going on?"

"Look, the nurse just brought a whole pot."

Kick watched in bewilderment as Neeva reached for her bed tray and wheeled it closer. "I don't get it," she said, approaching the bed. "What is this? Canyon Ranch? The nurse who called told me Irving tried to kill you. Where are the tubes, the heart monitor? Where's the plastic tent? You look terrific."

Neeva sat up and reached out to give Kick a kiss. "Oh, Kick. You see too many movies. Everything is wonderful. I had such a good time," she said. "Sit down. I'll tell you all about it."

"I think you better. You gave me the scare of my life. Was Irving in the apartment when you got there?"

Neeva propped herself on several pillows and smiled. The light reflecting in from the East River gave her skin a lovely glow. For the first time Kick noticed that Neeva was actually prettier without makeup than she was with it.

"Kick, everything bad I ever thought about Irving was true. He is a rat. After last night I have no qualms whatsoever about getting even with him. As a matter of fact, I think I'll make it a hobby."

"So what did he do?" Kick asked, settling herself in a perfectly dreadful chrome hospital chair at the side of Neeva's bed.

Once Neeva had seen that Irving wasn't in the apartment she had been in no hurry to pack. She hadn't wanted to go back to the empty penthouse until she was sure Kick was home. She fixed herself something to eat and watched the evening news. She was standing at the kitchen sink when she heard a key in the door and looked up to see Irving standing in the hall staring at her.

"You know, it's funny, Kick," she said, leaning on her elbow. "All the years I've been married to Irving I've always been just slightly afraid of him. Nothing serious, just a slight uneasiness when he entered a room. I was always studying his face to see what kind of a mood he was in. If he looked angry, I would immediately conclude that I had done something wrong— forgotten to pick up his shirts, left the top loose on a ketchup bottle, said something he didn't like. I don't know. It would never be anything earth-shattering—nothing I ever did, right or wrong would have shattered earth."

"You wanted his approval," Kick said.

"Exactly," Neeva said, nodding. "You know, at dinner parties I used to watch wives like me when someone was telling a joke. They would be watching their husbands. If the husband laughed, then the wife would laugh. Now I see I used to do the same thing."

Kick put her feet up on the metal siding of the bed. "So,

Irving's standing staring at you and you haven't seen him since he embezzled all your money. Weren't you furious at just the sight of him? I think I would have wanted to kill him, myself."

"I wasn't, Kick," Neeva said with amazement. "I didn't feel anything. No, that's not it. I'd say I felt something that wasn't anything. I felt complete indifference. For an instant I remember thinking, oh, shit, I ate the last can of tuna. That passed. I didn't care if he had eaten. I didn't care where he had been. If I had seen a pool of blood forming around his shoes I would have figured, what the hell, I don't have to wipe it up. I don't live here anymore."

Kick reconsidered Neeva's offer of coffee and helped herself.

Neeva sat up. "The indifference only lasted until he opened his mouth."

"What did he say? What could he say?"

"You have to picture the scene, Kick. There we are, staring at each other for what seemed like forever, and he says, 'What's for dinner?' Mr. Big Shot who's been cheating on me, stealing my money. Now, you have to remember my state of mind. Since I last clapped eyes on him, I had lost every cent I owned, consumed enough liquor to have been the star of the Navy Tailhook scandal, made an utter fool of myself in public and in front of my new business partner, and had sex with two total strangers. Whatever I had accumulated from a decade as the wife of a very prominent man is about to be packed in ten Gristede's boxes, and this gangster, who sits in his den and has phone sex with some bimbo he's screwing, while I'm in the other room, wants to know, 'What's for dinner?' "

Neeva plumped up her pillows and leaned back, clearly warming to the tale. "I didn't answer Irving right away. I kept on sponging off the already immaculate kitchen counter. I made sure all the cabinet doors were closed, wiped my hands on a tea towel, and then turned to face him again.

" 'Irving,' I growled in a voice right out of *The Exorcist*. 'Give me my money back.' I began to count the seconds.

"Well, before I got to four, he said, 'What money?' and walked into the living room.

"So I thought, 'Oh, Christ,' and folded the towel through the handle on the fridge. I realized he wanted to make me go through the whole bullshit routine. I'd have to go get the evidence, spread it out, make my case, thereby giving him time to get his defense lined up.

"Then I heard ice dropping into a glass. I crossed the foyer and stood in the living room door.

"I just looked at him and said, 'My money, Irving.'

" 'I don't know anything about any money,' he told me.

"So I said, 'All right. Let's try this one. Who's Sugar Tits?' "

"Sugar Tits?" Kick asked, trying not to laugh.

"That's what he calls the woman he's been seeing."

"Jesus, how did you know that?"

Neeva waved her hand impatiently. "I'll tell you later. This is more important.

"I asked about the other woman, Kick," she continued, "because just letting him know I knew about her would be liberating. I knew if I didn't, I would carry my rage away with me. I've seen what that does to women who know their husbands cheat on them. They never let their husbands know they know. They just take it. Look at the wives' faces in the newspaper when some public guy is caught cheating. That hard face, those dead eyes, come from swallowed rage. It's the look of murder turned inward. If they fight back they face solitude. I was already facing solitude. If I could put a face and a name on the other woman, make him admit what he'd done, I wouldn't have to live with my rage.

"I knew Sugar Tits was just the latest in a lifetime of sugary tits he's chewed on. Men don't just start in midlife. It's a pattern, the nature of the beast. I couldn't change him, but I wasn't going to pack that rage along with my mink and the microwave."

"If he wouldn't admit to stealing your money," Kick wondered, "why would he admit to Sugar Tits?"

"He didn't." Neeva shook her head vehemently. "He assumed

he was still dealing with the Neeva that let him push her around. He turned around, took a sip of his drink, made a face, and started to add more gin. I knew he was trying to think up an answer.

"That's when something snapped, Kick," Neeva continued. "I've always heard people say they were so angry they saw red. I never believed it. But I saw red literally, I physically saw the color wash behind my eyes like a rush of blood inside my head.

"He had his back to me at the bar. I had left a bread knife on the coffee table, where I ate my sandwich. I grabbed it without even realizing it and walked up to his back.

"I asked Irving to turn around. He took his time, selecting a perfect olive, dropping it in his drink. Slowly, he turned, and saw me holding the knife.

"'Put the knife away, Neeva,' he said, like he was talking to a child. 'You're so clumsy. You'll hurt yourself,' he told me.

"But instead, I pushed it against his chest.

"'Irving,' I said. 'I really don't care who you're screwing. The money is another matter. I can't go to the police. I can't go to the bar association. I can't go to a divorce lawyer, because no one is going to believe that the great Irving Fourbraz embezzles from his own wife. But if you don't give me my money, I'm going to call my friend who is the editor of the *New York Courier* and tell him what a swine you are and what you've done.'

"I hope you don't mind, Kick. Desperate times call for desperate deeds."

Kick opened her hands wide. "Be my guest."

"Well, it didn't work. He starts to laugh and says that he knows I don't know the editor of the *New York Courier*. I knew it would sound kind of silly for me to start going, 'Oh, no? This woman I'm going to stay with is dating him.' I mean, I don't have to give some silly high-school pom-pom girl argument when I've got the knife, right?"

"Good thinking," Kick said, thoroughly enjoying Neeva's tale. "So, I take it things moved on to a different tack."

"Right. Now, the way I knew about Sugar Tits was by listening in on the extension while he's in his den."

"Oh, okay," Kick said.

"Mind you, I'm still fondling this big bread knife, which seems to be helping Irving focus his attention. His hearing has improved from his usual wife deafness. I told him I had been listening to his phone calls for years, which wasn't really true, but I can see he doesn't doubt me. I told him I knew about the crooked deals he'd pulled, the payoffs he had taken, the clients he had cheated, the way he turns people into things they aren't and makes money off them. And I tell him I'm going to blow the whistle.

"I can see a little 'oh, shit' flicker in his eyes, but he's standing his ground. He takes a sip of his drink and says, 'Can't prove it.'

"He was right," Kick said. "A rat, but right."

"Yes," Neeva said, swinging her legs over the side of the bed and letting them dangle. "But then it hit me. You don't live with a man all those years and not know what really kills them. You bury it because you don't want to ever refer to anything that's painful. But this was different. So I sat down and crossed my legs and in a very soft, very low voice I said, 'Irving, I'm going to tell about your face-lift and your hair plugs. I'm going to tell them about how you were high on coke during the whole Ticky Shamansky trial.'

"That got him. Kick, I wish you could have seen the look on his face. Here he is listening to the sweet Chinese wife who always walked four steps behind and listened to the same goddamn fart jokes over and over again for years saying she's going to tell the world everything.

"He put down his drink and took two steps sideways away from my knife. I could see his right hand was balled up in a fist. I was sure he planned to punch me.

"Then he says—and this was so manly, so forceful—he says, 'You're a cunt, Neeva.' Cute, huh? Now, what does that mean, really? Calling someone a female organ. Here's Mr. Silver

294

Tongue of the talk-show circuit, with a vocabulary that keeps people out of the electric chair, and that's the best he could do."

"What did you say?" Kick asked breathlessly.

"I said, 'Irving, I'm going to tell them that you and your mistress call your penis Mr. Happy.'"

Kick couldn't help it. She burst out laughing, even though she knew Neeva had been through the most awful experience of her life. "Which threat bothered him the most?" she asked through her laughter.

"Actually, I think it was the hair plugs. At least that's when he started to turn purple," she said. "Also, the realization that I hadn't been lying about listening in on the phone. He knew that's the only way I could have known about Sugar Tits and Mr. Happy."

"Then what happened?"

"So . . . so," Neeva continued excitedly. "I guess he figured I meant business. He reaches for his drink and says, 'Look, Neeva, if it's just about the money, don't worry about it. You'll get your goddamn money, although I don't know what you need it for.'"

"Son of a bitch," Kick muttered. "What did you say?"

"Something like 'in a rat's ass.' I can't remember. Something vulgar. Kick, I can't tell you what a high I was on. I've never raised my voice to a soul. I never stood up to my mother. That would be like yelling at God. And I certainly never, never yelled at Irving. The way I would show anger would be to whine or go silent."

"So, go on," Kick said, reaching over to the bed tray and pouring herself more coffee.

"I gestured to him to sit down on the couch."

"With the knife," Kick clarified.

"Yeah, I was kind of pointing it at him. Kind of. Now he had at least admitted he had taken the money. So I asked him why. Why me? He's such a big shot he has to steal from his wife's dead mother's trust? I think I suggested he could have gone to the safe in his office, where he and Vivian stash his bribes."

"Ohhhhh, you were on a roll. Is there such a safe?"

Neeva waved away the question. "Oh, I don't know. But it makes sense, doesn't it?"

"Yup."

"So, I must have looked slightly crazy, because he began to back down. He says he had to have the money. That wasn't good enough for me. There was something about seeing him scared that made me stronger. Finally, the whole story poured out."

"You know, Neeva, something always seemed fishy to me. I wonder if he isn't in cahoots with the girl."

"Oh, Kick, you are so damn smart. That's exactly what's going on. Irv admitted it. He and this hooker were partners in an insurance scam. She provoked Keeko Ram intentionally. She practically pushed herself off that balcony. But there's more. Apparently, Irving spends a lot of time with hookers when he's in LA. That's how he met her. He didn't want to tell me that, but he cornered himself."

"What a doll," Kick said sarcastically, hating Irving Fourbraz more than ever. "Tell me more about Irving and this Lopez girl. It seems pretty obvious he was up a tree when she went with the Brits."

"Right. He can't get to her. She may tell on him and he can't do anything about it."

"Apparently, this happens a lot with stars," Kick said. "People like Lopez get them in compromising positions, sell their stories to whomever so it will look even more convincing in court. Usually, the poor celebrity settles out of court without ever knowing they've been set up. Even if they know it, it isn't worth the hassle or the publicity.

"And all this is accomplished with the help of someone sleazy like Irving who knows how to manipulate the media."

"Sickening, isn't it?," Neeva said softly. "The only thing he didn't count on was the girl double-dealing him with the Brits."

"But what about Irving? The nurse said he tried to kill you. What did he do, grab the knife away?"

"Oh, no." Neeva smiled, curling up against the pillows. "I put the knife down when he started telling me about the insurance scam. I figured if I let his mouth run, he would give me much better weapons than an old bread knife."

"Information is powerful," Kick said with a smile.

"The best."

"All right, how did you get here?"

"Oh, that. Well, I wasn't finished with him. I wanted him to confess his affair, which he did in glossy detail. The only thing he wouldn't tell me was her name. That's when we really started to yell at each other. Someone must have called the lobby. By the time building security got there, I was crying hysterically. Irving called me some pretty awful names. One thing led to another, I told security he had threatened me, so they called my doctor and he checked me in where Irving can't get at me."

"You can still come to my place," Kick offered.

"I know, Kick, and I can't tell you how much your help means. But this is better." She gestured toward the tray. "Room service, right?"

Kick smiled. She understood completely. She couldn't blame Neeva; sleeping in Lolly's old bedroom would give her the creeps too.

They both turned toward the door as a nurse materialized and whisked away the tray. As she started to leave, she turned back and smiled at Neeva.

"Dr. Jacobs just called the floor and said he wants you to stay at least until after the weekend, Mrs. Fourbraz. Are you feeling better?"

Neeva nodded sweetly. As soon as the nurse was out the door she whispered to Kick, "Good old Dr. Jacobs. He hates Irving too."

"It's a growth industry," Kick said. She stood up and began to pace. "Listen, Neeva, did you really mean it when you said you'd blow the whistle on Irving publicly?"

Neeva thought for a minute and then slowly shook her head. "I couldn't do it, Kick. It would make me look so awful. I wish I could, but I don't want to crawl through the mud just to splatter him with it."

"I could do the splattering for you," Kick said conspiratorially.

"How do you mean?"

Kick walked to the edge of the bed and took Neeva's hands. "This story has everything, Neeva. Sex, crime, a high-profile agent-slash-lawyer who everyone loves to hate. It even gives an inside look at how the celebrity-information racket works. I could have a field day with this, but I would need your help."

"But I don't know everything, Kick, and I can't prove what I do know."

"You wouldn't have to. Just point me in the right direction. I'll find people to prove stuff. I'll tell you who Irving's having an affair with if you'll team up with me on this."

Neeva sat bolt upright. "Kick," she gasped. "You know and you haven't told me?"

"I found out last night. I was going to tell you, but your situation here got top billing."

"Tell me," Neeva said excitedly.

Kick told her everything she knew about Baby Bayer. It wasn't much, but it was enough to turn Neeva's face beet red with anger.

"I met that woman," Neeva said through clenched teeth when Kick finished. "At Mortimer's with Jeffrey. No wonder she acted so odd when she heard my name."

"Ah, and what about Jeffrey? Have you told him about all this?" Kick asked, then returned to her chair.

Neeva suddenly looked away, clearly embarrassed at the mention of Jeffrey.

"Neeva? What's going on with Jeffrey?" Kick asked.

"I called him last night. He came to see me and well . . ." She looked up at Kick, a tiny smile playing at the corners of her mouth. "There wasn't anyone in the room. We talked for hours and, you know."

"Neeva," Kick said, wide-eyed. "You and Jeff?"

"Well, we began to realize that we'd always been a little crazy about each other, and one thing led to another."

"You did it right here?" Kick said, pretending to be shocked while secretly thrilled for Neeva. It was just what she needed after such an ordeal, and Jeffrey was awfully cute. She had watched him running in and out of the apartment for the past week with a twinge of longing of her own. "In a two-foot-wide hospital bed? You could have broken your neck."

"Oh, no," Neeva said seriously. "It's not dangerous at all if someone always stays on top. We alternated. It was just fine."

Their laughter was interrupted by a soft tapping at the door.

"Oh, dear," Neeva whispered, excitedly, pulling down the hem of her nightie. "He said he'd be back this morning. How's my face?"

"Glowing," Kick said, smiling from ear to ear.

Jeffrey Dunsmore, looking totally *GQ*, strode into the room carrying a huge bouquet of roses. He was wearing black trousers, a black cashmere turtleneck, and an emerald-green suede jacket. His coal-black hair shone in the midmorning sun.

"Good morning, ladies," he said with a broad grin.

"'Morning, Jeffrey," Neeva said, a bit dewy-eyed.

He walked to the bed and gave Neeva a lingering kiss. So lingering that Kick finally had to clear her throat.

"Did you get some sleep?" Jeffrey asked Neeva, putting the bouquet on the table next to the bed.

"Not much," Neeva said with a knowing half-smile.

Kick struggled out of the back-breaking chair and reached for her jacket. "I'm going to run, you two," she said. "I want to get started on our new project. You're quite sure you want to go through with this, Neeva?"

"Absolutely," Neeva said, turning to Jeffrey. "Kick wants to do a story to expose Irving."

"Way to go, Kick," he said, jerking a thumb upward.

"I have to be sure Neeva knows the repercussions could be

embarrassing at some point. The insurance scam would be the hook for it, but I'd like to do a complete personality profile on Irving. I would have to write things only Neeva knows. It could mean thoroughly trashing him, maybe even a call for his disbarment if I can document that he and the girl were blackmailing Keeko Ram. How would you feel about that?''

"Would you be able to work in the bit about the hair plugs and the name of his penis?''

"What?'' Jeffrey asked, bewildered.

"I'll do the best I can,'' Kick said, looking at Jeff. "Jeffrey, you're Neeva's partner. This might mean some uncomfortable publicity. How do you feel about it?''

Jeffrey looked down at Neeva's upturned face and then back at Kick. His black eyes were twinkling. "I think it's great. If Neeva's game, so am I. She's my only concern now.''

"I know it's none of my business,'' Kick said, "but inquiring minds want to know. When did this start?''

"You mean this?'' Jeffrey said, and he bent down and began kissing Neeva again. First he kissed her cheeks, then her mouth, then her neck, until she pushed him away, giggling.

"Yup,'' Kick said.

Jeffrey leaned against the bed, looking at Neeva as he spoke. "I guess it was when I saw her misbehaving at a club downtown. At first I was intensely jealous. Then I realized Neeva wouldn't have been there behaving like that if she wasn't terribly unhappy. I started to feel protective. I guess I've always been a little bit in love with her. The whole scene made me realize I had to make my move. I didn't want to lose her.''

"You lucky dogs,'' Kick said. "I'd better get going. By the way, Jeffrey, when I was clearing out Lolly's bedroom, I found an odd little statue that Lolly used as a necklace rack. I have a funny feeling about it. You might want to take a look at it.''

"I always trust those funny feelings, Kick. I'll be coming over later, anyway, after I make sure Neeva's all right,'' he said, putting his arm around her. Neeva snuggled into his shoulder and sighed happily.

Kick said good-bye and started to walk down the corridor. Then she stopped, walked back, and quietly closed Neeva's door. She couldn't be sure. Nothing was ever certain unless one saw it with one's own eyes. But her instincts told her that the minute she left, Jeffrey was no longer standing beside the bed.

33

*G*eorgina had awakened late, relieved to find that Tanner had
already left for work. She didn't want him to notice Selma
preparing the little luncheon she had planned.

She probably could have told him she had invited Rona for
lunch, but she didn't want to have to explain herself. Tanner
would never admit it when he felt threatened, but she would
recognize the tightness around his mouth, his overly solicitous
questions. He would have wanted to know why she was having
lunch with her editor. He would say there was no need. He had
everything under control. He had lunched with Irving Fourbraz
at the Friars just yesterday and worked everything out. No need
to complicate delicate publishing details by involving a middle-
level Winslow House employee. In other words, you girls
shouldn't bother your pretty heads with things the big boys can
take care of.

She threw back the covers and sat up feeling good about what
she had done. If it weren't for Rona, there would have been no

Winslow House involvement, and Georgina was going to at least let her friend know how much she was appreciated.

It was nearly eleven before Georgina arrived in the kitchen to find that everything was ready. She still had more than an hour to kill.

She walked to the house phone on the kitchen wall and buzzed the doorman.

"Arnold?" she asked when he answered the lobby phone. "My luncheon guest will be here at twelve-thirty. Her name is Miss Friedman. You'll send her right up, won't you?"

"Yes, ma'am. Just like I said before. I won't even take the time to buzz you. I remember what you said."

"I'm sorry, Arnold. I forgot I called you before. Please forgive me."

She hung up the phone and stood looking at the immaculate kitchen, thinking she was losing her mind. How could she have forgotten she had already called Arnold? He must think she was nuts.

She wasn't nuts; she was crazed with nerves. Rona Friedman would be the first person who could remotely be considered a friend from her old life to be in the apartment.

With nothing to do and feeling too nervous to sit still, Georgina strolled through the apartment looking at it with Rona's eyes. Rona still lived in a one-bedroom apartment too far over in the East Nineties to be at all chic. It was in a redone walk-up tenement that smelled of cabbage and Lysol. Rona kept her houseplants on the fire escape, which she laughingly referred to as her terrace.

Georgina stood at the glass wall in the living room that led out onto *her* terrace and cringed. It was huge and encircled the entire apartment. The twice-a-week gardener had just removed the summer plants and had replaced them with fall zinnias and marigolds already in bloom. When they died, he would come and get the pots. The twin hammocks in the glass gazebo at the southwest corner were still up, but as soon as it got cold, they, too, would be gone.

She turned and surveyed the huge living room with its stunning antiques and grand piano at one end, still thinking about the way both she and Rona had lived. This was a beautiful apartment, and yet, at the moment, she wished it were anything but. It would intimidate Rona. Even worse, Rona might think she was showing off, having her to her home rather than suggesting a restaurant.

She walked into the dining room. Selma had set the long, burnished table for lunch. She suddenly realized that, even though she and Tanner ate there every night when they were home, two place settings on such a vast piece of furniture looked ridiculous.

She quickly gathered up the exquisite English china and the heavy, monogrammed silver and carried them to the kitchen. They would eat at the butcher-block table. She had just set the butcher block with the blue-and-white kitchen china Selma and Grover used when the doorbell rang. She raced out of the kitchen and down the hall to catch it before Selma did, thankful that she had worn jeans and an old sweater.

She pulled open the door to see Rona standing in the outside foyer holding a heavy padded envelope.

"Wow," Rona said, smiling. "I've always wondered what these buildings were like inside. I just now realized you've got the whole damn floor."

Georgina wrinkled her nose. "I know. It's a bit much, isn't it? Come on in."

"I mean, it must go from Park to Lexington."

"Well, no, not quite."

Rona stepped into the front hall and held out the big envelope. "Here, some deathless prose from Winslow's fall list."

Georgina took the bag and cradled it in her arms. "Oh, Rona, you shouldn't have. Books are so expensive now."

Rona laughed. "Not when you get them from the storeroom on the fourth floor. It's one of the few perks in the publishing business. Free books. Right up there with getting the day before Christmas off."

"Nonetheless, it was sweet. I'll enjoy every one of them," Georgina said, leading the way down the hall, hoping Rona didn't know handpainted antique Chinese wallpaper when she saw it.

When they reached the end of the hall, Rona turned. "Holy cow, Georgie. That's Ming dynasty wallpaper. I hope you know the gold in that stuff is real."

Georgina looked up at the wallpaper as though seeing it for the first time. "How did you know that?"

Rona shrugged. "I edited one of those fifty-dollar decorating jobbies a couple of lists ago. Ask me about gold faucets some-time."

Georgina laughed. She had forgotten how easygoing Rona was and thought how pleasant it was to be with someone from her old life.

"Come on in the kitchen. I thought we'd eat there. It's cozier," she called, moving down the back hall. When Rona didn't answer, she looked over her shoulder. Rona was nowhere in sight. She turned and headed back to the front hall. Rona was standing in the archway to the living room.

"Rona?"

"Good God," she gasped. "Is that a terrace out there or a section of Central Park I haven't seen before?"

"It's a terrace, Rona. Come on into the kitchen."

Rona turned. "If it's okay with you," she said, "could I have a tour? I mean I haven't seen anything like this since my senior class trip to Blenheim Palace."

Rona said little during the tour, although she seemed to know more than Georgina did about the provenance of some of the older pieces, the fabrics the decorator had used, and the date of the huge silver service complete with three-foot swans on the breakfront in the dining room.

As they headed back to the kitchen, Rona paused.

"Georgie," she said quietly. "Would I be an utter dork if I said I'd like to have lunch in here?"

"Why . . . no . . . for heaven's sake. Really, you mean you'd really want to?"

"I really want to. There's someone I don't like a lot at the office. I'd enjoy being able to tell her about it, so I can watch her plotz."

"Plotz?"

"Drop over in a dead faint."

"Well, in that case . . ." Georgina said, stepping to the bellpull on the wall near the kitchen. "Let's do it right."

Selma appeared immediately in the doorway. "Yes, ma'am?" she inquired.

"Selma, this is my friend Rona Friedman. We've changed our minds about the kitchen. Could you set lunch up again in here?"

"Of course, ma'am."

"And, Selma, please tell Grover we'll have a nice, dry white. He can decide."

Rona was watching with great interest. After Selma slipped silently back into the kitchen, Rona said, "What's a Grover?"

"He's our butler. He doesn't usually serve lunch, but I think we need him. Don't you?"

"Absolutely," Rona said, trying to keep a straight face. "Does he wear white gloves?"

"Of course," Georgina said with mock hauteur.

"Good, I've never been buttled. I want everything I'm entitled to."

"He doesn't speak unless spoken to, either."

"Thank goodness there's some class left in this tacky old world."

"Come," Georgina said. "Selma will bring our wine out to the terrace. We'll sit there until lunch is served."

The two women stepped out into dazzling Indian-summer sunlight. Most of Manhattan lay at their feet.

Rona walked over and leaned her elbows on the parapet looking to the south. "This is like a movie," she said, shaking her head in wonder. "I knew people lived like this, but I never really believed it until now."

306

Georgina joined her at the waist-high wall. "It is amazing, isn't it? I still don't quite believe this happened to me."

"*Ahhh*, Georgie," Rona said, looking at her over her shoulder. "I knew I was right when I decided to root for my friends making it in life."

"I haven't made it," Georgina said wistfully. "This is all Tanner. He owns it all. All I did was marry him."

"Don't be so dismissive, Georgie. You made yourself into the kind of person someone like Tanner wanted to share it with."

Georgina smiled wanly. "I feel a little guilty at times. Like I don't belong here."

"Well, don't. You deserve it. Besides, think of the alternative. You're safe and secure. You have a man who obviously adores you. And you have all this." Her arm stretched out over the parapet, as though all of Manhattan belonged to Georgie as well.

Just then Selma stepped out onto the terrace carrying a tray with two glasses of wine.

"Come on, let's go sit in the gazebo. This sun is too hot."

They took seats opposite each other on the flowered settees that followed the curve of the glass enclosure and waited for Selma to serve their wine. "Luncheon will be ready in ten minutes, ma'am," she said quietly to Georgina.

"Thank you, Selma. Oh, and could you warm up the little rolls I made this morning? They're in the tin on the counter."

Selma nodded and disappeared again.

Georgina took a sip of her wine and put it down on the glass table at her side. "So tell me. How are you?"

"Fine, really," Rona said. "But getting a little tired of being a single woman in this town. My real fantasy is to move back to Vermont and take over my dad's weekly paper. He's thinking about retiring."

"So do it," Georgina said, suggesting her friend show a courage she herself didn't have.

"I'm not that brave, Georgie. I've spent the last ten years paying off my student loans and my Visa. I finally got the job I struggled for since I came here, and I end up working for a hydra-headed monster. I thought life would have gotten a little sweeter by now, but it hasn't. You're so lucky. You have so much to look forward to."

"Me? Rona, I'm married to a man who may make me a rich widow before I'm forty. I'm going to have to start all over again. Unless one considers facials and lunch a career."

"But you'll have your books . . ." Rona's voice trailed off.

"Book."

"Sure, at the moment. Soon you'll be starting on the next one. I think they said six in all. At least that's the number they were talking about in the meeting this morning."

Georgina pulled herself to the edge of her seat and stared at her friend. "What are you talking about?"

"Your series . . . to tie in with the television show."

Georgina jostled her head as though to clear the message she was receiving. "Back up, Rona, back up," she said sharply. "I'm absolutely bewildered."

"You don't know about it?"

"This is madness. What series? What television show?"

Rona took a deep breath, then slowly exhaled. "I thought that was why we were having lunch. I thought this was . . . I don't know, like a celebration."

"Rona, you must tell me," Georgina pleaded. "Since Tanner took this thing over, I've been completely in the dark."

"Join the club," Rona said, rolling her eyes.

"Rona . . ." Georgina felt as though she were smothering. Thank God she had asked Rona to come over. She wondered when Tanner had been planning to tell her about all this. "What have they committed me to?"

Rona took another sip of wine and began to tell her what was transpiring. Irving Fourbraz had gotten together with the chairman of Winslow House, apparently with Tanner's full acquiescence, and planned a whole campaign to build her into some kind of household celebrity.

Georgina sat listening in stunned silence. When Selma announced lunch, they walked into the dining room and took their seats at the beautifully reset table. Neither of them spoke until Selma and Grover had served the meal and poured more wine.

"I can't believe they didn't tell you about this, Georgie," Rona finally said, unfolding her oversized damask napkin and placing it in her lap. "Isn't it something you want to do?"

Georgina cleared her throat against the lump that had developed. She couldn't let Rona know how shocked she was, nor how angry she was with Tanner. Perhaps anger wasn't exactly what she was feeling. Hammered flat and helpless was more like it.

"Well, yes, I guess so," she said tentatively, picking at her salad. "Maybe I should be pleased."

"That doesn't sound like ringing enthusiasm, ducks."

"No, I guess not. I'm just having trouble absorbing it all."

"Oh," Rona said lightly, tearing off a piece of warm roll on her bread plate. "You'll feel better about it when you've had a chance for it to sink in. By the way, what are you wearing?"

Georgina looked down at her sweater. "I don't really know. I think this is a Donna Karan. I got it on sale."

"No, no, no. I mean to the party."

Georgina's fork dropped, hit her salad plate, bounced once, and flipped onto the terrazo floor with a clatter.

"Party?" she said, sounding like an automaton. "There's going to be a party?"

"Of course. Oh, God, you didn't know about that either," Rona said, holding her forehead. "It's . . . well, it's a week from today. Next Friday. At the Winter Palace, that big glass thing in the Financial Center. I was hoping you could tell me who's going to be there, because I won't be. It's just for the top Winslow brass and the press."

"This party . . . it's for me?" Georgina asked, staring into space.

"Of course it's for you."

"Why would they give me a party? My book won't be published for months. Isn't that when they give parties?"

"Oh, I'm sure there will be a lot of parties, love. This one is to announce all the deals they're putting together. Sort of a Heeeeere's Geor-geeeena!"

Georgina couldn't move. She sat very still and continued to stare. She was aware of an odd muffled feeling in her head and a slight throbbing in her ears. Numbly, she reached for the silver bell next to the floral centerpiece and rang for Selma. Before Georgina had even put down the bell, Selma's head peeped around the swinging door to the kitchen.

"Selma, would you bring me another fork," she asked.

"Certainly, ma'am," she said. "Will you be having dessert, ma'am?"

"Yes, thank you, Selma," she said in a monotone. "It's a lovely dessert. Raspberries in a very light Grand Marnier sauce, dusted with powdered sugar, with crème fraîche on the side. Crème fraîche is very simple to make yourself. Just take one cup of heavy cream, stir in . . ."

"Georgie?" Rona said, her eyes darting between Selma and Georgina.

". . . an equal amount of any good sour cream. Let the mixture stand overnight at room temperature."

"Georgina! Are you okay?" Rona asked.

Georgina fell silent but continued to stare. She vaguely heard Selma say, "Mrs. Dyson?"

There was a long, painful silence before Georgina could find her voice to speak. She turned to look at Rona, who appeared to be stricken with concern.

"Help me," she whispered. Her face went slack. "Help me, please. I'm suffocating."

34

A week after Irving's unfortunate confrontation with Neeva and the bread knife, she still had not returned to the Trump Tower apartment. That was fine with him. If he knew anything, he knew the law. She had moved out. The fact that she had moved out was going to save him a bundle in divorce court.

As he sat alone in his office waiting for Tanner Dyson's call, he pondered the chances of Neeva actually going public as she had threatened, then shrugged it off. He could control Neeva, always had. If indeed she had some inside track with Joe Stone at the *Courier*, one word to Tanner and any story she tried to peddle would be dead. Actually, anything she tried to pull with the media could be shot down. He hadn't spent his entire career sorting out how the world was organized without learning which buttons to push to get a story in or out of the news.

He was more concerned about what progress Tanner's reporter was making in London in getting Maria away from the Brits and back to the States.

For several days he had been extremely uneasy about his

having told Neeva as much as he had, but he knew Neeva well. She was too afraid of him to do anything. Besides, she had no proof of what he had told her. If she wanted her freedom, so be it. He wouldn't agitate her further.

As soon as Vivian buzzed the intercom and told him Tanner was on line one, he whipped up the phone.

"Tanner, good morning," he said boisterously, determined to start the conversation with news Tanner wanted to hear. "I've got a definite yes from the *Today* show and CNN to cover Georgina's party tomorrow."

"That's great news, Irving," Tanner answered, delighted. "Everything else under control?"

"Out of my hands, friend. Out of my hands. McKenzie Ross, the PR people, and the folks over at Winslow House have taken over. They're the pros. They know how to run these things. Is Georgina up for tonight?"

"She will be. All this takes some getting used to. I'm going to give her another pep talk tonight. She'll be fine."

"I hope so," Irving said, anxious to drop the subject and move on. Georgina Dyson wasn't his favorite client. She had balked at the whole idea of a huge promotional party, and Tanner was trying to change her mind. Frankly, Irving didn't give a flying fuck. He had bigger problems. Namely, his own. It was time to get to those. "By the way, Tanner, any word from London?"

"*Ahhh* . . . there's a little hitch there."

"Hitch?" Irving mumbled, feeling the perspiration forming at his hairline.

"The reporter I sent over has gone missing."

"What?" Irving shouted. "What kind of a lamebrain did you send? Reporters don't just go missing."

"You'd have to know this reporter. Baby Bayer has her own way of doing things. She's effective, but it takes time."

"Baby? Did you say Baby? Some name for a serious journalist, huh?" he said, choking back his panic. This was all he needed. Baby loose on the story. It had never occurred to him when he pushed Tanner to go after Maria that he would assign the one reporter who could screw up everything. "Look, Tanner, I've had second thoughts about all this," he said weakly. "This Lopez girl is a pretty cheap bit of business. Maybe there isn't such a big story there after all."

"I think you're wrong, Irv. This reporter is very clever. I think she's going to come back with the girl and a story that will stun us all."

Tell me about it, Irving thought.

Tanner turned away from the phone and began to speak to someone in his office. "Would you excuse me for a moment, Irving? I have to sign something."

"Sure, sure," Irving said impatiently. He sat, absentmindedly tapping a pencil on the glass top of his desk, cursing the potentially disastrous introduction of Baby into the whole mess. How much did she know? He had talked so much he couldn't remember what he had told her. It was one thing to tell her things while they were still lovers, quite another to have her furious at him. If she knew enough to keep Maria out of his reach, he'd be in real trouble.

He snapped to attention when he heard Tanner come back on the line.

"Now, Irving," Tanner said, sounding cautious. "There's another matter I feel duty-bound to bring up with you."

Oh, fuck, Irving thought. What's coming now?

"I had lunch at the Metropolitan Club yesterday. The topic of conversation at my table should be of some interest to you. It concerned your wife."

"My wife? What about my wife?" Irving asked, too quickly. He knew he sounded defensive. Had someone heard about her trip to the hospital? Was the word out around town that she had moved out on him? Or, worse than any of that, was she running her mouth about him?

"This is awkward, old man," Tanner said. "But you were very supportive during my marital troubles. I just thought you should know that people are talking."

"Why would anyone be talking about Neeva, for Christ's sake?

The woman's sick. She's been in New York Hospital for several days." He wasn't about to volunteer anything further.

"Oh? I didn't know that, Irving. What's wrong?"

"Just some female problems. Go on, Tanner, go on."

Tanner cleared his throat, obviously uncomfortable. "They're saying your wife has moved into the Riverton on East Fifty-seventh Street. She's living with Aubrey Dunsmore's son."

Irving swallowed hard. "Utter nonsense," he said, feeling as though someone had kicked him in the chest. He took a deep breath to get control. "Who's pushing that kind of garbage? What an outrageous bit of business."

"Well," Tanner said tentatively, "the people at my table don't usually carry idle gossip. I'd rather not name names, but they had some pretty telling details."

Irving didn't want the details. There wasn't any doubt in his mind that Tanner was telling the truth. Tanner Dyson was the most circumspect of men. While he loved gossip and was always an eager listener, he was not a carrier of tales unless they had a direct effect on someone he considered a colleague. Still, Irving found it impossible to do anything but deny what he was hearing.

"It's amazing how these things get distorted, Tanner," he said, his mind racing to find a plausible scenario to save face. "Neeva's working on the Lolly Pines auction with the Dunsmore kid. Someone probably saw them taking a break in some restaurant. Tell your friends they're dead wrong and shouldn't carry tales unless they want to spend a lot of money on legal fees. Jesus, the mouths on some people in this town."

"Sorry, Irving. I didn't mean to upset you. I just thought you'd like to know. I know I would if people were spreading such stories about my wife."

"I appreciate it, Tanner. It gives me a chance to nip this thing in the bud, right now."

"No problem, Irving. I'll get back to you as soon as we have word from London."

Irving hung up and sat slumped in his seat, seething. His mind reeled with thoughts of Neeva with the Dunsmore kid. How the hell could she? He was a little kid, for Christ's sake. Well, not so little. Irving had seen him at a Knick's game not long ago. He had had a model on either arm. He looked like a fucking movie star. Actually, he must be in his early thirties by now. He had a full head of blue-black hair and teeth like a Cossack. Maybe the kid was a fagola. He was too good-looking to be straight. Fags always liked Neeva. They hung around her at the gallery all the time. That's what this thing was all about. She moved in with this poofter for company. Irving knew the apartments in the Riverton. There wasn't one under eight rooms. The kid's trust fund probably didn't cover the maintenance, and he had conned Neeva into helping out with the rent. Ha! The laugh was going to be on him. Neeva didn't have a pot to piss in.

And neither did Irving.

35

In the sweeping Dyson apartment on Park Avenue, Grover and Selma tiptoed about, maintaining the hushed atmosphere of a private sanitarium.

Earlier that morning, Georgina had locked herself in her bathroom while Tanner did his hour on the treadmill in his gym.

Assuming Georgina was absorbed in some time-consuming ablution, he went into the dining room to take breakfast and read the morning papers. He had finished his hot lemon juice and freshly baked bran muffin and scanned the papers before he became mildly concerned that Georgina had not yet joined him.

He refolded *The Wall Street Journal* and walked back to the bedroom. He listened for a moment before calling her name. Then he softly rapped at her bathroom door. He pressed an ear against it, feeling a bit foolish, and called her name again.

When she didn't answer his second call, he tried the door. Alarmed to find it locked and nothing but silence from the other side, he rushed back to the pantry.

Fortunately, Grover had a master key. When Grover opened

the bathroom door, he stepped back respectfully to let Tanner pass.

Georgina was sitting on the quilted chaise lounge. She was naked. Her eyes were open, but they were dull and unfocused, staring off into space.

"Darling?" Tanner said, stricken. He sat down at the foot of the chaise and lifted one of her hands. "What's the matter? Georgina? Are you ill?"

She said nothing for an agonizing ten seconds. Finally, without moving anything but her mouth, she whispered, "No, I'm not ill."

Tanner reached for a silk dressing gown that had fallen to the floor and draped it around her shoulders. "Why are you sitting here like this? I was waiting for you to come in to breakfast."

"I'm sitting here because I am losing my mind."

"Georgina," he said, numb with shock and concern. "I'm going to call Dr. Willis."

"Don't do that, Tanner," she said. "He can't help me."

Tanner stood up in complete bewilderment. He had never seen Georgina in such a state. She was like a zombie. "Come to bed, my sweet. You're going to catch a chill in here." He held out his hand, speaking softly and clearly, so as not to alarm or startle her.

Georgina let him take her hand and gently pull her from the chaise. He put his arm around her and slowly eased her toward the door. Just before he reached it, he called out to Grover. "Grover, would you please step out of the bedroom. Mrs. Dyson is not dressed, and I want to put her to bed."

"Should I ask Selma to come in?" Grover asked from somewhere in the bedroom.

"Yes, Grover, if you would, please. Right away."

Beside himself, Tanner half lifted Georgina into bed. He pulled the dressing gown free and laid it on the bedside chair. Gently, he pulled the covers over her.

"Oh, my," he heard Selma say behind him. "Is Mrs. Dyson not well?"

"Would you find her a warmer gown, please, Selma. She seems

to have a fever." He felt her forehead for effect. It was cool and dry. He knew she didn't have a fever. Whatever was wrong with her, he preferred that Selma assume it was the flu.

He stood by the side of the bed as Selma slipped a long-sleeved silk nightgown onto to her arms and buttoned the front.

Georgina's eyes were closed now. She seemed to be sleeping. "Georgina, I'm going to call Dr. Willis."

Her eyes flew open. She reached up and grabbed his wrist. "No," she said curtly. "I don't want to see him. I want to see Rona."

"Who?" Tanner asked, totally bewildered.

"Rona Friedman. My editor at Winslow House."

"I don't understand," he said, unable to keep the calm tone he had maintained until now. "You are in a near-comatose state and you want to see your editor? That makes no sense."

"Please, Tanner. Please call her."

Tanner looked helplessly across the bed at Selma, who seemed as bewildered as he was, then back at Georgina. "Why don't I rub your feet, darling? You like that. It will relax you."

"I'm relaxed, Tanner. Don't rub my feet," she said in a monotone.

Tanner took a deep breath and clasped his hands together. "Well, then . . . the new Pavarotti CD. All your favorite arias. Why don't I put that on for you? Selma, would you go to the music room and bring us . . ."

"Tanner, please . . ." Georgina whimpered. "Please call Rona."

Tanner pretended not to hear her. ". . . the compact disc that's on my stereo. Then would you bring a tray for Mrs. Dyson. Some tea, I think and cinnamon toast fingers." He looked down at Georgina. "How about some eggs, darling. Poached is nice. Or coddled. You love coddled eggs."

"Tanner, I can't stand it anymore. Please call Rona."

Tanner sighed deeply. "All right, Georgina, all right," he said reluctantly. "Then I'm going to call Dr. Willis. I'm very concerned. You may have a flu bug or something. It would be unthinkable if you weren't up to the party tomorrow night."

Rona swung into her office and jumped. Jason Fourbraz was sitting in her desk chair with a pair of jumbo-paper-clip fangs protruding from his upper lip.

"Damn it, Jason," Rona said. "Don't do that. Not this morning. Today is going to be terrible."

Jason removed the paper clips and pinged them into the wastebasket. "It already is," he said.

"Sweet Jesus, what's happened?"

"The reptile that walks like a woman just called."

"Tell me you are being your droll, sarcastic self, please, Jason," Rona said frantically, as she tossed her coat onto the coat tree.

"It gets worse."

"Get out of my chair so I can put my head down," Rona said, shoving Jason's shoulder. "How much worse? Am I supposed to call her back?"

Jason slid around the corner of the desk and threw himself into a chair. "No. You are supposed to call Tanner Dyson."

"What? Georgina's husband called Pearl?"

"No, he called my father. My father called the chairman. The chairman called Pearl. Pearl called you to tell you to call Tanner, but you weren't here yet, and I was walking by and took Pearl's call. That makes you dirt and me Mr. Wonderful for getting to work on time."

"I know what this is all about, Jason," Rona said, holding her head. "This is the beginning of the end. Somehow, when all this is over, I'm going to be the one who has to sleep on the wet spot."

"When what's over, pumpkin?"

Rona lifted her head and sighed with a long sad whoosh of resignation. "Georgina Dyson is going to refuse to go to her own party. Pearl's got wind of it, and somehow, I don't know how, she'll find a way to blame me."

"Way to go, Georgina," Jason said, pumping the air with his

fist. "That ought to get her party more ink than Tanner's plan to set fire to the Mormon Tabernacle Choir during the cocktail hour."

"This is not funny, Jason," Rona said with more than her usual morning irritability.

"How do you know she's not going to go to her party?" Jason asked, turning serious for a change.

"Because Georgina and I have been speaking every morning since I had lunch with her."

"Doesn't she have any friends?"

"Thanks, Jason," Rona snapped. "Sure, she has friends. They all belong to her husband. She's completely overwhelmed by all this promotional stuff."

Jason stood up and leaned against his mail cart. "Oh, please God, someone overwhelm me with promotion. I've had one hundred-dollar gig in two months. I'm ready to give up jazz and turn to Muzak."

"I'm sorry about your fame problem, Jase, old bean, but I've got a bigger one," Rona said, reaching for the phone. "Now, if you'll excuse me. I have to make my call."

"This is so exciting," Jason said, swinging up out of the chair. "I love this kind of stuff—squandered money, ruined careers, hypocrisy exposed."

"I don't find it exciting. I find it terrifying and the thought of looking for a new job deeply depressing."

Rona had just put her hand on the phone when it rang. With a sinking heart she knew it was Pearl. "Rona Friedman," she answered, trying to sound rushed.

"Ms. Friedman, this is Tanner Dyson."

"Why, hello, Mr. Dyson," Rona said, taken aback.

"I'm calling at my wife's request. I thought she should see a doctor, not an editor, but she was adamant. Would it be possible for you to see her at the apartment? I confess, I'm . . . concerned."

Rona hung up wondering what fresh hell this was. Whatever

was going on, her first loyalty was to Georgina. She was an author; she was her friend.

As she made her way out of the office and hailed a cab on Sixth Avenue, she realized that underneath her concern she was feeling . . . angry. She truly cared about Georgina, but she had to be honest with herself. She deeply resented the way Georgina was behaving. Rona had dealt with authors who wept with joy when the publicity department got them on a 2 A.M. radio station in West Virginia. One of her authors, a man who could actually write, paid for his own little advertising stickers. He and his nine-year-old kid spent nights and weekends plastering them all over Manhattan to promote his book that nobody read anyway.

Now here was Georgina with an adoring husband handing her a celebrity career without her even having to get out of bed, and she was thrashing around like some princess on a painful pea. Rona wished she had given her the facts of life at lunch the week before, when Georgina practically passed out at the news of her party.

The surge of righteous indignation stayed with her all the way to Georgina's unthinkably luxurious apartment and through the business of being announced and getting admitted by a grateful Selma. But when she was ushered into the bedroom and saw with her own eyes how wretched Georgina felt, her heart began to melt.

"Georgie," Rona said. "What can I do to help?"

"I'm panicking, Rona. We need to talk."

"You're not going through with the party, are you?" Rona asked.

Georgina's face fell. "I can't. It's so phony; it's just not me."

"I figured this was coming," Rona said. "But for pity's sake, Georgie. Can't you put up a front? You do realize the enormous amount of effort a lot of people have gone to on your behalf."

"For their own enrichment," Georgina said defensively.

"Get real, girl," Rona snapped. "What other reason is there? This is business. This is the way salaries are paid. Mine included, incidentally."

"Please don't be angry at me. It's just . . .". Georgie's voice trailed off.

"What, Georgie? You can tell me. I'm not angry. Just disappointed. This was going to be a very big deal. There are people who would kill for the opportunity that's being handed to you."

"I know, I know," Georgina said, waving her hand. She raised her head and looked at Rona with pleading eyes. "That's the problem. It's being handed to me: nothing is mine. Rona, Tanner controls everything I do. At first it was how I looked, what I wore, what the house looked like, who we saw. I wrote that book because I wanted to feel that I was worth something. Now he's taken my book away from me."

"It seems to me you went along with it all, Georgie."

"Yes," she said solemnly, "I did. I thought that's what I was supposed to do. What a wife is supposed to do. Rona, you remember what I was like. I was huge. Tanner doesn't even know that part of my life. I've burned any pictures, buried it all. In those days I had nothing but a little talent with food things. Tanner had everything. I need something that's mine."

Rona put down her glass. Little in her life had prepared her for giving what would amount to marital advice to Georgina. One of the things she prided herself on was never involving herself in other people's personal lives, certainly not the authors she worked with. Her job was to turn out readable books, on time and with no errors, if humanly possible. She had never been married nor particularly in love, other than a heavy crush, but in the course of her work she had read and edited enough romance novels to learn the things a woman had to do to resolve conflicts in her emotional life. If a woman was miserable watching *Celebrity Bowling* in a trailer or sipping French wine on her yacht, she had to find the roots of her own unhappiness and take charge.

"Do you love Tanner, Georgie?" she asked, diving into the dark and dangerous waters in which friendship is supposed to let women swim.

"Yes."

"Do you want all this?" Rona asked, sweeping her arm to indicate more than just the apartment.

"Yes, if that means having Tanner."

"Do you want to be a famous author with your own show and lectures and book signings and all the bells and whistles that go with fame?"

Georgie looked out through the windows over the park, then back at Rona. "No," she said. "I just wanted to write my little book, see it published, and maybe have someone write me a note saying hairspray really does get out ballpoint pen stains."

"Do you think Tanner knows how you feel?"

Georgina thought for a moment. "No, he probably doesn't."

"Okay, now pay close attention. Sometimes the simplest advice takes a lot of digesting. I think I know how you can solve your problem with Tanner. How you can get him to stop giving you things you don't want because he adores you and wants to make you happy."

Georgina leaned forward. "How? How can I make him understand how miserable I am?"

"Tell him," Rona said.

Georgina Dyson's big "coming out" party didn't happen. Its cancellation less than twenty-four hours before the event cost her husband over one hundred thousand dollars and thoroughly infuriated her publishers at Winslow House and a large grocery chain that had tied into the event. The management of the Winter Palace was not amused, the Tewesbury Consort got an unexpected evening off, and God's Love-We Deliver was able to serve several hundred grateful and surprised AIDS shut-ins roast beef, jumbo shrimp, glazed Virginia ham, and risotto Parmesan. The petit fours and marzipan raspberry tarts went to the Salvation Army Food Center. The media that had scheduled coverage didn't care. They moved out into the city to cover less earthshattering events.

36

The night Georgina's party had been planned for, Kick and Joe returned to the penthouse after a celebratory dinner with Jeff and Neeva at the elegantly minimalist apartment they were sharing in the Riverton. The evening had been one of the happiest Kick could remember. It had started with the general excitement about her doing a piece on Irving. Then there was the news that the little statue Kick had uncovered in Lolly's bedroom was, in fact, a genuine Rodin bronze, an obscure early work thought lost to the art world. They all toasted, amid much laughter, "the most expensive jewelry stand in the world." Thanks to Jeff's clever sense of public relations, news about its thirty-year stay on Lolly's dresser and its upcoming auction by the Chandon Galleries would shortly be on front pages around the world.

Giddy with her good fortune and Jeffrey's superb wine, Kick reached across the backseat of the cab as it pulled up in front of the Barrington and tightly clasped Joe's hand.

"It's time," she said, watching his face turn from its normal sweet expression when they parted to excited disbelief.

"You mean it?" he said, jamming his hands into the pocket of his jacket to find a few crumpled bills.

"I mean it."

"You'll be gentle?"

"Out," she commanded, pulling him across the seat and out the open door.

"Wait," Joe said, laughing as he stumbled onto the pavement. He stepped to the open window opposite the driver and shoved a handful of bills at him.

In the elevator they maintained a cool silence as Frank, the night operator, pretended to be oblivious to the fact that the lady staying on in Penthouse 3 was bringing a gentlemen home with her at eleven o'clock at night. Kick smiled quietly, knowing the news would be all over the building by morning.

As she pushed open the door, the ringing phone echoed eerily through the empty rooms. Kick picked up the foyer extension.

"Kick, this is Fedalia Null."

"Oh . . . oh, Ms. Null . . . Fedalia, hello," Kick said, frantically signaling to Joe as he closed the door. "Could you hold on for a minute?"

Kick jabbed at the hold button and looked at Joe. "Joe, it's Fiddle. She probably doesn't like the Lolly piece," she said with a shrug.

"So she doesn't like it. No big deal," Joe said. He was already on the landing, gazing at the cavernous apartment. "This is amazing. Let me look around. Go on—talk to Fedalia," he said as he disappeared up the stairs.

Kick pinched the bridge of her nose and squeezed her eyes shut for a second or two to clear her head before she released the hold button.

"Yeah, Fiddle, hi. I'm here. Sorry."

"Sorry to call you so late, Kick. I promised Joe Stone I'd get back to you as soon as possible on your Lolly Pines piece. I just read it. It's nice work, Kick. Very nice. You must have cared for her a great deal."

"Oh," Kick breathed. "Right. Gee, thanks. Yes, I did, a lot."

She felt her heart picking up speed. Was it the authoritative clip of Fiddle's speech? Was it the memory of the way she felt the last time she heard it that awful day that Fiddle and Irving Fourbraz, acting in concert, fired her?

"I was delighted Joe got in touch with me about you. I've often wondered what happened to you."

For lack of any other place to sit down, Kick leaned against the foyer wall and slowly slid to the floor. From Fiddle's friendly tone, she was prepared to, at last, hear some good news about her writing.

"Look, Kick, as much as I liked your piece, I'm afraid it's not for us. We're really into more of the exposé kind of thing these days. We've found that our base circulation has, in the last year, turned toward the . . ."

Kick sat on the cold floor, listening as Fiddle droned on, her mind suspended in a kind of numb limbo. Coming through the phone was a boring mush of circulation figures, demographics, examples of the type of readers *Fifteen Minutes* wanted to appeal to, the zeitgeist of the nineties . . . blah, blah, blah . . . bullshit!

Someday she would be able to piece together the combination of circumstances that had, in the course of Fiddle's phone call, changed her attitude about her work. Perhaps it was hearing her article being turned down again by an editor who had so painfully rejected her in the past. Why was Fiddle in such a rush to give her bad news that she had to call at 11 P.M.? Kick had come home so full of high spirits. Neeva and Jeffrey seemed deliriously happy. The auction would be a real smash now, with the authentication of the Rodin head. And the best part was that upstairs, waiting for her, was a man who was falling in love with her, a kind, intelligent, sexy grown-up, who was doing more for her self-confidence than fifteen Fiddles would ever do.

As she listened to Fiddle, it dawned on Kick that if she didn't do something to control her own destiny, she was doomed to a life of rejections. Everyone gets rejected, but she had endured hers without raising a finger or her voice. Since Lionel's betrayal she had assumed the role of victim. She thought of the advice given to tourists in New York: If you carry yourself like a victim, you're going to get in trouble. If you think you're going to get hurt, you will.

She might not have been as experienced as Fiddle Null. She might not run a major magazine and have power over others' lives. But she knew her work was just as valid as anyone else's.

There were writers around town who would sell their souls just to get Fedalia Null to return their calls. And Kick had her right there.

She got up off the floor and picked up the base of the phone so she could pace. "I appreciate your reading my piece, Fiddle," she said, interrupting Fiddle's flow of words. "I guess I'll put Lolly on hold. I'm anxious to get on to the piece I'm doing now."

There was a slight pause as Fiddle shifted gears and digested what Kick had just said. "Oh?" she said. "What are you working on?"

"I don't think it's something you'd want to do, Fiddle. It's a none-too-sympathetic profile on a friend of yours."

"A friend of mine?" Fiddle asked warily.

"Yes," Kick said, plunging ahead. "I have very good information that there is a scam going on. It involves some of the biggest names around." It was a stretch to hint that she was further along with the Irving project than she was, but, what the hell, she had nothing to lose. The more she assumed the whip hand in the conversation, the more confident she became.

"You said 'a friend of mine,'" Fiddle said, pressing.

"Irving Fourbraz is in big, big trouble," she said, then counted her heartbeats, waiting for Fiddle's reaction.

"Hot damn," Fiddle said, exhaling loudly. "It's high time someone nailed him. That man has been conning us all for years."

"You mean he's not your big buddy?" Kick asked.

"Buddy? I loathe the man. Everyone knows he's a sleaze. We've all had to suck up to him because he controls so much talent. Wow, Kick, good for you. This is exciting."

"I think so," Kick said, as calmly as her nerves permitted.

"Have you sold it to anyone yet?"

"No. I thought I'd wait to see how it turned out."

"I want it," Fiddle said briskly. "What do you need?"

The old Kick would have groveled with gratitude. But the new Kick was already in residence. "I'll make you a deal, Fiddle," she said, exhilarated with her new clearheadedness. "There's a very important source I need to talk to. If the magazine will spring for a round-trip ticket to London and a few days of expenses, I'll give you first refusal."

Fiddle laughed. "Cool move, kid," she said warmly. "Done is done. When do you want to leave? I'll messenger you your ticket."

Kick had taken off her pumps during the phone call. As soon as she finished making arrangements with Fiddle, she slammed down the phone and raced up the stairs, sliding around the corners of the landings in her stocking feet.

As she hit the third floor landing, she started shouting. "Joe, where are you? Joe, you aren't going to believe this!"

She slid the last ten feet through the open office door and, having grabbed the edge of a file cabinet to stop herself, stood slackjawed with surprise at what she saw.

"What in the world . . ." She stopped in midsentence as she stared up at the ceiling. The huge glass dome was completely open to a charcoal-colored sky. A velvet sea of stars winked down at her. She took a couple of mincing steps and felt grit, like pebbles, under her feet.

Joe was sitting on the mattress of the pullout couch, a coffee mug in one hand and the office bottle of brandy in the other. His head was back and his mouth slightly open as he stared up at the open ceiling. "I don't believe this," he said in a hoarse whisper. "This is the damnedest thing I've ever seen."

"But how . . . how did this happen?" Kick asked, blinking at him in the deep blue shadows.

Joe turned and pointed to the wall beside the couch. "This thing," he said, indicating the metal gadget Kick had noticed earlier only because it poked her in the back.

"When I pulled out the couch, I saw this thing and started fooling with it. Look." He got up and stepped to the gadget. There was a rusty lever under the wheel. "It's all on some Rube Goldberg kind of device. See?" He released something on the wall, and an agonizing groan came from over their heads.

Kick looked up again and saw the giant glass panels begin to close. Years of dust and debris began filtering down through the air. She put her arms over her head. "Joe, stop it. The whole damn thing is going to collapse on us," she shouted.

"And look here," he said, excitedly pointing to the metal cables that rose from the wheel. "This regulates the pitch of the panels. Watch."

"No, don't," she shouted again, but she was already laughing. "You'll kill us both. Leave it like it is and get me a brandy, while I sweep up this mess."

Joe grabbed a coffee mug from near the hot plate and poured her a drink, while Kick found a broom in the hall. She swept the floor and shook out the bedclothes on the couch. When things were relatively back to normal, except for the open roof, they sat down side by side on the edge of the bed and stared up at the sky in a kind of speechless amazement.

Kick leaned back against Joe's shoulder. She said nothing when he reached over and took her glass and set it on the floor. She said nothing as he carefully unbuttoned her silk blouse and loosened his tie and shirt.

Slowly, silently, they undressed each other. Joe reached down to the foot of the bed and pulled an old down comforter over their naked bodies. For a long time they lay entwined, listening to each other's breathing, staring at the stars.

"How did it go with Fiddle?" Joe asked in a soft monotone.

"She can't use the Lolly piece, but she's interested in my Irving story," Kick answered in a similarly inflectionless voice.

"How interested?"

"A ticket to London will be here in the morning."

"That's great. When will you leave?"

"As soon as I can," Kick said, moving even closer as he slowly ran his hand down her body.

"Are you cold?"

"Not anymore."

"Will you miss me?" he asked, his lips against her forehead.

"Can't tell."

"Why not?"

"We haven't done it yet."

"Done what?"

"You know," Kick said, giggling.

Joe turned and began to kiss her, covering her body with his. "You mean this?" he asked, moving his mouth down her neck and across her shoulder to her breast.

"Not exactly," she said, arching her back and giving in to the warm feeling racing down her inner thighs.

He spent what seemed like a heavenly eternity kissing her nipples and elbows and thighs, and then he parted her legs with his knee and moved fully on top of her. "Is this what you mean by 'it'?"

"Well . . . not quite."

He kissed her again, deeply, and when he entered her, she gasped his name.

"This?" he said, moving slowly inside her. His breathing matched hers.

"Right," she said. Her entire body was tense with desire. "This is what I had in mind."

They made love for the rest of the night, under the stars, going to places Kick had ached to go to for so long and had begun to believe she would never experience again.

When she awoke at dawn, she was still in Joe's arms. Gently rolling over on her back, careful not to wake him, Kick stared up through the roof. The sky was full of gold metallic streaks and yet the stars were still out.

She lay very still, watching the stars disappear one by one, like tiny lights being switched off by a watchman who knew the night was over.

330

She wondered how long the roof had remained closed and if Lolly had known—or remembered—about the contraption that opened the ceiling. She wondered if Lolly had ever made love in this extraordinary place or if, in search of peace and solitude, she had ever opened the roof and stared at the stars.

Lolly had been from another generation, one that was pushed and shoved into marriage. How terribly determined she had to have been to live the life she lived, famous and powerful and alone.

Maybe this room sustained her when she felt she was losing her grip on the control she demanded. Maybe this was where she found her strength. There couldn't be any place else like it on earth.

She got up and slipped on Joe's big shirt against the crisp morning air. From the chair at Lolly's desk she could see brighter rays of sun streaking the eastern sky.

She knew what would happen when the penthouse went on the block at the end of the year. She pictured the wrecking crews, hired by rich yuppies, crowbarring out the glass and metal framework, thinking the effect weird and old-fashioned. Heaven only knew what would replace the tower room, a gym probably, with a Jacuzzi or a hot tub and a StairMaster. Perhaps, because the whole apartment was so big, someone would chop it up into studios and charge a fortune for one room.

Kick had never been interested in owning things. She traveled light and preferred it that way. Being responsible for Lolly's things had felt burdensome to her. But in that moment she knew what her dream was. Yes, she wanted to write, and success at her chosen profession was important to her. She also wanted a home, and someone to share it with.

37

Kick had been waiting for nearly an hour in the stately lobby lounge of London's posh Claridge's hotel. From where she sat she had a clear shot at anyone coming in the main entrance.

She didn't care if it took all night, she was going to ambush Baby Bayer. If Baby hadn't found the Lopez girl by now, she had to at least have an idea of where she was.

Joe had managed to find out that Baby was staying at Claridge's. The mention of the venerable old hotel sent Kick racing for her trusty B list. Once again, it didn't let her down. Guy Hunting, a charming trainee at the hotel she had met on a trip some years earlier, was now the night manager there, and to her delight he remembered her the minute she called from the U.S.

There'd been a sharp intake of air when Kick asked Guy if he knew anything about Baby's activities since she had arrived. Guy told Kick that during her relatively short stay at the hotel, Baby had made herself quite well known to the staff. She had been seen in the lounge and elevator with a well-known member of the international paparazzi, an Italian known simply as "Paco," who specialized in sneaking up on the royals with a long lens and selling the pictures to tabloids all over the world.

Guy had made a quick check with room service and called Kick back. Baby and the photographer had spent three days in her room ordering quantities of food and champagne and dispatching porters to a nearby pharmacy on several occasions.

When Kick had arrived at the hotel at ten o'clock that night, Guy Hunting had been waiting for her at the front desk. Tall and lanky with a huge Adam's apple and an infectious laugh, he was wearing a severely tailored dark blue suit and a silver tie, a nice upgrade from the bellman's uniform she remembered him wearing the last time she saw him.

He took Kick's hands and kissed both of her cheeks.

"Let me look at you," he said, releasing her and holding her at arm's length. "Now, why did I expect a skinny teenager? You're all grown up and gorgeous."

"Thank you, Guy," Kick said, laughing. "You look pretty grand yourself."

He looped his arm through hers and guided her over to a tall potted fern in the corner of the lobby where they could talk.

"Darling," he whispered dramatically. "Your Ms. Bayer and her friend have gone out. I happened to see them leave a few minutes ago."

"Oh, rats," Kick whispered. "I wonder what I should do?"

"If you want to freshen up, your room's ready for you."

"I'm afraid if I go to the room, I'll fall asleep. I, uh, didn't get much sleep last night."

"Let me get you a good table in the lounge, my dear," Guy said, taking her elbow. "Depending on your patience, you could just wait until they return."

Guy settled her comfortably. She promised to let him know if she needed anything more, and he went back to work.

She was finishing her second cup of tea when, out of the corner of her eye, Kick saw the captain approaching her table.

"Ms. Butler, you have a telephone call," he said.

She turned to see that he was holding a telephone out to her. "For me?" she said, startled. "Thank you."

The captain set the phone on the table next to her chair and disappeared.

"Kick? Guy Hunting here. I thought you'd like to know that the lady you're looking for has just arrived. The front desk just called me."

"You're kidding," Kick said, looking anxiously toward the lobby. "Where is she?"

Guy chuckled. "I'm afraid she's still outside. They're having a spot of trouble getting her out of the car. It appears she and her friend have been to a party."

"Do you think I should go out?"

"That might not be a bad idea. If she gets upstairs in her present condition, you may not see her for some time."

"Thank you, Guy, you are a darling."

As she stepped through the massive front door, the doorman was nowhere to be seen. She stepped onto the sidewalk and looked to her right. A taxi was haphazardly parked several feet from the curb. Standing by the open curbside back door was the doorman, a policeman, the driver, and a tall man with dark slicked-back hair who looked like the men one sees in the paper carrying the casket at a Mafia funeral.

A pair of women's legs clad in black fishnet hose and gold sling pumps protruded from the open cab door.

As Kick moved cautiously toward the scene, she saw a handbag swing out of the open door, narrowly missing the pallbearer's crotch. Over the low but heated conversation the men were having, she heard a woman scream, "Just fuck off, goddamn it. I said no."

Kick moved closer until she was standing only an arm's length behind the policeman. No one paid the slightest attention to her.

"Ma'am, if you'll just step out, please," the policeman said, addressing the pair of legs.

"Let me try, Officer," the pallbearer said halfheartedly.

"The fuck you will, you freeloading scumbag. I'm tired of giving you money. If you don't have cab fare, it's not my problem."

The doorman bent down and spoke to the woman. "Miss Bayer, I'd be happy to take care of the fare," he said solicitously.

"And put it on my fucking bill? No way, Jose. Tell that cop to take this freeloader to jail," the woman shouted.

The doorman shrugged and backed away. By now, Kick had figured out that the dark man with the slicked-back hair was Baby's new lover, Paco. He was good-looking in a sinister way. Apparently, he was ready to give up on Baby. He nimbly dodged another sudden assault on his groin as one of Baby's high heels shot forward. He backed up, slapped his forehead with his open palm, and began to pace the sidewalk in a loose circle, apparently waiting for someone to put an end to the impasse.

Kick knew she had to make a move.

"Excuse me," she said, in a bright, take-charge voice as she elbowed her way between the doorman and the driver. "I'm a friend of Miss Bayer's. How much is the fare?"

At the sound of Kick's voice, a yellow mop of hair suddenly emerged over the extended legs. "Who the fuck are you?" Baby asked, looking up at Kick. There were great smudges of black mascara circling her big, suspicious eyes. She looked like a raccoon on speed.

Kick leaned through the door. "I'm Kick Butler," she said in an urgent, low voice. "I'm a friend of Joe Stone's."

Baby's mouth opened and then shut. "Oh, shit," she croaked. "Tanner's sent you to get me. I knew it . . . I knew it. This is all that fucking Italian's fault."

As Baby began to cry, Kick quickly turned and pressed some bills into the driver's hand. "Better count it. I'm a bit rusty on English money."

The driver looked down and smiled. "This is fine, mum. Thank you very much, mum."

Kick leaned back through the door. Baby was now sitting

335

upright and blowing her nose into the gold chiffon scarf that was thrown over a black strapless evening dress.

"Come on, pal," Kick said. "The cabbie wants to leave. And don't worry. Joe didn't send me. You're okay."

Baby mumbled something into her scarf.

"Sorry?"

Baby dropped the scarf and jerked her head toward the street. "Lose the goombah," she said. "His name is Paco. Tell him to get his goddamn cameras out of the trunk and fuck off. Then I'll get out. I don't want him coming into the hotel with me."

Kick nodded and pulled her head out of the cab, wondering if Baby used the F-word quite as much when she was sober. She turned to Paco, who was still walking in circles. "Are you Paco?"

"Yeah," he said, sneering. "You gotta problem?"

"Would you get your gear, please. Miss Bayer would like you to leave."

"Who says?" He scowled, his handsome face twisting into a fist.

"She says," Kick said, firmly. "She won't get out of the cab until you leave."

"She's drunk."

"She is, and she'll still be drunk after you've gone."

"Don't get wise," he groused, walking to the back of the cab, where the driver was unloading a bulky black camera bag. Paco hefted the heavy bag and walked back toward Kick. "I don't know what's she's so mad at me for. She's the one who bitched and moaned about going to Lord Mosby's party. I *told* her I had to work."

"Thank you for escorting Ms. Bayer to the party, Mr. Paco," Kick said, in her best Sister Mary Immaculate voice, making sure she was speaking loudly enough for Baby to hear. "It wouldn't have been right for her to go alone. She's a very important journalist, you know."

"So she says," Paco said, his eyes following a V path, down and then up Kick's body. "What are you, her nurse?"

"No, just a fan," Kick said, moving back to Baby, who had

336

eased herself out to the edge of the backseat, stuck her head out the door, and was listening.

"Don't bother telling him who I am," Baby snapped. "All he cares about is a free fuck and his goddamn pictures."

Kick pulled the last large pound note she had out of her bag and handed it to Paco. "Have a drink on me, Mr. Paco," she said. "I'll take care of Ms. Bayer."

Paco took the note, looked at it for an instant, and turned. "Smartass broads," he muttered as he walked away.

Getting Baby through the entrance and into the lobby was like trying to stuff an oyster into a slot machine. She didn't seem to have any bones, and her feet kept rolling off her shoes.

Suddenly, Baby stopped dead in her tracks. "What'd you say your name was?" she slurred.

"Kick. Kick Butler."

"You sure I don't know you?" Baby asked squinting up at Kick's face.

"Maybe. I used to work for Lolly Pines."

"Lolly Pines?" Baby whooped, suddenly almost sober, looking as if she remembered. "You worked for Lolly Pines?"

"Yes. Sure did."

Baby leaned forward, attempting to reach Kick's ear, but missed and stumbled against her shoulder. *"Shhhh,"* she said, pulling back. "I'll tell you a little secret. I'm going to replace Lolly Pines. Let's go get a drink."

Now Kick knew Baby was out of her skull. She caught Baby's arm as she lurched toward the lounge. Kick took in the wild eyes, the extensive show of upper body flesh, and the mass of tangled hair. "Not a real shiny idea, Baby. Let's go up to your room. We'll order room service. Okay?"

"Ha. Room service." Baby hiccuped as she wobbled toward the elevator with no further protest. "They cut me off. Said I owed two thousand dollars. We had a minibar, but they stopped putting booze in it. You ever hear of that? Fancy-ass hotel like this cuts off your room service? Takes away your minibar? Fucking snots."

337

Kick propelled Baby into the elevator cab and turned her around to face the front. "What floor are you on, Baby?" she asked, throwing a nervous smile to the elevator operator.

"She's on the third floor, ma'am," the operator answered with faintly concealed disdain.

Kick helped Baby get the key in the door to her room and walked in behind her. She could immediately see that Baby had treated herself very, very nicely. She had a two-room suite with a lovely view. From the entrance hall Kick could see that both rooms were furnished with real antiques and were an utter shambles. There were panty hose looped over the lampshades. Shoes were scattered around the Oriental rugs, and piles of clothes were thrown everywhere. It appeared as though a maid had been in to make the bed and, in disgust, had left anything personal right where it lay.

Once inside, Baby made a beeline for the bedroom and collapsed onto the canopied bed. Kick followed her in. Through an open door she could see a bathroom in chaos.

Kick stepped to the side of the bed and pulled off Baby's pumps, more in an effort to save the pale satin bedspread than to make Baby more comfortable. She placed them under the bed and straightened up.

"Why are you being so nice to me?" Baby moaned, pulling a pillow over her head.

"You looked like you could use some help out there. Just call it sisterhood," Kick said, feeling not a little guilty. Being nice to Baby had nothing to do with sisterhood. It had to do with coddling Baby into telling her what she knew about Maria.

Baby lifted the pillow off her head. "Sisterhood sucks," she snarled. "It's naive, sentimental, and dated. That crap only works when you need the name of a good gynecologist or a recipe for lasagna. When you get to where I am professionally, women cut you no slack. Men just want to fuck you. Women kill."

Kick was too jet-lagged to figure out where Baby was professionally. Clearly she ranked herself somewhere between Oriana Fallaci and Clare Boothe Luce. She was dying to ask Baby why she thought she was going to be the one to replace Lolly. She couldn't imagine what could have given her such a crazy idea. "I like my women friends," Kick said. "I've always found them very supportive."

Kick waited for Baby to say something from under the pillow, then tried a different tack. "Maybe I better roll along, Baby," Kick said, testing. "You probably want to get some sleep."

Kick picked up her bag. She was halfway across the room when she thought she heard Baby laughing. She turned. The odd sounds coming from the massed pillows were sobs. Baby was crying.

Kick walked back to the bed and pulled the pillows away from Baby's head. Baby's hands flew up to cover her face. Great, gasping sobs shook her body. The raccoon eyes had begun to melt down her cheeks.

"What's the matter, Baby?" Kick asked calmly, figuring Baby was on a booze-induced crying jag.

"Don't go," Baby snorted between sobs. "Please don't. Stay with me. I can't stand to be alone. I'm in such trouble."

Kick dragged a slipper chair up to the side of the bed and sat down. "Okay. For a while," she said. "Now, what kind of trouble are you in?"

Baby gulped a body-shuddering mouthful of air and began to settle down. "I'm a total fuckup, Kick. I've ruined everything . . . everything," she whimpered. "I've just thrown everything I ever wanted down the toilet for Paco. Son-of-a-bitch bastard slime." She pushed both fists into her eye sockets.

"You're really crazy about him, huh?" Kick asked wryly. "Maybe now that he's gone, things will get better."

Baby let out a howl that would have served her well in childbirth. "Don't say he's gone," she screamed. "I want him. I can't live without him." She threw herself back against the headboard. "Now I've lost him, and I've blown my chance at getting Lolly's column."

Now, that's what I want to hear about, Kick thought. She slowly pulled off her boots. It was going to be a long night.

Baby began by telling Kick about the deal she had with her publisher. If she could get a call-girl media creation named Maria Lopez to come back to New York and give her her story, she could have Lolly's column. Something, she claimed, she wanted more than life itself.

A columnist named Abner Hoon at the *London Gazette* had the Lopez girl hidden out. All Baby had to do was arrive in London, get hold of Hoon, trick him into telling her where the girl was, and pounce on her.

"So what did this Hoon person think you were doing in London?" Kick asked innocently.

"Oh, now this was really clever," Baby said, bouncing excitedly among the pillows. "I told him my publisher wanted to do a big profile on him, and because we knew each other—Abner Hoon and I go way back—I was here to interview him."

"And he bought that?"

"Bought it," she whooped. "I thought he was going to have an orgasm on the phone. He couldn't see me soon enough and wanted to know when could I meet him at this pub all the Fleet Streeters hang out in called El Vino. What a dump."

Kick sat back and pictured the scene. From the sound of it, the party-hardened crowd who made El Vino their second home had seen it all—that is, until the arrival of Baby Bayer. Booze hounds who had never squinted further than the rim of their whiskey glasses probably stiffened to attention when Abner Hoon swung through the door that first night with the blond American reporter on his arm.

"They loved me." Baby sighed, wiping more mascara on the lace-encrusted linen pillowcase that was cross-hatched with smears of makeup. As she told her story, she got up and stripped off her dress. On the floor next to the bed she located a see-through fuchsia peignoir with black marabou feathers at the wrists and throat. As Kick watched her flouncing around without missing a beat of her tale, she could see why the jaded crowd of Fleet Streeters must not have been able to take their eyes off Baby.

Baby was infinitely watchable. If a man had any latent pedophilia stirring in his loins, Baby's deceptively angelic face and child-woman body would release the demons of hell.

As she flopped back on the big bed, the little black marabou feathers closest to her face lifted and floated about her cleavage and chin as she talked. From time to time a hairlike feather would stick to her wet magenta lips, an annoyance that would have driven Kick nuts. Baby, however, would lanquidly reach up, slowly pull the strand away, and keep right on talking. "They crowded around me, just hanging on everything I said," Baby recalled, in a dreamy baby-girl voice. "It's like I was Henry Kissinger or something. I don't know you at all, Kick, but you're a woman. Do you know how it makes you feel to have that kind of male attention all at once?"

"I can't say I've had the experience," Kick said. "It must have been fun."

"Fun?" Baby yelped. "It damn well turns you on. But you should have seen what it did to Abner Hoon. He was like a goddamn peacock. Like I'm his property. Boy, was that a performance."

"I'll bet," Kick said, smiling.

"Usually I can tell if a guy is light in the loafers, but guys like Hoon baffle me. If there's one thing that drives me crazy, it's a bisexual homosexual. I just don't know what to do with them.

"By the second night, the situation at El Vino was out of his control. He started to get all snippy, because what he wanted was to be telling me the story of his life for my so-called article. He's starting not to like me. You understand, I need to have him like me, a lot, but I can't help myself."

Kick frowned, deciding to push a bit. "Has he mentioned Maria Lopez at all?"

Baby's big blue eyes squeezed into slits. "No, damn it, and I know if I had paid attention to him, he wouldn't have been able to resist bragging. You see, he thinks Maria is valuable because her black book is full of the names of clients who are royals and members of parliament."

"And it isn't?" Kick asked.

Baby bit her upper lip for a moment and stared out the window. Finally, she turned back to Kick. "You've got to promise me you won't tell anyone if I tell you something real personal."

Kick didn't want to promise her anything and figured she wouldn't have to. If working for Lolly had taught her anything, it was that people who had secrets couldn't bear not to share them. "Go ahead, I'm fascinated."

"This girl Maria was represented by a very big New York lawyer. We were having an affair, and as a favor to him, I wrote an item saying that Maria had a lot of fancy English clients, just to hype her story. Abner saw it and called me, and I kind of let him think it was true."

"Abner still believes that?" Kick asked.

"I guess so. Eventually, I was going to tell him it wasn't true so he'd lose interest in Maria and let me have her. But I was having such a good time, I didn't want it to end. I wouldn't have any excuse to stay once I got the girl."

"Wouldn't he have been angry that you'd lied to him?"

"No problem. I'd just tell him Irving was feeding me bad information."

"Irving? That's your lover?" Kick asked coolly.

"Irving Fourbraz," Baby said, preening. "You know who he is, of course."

Kick forced her eyes to widen in feigned veneration. "Of course. Heavy."

"He's not my lover anymore. Our thing is over. I hate him now. He lied to me."

"Thing," Kick said dully, thinking about Neeva and how Baby's "thing" had torn her life apart.

"So," Kick said casually, "there you are in the pub with all these guys around you and you're ignoring Abner. What happened? Did he get mad and walk out?"

"Oh, no." Baby sighed deeply and began to twist the feathers at her throat. "Paco happened."

Baby took Kick back to the scene on the third night at El Vino. She had promised herself she would concentrate exclusively on Abner. She had wasted enough time flirting and was getting nervous about not accomplishing anything. She was standing at the bar, her back to her drooling suitors, telling Abner how brilliant he was, when she glanced down the bar. There, framed in the door, was the Great Dark Man of her fantasies coming out of the night. A murmur stirred the crowd. The few other women there gasped and clutched their throats. The Prince of the Paparazzi—Paco—walked into El Vino, all black leather and Italian-brewed testosterone, the nostrils of his Roman nose flaring as he sniffed the potential for adventure in the smoky room.

In the length of time it took him to order and lift a glass of gin and bitters to his pouting lips, Paco caught the scent of Baby Bayer.

Their eyes locked and held. Baby felt her inner thighs begin to tremble. Her stomach tightened and her lips parted ever so slightly. Abner had his back to Paco and was too involved with his own monologue to know what was going on. He assumed he was the cause of Baby's rapt expression.

To hear Baby tell it, within seconds of their eyes locking, cymbals clanged and her bikini Calvins began to dampen.

"You hear about people who take your breath away," Baby said, all dreamy-eyed in remembrance. She was now lying flat on her back staring at the ceiling. "That's the way I felt. I literally couldn't breathe. I couldn't speak. I couldn't move. Abner was jabbering away. He could have been telling me where Maria was, I wouldn't have noticed. It took him a minute or two to realize that I was holding on to the edge of the bar to keep from fainting. He asked me if I was all right. I didn't even answer him. I couldn't stand it anymore. I asked Abner to excuse me. I guess he thought I was going to the john. I walked straight down the bar and stood in front of Paco. He looked down at me. I mean, you saw how big he is. I felt like a toy next to him. He looked down at me and said,

343

'Who are you?' I told him. Then he said, 'I am Paco. Let's go.' So we did."

"Baby," Kick exclaimed. "Just like that? You walked out on Hoon?"

"No, I *ran* out on Hoon," Baby corrected. "I left my handbag on the bar and my coat in the checkroom and walked right out into the rain. We hadn't gotten halfway down the block before Paco grabbed me and pulled me into this alley. He pushed me up against the wall. Before I knew it he had his tongue down my throat and his hand up my dress. I'm so hot I don't care. He pulled down my panties and fucked me right there. Kick, he was the size of an eighteen-ounce can of Molson Light."

"Jesus." Kick gulped.

"While we're doing it," Baby continued, "and I mean really doing it"—she pounded a fist into a palm—"I'm so crazed I start to come. I guess I was making a lot of noise. For some reason, I looked over his shoulder, which would have been impossible if he wasn't lifting me up with both hands under my butt—and what do I see?"

"Don't tell me," Kick said. "Abner."

"You got it. Abner. He's standing in the light at the end of the alley with my handbag dangling from one finger. I thought his eyes were going to come out of his head."

"What did you do?"

"What could I do? I came. You talk about rockets. It was the fucking Fourth of July. I'm holding on to Paco, shaking like some rag doll. I don't know if he came or not 'cause he's still hard. I've got my legs around his waist with him still in me while he's carrying me out of the alley, leaving my shoes and panties on the ground. When we get out to the street, Abner is gone. My handbag is sitting in a puddle on the sidewalk. Paco bends and picks it up without missing a beat. It's the first walking screw I've ever had. The guy has legs of steel. He walks us up to his car about a half a block away, pulls out, and dumps me into the front seat.

344

"The next thing I know we're walking through the door here. We didn't leave for two days, three days. I can't remember."

"Whew," Kick said, slowly shaking her head. "Remind me to pay more attention next time I'm in Rome. So, what happened this evening, then? Did you two have a fight at the party?"

"*Oy*," Baby said, slapping her forehead. "A fight? I wish it had been just a fight."

Baby explained that when she finally emerged from her sexual black hole, it dawned on her that she was in deep trouble. There were several urgent messages from Tanner, who wanted to know how she was progressing. There were other messages from men she had met at El Vino's asking for dates. There were no messages from Abner.

She tried to reach him both at his flat and at the *Gazette* only to be told, after identifying herself, that "Mr. Hoon was taking no calls." Baby panicked. It was imperative that she get back in Abner's good graces.

When Paco said he was going to a party at Lord and Lady Mosby's that night, she begged him to take her. Lord Mosby owned Abner's newspaper. Abner was sure to be at the party.

As Baby began to tell Kick what had happened at Lord Mosby's, she began to cry again. Kick found a box of tissues on the bed table and handed her one so she could blow her nose properly.

"I should never have insisted on going to that party," she said. "I should have known better, but I had been screwing for days and my brain wasn't working. Paco wasn't going because he was invited. He was going to stand outside this gorgeous town house in Belgravia like a stray dog with all those other cretins, firing away at the celebrities. He thought I knew that. That's why he was so reluctant to take me. But *noooo*, I begged and whined to go. It was so awful."

"I take it you ran into Hoon," Kick said.

Baby nodded her head vehemently. "It was so humiliating. You have to realize, I originally met Abner at this spectacular party at a mansion on Long Island. Do you know who the Garns are? Tita and Jourdan Garn?"

Kick nodded with a twinge of sadness. That would have been the weekend Lolly died. So much for Baby going back a long way with Abner.

"Anyway, he saw me at the Garns' just surrounded by everyone who was anyone. People simply wouldn't leave me alone. Dan Rather, Diane von Furstenberg, Walter Cronkite, Brooke Astor, absolutely everyone wanted to chat. Abner saw me as this media star. I stayed over that night in one of Tita's guest rooms. Abner sent a car for me the next day, invited me to lunch. You know, buttering me up. So you can see how dreadful this trip has been. First he sees me with my dress over my head getting boffed in an alley by some Italian gorilla I had just met, then—and frankly, this was worse—he sees me standing outside Lord Mosby's with this jerk, dressed to the nines and begging some footman to let me go in. It's dark. It's cold. All the photographers have grass and flasks of scotch. We're all drinking pretty heavily to stay warm. We were out there for more than two hours, and I'm getting drunker and madder by the minute."

"So what happened when Abner saw you outside Lord Mosby's?"

"Shit," she said, burying her face in her hands. "It was so awful. He got out of his car right in front of me. He didn't say a word. He goes up to a footman and says something. The next thing I know, the footman comes over and says, 'Girly, you take your business elsewhere. You're in the wrong neighborhood.' That's when I wigged out. I was so freaked that Abner had done that, I started running up the steps after him screaming 'cocksucker.' Paco finally got me into a cab. He yelled at me all the way back to the hotel. When we get here, he didn't even have the fare. Well, you know the rest."

"*Ummm,*" Kick said thoughtfully. "I'd say you burned a few bridges, Baby."

"Now you see why I'm so upset. I've lost everything, Paco, Abner, any chance of finding Maria. And when this gets back to my publisher, and you know it will, I'm screwed out of getting Lolly's column and probably out of a job."

Kick stood up and walked to the minibar, hoping there might at least be some peanuts or a candy bar. She was starved. She hadn't eaten since the mystery-meat meal on the plane hours before. She was also dog tired. The minibar had one last can of club soda in it. She popped off the top and walked back to her chair. "Wanna split this?" she asked, holding up the can. Baby shook her head.

"Well, Baby, I'd say you have a problem."

"Don't tell me," she cried. "I don't know what to do. I'm crazy about this guy. I've charged so much on my bill here, Tanner will probably fire me for that alone. I've just got to find that Maria Lopez. But how?"

Kick took a big swig of club soda. "Baby, we both need to get some sleep."

"Are you staying here?" Baby asked hopefully.

Kick nodded and took another swig.

"Oh, goody," she said perkily. "What's your room number? I'll call you in the morning. We can get together and think up something."

"Well . . . I don't know . . ." The thought of a whole day of girly face time with Baby made her eyes sting. Yet now that Baby had admitted her true feelings about Irv . . . "You know what? I'd love to hear more about Irving Fourbraz. I'm thinking about doing an article on him. Maybe you could tell me some . . . ah . . . personal details."

"Sure. I've got some real dish," Baby said blithely.

"I'll call," Kick said, picking up her bag.

Kick wanted to get out of there. She wanted a hot bath and clean sheets. Kick patted Baby's shoulder and said good night.

When Kick reached the elevator at the end of the hall, she turned to see Baby standing in the door in her ridiculous nightie, looking little and sad and trusting. Kick didn't know Baby well, but she was certain it was an act.

The room Guy had arranged for Kick was two floors up from

Baby's but small in comparison with her suite. Still, it looked like heaven to Kick. There was a basket of fruit sitting on the dresser with a welcoming note from Guy.

Kick smiled, thinking how nice he was. She picked up the bedside phone to call and thank him.

"No problem, darling," he said. "How did you do with the ludicrous Ms. Bayer?"

"Oh, fine, I guess. She talked, I listened. But she didn't have the information I wanted."

"What is it you needed to know? Would it be anything to do with Abner Hoon?"

"Guy, what do you know about Abner Hoon?"

"Well, darling, I saw him bring Ms. Bayer back to the hotel a few times. I know him only vaguely, but we do move in the same, *um,* rarefied circles."

"He's hardly your type, is he?"

"Well, no, but he's got a little country hideaway, where he throws some interesting house parties."

Kick froze. Country hideaway? Suitable, perhaps, for hiding kidnapped call girls?

"Guy, I need to know where Hoon's country place is. It's crucial to a story I'm working on. The thing is, if I get to the person I think he's got stashed there, he'll be pretty upset, so I'd like to keep this confidential."

There was a long silence at the other end of the line. Then Guy began to give directions to Abner Hoon's country house in Kent.

After she hung up the phone, Kick was too excited to sleep. She drew a deep, hot tub of water and poured in all of the little guest bottles she found on the bathroom counter—bath gel, shampoo, bubble bath, and hair conditioner. She always figured it was all the same stuff no matter what it said on the label.

She undressed, selected a ripe pear from the basket, and sank into the warm folds of thick foam. It took only a minute or two for her to begin to feel the effect. As always, the combination of fatigue, tension, stress, and uncertainty made her feel as though someone had beaten her up. Every muscle pulled, every bone ached, and nothing cured the feeling quite like a hot, frothy soak. This evening had to have been one of the stranger nights of her life.

She had found Baby and Maria in virtually one fell swoop.

As shocked as she was that Baby had been offered Lolly's column, she had to accept the possibility of her getting it. Baby had a shot at one of the best jobs in American journalism. All she had to do was control herself. Abner surely would have led her to Maria if she had been able to.

Poor Baby, so fearless and vulgar, and so pathetic in her need to be taken seriously.

Kick sat up and ran that thought through her head once more. Fearless . . . vulgar . . . pathetic . . . Also, driven to have the world pay attention. That was exactly what someone needed to be a good gossip columnist. Maybe Tanner Dyson knew what he was doing after all.

38

*A*bner Hoon's elaborately "thatched" cottage was set a few hundred yards back from the road, just as Guy had described it. There was a small front gate and a flagstone walk leading to a brass-fitted door. Kick said good-bye to the nice man who'd given her a lift from the pub near the train station—there hadn't been a taxi to be seen in the village—and marched up the drive.

"I'm not here to harm you," she muttered. "I know you are in trouble, and maybe I can help." Nah, she thought. Maria wouldn't buy that line. She probably didn't think she was in any trouble at all. Maria wanted money and fame. Holing up in Abner's country house was her idea of how to get that. Kick couldn't offer her money, but she could offer her a level of fame. *Fifteen Minutes* was a magazine that Hollywood agents, talent scouts, people in the music industry, and millionaires who liked notorious girls read. She could suggest that her magazine might hire an Annie Liebowitz to take a great picture of Maria walking on a beach in a six-hundred-dollar silk shirt that the people at Michael Kors would let her keep. Being in *Fifteen Minutes* offered a certain degree of credibility. People like Maria were short on that, and it probably bothered her. Maybe that was the way to go. She would tell her that once Irving got through with her for selling him out, no one would believe her. Irving had such powerful friends that he would reduce her image to that of nothing more than a money-grubbing little hooker. The only way to neutralize the damage would be for her to strike first. But what if Maria was too bone dumb to get it? Kick wished she had been able to do some homework on the woman. That was a lesson she would remember for the future.

When she reached the doorstep, she squared her shoulders and rang the bell once, then twice. She listened to her own rapid breathing. She rang again and listened.

Inside she began to hear the sound of hard heels on bare wood coming closer.

"Who's there?" a woman's voice called.

"Hello, hello," Kick chirped, trying to sound like a neighbor dropping by with a Tupperware container of raspberry fool. "I'm a friend of Abner's."

"You sound American. Where are you from?" the voice asked.

"Where am I from?" Kick mouthed silently. Where the hell should I be from? What did the person on the other side of the door want to hear that would make her open the door? Should she say, "My car is broken down," or maybe, "You've just won the Publisher's Clearinghouse Sweepstakes?" No, she thought, the truth should be intriguing enough. "I'm from New York," she called.

The door sprang open so fast Kick jumped. Standing in the door in a pair of black stretch pants and a man's plaid work shirt was a dark-haired young woman with a tense, unmade-up face.

"Hi there," Kick said perkily. "My name is Kick Butler. Are you Maria Lopez?"

"Yes," the woman said, in a voice pinched with hysteria. "Please, please, please come in. I'm so bored I could die."

* * *

351

Late that afternoon Kick walked her odd-looking guest across the lobby at Claridge's and straight into the lounge. Overjoyed to be freed from her rural incarceration, Maria had gotten herself up to look like Charo doing a lounge act in the Poconos. Her hair had been puffed and teased into an explosion that made her look as if she had a Yorkshire terrier sitting on her head. She wore a silver lamé bustier and miniskirt. Her high, lace-up white boots had tiny flowers embroidered up the sides. She completed the effect with a fake-fur cubby and black-net wrist gloves.

The captain showed them to one of the best tables and took their drink order himself without batting an eye.

"Now, Maria," Kick said, after their drinks had been served. "This woman you are about to meet is going to want you to tell her pretty much what you told me on the train ride back. You might want to start with how Irving Fourbraz and you first met."

Maria leaned forward, displaying an inappropriate amount of cleavage for the late afternoon. "You mean tell her about screwing Irving in his room at the Beverly Hills Hotel?" she asked.

"That's right," Kick said. She felt good about the deal she'd cut with Baby when she phoned her from Kent. Baby had screamed a little when she heard that Kick had Maria, but she calmed down when Kick explained how they could both get their stories and come out ahead. Baby would run with the headlines, Kick would follow up with an in-depth magazine piece. Both ways, Irving would lose.

"Ah, there you are," Kick said as Baby approached their table. She turned to Maria. "Maria, I'd like you to meet Baby Bayer of the *New York Courier*. Baby, this is Maria Lopez."

The captain held the empty chair next to Maria. As Baby sat down, she reached out and squeezed Kick's shoulder. "Thanks, pal," she whispered.

Kick sat back to listen, one more time, to the story Maria had hoped to sell to the highest bidder, until she had been treated so badly, stuck away in hospitals, and left to molder in a village in

Kent. All she wanted was appreciation, revenge, and her Warhol formulation. That was exactly what Kick had had to offer her, one girl to another, in the lonely country cottage with no TV.

Early the following evening, Kick sailed past the customs counter at JFK. She pushed through the swinging doors to the outer terminal and was about to turn right toward the cab stand out at the curb. She stopped short as a cardboard sign rose up in front of her face. Someone had written *Miss Katherine Butler* on it with magic marker.

Kick pulled back in surprise. She identified herself to the driver holding the sign and followed him toward the private car entrance.

A long black stretch was sitting at the curb with the back door open. She could see a pair of corduroy legs extending from the seat.

She bent down and looked in. "Joe," she cried in delight. "You didn't have to do this."

Joe leaned over the bouquet of roses on his lap and helped her into the backseat. "Welcome home, champ," he said with a broad grin.

Kick kissed him and pulled her long coat free of the closing door. She leaned back and sighed. "This is bliss, you darling person. I'm exhausted."

Joe bent forward and lifted his briefcase from between his feet. He pulled out a copy of the *Courier* and handed it to Kick:

"Ram Scam?" she said, reading the huge black headline over a brooding photo of Keeko Ram. At the bottom was a picture of Maria in the doggie hairdo and one of Irving leaving his office with his briefcase over his face. "I guess Keeko Gate wouldn't have worked."

She opened the paper to see Baby's story spread across two pages. Baby's face grinned out from the first column.

Kick hurriedly scanned the story. Baby had really hyped it, implying there'd been a massive search for Maria throughout

England and a hair-raising escape by night from a love-crazed Abner Hoon. Maria's boring stay at the Hoon cottage had been turned into a gruesome imprisonment fraught with days of prayer and longing for her mother and nights filled with terror.

Kick was happy to see that Baby had, as promised, limited Irving's role in the drama to a box in the right-hand corner of the second page. What she had written was damning enough but gave few details.

"Check out the Grapevine page," Joe said.

Kick flipped to page ten and read aloud the item Joe pointed to.

"An astounding in-depth look at the world of megalawyer Irving Fourbraz will be featured in the December issue of *Fifteen Minutes* magazine. Authored by freelance journalist Katherine Butler, the profile will be the first . . ." She stopped reading.

"Did you do that?" she asked Joe, trying not to smile.

"Actually, no. Fiddle called that in."

"Wow." Kick sighed. She folded the paper and turned to Joe. "Quite a splash. Baby must be thrilled."

"I hear Tanner called her in London this afternoon and told her to start turning in copy for Lolly's column."

Kick smiled. "You know, at first I had mixed feelings about that. But now I realize Baby is perfect. When does she start?"

"In a couple of weeks."

"Really?" Kick asked, surprised. "Why so long?"

"I don't know. She told Tanner she wanted to stay in London a bit longer. Something about chasing down some other story."

Kick smiled. The only thing Baby was chasing down was Paco the paparazzo. By the time Kick had checked out of Claridge's, they had gotten back together. As Guy walked her to a cab to the airport, he told her that Tanner had okayed Baby's exorbitant bills and Baby had her room service back.

"Guess who's having a hissy fit?" Joe asked with a chuckle, as the limo zoomed onto the parkway and headed for Manhattan.

"Any number of people, I suspect."

"Abner Hoon. He's got Mosby's solicitors screaming libel so

loud, we don't even need to pick up the phone. I personally think it's the implication that he had the hots for Maria that's got him so riled. You may end up having to give a deposition or two before this is over."

"Lemme at 'em," Kick said forming fists and punching the air.

"You're full of beans," Joe laughed, grabbing one fist and flattening it with a kiss in her palm.

Kick turned to face him. "Oh, Joe, I had such fun. I can't tell you. I can't wait to really get going on my Irving piece."

Joe let go of her hand and patted his pockets. "Ah, here it is," he said, pulling a piece of folded bond from the inside pocket of his tweed jacket. "I've got the list you phoned about. If you talk to everyone on here, you should have what you need."

Kick took the list and glanced at it. "Wow," she breathed. "You found Ticky Shamansky."

"He's the oldest living pool boy in Las Vegas."

"And he'll talk to me about Irving?"

"Everyone on that list will talk, Katherine."

Kick turned to him again. "What's with the Katherine stuff? Even the driver's sign had Katherine on it."

"It's time. Fiddle agrees with me."

Kick's eyebrows shot up. "You and Fiddle dishing about me, while I'm working my buns off?"

Joe nodded toward the list in her hand. "You have Fiddle to thank for more than half of those names. She's been doing business with Irving long enough to know where all the bodies are buried."

Kick looked at the list again. She recognized many of the names. Some surprised and delighted her. "Tanner Dyson? He'll talk?"

"Yup. He's pretty disgusted with Irving. Says he hoodwinked him into sending Baby to London by promising there'd be more dirt than actually turned up. Something about an old enemy."

"Who is this Rona Friedman?" Kick asked, pointing to another name on the list.

"She's a former editor at Winslow House. I'm not sure what her connection is, but Tanner felt she could give you some of the publishing side of Irving's life."

"You said 'former.' What does she do now?"

"She and Tanner's wife are starting some kind of business together. Maybe he hopes you'll plug whatever they're doing in your story."

"Whatever it takes," Kick said.

Joe put the roses in his lap on the jump seat. He reached over and pulled Kick's head down onto his shoulder.

"I missed you," he whispered against her forehead. "I haven't been able to look at my bedroom ceiling since you left. I keep seeing stars in the cracked plaster."

Kick sat bolt upright. "Oh, my God, the auction. Poor Neeva. I haven't called her. She must think I don't give a damn."

"I'll be assigning a reporter to cover it. I hope you'll give him a break with a little background interview. There's going to be a lot of competition, particularly with all the publicity over the Rodin."

Kick returned to his shoulder. "What do you think it will go for?" she asked.

"The question, my love, is how are you going to feel about being rich?"

Kick snuggled further into Joe's side. She hadn't given much thought to the fact that come next weekend that might be true. Oh, it was nice to know she wouldn't ever go hungry or have to sleep on the streets. But being rich wouldn't give her what she already had. She knew it was perverse not to crave money the way other people did. All around her were people who thought money would make them happy, turn them into swans. She'd never cared about being a swan. All she'd ever wanted was to be was a happy, confident duck.

They rode in silence until the car pulled out of the Midtown Tunnel.

"Uptown or downtown?" the driver asked through the open partition.

Joe looked down at Kick's upturned face. "Up to you," he said.

"Let's go look at some stars," she said.

"Uptown, please," he called to the driver. "I'll cover any speeding tickets."

39

Someone threw a premature puff of confetti off the balcony of the auction hall when Jeffrey Dunsmore bellowed into the microphone. "Eight hundred and fifty. Do I have any advance on eight hundred and fifty?" He paused and listened for another bid. The only sound in the room was a hushed rustle of programs and whispers. "Sold," he boomed, bringing the hammer down with a resounding crack. "For eight hundred and fifty thousand to number forty-seven."

Then the confetti poured down onto the cheering heads and waving arms in the big room. Several photographers raced down the aisle, firing away at the stage, at Jeffrey, and at a smiling man in the second row holding paddle number forty-seven.

With the last crack of Jeffrey's hammer, the auction came to a triumphant close. Lolly Pines had made Kick Butler a wealthy woman.

In her seat in the last row, Kick's hand flew to her mouth. She watched, nearly paralyzed, as two men in gray coveralls wheeled away the velvet-draped pedestal holding the Rodin head.

Jeffrey had saved the Rodin bust for last, knowing that would hold the overflow crowd in their seats. He and Neeva had done an incredible job. Between the advertisements they bought and all the free publicity, both about the head and the fact that everything had belonged to Lolly Pines, the auction had been an eye-popping success.

Kick had waited for the last minute, slipping in a side entrance and taking the last available seat in the back. She knew Joe wanted her to talk to his reporter, but she didn't really want to, and Neeva had agreed to fill in.

She had very much wanted to be by herself. She had watched, transfixed and filled with nostalgia, as each lot came on the block. The beautiful old Chippendale clock was the first big-ticket item. To her shock, Jeffrey opened the bidding at thirty thousand dollars and swung his head back and forth as two dealers fought the price up over one hundred thousand.

The barely visible painting that had hung in the foyer had been cleaned and reframed. It went for an astonishing seventeen thousand. Clearly, there were people in the room who knew a lot more about what was being sold than Kick did.

She was amazed. People bought anything. Old photos, truly tacky mismatched china and glassware, even an old cardboard box of odd tablecloths and napkins went for several hundred dollars.

She had cringed when the men wheeled out a box with old jelly glasses and canning jars. Jeff had reached in and held up one of a dozen Shirley Temple milk glasses until some collector screamed a final bid of six hundred.

Kick had been keeping a running tally, until the Pembroke table came up. She remembered the table, dirty, covered with white rings, and heaped with junk. When Jeffrey brought the hammer down at three thousand and something, Kick dropped her head into her hands. All in all, the total looked like it would be well over a million. Right now, she couldn't keep up. She'd let Neeva fill her in later.

After the Rodin was wheeled away, she remained in her seat as people pushed their way up the aisle. Never had she been so grateful for anonymity. She didn't think she would like how people would react if they knew she was the major beneficiary.

She gathered up her coat and bag and headed up the aisle to go backstage and find Neeva and Jeffrey. She had a lot to thank them for.

Kick found them in each other's arms, twirling around in a gliding little dance of pure joy. When they saw her, the two of them pulled apart and raced to embrace her.

"Do you believe it?" Neeva said, half laughing, half crying.

"No," Kick said, laughing.

"Congratulations, girl," Jeff said, nearly lifting her off the ground.

"We've got champagne. Come on," Neeva said, pulling at Kick's sleeve.

The party had already started. The staff Jeff and Neeva had hired were standing around hooting and slapping backs and drinking champagne out of plastic glasses. Kick was taken aback to see the large portrait of Lolly that had once hung over the penthouse fireplace leaning against the back wall.

"Jeff," she said, turning. "You didn't sell that?"

Jeff smiled. "Nope. I pulled it at the last minute. It occurred to me that you might want it. I auctioned it to myself. Amazingly, I won."

Kick studied the portrait. "I'm glad you did that, Jeffrey. Thank you. That means a lot to me."

"I'll have the guys drop it off tomorrow," Jeff said. "Now, sit down, you two. I'll get some bubbly."

Neeva and Kick walked to a row of steel folding chairs against a brick wall and collapsed into two of them. Off to one side sat all of Lolly's things, tagged and waiting to be crated. It was the first time Kick had seen them like that, and it made her sad.

"Oh, Neeva, look at them," she said, biting her lower lip. "It looks like they're all saying good-bye to each other. They were together for such a long time."

"Don't start," Neeva said, laughing. "Those things are all

going to wonderful homes where they will have long and happy lives."

"I know," Kick said downheartedly. "Still . . ."

"Here you go, Miss Gotrocks," Jeff said, handing a glass of champagne to Kick.

Kick took the glass and looked at Neeva. "What about yours?" she asked.

Neeva shook her head and smiled. "Can't."

"I've got to sign some stuff," Jeff said, bending to quickly kiss Neeva's cheek. "Be back in a shake."

They both watched as he jogged across the stage and disappeared into the wings.

Kick took a sip of her champagne and turned to Neeva. "What's with you and no drink?"

Neeva looked down at her hands. "I'm not drinking because it isn't good for babies and other growing things."

It took a moment for Neeva's words to sink in. When they did, she let out a little squeak. "Neeva," she said. "You're pregnant?"

"Well, I don't know. But we're trying real hard. Jeffrey wants to get married right away. You and I know that's impossible. Irving's going to make my life even more miserable once I ask him for a divorce."

Kick drank off the rest of her champagne and put her glass down on the dusty stage floor. "I have a feeling Irving isn't going to give anyone a hard time once my piece comes out."

"Kick, I completely forgot. How's that going?"

"I'm amazed. People have been so cooperative. Not the least being you, my buddy," Kick said, patting her shoulder. "The leads you gave me on his early life were terrific. I still haven't located his first wife, though, which is a pity. I'm just about finished. Only one more interview to go. Tonight at six."

"Oh? Who's that?"

"Tanner Dyson insists I speak to some woman who worked at Winslow House. I've been putting it off. I can't imagine she could have anything more to add. I've got enough now to hang him."

"Can I watch?" Neeva asked.

"The man could do some time for extortion, alone. That's why I think you'll be able to get your divorce without a lot of hassle."

"Poor Irving." Neeva sighed.

"Poor Irving my left ventricle," Kick snapped, gathering up her things and standing up. "He's earned every minute of it. Wait until you read my piece."

Neeva stood and put her arms around Kick again. "Jeff will call you in the morning. You'll have to tell him where to back up the truck."

Kick pulled back and looked at Neeva. "The truck?"

"With the money."

Kick laughed. "Yikes, the money. I guess I haven't absorbed all this yet."

Neeva locked her arm through Kick's and walked her to the edge of the stage. "Have you thought about what you're going to do with it?"

"Well, I have to find an apartment. The penthouse goes on the block at the end of the year, and I gotta be out of there. Then, of course, there'll be little Mister or Miss Dunsmore to spoil."

"Oh, Kick . . ." Neeva said, taking both Kick's hands. "Just think, a baby. I've never known a baby. Irving refused to even discuss the possibility, and of course I never questioned him. But I like babies. I smelled one once. A woman I worked with had one. She handed it to me right after he had his bath. That was very, very nice."

Neeva let go of Kick's hands. "Bye, sweetheart. I'll speak to you tomorrow."

Halfway up the aisle, Kick turned and looked back. Jeffrey had reappeared and was standing in a pool of light with his arms around Neeva. He was kissing the tip of her nose.

Kick decided she had enough time to walk to the Dysons' apartment on Park. It was a brisk, cold October night. The stars had just come out, reminding her of the open roof of Lolly's tower and making love to Joe there. Joe had brought a couple of quilts from his apartment, and it was like making love out-of-doors.

Joe was now a constant in her life. She didn't know how she could have even begun to do the Irving piece if it weren't for him. He had paved her way with people who probably wouldn't have spoken to her on a dare. If the piece worked, Joe deserved a lot of the credit.

"We're a great team," he had said just the night before as they lay in each other's arms. "We should make it permanent. You're going to be homeless, and I have a nice warm apartment. How about it?"

Afraid of what was coming next, Kick reached up and put her hand over his mouth. "Don't," she had said. "Not yet."

"Okay," he whispered, kissing her fingers. "I can wait."

She knew the night he picked her up at the airport that someday he would ask. She knew he loved her. And she loved him too, in a very sweet, gentle way, but it wasn't exactly passion. Not like it had been with Lionel.

"Shit," she hissed out loud, kicking a lingering leaf skittering across the pavement. Why was she still thinking about Lionel? Why couldn't she exorcise him once and for all? She thought she had, several times. Now that she was writing full time, well aware that the world would see her work, the memory of Lionel rose up to challenge and haunt her. Every time she sat down at the keyboard, she pictured him reading and judging what she was writing. It wasn't fair to Joe. She had told him more about Lionel. He had listened patiently, even when she admitted she was still holding on to the pain. He had to have known she was measuring him against Lionel, but he never complained.

The doorman at the Dysons' building tipped his hat and held the door for her.

"Dyson," she said. "I'm Ms. Butler."

"Go right up," he said pleasantly. "Ms. Dyson is expecting you."

Kick rode up in the elevator hoping the meeting wouldn't take too long.

A uniformed maid answered the Dysons' door. Over her shoulder, Kick could see a stunning blond coming up the hall toward her.

"Hel-ooo," the woman called, as the maid disappeared with Kick's coat.

The blond was wearing a long emerald-green velvet hostess gown that showed a flash of pink satin lining as she walked.

"I'm Georgina Dyson, Kick," she said, shaking Kick's hand and smiling a dazzling rich-lady smile.

"Hello," Kick said, returning her smile.

"Come in to the drawing room. I want you to meet my partner."

Kick followed Georgina down the hall and into one of the most beautiful rooms she had ever seen outside of *Architectural Digest.* The twinkling lights of the skyline beyond the wraparound windows looked like something in an old Fred Astaire musical. The room was nearly all white with accents of peach and mint. It was a room to eat, not sit in.

"This is Rona Friedman," Georgina said as a small woman in her early thirties rose from the couch. In contrast to Georgina's cool elegance, Rona was wearing a jeans jumper and a white Fruit of the Loom T-shirt.

"Hi, Kick," Rona said, shaking Kick's hand. "I understand you used to work for Lolly Pines?"

"Hey, now there's an icebreaker," Kick said, taking a seat on the other end of the couch. "Did you know Lolly?"

"We wanted her to do a book for us. It must have been three years ago now. We had several meetings about it. I remember she would only meet at lunch. Either La Côte Basque or La Grenouille. Only once, we met at her huge old place up on Central Park West. That was the first time I met Irving Fourbraz."

"Was anyone else there?" Kick asked, wondering if she should take out her notebook.

Rona looked at the ceiling. "Let's see, it was me, my boss, Lolly's assistant, and Irving. He was acting as her agent."

"Yes, he was her lawyer as well," Kick added.

Georgina was sitting demurely on a chair on the other side of the coffee table, listening. "Kick, a drink?"

Kick was about to say no when she looked toward the archway and saw a butler in a tux entering the room with a tray of drinks. He walked directly to her and lowered the tray. There was a selection of juices, flutes of champagne, short glasses of whiskey on the rocks, and tall glasses of plain club soda. There was a nice touch of excess to it all. Whatever no one drank would get poured down the sink.

Kick selected a club soda, and the man moved on to Rona and Georgina. Georgina selected a flute of champagne and looked up at the butler. "If Selma is finished in the kitchen, Grover, I'd like to show our guest the display before it melts."

"She's finished, ma'am," the butler said.

"Kick, excuse me for interrupting, but we have something I thought you'd like to see," Georgina said, standing up. "Bring your drink. This won't take a minute."

Slightly mystified but none the less interested, Kick picked up her club soda and followed the other two women.

The kitchen seemed to be several football fields away. They entered it through a long, service pantry with high glass cabinets filled with enough bone china to serve a state dinner.

Kick stepped into the kitchen to see a worktable more than fifteen feet long. She didn't know what to make of what she saw. Mounted on the table in a mind-boggling profusion were baskets of dozens of sausages and salamis; pyramids of darkly golden loaves of bread; earthenware bowls filled with pasta flecked with pork, meatballs, fried zucchini, tiny balls of fresh mozzarella, seafood salad, marinated yellow and red peppers, platters of roasted eggplant dripping with olive oil and basil; plates of sardines and smoked fish; ravioli with spinach and ricotta; scampi with capers; and a dark brown roasted rack of veal.

The whole stupendous mass was surrounded by klieg lights on tripods that made each dish shine with almost unreal color.

"This is one of the most beautiful things I've ever seen," Kick said, in awe. "Are you having a party?"

Georgina and Rona exchanged glances and laughed.

"I don't think anyone would want to eat this," Rona said. "The veal has been sprayed with motor oil. The crust on the bread is actually painted. See the shine on the eggplant?"

Kick nodded, moving closer.

Rona turned to Georgina. "I forgot. What did you use on the eggplant?"

"Purple magic marker and hair spray," Georgina answered proudly.

"Would you like to tell me what I'm looking at?" Kick asked.

Georgina made a sweeping gesture over the top of the table. "This is the January cover of *Fabulous Foods* magazine."

"Tanner said you'd just gone into business together," Kick said. "What do you call putting all this together?"

"Food design," Georgina said.

Just as Kick had suspected. The women wanted her to work a mention of their new venture into her story in return for the interview. If she could, she would. It was no larger a breach of ethics than paying for Maria Lopez's train ticket. Who knew? It might be worth it.

"Isn't *Fabulous Foods* a part of the Bartley Communications Group?" Kick asked, making small talk and wishing they could go back into the other room and get on with the interview.

"Not anymore," Georgina said, smiling across the table at Rona. "Rona and I and the nice people at the Allied Bank own it now."

"Actually, we're in hock up to our eyeballs, but we'll dig our way out," Rona said with great confidence.

Kick folded her arms and slowly walked around the table, admiring the show. "Excuse me, Georgina, it's none of my business, but I wouldn't think that Mrs. Tanner Dyson would have to come within a country mile of a bank loan officer."

"You're quite right to think that, Kick," she said, not taking offense. "But when Rona and I bought *Fabulous Foods*, it was with the understanding that my husband would have nothing to do with it."

"Georgina had a tiny control issue with her husband," Rona added. "She had one project that Tanner sort of macromanaged. It caused a problem."

"For a while," Georgina interrupted. "Until Rona put some sense into my head. Let's go back to the other room and let Grover strike these lights. This thing has to last until tomorrow morning."

On the way back to the drawing room, Rona explained how she and Georgina had worked together years ago on the food magazine they had just bought and then gotten reacquainted when Georgina submitted a book to Winslow House.

"I'm somewhat familiar with all that," Kick said as they all took their original seats. "It's probably rude of me to bring this up, Georgina, but the big promotional piece on you in the *Courier* Sunday magazine bumped an article I had written about Lolly Pines."

"Oh, dear," Georgina said. "I'm sorry. I'm afraid that was my husband's doing."

"Whatever happened to that book?" Kick asked. "Wasn't there supposed to be some big party for you earlier this month? As I remember, it was canceled at the last minute."

"It was something I didn't want to do," Georgina said.

"Georgie is one of those rare birds who is uncomfortable with fame. At the time, her husband didn't understand that," Rona said, glancing at Georgina.

"I was too much of a people pleaser to tell him."

"Usually, controlling men don't change," Kick said. "What happened?"

Georgina began to laugh. "It was all so ridiculous. I made myself so miserable, and there was such a simple solution. I sat Tanner down and told him that I was terribly unhappy. That I felt helpless and out of control. I told him I knew he loved me, but I wanted to do things for myself."

"And he stopped?" Kick asked, amazed.

"Just like that," Rona said, snapping her fingers. "He had no idea he was making her unhappy. He thought he was making things easier for her. She just had to be brave enough to tell him how she felt. He's smart. He adores her. He got the message."

Kick shook her head and smiled. "What happens if you start to go broke with your new venture? Will he rescue you?"

"Nope," they said in unison.

Just as their laughter died down, they heard the sound of the doorbell. From Kick's seat on the couch, she could see the butler moving up the long hall and admitting a tall young man.

"Ah," Rona said, jumping up excitedly. "Perfect timing."

She hurried out of the room and returned seconds later with the young man who had just arrived.

"Georgie, you already know Jason," she said, her hand resting lightly at the young man's back. "Kick, this is Jason Fourbraz. We worked together at Winslow House. He's the main reason I wanted to talk to you."

The minute Jason Fourbraz sat down, Kick turned a new page in her notebook and began to scribble frantically.

The young man was a gold mine of information. As much as he hated his father, he seemed to have made a lifetime study of the swath Irving had cut through the world. He told her a great deal that was new to her and more that confirmed some of the interviews she had already done. He offered to let her look at early photographs and clips he had saved and offered more names of people to contact.

At one point, Kick looked up from her notebook to see that Georgina and Rona had slipped out of the room to give them some privacy.

When there was a lull in the interview, she felt it was time to ask about his mother. "Jason, I'd love to talk to your mom. I know she's a writer. Is she still doing that?"

"Yeah." He nodded calmly. "She keeps at it. Her own stuff plus the work she does for my father's clients."

"What kind of things does she write for his clients?" Kick asked, still scribbling.

"She ghostwrites novels," Jason said. His tone had gotten

softer when he began to speak about his mother. "The first one wasn't easy, because she had to copy a certain style of writing and the book she had to imitate had won a National Book Award and made the author famous. He had fallen in love with the image of himself my father created and couldn't write another word. She wrote two more books for that jerk."

"Lionel Maltby," Kick said in a flat, zombielike voice, speaking more to herself than to Jason.

"That's right," Jason said. "Do you know him?"

"I thought I did."

"Well, for my money he's a fraud and an asshole to boot. He has never admitted my mother is alive. When she was doing the books, he wouldn't even speak to her on the phone. Everything had to go through my father."

"*Allaranta's Hands* was published not too long ago," Kick said, regaining her voice. "You mean your mother is still working for your father?"

"Yup," Jason said with a shrug. "The money is good. It got me through Juilliard, and it pays for household help so she can work on the stuff she really wants to write."

Kick put down her pencil. "Tell me, Jason," she asked. "That first book your mother had to copy. That must have been *The Arms of Venus*?"

"Yes, that's the only one that bastard wrote before my father got a hold of him.

"You know, I completely forgot I had told Rona about my mother and Lionel Maltby, but when she said you were doing a piece on my father, I couldn't wait to talk to you. My mom once wrote to Maltby asking him for a blurb for the cover of one of her romance novels, and he never even answered her. I think it was because if he did, he would be admitting that he knew her, and here she had been saving his professional ass for years.

"My mom could get in trouble if she told anyone about this. But I've never signed a confidentiality contract. And she says she's tired of the work. She doesn't need the money now that I'm paying my own bills. And her romances sell better than Maltby's books anyway. So I think it's time. You're welcome to use this in your article. Just don't let anyone know it came from me."

"Jason," Kick said, forcing a smile. "Would you excuse me for just a minute?"

By the time he said, "Sure," Kick was halfway across the room. She bolted down the hall, figuring there had to be a powder room near the front door. As she passed the pantry, she was vaguely aware of Georgina and Rona sitting at the counter drinking coffee.

She found the bathroom just in time, slammed the door, and dropped to her knees in front of the toilet to be sick.

She stayed on the floor for a long time, her cheek resting against the cool top of the toilet seat, until she was sure it was over.

As she rose to return to the living room, her knees wobbled a bit, but her head had never been more clear. Maltby didn't even write his own books. He was a total fraud. The last illusion had been stripped away. She was free.

Epilogue

*K*ick stood alone in the tower room.

The contractor had promised her all the renovations would be finished in time.

The results from Neeva's tests showed that Jeffrey Dunsmore, Jr., was due in August. A month after Neeva's divorce would become final.

Kick knew exactly how she wanted the tower room to look for Neeva's wedding. Weather permitting, she wanted the new glass dome open. The newly white walls would be swagged with fat garlands of ivy and huge white peonies. The service was planned for just after sunset. The light from the dome and dozens of silver floor candelabrum holding high white tapers would make the room glow. Even if it rained, the new beveled glass and brass fittings of the dome would be just as spectacular.

Fiddle had promised to do all the photography to illustrate the piece she wanted Kick to do on Jeff and Neeva and the runaway success of the Chandon Galleries. Georgina and Rona would handle the catering, now that they could relax a bit. *Fabulous*

Foods was thriving in their more up-to-date hands, and there was no question they'd be able to pay off their debt by the end of the year.

After the wedding, the tower room would be restored to the bedroom Kick had designed for herself. Joe was welcome at any time.

She'd been living and working in her old bedroom on the second floor while the renovating continued. The only time she had had to take her laptop to another room was when the men came to repair Thelma and Louise. She could have asked the building to do it, it really wasn't her responsibility, but not wanting to wait for months, she found and paid for the stonemasons herself. Now Thelma had fresh new talons. Louise's beak had been replaced, and both of them had been sprayed with some kind of preservative to prevent them from pitting.

Kick had worked in the kitchen during the gargoyle's cosmetic surgery. As a permanent contributing editor at *Fifteen Minutes,* she was now on her fourth assignment.

Her article on Irving Fourbraz had changed many lives. To her amazement, the person who seemed the least affected had been Irving Fourbraz. Believing as he did that any publicity is good publicity, he had shrugged off the allegations of extortion and duplicity and hired lawyers to sue everyone Kick quoted in her article. She wasn't worried about those lawsuits, as she had scrupulously taped all her interviews and quoted precisely.

Satisfied that the tower room was just the way she wanted it, Kick turned and headed downstairs to get the morning papers. The workmen were used to seeing her in her writing uniform: white athletic socks and one of Joe's old T-shirts that came to her knees. As she went softly down the stairs, she called good morning to the men replacing the dental molding in the foyer.

The stack of newspapers on her doorstep loomed ominously. The workmen thought it was amusing that she subscribed to six newspapers. She had no choice. The war Baby was waging with competing columnists was too much fun to miss, and she had to read them all.

Baby had started, her second week on the job, with a slam at Liz Smith of *Newsday*, the mother lion of all the New York columnists. Baby had written that Liz must be on Madonna's payroll considering all the gratuitous plugs for the singer in her columns. Baby then wrote a parody of a Smith column in which the only two names mentioned over and over again were Frank Sinatra and Elizabeth Taylor.

Baby persisted in needling Liz Smith until Smith reached out one big lion's paw and cuffed Baby with the Paco story from one of her London tipsters. Kick saw Abner Hoon's fine hand.

The Liz Smith column about Baby's romance with Paco was particularly painful for Baby. After Baby had left London, Maria Lopez had lingered long enough to do the El Vino eye-lock with Paco and ran off to St. Tropez with him, where he was long lensing newly wed Brigitte Bardot in her fifty-eight-year-old birthday suit.

Hurt and tasting blood from Liz's counterattack, Baby moved on to a softer target and mortified the gentlemanly Billy Norwich at the *Post* by writing a column in baby talk taunting him for dozens of gratuitous mentions of a dog that belonged to one of his restaurateur friends. The column started, "Yucky puppy should go pee-pee on pencil pusher's pumps." It took a stunned Norwich a few days before he struck back with a story his friend Ian McCaulley told him about Baby's use of his apartment during her romance with "a certain married megalawyer." Apparently, Norwich knew of Irving's new hobby of suing and pulled his punches.

Then, in a near suicidal move, Baby bore down on the *New York Post*'s Cindy Adams, referring to her as the South Street Maggot Mouth. Cindy, who was known for having a faster retaliation time than the Israeli Air Force, did not wait to bury a Baby barb among the restaurant plugs and colorful "only in New York" items. Adams walked straight onto the *Joan Rivers* show and told, in vivid detail, the story of Tita Garn's party, where "someone" spotted Baby stuffing a designer skirt under her dress—only by then the designer's skirt had turned into a full suit.

Abner Hoon had struck again.

Readers in five boroughs ate it up, and the media moved in on Baby, all but drowning her with interviews, items, and feature stories on her lifestyle. There were *Time* and *Newsweek* articles with headlines such as "New York Columnists Loaded for Bayer." Kick's favorite was *Variety*'s "Teeny Weeny Meanie Terrorizes Titans of Talk."

Baby was in her element at last. She conned Tanner Dyson into hiring two large black men with shaved heads whose only function was to walk backward in front of her when she entered a room, holding huge floodlights focused on her as she moved.

Kick and Joe thought it was hilarious. The *Courier*'s circulation soared, and Fiddle asked Kick to do a piece on Baby.

Kick was still thinking about it that day as she snapped open the *Courier* and turned to Baby's column.

At the top of the page in bold script letters was the name of the column, *People Will Talk,* with a long-lashed cartoon bear draped provocatively over the middle stroke in the *W.*

Halfway down the page Baby grinned out, wearing one of the "young designer" outfits she had begun to favor, a satin jacket tortured with trapunto and dripping sequins. On either shoulder sat two enormous gold epaulets embroidered to look like dominos. She now wore her hair in a rich-washerwoman's style, piled on top of her head with tendrils dripping around her cheeks and forehead.

How Many Times Can a Columnist Be Wrong? Let Me Count The Ways . . . Baby began, and launched into an attack on this week's target—Richard Johnson at the *Daily News.*

Kick folded the *Courier* and picked up the rest of the papers to read over coffee in the torn-up kitchen. As she passed the archway to the living room, she glanced in. The workmen removing the wallpaper had discovered two sconce outlets long plastered over on either side of the fireplace: a perfect spot for the portrait that was resting, wrapped in brown paper, against the far wall.

Kick finished going through the rest of the papers at the kitchen counter. The other columnists seemed to be easing up on Baby for the day, and there wasn't much else happening.

Much as she would have liked to take a day off, Kick couldn't. Her new piece on Lionel Maltby was due on Monday. His wife had caught him in bed with a *Columbia Journalism Review* staffer and tried to kill them both with a small-bore hunting rifle. Fiddle thought that incident and Maltby's refusal to comment on the allegations in Kick's Fourbraz piece gave a profile on Maltby a fresh lead. At least now, Irving wouldn't interfere.

This time Kick had not attempted to interview the former novelist. She was writing her piece using information gleaned from former lovers and the IRS, plus the stuff she had on her tapes from two years before.

She had just poured herself a fresh cup of coffee to take upstairs to her workroom when a workman appeared in the kitchen doorway.

"Miss Butler, you want to come in and take a look?"

Kick nodded and picked up her coffee mug.

She walked down the hall and through the archway to the freshly plastered and painted living room. Snow was falling over the park beyond the new windows.

She stood in the middle of the room and looked at the portrait the workman had just hung over the fireplace.

"Oh, my . . ." she whispered, feeling a slight shiver run up either arm.

Lolly smiled down at her, frozen at forty. Her dark hair and eyes gleamed; the soft light from the new sconces made her gray-silk ball gown glow. Around her neck was an emerald choker that had not been found among her belongings and, Kick suspected, had existed only in Lolly's mind and the artist's eye.

She moved closer, imagining Lolly on a red velvet banquette in the sky. There would be a big white Hollywood phone on the table—no mingy cellular job would do for Lolly in her celestial court. She would have read every one of Baby's columns and been begrudgingly proud. Kick looked around to see that the workman, sensing that she might have wanted a moment alone, had slipped from the room.

In the quiet room, alone with her benefactor, she raised her coffee cup to the portrait. "Oh, Lolly," she whispered. "Have I got some dish for you."